Glimmers of Change

Book # 7 in The Bregdan Chronicles

Sequel to Carried Forward By Hope

Ginny Dye

Glimmers of Change

www.BregdanChronicles.net

www.GinnyDye.com

www.AVoiceInTheWorldPublishing.com

ISBN 1503282902

Printed in the United States of America.

For my sister, Jan -

You inspire me every day!

A Note From the Author

My great hope is that *Glimmers of Change* will both entertain and challenge you. I hope you will learn as much as I did during the months of research it took to write this book. No one was more surprised than me when it ended up portraying just the first 8 months of 1866. The first five books of The Bregdan Chronicles each covered a year. That hasn't been possible with the last two books.

When I ended the Civil War in *The Last, Long Night*, I knew virtually nothing about Reconstruction. I wasn't even sure it could carry an entire book. Just as with *Carried Forward By Hope*, I've been shocked and amazed by all I learned as I researched and wrote *Glimmers of Change*.

Glimmers of Change is perhaps the most difficult book I have ever written. I think you will understand just why it was so difficult by the time you are done, and why I shed so many tears during the research for this book.

Though I now live in the Pacific Northwest, I grew up in the South and lived for eleven years in Richmond, VA. I spent countless hours exploring the plantations that still line the banks of the James River and became fascinated by the history.

But you know, it's not the events that fascinate me so much – it's the people. That's all history is, you know. History is the story of people's lives. History reflects the consequences of their choices and actions – both good and bad. History is what has given you the world you live in today – both good and bad.

This truth is why I named this series The Bregdan Chronicles. Bregdan is a Gaelic term for weaving: Braiding. Every life that has been lived until today is a part of the woven braid of life. It takes every person's story to create history. Your life will help determine the course of history. You may think you don't have much of an impact. You do. Every action you take will reflect in someone else's life. Someone else's decisions. Someone else's future. Both good and bad. That is the **Bregdan Principle**...

**Every life that has been lived until today is a part of the woven braid of life.
It takes every person's story to
create history.
Your life will help determine
the course of history.
You may think you don't have
much of an impact.
You do.
Every action you take will reflect
in someone else's life.
Someone else's decisions.
Someone else's future.
Both good and bad.**

My great hope as you read this book, and all that will follow, is that you will acknowledge the power you have, every day, to change the world around you by your decisions and actions. Then I will know the research and writing were all worthwhile.

Oh, and I hope you enjoy every moment of it and learn to love the characters as much as I do!

I'm already being asked how many books will be in this series. I guess that depends on how long I live! My intention is to release two or three books a year, each covering one year of history – continuing to weave the lives of my characters into the times they lived. I hate to end a good book as much as anyone – always feeling so sad that I have to leave the characters. You shouldn't have to be sad for a long time!

You are now reading the seventh book - # 8 (*Shifted By The Winds*) will be released in the Spring of 2015. If you like what you read, you'll want to make sure you're on my mailing list at www.BregdanChronicles.net.

I'll let you know each time a new one comes out so that you can take advantage of all my fun launch events!

    Sincerely,
Ginny Dye

Chapter One

January 1, 1866

Carrie stiffened when she heard rustling in the thick brush. She stopped on the path and strained her ears, peering into the darkness, forcing herself to breathe naturally. She scolded herself when silence echoed back at her. "What do you think is out here?" she muttered. "You know these woods like the back of your hand. It's probably nothing more than a rabbit or a raccoon."

Her voice seemed to crack the brittle cold stealing her breath. The fog pouring from her mouth seemed to hang frozen. She clutched her coat to her more closely, grateful she had put on two pairs of riding pants after she had crawled out of her warm bed, evading Robert's groping hands before he rolled back over and continued sleeping. Her husband had looked so warm and inviting with his black, tousled hair spread over the pillow, but her desire to greet the new year had propelled her down the stairs and out through the back kitchen door, closing it softly so no one would be disturbed.

Shaking her head at her imagined fears, Carrie forced herself to continue moving down the barely visible trail. Stiff frost crackled under her feet as frozen branches pulled strands of her wavy black hair out of the careless bun she had created. She would be back in plenty of time to look presentable for the New Year breakfast celebration.

Within minutes, the path opened into a small clearing, leaving behind the sheltering embrace of the woods. Carrie caught her breath as she looked up into the canopy of stars spread above her, the tiny orbs glistening and dancing in the frigid air, the belt of the Milky Way holding them close in what looked to be an endless cluster. "Good morning," she whispered. The still air echoed back her soft words, a tiny sliver of dark blue appearing on the horizon as dawn advanced to claim the day.

Carrie turned away and headed for the concealed path that would take her down to the river, her heart suddenly beating faster with anticipation, her lips curved into a smile. She had welcomed the New Year at this same spot since she was ten years old and learned how to miss all the creaking boards as she snuck out of the house. Her father had laughed when she returned that first morning, her eyes sparkling with the fun of her adventure. Her mother had been horrified at more evidence of her independent, wayward daughter and proclaimed it would never happen again. Carrie had not missed a year after that.

She found the spot but paused and stared in the direction of Richmond. Yes, in fact, she had missed years. All the years of the war that kept her from home rose up in the darkness and threw painful memories into her mind and heart. Carrie shook her head impatiently and started down the path, not needing any light to navigate the gently sloping trail. She knew the memories and images would always be there, but today she had come to prepare for the New Year that lay ahead.

She could hear the lapping of gentle waves as she broke out onto the shore and looked toward the boulder she always came to. Suddenly, she stiffened, alarmed by the realization she wasn't alone.

"About time you got here."

Carrie laughed in disbelief and relief. "Rose?"

"I hope you have a lot of clothes on. It is brutally cold. I've been rethinking my decision to join you," Rose said ruefully, a slight tremor in her voice revealing how cold she was. "I could be home in bed with Moses," she said wistfully. "He told me I was crazy to come, but then he pushed me out of bed so I wouldn't miss it."

Carrie hurried forward and settled down on the boulder beside her best friend and half-aunt. "How long have you been here?" she asked with delight.

"Long enough to feel like a solid block of ice," Rose replied, pulling her coat closer. Her voice was muffled by the thick scarf wound around her face, leaving just enough space for her to peer out.

Carrie chuckled. "Greeting the New Year sunrise is not for the weak of heart."

"It's not for *sane* people," Rose retorted.

Carrie cocked her head. "We could definitely debate whether you fit that description, but I'll let it go in the spirit of new beginnings," she parried playfully. "How did you know I'd be here?"

"You've been doing this since you were ten years old," Rose said smugly. "I bet you thought no one knew you came down here. I heard you from my room every single time."

"Why didn't you join me before?" Carrie cried. Then she answered the question herself. "Because you were my slave, and you didn't know if you would be welcome."

"That was part of it," Rose agreed easily, "but the real reason was that I didn't see any point in leaving my bed when I was so warm." She paused and gazed at the horizon that was beginning to glow. "This year is different, though." Her voice sounded sad and a little strained. The silence grew until the only sound came from the waves pulsing and whispering. "I don't know when we'll be together again," she finally said.

Carrie reached over and grabbed her hand. "Sometimes I wish I could give up my dream of becoming a doctor," she admitted. "It would be so much easier to stay here on the plantation with Robert and you and Moses. There are moments I can't breathe when I think about being back in a city as big as Philadelphia, away from everyone I love." Her voice trailed off as tears flooded her eyes.

"You'll have Janie," Rose reminded her.

Carrie blinked back the tears and smiled as she thought of her close friend, who had stayed behind in Philadelphia when Carrie had returned home for Christmas. She received a letter from Janie a few days before Christmas with glowing words that described living at Abby's home, and the three other women medical students who shared the house with her. Janie could hardly wait for Carrie to arrive in the spring. "Yes,

I'll have Janie," she agreed softly, "but no one can ever replace you. I always feel like a part of me is missing when we're not together."

Rose gripped her hand tightly. "I feel the same way." She stood abruptly and faced the glimmering horizon. "Enough of this," she announced. "You're not leaving for three months. It's going to be a dismal winter if we spend every minute dreading being apart again." She waved her arms toward the puffy clouds hovering above the stark tree line, just beginning to turn purplish gold. "I suggest we focus on making the most of every day we have. It's not like it was during the war. It won't be years and years, because you'll be home every few months."

"Well said!"

Carrie and Rose both jumped when another voice rang out into the cold air.

"Abby?" they said in unison.

"Who else would be crazy enough to come out here when it's this cold?" Abby shivered dramatically as she stepped forward to give them both a hug.

"How did you...?" Carrie began.

"Your father told me about your annual tradition," Abby replied. "I had already decided to join you last night, but Thomas had to push me out of bed to actually get me here. I would have been down here earlier, but the idea of my feet hitting the cold floor kept me in bed longer than I should have," she said.

"Moses had to push me out of bed, too," Rose admitted.

"Soft! You're both soft," Carrie scoffed. "Robert never even knew I left our bed."

"Rose and I decided years ago that you are the only truly insane one of the three of us," Abby said agreeably. "We don't let it bother us." A thick hat concealed her twinkling eyes, but her voice was full of warm laughter.

Carrie laughed and grasped both their mitten-covered hands. Rose and Abby were the two strongest women she knew. Abby had been defying tradition for years. Rose had escaped slavery and become a fabulous teacher, wife, and mother. Both of them had survived the challenges and pain with their compassion and humor intact.

She turned to Abby. "Have I told you recently how very glad I am you married my father and became my mother?"

"I don't keep count, because I'll never hear it enough," Abby replied joyfully. "When your father told me you would be down here for the sunrise, I knew I wanted to share it with you. To have Rose here, too, is just icing on the cake. I can't believe I get to watch the sunrise with my two favorite women."

Rose laughed happily. "My feelings exactly!" She waved her hand at the horizon. "It's time to get quiet and contemplative," she said softly. "The sun is about to make its appearance."

The three women stood together, hands clasped, as the clouds turned from purple to a bright glowing pink, the still hidden sun shooting up shafts of light that pierced the clouds and turned the sky to a brilliant cobalt blue.

Carrie leaned over and whispered soft instructions to each of them.

Silence reigned as they watched the cobalt blue change to a brilliant turquoise, the clouds beginning to wisp across the sky as a light breeze began to blow. They held their breath in unison as the first sliver of sun peeked over the horizon, and in moments seemed to jump upward to claim a new day.

Carrie laughed and raised her hands as the golden orb glowed down on them, Rose and Abby imitating her movement.

"Happy 1866!" they yelled in unison. "Hello New Year! We're so glad you're here!"

Carrie grabbed their hands again and began to spin them all in a circle. "I've always danced alone," she cried. "This is so much better!"

Laughter rang through the morning air as the three women danced joyfully, the sun pouring down on them, the lapping waves seeming to keep time with their dancing.

The three women were laughing and talking as they ran into the kitchen, gasping with delight when the warm air enveloped them.

"What you crazy women doin'?" Annie demanded. "Anybody with a lick of sense knows it be too cold to be outside this mornin'."

"Sense is highly overrated," Carrie responded playfully. "Happy New Year, Annie!"

"Hmph. You would certainly be the one to know 'bout not havin' any sense," Annie scolded. "I declare, Carrie Borden, you do more crazy things den anybody I ever saw." She eyed Rose and Abby. "And I bet she talked the both of you into whatever has your faces beet red and your hands shaking all over. Your husbands know where you be?" she demanded. "I know Robert done given up on changing Miss Carrie."

Rose laughed as she stepped forward to hug her mother-in-law. "We surprised Carrie down by the river for her annual tradition of watching the sunrise. It was glorious! Moses had to push me out of bed..."

"Just like Thomas did," Abby admitted, her eyes dancing.

"But I'm so glad he made me get up," Rose cried. "I wouldn't have missed it for anything!"

Annie stared at them for a long moment, her eyes soft with affection. "Crazy. You three ain't nothin' but plumb crazy." She waved her hand toward the table. "Take your coats off and hunker down next to the fire. I'll have coffee ready in a minute."

"We won't mess up your preparations for the New Year breakfast?" Abby asked. "We don't want to be in the way."

"Ain't no bein' in the way," Annie replied. "Polly gonna be here in a few minutes. We done got plenty of time. Now," she said briskly, "get out of them coats and get warm before you catch yourselves a cold." She bustled over to the stove and picked up the coffee kettle. "Crazy," she muttered again as she poured three cups of the steaming brew.

Abby held her hands toward the fire, smiling as the flickering flames chased away the last of her tremors. "I don't believe anything in the world is better than finally feeling warm after you've turned into a block of ice," she murmured. She reached for the thick mug Annie handed to her. "Thank you."

Silence fell on the kitchen as Annie bustled about with preparations for breakfast. The only sounds were the crackling of flames and the clinking of pots and pans. Gradually, the smell of frying bacon and the warm scent of biscuits filled the air.

Carrie gripped her cup tightly as she gazed into the flames, letting the warmth seep through every pore of her body. She tried to reclaim the sheer, exuberant joy she felt when the three of them danced in celebration, but reality insisted on intruding.

"Carrie?"

Carrie turned when Rose's voice broke into her thoughts. "Yes?"

"What's bothering you?"

"That was an awful big sigh," Abby agreed.

Carrie flushed. "I didn't realize I made a noise." She stared into the flames again for a long moment and then looked at them with troubled eyes. "1866 is going to be a hard year," she said. "It's fun to celebrate it arriving, but I'll admit, I'm afraid of what it's going to bring."

"Harder than the war years?" Abby asked, reaching over to take her hand. "I know you suffered so much more during the war than Rose and I did."

"We all suffered," Carrie answered. "Everyone in the country suffered, just in different ways."

"Then...?" Rose asked softly.

Carrie gazed back at the flames, wishing some spark of comfort would leap from the fire, but the cold grip of reality held her tightly. "I guess I don't really think the war is over," she finally murmured.

"I'm afraid you're right, Carrie."

The three women looked up as lanky, red-haired Matthew Justin walked into the kitchen. "Good morning!" they said in unison.

He sniffed appreciatively as the warm aromas hit him. "Do you think a starving man could have a before-breakfast biscuit?" he asked hopefully, reaching his hand toward the basket.

"Only if that starvin' man don't mind bein' without a hand," Annie said calmly, lifting a large butcher knife from the counter.

Matthew snatched his hand back with an easy laugh, his blue eyes dancing with fun. "Can't blame a guy for trying." He settled down next to the fire in the last remaining chair and held out his hands. "I'll stay here where I can at least smell them."

"And I be stayin' where I can keep an eye on them," Annie retorted.

Matthew shook his head dolefully. "Were you this hard on Moses when he was growing up?"

Annie snorted. "That boy grew so big, so fast he be hungry all de time. I had to watch every morsel of food to make sure his sisters done got anythin' at all!"

"He's *still* hungry all the time," Rose said. "And Little John is not even three, but he's going to be just like him. I swear he grows every day."

"Gonna be just like his daddy," Annie agreed, happiness crinkling her eyes. "Y'all best plan on growing a lot of food, because it gonna take a lot to fill them two up."

When the laughter faded away, Abby turned to Matthew. "What did you mean when you said Carrie is right about the war not ending? Have I missed something?" she asked, only her gray eyes showing her concern. "I do believe the war ended at Appomattox last year."

Carrie, watching carefully, saw something in Abby's eyes that was far more than concern. It looked more like knowledge.

Matthew frowned, reaching gratefully for the cup of coffee Annie handed him. "Thank you," he murmured, before he turned to Abby. "I wish that were true," he said heavily. He stared into the flames for several long moments before he looked up. "I'm afraid that Appomattox ended just one phase of the conflict. From everything I can tell, the Confederates have returned home and initiated a new struggle to maintain the political and social dominance they enjoyed during the war."

Carrie's heart quickened. She and Matthew had started this discussion the day before. She wanted to refute his conclusions, but the evidence was piling up that he was right. She'd had no trouble waking up for the sunrise, because her heavy thoughts had kept her awake most of the night. "So it was all for nothing?" she said hoarsely.

"Weren't for nothing!" Annie snapped. "Ain't I free? Ain't Moses and Rose free? Ain't little John and Simon and Hope gonna grow up free?"

"You're right," Carrie said instantly. "I'm so glad for that, but I worry what kind of world all of you are going to live in."

Annie planted her fist on her hip and stared at them. "It be somethin' I wonder 'bout every single day, but you ain't gonna come up with an answer to it this mornin'. And I don't aim to let dark thoughts spoil our New Year's breakfast." She stared at all of them, her dark eyes taking in their rumpled appearances. "Mr. Matthew look pretty good, but you three women look like you crawled out of bed and forgot to do anything. I ain't gonna let such sorry lookin' women sit down at the breakfast I be workin' so hard on. Polly will be here in a minute to help me finish up. You three go upstairs and do somethin' to yourselves. While you be there, you gots to wash out any dark thoughts before you come back down." She took a deep breath. "Now, you three think you can do that?"

Abby laughed, stood, and walked over to plant a warm kiss on Annie's startled face. "You're right as usual, Annie." She beckoned to Carrie and Rose. "We have orders to follow."

Carrie followed willingly, wondering about the look of relief in Abby's eyes when Annie ordered them to leave.

Carrie felt like a new woman when she settled down at the breakfast table. Her unruly black hair had been tamed. She didn't have much of a wardrobe left after the war, but she knew her green gown matched her eyes. All it took was one look into Robert's deep brown eyes to know she looked good. It had also taken only one look into his eyes to make her forget the country's troubles. She could hardly believe the vibrant, handsome man standing in front of her was the same emaciated, disease-wracked man the war sent home to her more than eight months earlier.

Her gratitude intensified when she thought of how many people all over the South had lost their homes and everything they owned during the war. The wonder that Cromwell Plantation had survived filled her every day. She sat quietly as the seats around the table filled with her favorite people in the world—Robert, her father, Abby, Rose, Moses, little John and baby Hope, Jeremy, Matthew, June, and Simon and little Simon.

A sudden blast of cold air swirled through the room before Gabe, Amber, and Clint entered the house, joining her list of favorite people.

Brilliant sunshine illuminated the dining room and turned the crystal chandelier into dancing droplets spiraling over their heads. Christmas greenery still adorned the windows and fireplace mantle, releasing a fragrance that competed with the smells from the kitchen. A blazing fire shot warmth through every corner of the room. The Christmas tree would come down tomorrow, but for one last day, it occupied the center of the living room, its splendor standing guard over everything.

Carrie smiled when Robert reached down to take her hand. "It's a miracle we're all together," she said softly. "This time last year, you were freezing out in the Petersburg trenches." Her stomach clenched as she remembered the box of amputated hands and feet she collected after many of the men were brought into Chimborazo Hospital. She had used the horror to gather shoes, socks and gloves from the impoverished Richmond residents, but she knew the suffering had been far greater than their offering.

Robert's face darkened for a moment with the memories, but his eyes cleared quickly.

Carrie squeezed his hand more tightly. The nightmares still came, but they were fewer and further between. Most importantly, Robert could talk about them. That, more than anything, seemed to release their power over him. She doubted they would ever go away completely. The horrible images that filled his mind would fade but never totally disappear. She carried so many of the images herself from her years in the hospital, intensified now by the memories Robert shared with her of his battlefield experiences. The war had shaped all their lives. Nothing would ever change that reality, but she also believed time would heal.

She gazed around the table again, once more overcome with gratitude. Baby Hope, snuggled in Moses' huge arms, filled her with warm faith for the future. She pushed aside her fearful feelings, fighting to focus on all the things she had to be grateful for.

Thomas Cromwell spoke the words in her heart. "It's nothing short of miraculous that we're all here together. So many families will never again have what we are sharing."

A long silence filled the room as they thought of the hundreds of thousands of men, both North and South, who were killed during the long war; the millions of family members who lost loved ones; the scores of men who would live the rest of their lives as amputees, or battling illness because their bodies were too weak to fight off infection.

"We have so much to be thankful for," Thomas continued as his gaze swept the room, his eyes taking in all his family members, both black and white. He took a deep breath. "The beginning of a new year always brings hope. Maybe this year, we, as people, might make decisions that will make our country, and our world, a better place. This time last year, we were all separated, some of us fighting on different sides of the conflict that ripped our country apart." His eyes rested briefly on Robert, Moses, and Simon. "We have a new chance to get things right. Perhaps the fact that we are all sitting together to celebrate the beginning of 1866 is the biggest reason of all to have hope."

Carrie smiled, her father's words piercing her heart with their simple truth. Her father was right. Annie was right. Every slave was free. There was a new chance to create a country of equality and compassion. Change would be difficult, but that didn't mean it wouldn't happen.

Abby reached for Thomas' hand. "I joined the abolition movement in 1832. The movement itself started in the 1820s, but it really gained force in the thirties. I was only eighteen years old, but completely convinced slavery was wrong. In my naiveté, I believed we would have the slaves freed within a few years. It seemed so simple to me, because it was clearly the right thing." She smiled ruefully. "I never could have guessed it would take thirty-three years and a brutal war to accomplish freedom for the slaves. So many people, both black and white, have paid a huge price for that freedom, but we've only begun."

Carrie stiffened, knowing she was hearing truth, but wanting to block out Abby's words.

"is going to be an exciting year, but I don't believe it's going to be easy," Abby continued. "A whole way of life has been changed and is being challenged. Slavery is dead, but that doesn't mean the beliefs that established it aren't alive and well. It will be up to those of us around the table to work to change those beliefs." She took a deep breath and smiled warmly. "Only by changing beliefs will actions be different. The great news is that it can be done. It won't be quick, and it won't be easy, but we will achieve equal rights for everyone if we simply refuse to give up until it is so."

Another long silence filled the room as her words sunk in, giving both purpose and hope, along with a clearly heard warning.

It was Moses' deep voice that finally broke the silence. "Here's to 1866," he said firmly.

"Here's to 1866!" reverberated around the room as everyone echoed back his words.

"I say it be time to eat," Annie announced from the doorway. She waved her hand at Abby and Carrie as they started to rise. "Me and Polly don't need no help bringing in the food." Then she grinned slyly. "That don't mean we won't take help cleaning up all the mess, though."

Laughter rang around the table as platters of food were carried in. The table was soon groaning under the weight of Virginia ham, cornbread, scrambled eggs, baked apples, cranberry sauce, steaming biscuits, and deep bowls of blackberry and strawberry jam.

Everyone waited for Annie and Polly to slip into their seats before they began to eat.

Robert finally leaned back with a groan. "Now *that* was a meal to start a new year!" he announced. "It's a good thing I decided to take a day off from the stables. I'm certain I couldn't move if I had to."

Clint nodded his head toward the window. "The horses agree with you. They seem to be enjoying their day off."

Everyone began laughing when they peered out the bay window overlooking the pasture. The horses, their fur thick against the cold, seemed to be playing a game of chase through the stiff brown grass. Tails held high, their faces tilted toward the sun while steam blew out of their nostrils, twenty-one horses charged around the field.

"Granite is having a ball," Carrie said laughingly, holding back the choked feeling that rose in her throat as she thought of leaving her tall gray Thoroughbred again in the spring. Once, all she had wanted was freedom from the plantation and a chance to make her way in the world. After four years of war and separation from all she loved, it hurt her to think of leaving it again.

"Your thoughts, Carrie?" her father asked.

Carrie gazed at him, aware of what he was really asking. Another New Year tradition was to share your dreams for the upcoming year. Some people called them resolutions. Her father had taught her to shy away from that word because he believed it set people up for failure when they inevitably couldn't, or wouldn't, accomplish them. All her life, the dreams her father encouraged her to have had driven her forward into action. In different company, she may have blithely shared her dreams and then passed the baton. As she looked around the table, she realized that more than anything she wanted to speak honestly.

"I'm wishing becoming a doctor didn't mean I have to leave the plantation," she said. "It hurts my heart to think of leaving all of you." She paused and swept her gaze around the room. "I've actually thought about not going to medical school, though Robert has done nothing but encourage and support me." She stopped again, wondering if anyone would respond. She quickly realized they would remain silent until she had finished, giving her time to communicate her thoughts. That knowledge, perhaps more than anything, made the idea of leaving even harder. How could she leave this group of people who loved and accepted her so completely?

She swallowed hard against the lump in her throat and continued. "Yesterday, I had an emergency patient at the clinic." Carrie smiled slightly as she called the small room tacked onto the schoolhouse her *clinic*, but she also knew that without it, medical care would be unavailable for everyone in the area. It was humble but crucial. "He lost his arm two years ago during the war. Suddenly, for no reason I can tell, it's hurting him terribly and has become red and inflamed. He's in agony." She took a deep breath. "I was able to give him something for the pain, and we're working to battle the infection, but I realized I still have so much to learn before I can truly help people the way I want to. The only way to get that knowledge is to go to medical school and learn from people who know more than I do."

Carrie held back the tears that threatened. She breathed a sigh of gratitude when Robert took her hand and squeezed it firmly, giving her courage to continue. "Abby and Rose have taught me so much about courage. People think I'm brave, but I've always had the support of my family for everything, even during the war. Abby fought so many challenges on her own for so long." Her face lit with a quick smile as she looked at Abby and her father. "I'm so glad both of you have each other now."

Her eyes swept to Rose. "After escaping slavery, you left Abby's home in Philadelphia to move down to teach school in the contraband camp. It would have been so easy to keep going to the Quaker School and live in the comfort of a wonderful house. Instead, you moved into a shack so you could teach and make a difference."

She couldn't hold back the tears as she finished. "It's my turn now. I've got to leave the things I hold precious so I can make a difference. I have so very much to learn. I know there are people, even in Philadelphia, who will think it horrible that I have left my husband to go to school." A tear slipped down her cheek as she turned to look at Robert. "It still amazes me that you'll let me go."

"I think we determined several years ago that *letting you* has nothing to do with it," Robert responded blandly, his eyes dancing with fun. "Having said that, I'm so proud of you I could almost burst. My wife is going to be a *doctor.*"

Laughter rolled around the table as everyone nodded in agreement.

The burden completely lifted from Carrie's heart as these people she loved so much looked at her with love and pride. They had survived four years of war and reunited stronger than ever. Life would call all of them away at some point, but there would always be times like these when they came back together, giving each other the strength to do what they needed to do.

"We're all so lucky," she said softly. "So very, very lucky."

"Amen to that," Abby said.

"Robert?" Thomas asked.

Robert leaned back in his chair, his muscular arms crossed across his chest, his brown face attesting to all the hours spent outdoors in the stables. "Now that the war is over, horses are going to be needed more than ever. Especially in the South. I intend to make the horses from Cromwell Plantation the best in the region. We've made a good start." His eyes rested with pride on Clint, his young protégé. "We've got a long way to go, but we'll get there." He nodded his head toward Moses. "Your turn."

Moses polished off another biscuit before he began to speak. "Last year's tobacco crop was a huge accomplishment, since we had to plant so late because of the war. This year's crop is going to be even better. I've talked to the men. We're going to plant every acre of Cromwell that can be planted. The war was a huge financial hit, Thomas, but the value of tobacco is even higher now. By the time spring arrives, we'll be at full speed."

Carrie smiled at the look of pride on her father's face, marveling again that he had come so far. Before the war, he had simply not been able to see blacks as anything but the inferior race white men were supposed to control. That he had given half of Cromwell to Moses, accepting him as his brother-in-law, was a huge testimony to the ability of people to change.

It was Rose's turn. "The school is growing. This cold may be hard to battle with the woodstove, but it has also made it possible for more of the children to come to school. They don't seem to mind staying bundled up through the day. Almost every student can read now," she said proudly.

"Tell them about Sarah," Moses urged.

Rose laughed. "I've been trying to get the parents to come to school, but so many of them are too tired after a long day of working, or," her eyes darkened with quick anger, "they can't get passes off the plantations they are working on."

Carrie grimaced, knowing that tension was growing between the planters and the freed slaves. The planters were trying their best to operate things the way they had during slavery. The slaves were trying their best to live in the freedom they had fought so hard for. A portion of her fears came from the understanding that things would have to come to a head at some point.

Rose shook off her anger. "Sarah is five years old. She came into school right before Christmas and told me she had taught her parents how to read." She grinned with delight. "I sent her home with more of the books that were shipped down, so they can all read together at night. She's inspired the other children to do the same thing."

Everyone clapped with delight before Rose turned to Matthew. "Your turn."

Matthew shook off his somber look and smiled brightly.

Carrie watched him closely, knowing Matthew was trying to hide far more than he was going to be willing to say. She was so grateful for her strong friendship with the journalist from West Virginia. He had survived horrors during the war, but he had not lost his passion for using the written word to communicate truth and affect change.

"This time last year, I was still covering horrific battles, wondering when it all would end. I'm so grateful the war is over. I realize we have a new battle to fight now, but I'm also convinced that newspapers and the stories I will write for my book can help change how people feel. I *have* to believe it," he said, his voice bordering on desperation even as he fought to sound casual.

"What aren't you telling us?" Moses asked perceptively.

"What makes you think I'm not telling you something?" Matthew asked lightly.

"Because your eyes and your voice aren't saying the same thing," Moses said. "You might be able to pull off a charade with another group of people, but I'm afraid we all know you too well."

Matthew smiled slightly as he searched for words. "I wanted to wait until after our celebration breakfast," he murmured.

Robert nodded at the empty platters on the table. "I'd say it's over," he observed, watching Matthew closely. "Moses is right. What are you not telling us?"

Just then, the pounding of hooves sounded outside, the noise increasing as it drew closer.

Thomas' face set in stern lines as he stood. "We're not expecting company." He kept his voice calm. "It's probably nothing, but I think it best if all of you stay inside. I'll take care of it."

"But, Thomas..." Moses began, pushing back from the table.

"That especially includes you, Moses," Thomas said firmly. "You're part owner of the plantation, but I don't think our visitors, whoever they are, have come to talk to you."

The tension around the table increased as Thomas strode across the room, grabbed his coat, opened the door, and stepped out onto the porch.

Chapter Two

Thomas stood erect at the edge of the porch. His silver hair glistened in the sunlight, his handsome face displaying none of the tight concern clenching his gut. He had heard the rumors swirling through Richmond in the weeks before he came out to the plantation for Christmas. The news Matthew brought, the same news he had not been willing to share with everyone during the holidays, had lent weight to the rumors. Thomas, Abby and Jeremy agreed with Matthew's decision not to infuse darkness into the celebration. Though Thomas had hoped nothing would happen, he was prepared for any contingencies. No one but he knew a pistol was tucked into his coat pocket.

Within moments, a group of six horsemen cantered around the final bend, slowing as the horses in the field stopped playing and watched them. All the men were bundled tightly against the cold, scarves concealing their identities.

Even through the thick layer of clothes, Thomas could feel the anger emanating from them as they continued to ride forward. He forced himself to remember the hospitality Cromwell Plantation had always been known for. "Happy New Year, gentlemen," he called as the horses came to a halt, their bridles jingling as they bobbed their heads.

"I guess *you* would think so, Cromwell," one of the men answered caustically.

Thomas stiffened but chose to not respond.

"There aren't many plantation owners in the South who still have horses like this, Cromwell," another man said bitterly. "I guess the stories of you selling out to the North are true."

Thomas recognized the voice immediately. Jonathan Sowell owned the plantation ten miles down the road. He knew Sowell had lost everything during the war, including his two sons. He still remained silent.

"Don't you have anything to say?" Sowell taunted, pulling down his scarf so Thomas could see his brown eyes glittering with rage.

Thomas took a slow breath, willing his body to stay relaxed. "I learned in my years serving in the Virginia government *during the war* that it is impossible to reason with bitterness." He decided to let the reminder of his service be the only response to their accusations. "I don't imagine all of you came to wish me and my family a Happy New Year, so what can I do for you?"

Sowell moved his horse closer to the porch. "You and your *family*, Cromwell? Would that include the niggers that used to be your slaves? And that daughter of yours who is treating niggers in the same clinic where she treats white people?" He sneered. "We've been hearing things."

"Did you come just to ask me questions?" Thomas responded evenly, clenching his fists within his pockets and closing one over the pistol. "It seems like you could have picked a day that wasn't quite so cold."

"No, we didn't come to ask you questions." Another man pushed his horse forward, his scornful voice ringing in the frigid air.

Again, Thomas recognized the voice. "Hello, Daniel." In spite of his concern and his growing anger, he felt sympathy for the band of men grouped in front of the porch. All of them must have suffered horribly during the war. He couldn't identify them all through their scarves, but he was quite sure they had attended parties together in the past. Daniel Cannon owned the plantation eight miles due west of Cromwell. The limp hang of his jacket confirmed the rumors of him losing his left arm at Gettysburg. He also lost two of his three sons, with the third returning home an alcoholic.

"Questions don't mean a thing," Daniel continued, ignoring the greeting. "We came to *tell* you a few things." His slurred words revealed he had developed his own drinking problem—or perhaps he had needed the false courage to make this visit.

"That right?" Thomas asked. "I don't believe I have a need for anyone to tell me how to live my life."

"If you want a life to live," Daniel snarled, "you'd best listen to us."

Thomas battled the bile rising in his stomach as the combined hatred of the men rose to engulf him, but his face remained impassive.

"We used to all be friends," Sowell said hastily, obviously trying to take back control of the conversation, "but things have changed, Thomas." His voice was both harsh and pained.

"Evidently," Thomas responded blandly. "Since you seem to have something to say, go ahead and say it so I can go back in to my family." He was quite sure all of them were clustered close to the front door listening to every word being said. He relaxed a little with that realization, knowing he wouldn't have to face anything alone if the men decided their message would be more than words.

"We heard about you giving four hundred acres of Cromwell to them niggers you got working here," Daniel snapped.

Thomas continued to stare at them silently.

"You've got to take that land back, Cromwell," Sowell stated angrily.

"I believe I can do whatever I want with the land I own," Thomas replied.

"Not when it impacts the rest of us," Sowell snapped. "You got every nigger in the area thinking we should be giving them land. They seem to believe they were better than they were before the war."

"They're free now," Thomas reminded him. "You don't own them anymore. They are *choosing* to work for you."

Sowell snorted, his face twisting into an angry grimace. "*Free!* I don't care if a piece of paper from a government that destroyed my home makes them free. They're nothing but niggers, and I plan on treating them the same way I always did."

"Then I predict you will have some problems."

"Only because you have put crazy ideas in their heads," Sowell seethed. "You're paying your niggers more than we can pay, and you're giving them profits. I always thought you were a sound businessman, Cromwell. Now I'm questioning your sanity."

"Question it all you want," Thomas replied, willing his voice to remain even and reasonable. "While you're questioning it, you may want to ask which plantation in the area had the biggest tobacco crop this past year. You might ask which plantation had the highest profit margin." His voice grew firmer as he stepped up to the edge of the porch. "The blacks are all *free* now, gentlemen. You can't do things the same way they used to be done. If you treat your workers fairly and make it worth their while to work hard, you'll find you can make as much money as you did in the past." He paused, remembering Abby's words that beliefs would be difficult to change. "I know all the change is incredibly difficult, but I honestly believe we can rebuild a South that is even stronger and more viable than before."

A short silence met his words as the six men stared at him. He thought he saw a flicker of wary understanding in Sowell's eyes, but Cannon extinguished it with his next words. "What is going to be incredibly difficult, *Cromwell*, is life for you if you don't change your ways. We're here to tell you to take back that land from the niggers and to pay the same wages the rest of us are paying."

"And if I don't?" Thomas asked, his voice calm, his eyes hard as stones.

"Then you and your family will pay the price," Cannon said, rage glittering in his eyes.

Whatever Thomas had seen flicker in Sowell's eyes disappeared when Sowell added onto Cannon's announcement. "And don't think this is just about the plantation. We know what you and your Yankee wife are doing in that factory in Richmond. There are lots of people angry that you are paying the niggers higher wages than other places. You won't get away with it."

Thomas had heard all he was going to listen to. "That's enough," he said shortly. "What I do with my plantation and my business is no one's concern but mine and those who choose to work for me. I won't come down the road to tell you how to live your life, and I won't have you coming here to tell me how to run mine." He stepped back from the edge of the porch. "Your time here is over. You know the way to the entrance."

"I told you he wouldn't listen," Cannon snarled, his hand snaking toward the rifle strapped to his saddle. "I guess we haven't stated our message as clearly as we meant to."

At the same moment Thomas pulled his pistol from his pocket, the door to the house opened. Robert, Moses, Jeremy, and Matthew stepped out onto the porch, rifles pointed at the group of men.

"There are five of us and six of you," Robert stated quietly, anger flaring in his eyes. "One of you will have a chance to ride away if Daniel Cannon or any of you touches the rifle on your saddle." He stepped closer to Cannon, holding his rifle steady, his years as a Confederate officer showing in his stance. "I believe Mr. Cromwell has asked you to leave. I suggest you do."

Cannon moved his hand away from his rifle, but the rage in his eyes intensified. "We'll leave," he growled, "but don't think this is over." His glittering eyes settled on Moses standing tall on the porch, his rifle held steady. "I can't believe I'm living to see the day a nigger would stand on the porch of Cromwell Plantation holding a rifle." For a moment, intense grief mixed with his anger. "Everything I ever worked for has disappeared." Rage flared again to dissolve the grief. "It's not over. We may have lost the war, but there are many of us who are going to do whatever it takes to reclaim our lives and our fortunes. We're especially not going to let any traitor Southerners or Yankees stand in our way!" With that parting shot, he spun his horse and galloped down the road.

The other five hesitated only a moment before pulling their horses around and following him down the drive. The pounding of their hooves on the frozen ground sounded like gun shots as they disappeared around the bend.

Thomas put his pistol back in his pocket as the other men lowered their rifles. "Well," he said, taking a deep breath to steady himself. "I knew it wouldn't be easy," he finished matter-of-factly.

Robert chuckled as he stepped up to put his hand on Thomas' shoulder. "You handled it well," he said admiringly. "I'm afraid I would have already put a bullet in Cannon." He stared down the road. "Has he always been like that?"

Thomas shook his head heavily. "No. Daniel and I played together as boys. I attended functions at his plantation, and he attended many at Cromwell." He stared off into the distance as the sound of the drumming hooves grew more distant. "The war changed him. Losing everything, including his two youngest sons, changed him." He shook his head. "I disagree with his conclusions, but I sympathize with his pain and anger."

"They're not going to stop with words," Matthew said.

Robert stared at him for a long moment. "Does this have to do with what you didn't want to tell us at breakfast?"

"Yes," Matthew admitted.

"I think now might be a good time to fill everybody in," Thomas said, a spark of humor flaring as the tension of the moment passed. He turned to gaze down the road. "Should I expect them back tonight?"

"No," Matthew answered. "They know you have too much backup."

Thomas swung back around and stared into Matthew's face. "You're serious."

Matthew nodded, his blue eyes grim. "This stuff is happening all over the country."

Thomas took a deep breath. "Let's go back inside. Whatever you have to tell everyone would best be told around a warm fire. Now that the moment has passed, I am freezing!"

After Annie passed around a tray of hot coffee mugs and several thick logs fueled the flames throwing welcome warmth into the living room, Thomas turned to Matthew. "It's time for you to tell everyone what is going on," he said gravely.

Matthew took a long sip of his coffee and gazed around the room, wondering how there could be so much light and beauty in the midst of another darkness covering the country he loved. "I take it you have not received news about the Black Codes." He hesitated for a moment. "Thomas, Abby, and Jeremy already know what I'm about to say. We decided to keep it amongst ourselves through the holidays because we didn't want to ruin them."

Carrie was the only one with comprehension on her face. "I received a letter from a friend who mentioned Black Codes, but she didn't go into an explanation. She just seemed terribly indignant." She glared at her father. "As am I. You had a pistol in your pocket when you went out onto the porch. You suspected something would happen, but you went out there on your own."

Thomas reached over to take her hand. "I suspected, but I didn't know for sure. The only thing I was fairly sure of was that I would have backup if I needed it. I'm glad I was right about that." He gripped Carrie's hand tightly. "We've all been through so much, Carrie. I thought it was only fair to let us have our first Christmas since the war ended without more bad news."

Carrie's eyes softened. "I suppose I would have done the same thing," she admitted reluctantly. Then she turned back to Matthew. "So my friend had a right to be indignant about the Black Codes?"

"She had *every* right," Matthew said, anger flaring in his eyes, turning the blue almost black. "Abby, you asked me this morning what I meant when I agreed with Carrie that the war wasn't over."

"And you told me you were afraid that Appomattox ended just one phase of the conflict. The Confederates have returned home and initiated a new struggle to maintain the political and social dominance they enjoyed during the war," Abby replied.

Robert, adding another log to the fire, spoke over his shoulder. "I'm thinking you must have concrete evidence of that, because you're not one to speak lightly."

Matthew nodded heavily. "I'm not surprised the news hasn't reached the plantation. I also know how hard Thomas, Abby, and Jeremy have been working to open the factory. I shared part of this news with them before we came out for Christmas."

"We *had* been rather preoccupied," Thomas admitted. "I'm almost ashamed the news came as a shock. Please tell everyone what is going on. I'd heard rumors around town, but I haven't taken the time to stay current with everything in the country. I thought I was doing myself a favor after the constant pressures of political work, but now I'm afraid I've put myself and my family at a serious disadvantage because of my ignorance. Each person in this room needs to know the truth."

Abby reached over to squeeze his hand. "We're all adults responsible for our own information," she said softly. She turned back to Matthew. "Please don't hold anything back. Now is not the time to protect us."

"All of you know President Johnson has allowed political conventions in the Southern states to resume," Matthew began.

Carrie nodded, a resigned expression on her face. "I at least know that much... As far as I can tell, they have, for all intents and purposes, set up almost identical state governments to the ones that led us into secession. As much as I can sympathize with the Southern aristocracy fighting to regain control, I fear Johnson is doing nothing but fostering the same attitudes and beliefs that led us into the war in the first place."

"Northern Republicans would agree with you," Matthew answered.

"I agree with my astute daughter. Rather an odd position for a Southern politician to be in," Thomas said, an amused twinkle in his troubled eyes.

"I have a feeling that when all is said and done, many rational Southerners are going to find themselves aligned with Northern Republicans," Matthew said. "The South is doing all they can to make sure that emancipation for the slaves does little to actually change things."

"The Black Codes." Carrie said, leaning forward. "Please explain them."

Matthew nodded again and pulled some papers from his pockets. "Conventions in Mississippi, South Carolina, Georgia and Florida have already passed a form of Black Codes. I can assure you the other Confederate states will follow. Basically, it means they included language in their new state constitutions which instructed the legislature to guard them and their states against any evils that may arise from the sudden emancipation of the slaves."

"Can you be more specific?" Moses growled, his dark eyes flashing, his face a mixture of anger and pain.

Matthew exchanged a long look with him before he opened the sheaf of papers he held. "I'll read some of them in a minute, but the gist of their purpose is to restrict black people's rights to own property, conduct business, buy and lease land, and move freely through public spaces." He paused, an anguished look in his eyes. "These states have mandated that a black who is not working is a criminal..." his voice trailed off, his face saying he didn't want to continue.

"Just tell it to us straight, Matthew," Moses said, his voice once more under control. "We already know it's going to be bad."

"Yes, it's bad. Once blacks have been designated as criminals, they can be hired out as convicts for labor, either to the plantations or for public works projects," Matthew said flatly, only his eyes showing his disgust as he struggled to control his voice.

"So they have reinstated a new kind of slavery," Rose said, horror and bitterness lacing her words.

"It looks that way," Matthew admitted as he exchanged a long look with Robert, their years of friendship making words unnecessary for communication. It had taken many years for them to be on the same side in regard to slavery. He knew they both felt terrible for the freed slaves, but he also knew they could only imagine what it was truly like for them.

"Read some of them," June said, edging closer to Simon, as if her husband's presence would protect her from the harshness. "The happiest day of my life was when Moses set me free from the plantation. I aim to live with my husband and raise my little boy in freedom. We have to know what we're up against."

Matthew sighed and held up the papers. "This is written in typical legal mumbo jumbo, but I'm going to read it just as it is in the Mississippi Constitution. This section is in regard to the vagrancy laws..."

> *That all freedmen, free negroes and mulattoes in this State, over the age of eighteen years, found on the second Monday in January, 1866 or thereafter, without lawful employment or business, or found unlawfully assembling themselves together, either in the day or nighttime, and all white persons so assembling themselves with freedmen, free negroes or mulattoes, or usually associating with freedmen, free negroes or mulattoes, on terms of equality, or living in adultery or fornication with a freed woman, free negro or mulatto, shall be deemed vagrants, and on conviction thereof shall be fined in a sum not exceeding, in the case of a freedman, free negro or mulatto, fifty dollars, and a white man two hundred dollars, and imprisoned, at the discretion of the court, the free negro not exceeding ten days, and the white man not exceeding six months.*

"So they're even punishing sympathetic whites," Jeremy said after a stark silence filled the room for long moments. "They're covering their bases."

"Just like they did with the Fugitive Slave Act," Abby said with disgust. "I've had almost two weeks to absorb this, and it's still as horrifying as the first time I heard it!"

"I done come a long way with all of Rose's schooling, and I almost be able to read, but I'll admit I not be sure what you just read, Mister Matthew," Annie said slowly. "Could you put that into plain English for me?"

"Of course, Annie," Matthew replied. "Don't feel badly. Most educated people have a hard time understanding this convoluted language," he said with a smile. "It's basically saying that a black person can be detained for any number of reasons, put into prison, and then hired out to local plantation owners as labor to pay off the fines they can't afford. If a white person tries to help them, they will go to prison or have to pay a big fine."

"That be for any black person, or just the ones that used to be slaves?" Polly asked keenly.

"I'm afraid it means any black person," Matthew answered honestly. "The days of things being better for blacks who were free before emancipation may have ended. I don't believe anyone will make a distinction."

"That's the reason we left Maryland," Gabe said angrily. "They were wantin' to take Clint and Amber and force them into labor by taking away our custody. We left our home to get away from that. Now you're telling me the entire South is going to be like that?" His voice was twisted with disbelief.

Matthew looked at him, knowing there was nothing he could say to ease the anguish in Gabe's eyes.

"They're also talking about mulattoes," Jeremy observed. "That means me."

"You have to stay out of Richmond," Rose cried as she edged closer to her twin. "You won't be safe there."

Jeremy reached out to take her hand. "I can't hide here on the plantation, Rose," he said gently.

"Why not?" Rose asked, desperation edging her voice as her eyes filled. "I've only known you for eight months. I won't let some ignorant bigot take you away from me."

Jeremy squeezed her hand tightly. "I have a factory to run," he reminded her. "But more importantly, I refuse to live my life in fear. If we all run in fear, or give in to the mandates of the Black Codes, we'll be letting them win." He smiled softly as he gazed at Rose's mutinous look. "All of us are going to have things to battle in the years ahead. I counted the cost before I decided to acknowledge my heritage. I knew there was risk involved, but I wouldn't change my decision if I could make it again. I choose to live in honesty, and I'm proud to have the most wonderful twin in the world."

The tears in Rose's eyes spilled over. She turned to Matthew. "Have these laws passed in Virginia?"

"Not yet," Matthew said slowly, but he refused to give her false hope.

"But they will," Rose said flatly. Matthew's silence was her answer.

"There's more, isn't there?" Carrie's voice broke into the silence. "Tell us everything. We can't protect ourselves or fight if we don't know it all."

Matthew waved the thick sheaf of paper. "I'll tell you parts of them, but that's why I brought this with me for all of you to read. The other states have worded things a little differently, but they basically all say the same thing." He sighed heavily. "Whites can avoid the code's penalty by swearing a pauper's oath, but the sheriffs of each county have been mandated to hire out the blacks to whoever will pay their fine and all costs."

"Meaning the plantation owners buy them again," Simon said, rage filling his voice.

Matthew nodded. "There is also a special tax on blacks between the ages of eighteen and sixty. Those who cannot pay can be arrested for vagrancy."

"And sent back into forced labor," Rose said, the horror growing in her voice. "Most of the freed slaves just starting out can't pay a tax like that."

Matthew plunged ahead, his expression saying he wanted to get it over with. "Another law allows the state to take custody of children whose parents are deemed not able to support them. These children will be *apprenticed* to their former owners." His voice deepened. "These apprentices can be disciplined with corporal punishment. They can also recapture apprentices who escape and put them in prison if they resist."

"But what about the Thirteenth Amendment?" Carrie gasped. "Our country abolished slavery and involuntary servitude."

"Mississippi rejected it on December fifth," Matthew responded. "The others will follow them. They believe

President Johnson's willingness to give them their way has opened the door for them to ignore the amendment. They don't believe there will be any consequences."

A deep silence fell on the room as everyone struggled to absorb Matthew's news.

"I'm sorry," he said finally. "I wish I had better news."

"Of course you do," Moses said heavily. "No wonder you have been holding this back. It certainly would have put a damper on our holiday spirit." He shook his head. "I'm trying to understand what this will mean for all of us, for the South, and for our country as a whole."

"It's infuriating!" Abby broke in. "I don't understand how President Johnson can allow all this to happen. What was the point of four horrible years of war? What is Congress going to do about it? I have friends in the Senate who have to be livid about this."

Matthew nodded. "You're right, Abby. Congress just reconvened. There have been a lot of senators who have tried to change our president's course of action, but until Congress came back together, they could do little more than suggest, urge and pressure. President Johnson has listened to no one." He held up the sheaf of paper. "This is the result," he said, his voice filled with disgust.

"It's almost as if they believe slavery will be reinstated," Robert said slowly, his voice thick with disbelief. "They are simply creating a different name for it."

Matthew nodded again. "I believe you're right. Abby said it best at breakfast—we have changed the laws, but that has not changed people's beliefs. Losing the war may have actually intensified them. However irrational, the South blames the blacks for the war and for their defeat."

"That's ridiculous!" Carrie cried. "It was the white people who created slavery in the first place."

Moses was the one to answer her outburst. "I don't believe rational thinking figures into all this," he said bluntly. "If they blame the blacks, they have to blame the ones who fought against them even more." He gazed hard at Matthew.

Matthew remained silent for a long moment. "It's worse," he finally admitted, taking a deep breath. "There are white vigilante groups forming around the South."

"So, Jerrod was telling the truth," Simon said bitterly.

Everyone turned to look at him.

"Jerrod was a fella who came through a few weeks ago from Mississippi. He was looking for work, but we don't need anyone right now. He told us he thought he might have been safe here on Cromwell, but since there wasn't any work, he was going north as far as he could. He told us about blacks being killed by groups of white men who descend on homes." Simon's face hardened. "Folks are being hanged, beaten, and whipped." His voice cracked as he looked at Matthew. "It's true?"

Matthew looked far older than his years as he answered. "I'm afraid it's true." He stood and paced to the window, gazed out for a long moment, and then swung back to stare at the group. "We knew it would be hard..." he began.

"Hard?" Rose cried. "This isn't *hard*—this is slavery under a new name." She gazed down at John, who was curled up in the chair fast asleep, and clutched Hope closer to her chest. "I thought I was going to have a chance to raise my children as free people. Now, I have to worry that someone could snatch them away from me and sell them to some planter as apprentices!" Her eyes shot around the room. "It could happen to little Simon or any of the other children here on the plantation." Fear twisted her face. "It's not right..." Her voice broke as she buried her face in Moses' shoulder. "It's not right..."

Carrie and Abby moved as one, kneeling in front of Rose and taking her hands as Moses wrapped a protective arm around her shoulders. They said nothing because there were no words to assuage the fear and agony she was feeling. Support was all they could offer.

"Congress will fight it," Matthew said, a note of desperation in his voice.

"When?" Robert asked.

"I already know of several Republican senators who have drafted a civil rights act that will fight the Black Codes."

"And who will enforce them?" Jeremy asked. "President Johnson seems not to care what the Southern governments are doing. He just seems to let them do whatever they want."

"I know that's what it looks like," Matthew agreed. "I think even our president is appalled with the Black Codes, but he has alienated so much of the North with his policies that his only hope for re-election is Southern support."

"So that's what it comes down to?" Carrie asked angrily. "Once again we sell out the rights of an entire people for political gain?" Her voice cracked. "What can we do?"

"We continue to fight for equality," Abby said firmly. She lifted Rose's tear-stained face so she could gaze into her eyes. "We continue to fight for the rights of every living being. We continue to fight for ourselves, for our children and for the generations that will come." She smiled slightly. "It's either that or roll over and let them have their way."

Matthew watched as the spark reignited in Rose's eyes.

"Only over my dead body," she murmured as she straightened her shoulders and lifted her chin.

"There are plenty of Republicans in Congress who are going to fight this," Matthew said encouragingly. "It's going to take some time, but I don't think they will allow this to continue."

"Can they stop it soon?" Jeremy asked.

Matthew hesitated. "President Johnson's policies have picked up a lot of momentum," he responded honestly. "It's going to take some time to turn them around."

"Is there enough Republican support in Congress now to block President Johnson?" Abby asked. "I can't believe I even have to ask that question, but I've been so focused on the factory that I no longer know the answer."

"I don't know," Matthew said. "It may have to get worse before it gets better. There are Republicans who want equality for the blacks, but they are worn out from the years of war. They want to believe things will get better if they let the South figure things out."

"*That's* working well," Carrie interjected.

"Then there are the Republicans who are livid with Johnson," Matthew continued. "They refuse to let the years of war be for nothing. They will fight him with everything they have, and work to convince everyone else to join them."

"Politics..." Jeremy muttered. "It was the politicians who allowed slavery and got us into the war in the first place."

"Yes," Matthew agreed. "But it's the only system we have to create change. Against all odds, it was politicians who declared emancipation for the slaves. They created the Freedmen's Bureau. I have to believe they will see it through." His voice grew stronger. "*We* have to believe they will see it through. And we have to do everything we can to help make it happen."

Abby focused her clear gaze on him. "You have a plan."

Matthew smiled slightly. "I'm going to make sure everyone in the North knows what is really happening down here. I'm not going to let it slip to the backs of their minds. In addition to writing the book I've been commissioned to write, I've been offered the opportunity to write a column for the major newspapers in the North. I said yes."

"That's wonderful!" Abby cried.

"It will give me a platform to let people know what is really happening."

"And in the meantime?" Jeremy asked.

"In the meantime, everyone has to be careful," Matthew replied reluctantly. "We're *all* in danger. We need to be aware, and we need to be careful."

"Will that do any good?" Moses asked bitterly, almost as if he didn't expect an answer.

Matthew gave him one anyway. "In spite of the threats this morning, you are safest here on the plantation. Even though Thomas will be in Richmond, Cromwell Plantation is well-respected. I believe everyone will think twice before they come here. I'm sure it doesn't hurt either that everyone in the area knows the entire work force served as soldiers who saw battle. They may hate you more for it, but they aren't going to want to come under your fire."

"So the fight continues," Moses said wearily. Then he straightened his shoulders. "It's not like I didn't know it would, but I guess I hoped for a longer respite."

"We'll take care of our own," Simon vowed.

"We'll be ready," Gabe said gravely.

"And I'll stand with you," Robert said. "This isn't just a black fight. It may have taken me a while to understand basic human rights, but all of you are my friends and family. I will do whatever it takes to help protect you."

"And yourself," Matthew reminded him. "Your very attitude makes you a target." His eyes swung to Thomas. "Just like it does for you and Abby." Then he looked at Jeremy.

Jeremy held up his hands. "Don't worry. I know I'm a target. I won't run and hide, but I'll be as careful as I can be."

Carrie took a deep breath of the crisp, cold air as she and Robert stepped out onto the porch under the glitter of millions of twinkling stars. It was still frigid, but a soft breeze had blown away the brutal cold of that morning.

Robert smiled down at her. "Sure you want to do this?"

"Absolutely!" Carrie responded. "We haven't taken a nighttime ride in a long time."

"And remind me why we have chosen one of the coldest nights of the year?"

Carrie laughed. "Getting soft on me?"

"I would prefer to say I am getting older and wiser as I age," Robert responded smugly. "Not something you would recognize, though, I'm afraid."

"Insult me all you want," Carrie scoffed. "You're still going to have to keep your promise. Not to mention the promise I made to Granite when I slipped outside earlier to give him his New Year's carrots. Soft or not, we're going for a ride."

"Annie told me I couldn't talk you out of it," Robert said with resignation, although his eyes lit with laughter as he grabbed her hand.

"You'll be glad you couldn't," Carrie promised. "I have something to show you." She hoped the slightly warmer air hadn't taken away the surprise she had for her husband. The crunch of frozen grass under her feet indicated it had not.

Minutes later, they were mounted, shunning saddles and riding bareback to take advantage of the horses' body heat. Granite pranced excitedly, his arched neck glistening in the lantern light of the barn. Robert was mounted on Diamond, a bay mare given the name because of the single white marking that decorated her forehead. Her expression was one of confusion as she gazed wistfully at the rest of the horses staring at them from their protected stalls. Clearly, she did not share Granite's anticipation of going out into the dark cold.

"Where are we headed?" Robert asked.

Carrie held a finger to her lips, beckoned him to follow, and pushed Granite into an easy canter, once again giving thanks she had turned her back on sidesaddle riding. Being astride Granite in warm breeches was the only way to ride. Her friends in the South still looked askance at her when they met on the road, but women in the North had embraced the freedom years ago.

She took long breaths as they cantered side by side down the road leading toward the woods. Carrie could feel Robert looking at her curiously, but he said nothing. She knew he expected her to take them down to the river. Instead, she was heading toward a thick patch of woods she suspected Robert had never explored. She was glad the Christmas snow had melted away before the latest wave of cold swept in. It had been years since she was in this part of the plantation, and she was certain she couldn't have found the trail if it was buried under snow. As it was, she worried it would be too overgrown for her to find now.

Carrie slowed as she reached the edge of the woods, her eyes trying to penetrate the darkness and heavy brush. She breathed a sigh of relief when she saw a faint trail leading deeper into the trees. Holding up her hand for continued silence, she edged Granite forward at a steady walk. Moving slowly, they dodged overhanging branches and made their way carefully around fallen trees. The glow of the half moon was just enough to light the way. The frozen ground echoed back the thud of hooves, and brittle branches snapped in the cold as they pushed through them. Finally, they broke out into a clearing. One look told Carrie her surprise was waiting.

"I didn't even know this was here!" Robert exclaimed as he gazed at the small lake nestled in the woods.

"I hoped you hadn't discovered it," Carrie said with delight.

"This is a great surprise."

"Oh, this isn't your surprise," Carrie murmured as she swung off Granite's back and tied him to a hanging branch. She waited for Robert to dismount and tie Diamond; then she took his hand and led him forward to the edge of the lake. "*This* is your surprise," she announced, waving her hand over the lake. The lake caught the moon and sent it shooting back as diamonds glittered from along the entire shoreline.

"Look at that..." Robert said slowly, amazement filling his voice as he leaned down. "The whole lake is surrounded by ice sculptures! I've never seen anything like it."

Carrie nodded happily. "The conditions have to be just right. If the air is cold enough, and the wind blows strongly enough, the water forms ice sculptures on everything it hits. I discovered them for the first time when I was thirteen." She paused. "I've never shared them with anyone but you." She gazed up at Robert, her eyes soft with love. "I used to dream of bringing my husband here to see them. This is the first opportunity."

Robert leaned down to kiss her warmly, holding her face as he peered into her luminous eyes. "You are one in a million, Carrie Borden. Thank you for loving me," he whispered.

Grabbing her hand, he began to walk along the edge of the lake. "This one looks like a cluster of grapes."

"A cluster of grapes full of diamonds," Carrie agreed. "Look how they are reflecting the stars." She pointed further to the right. "That one looks like a heart. See how it is wrapped around the branch suspended above the water?"

"Magnificent," Robert muttered, his head swinging as he tried to take it all in. "I don't believe I've ever seen anything more beautiful," he murmured.

Carrie felt the sudden tension grip his body. "Robert?" She knew so many different things could trigger the pain and agony of the last four years.

Robert stood on the shoreline and took several deep breaths until he could speak. "This time last year I was hauling frozen carcasses out of the Petersburg trenches. Men I had eaten with the night before had frozen to death," he said slowly, his voice laced with pain. "I just can't believe there can be so much pain and fear in the midst of such beauty," he muttered as he leaned down again to touch an ice formation that looked like a bird in flight. "It seems to me that if people could simply absorb the raw beauty of God's world they would find a way to live in harmony. They would see their own fears and greed as being so tiny and unimportant if they could truly grasp God's power."

Carrie knew his thoughts had never strayed far from Matthew's announcement this morning. Somehow all of them had been able to push aside the reality and bring laughter to the rest of the day as they played games and ate around the fireplace, shoving aside their turmoil for the children's sake. But she had seen the trouble lurking in her husband's eyes. She knew it was more than memories of the war. "You're afraid it will come to Cromwell," she said.

Robert looked down at her. "I think 1866 is going to be a year of challenges," he finally acknowledged, but he said no more.

Carrie tried to swallow the surge of panic that rose in her throat as she wrapped her arms around Robert, letting him hold her close. "I don't want to leave you," she whispered.

"You're not going anywhere for three more months," Robert said roughly, his lips pressed against the top of her head as he rubbed his hands down her back.

"One day, or four months. I can't imagine saying goodbye again. I can't imagine not knowing what is going on with you every day." She fought against the images of marauding vigilantes sweeping the countryside.

Robert held her back and stared down into her face. "We will not let fear rule us. If we do, they will have won. We have to live our lives as if there is no fear."

Carrie held his eyes, trying to slow the pounding of her heart. Finally, she managed a small smile. "Old Sarah used to tell me that fear does nothing but keep me focused on the past or worried about the future." Her smile grew as she remembered. "She told me if I could acknowledge my fear, I would also realize that *right now* I was okay. That right now I am alive. That right now I can see the sky and all the ice sculptures nature has created. That *right now* I am with the man I love more than life itself."

She felt her anxiety lift as she spoke the words. Once more she turned her face up, losing herself in a kiss that completely blotted out her fears.

Chapter Three

Janie was shivering uncontrollably as she walked the last block toward home. She was wearing two layers of clothes, had on her warmest coat, and was bundled with gloves, scarf, and a warm hat, but she was sure nothing could keep out the biting cold. She was quite sure it was cold in Richmond, but she was also convinced she had never been in a city as cold as Philadelphia. Gray snow, turned grimy by coal dust, blanketed everything in sight. Workers had tried to clear the sidewalks, but there was simply nowhere to put the mountains of snow that had been piling up for the last two months. The sixteen inches that fell shortly before Christmas had been packed down by sidewalk traffic, but her feet kept pushing through, causing her to walk very slowly. Her thick boots were no match for the cold that had seeped through to every pore of her body.

The sidewalks were peppered with people, but no one spoke. Heads down, hands shoved deep in pockets, everyone was simply intent on getting where they were going. Janie was so grateful she had a home to look forward to. She wondered how many of the miserable looking people were going to a home that was barely warmer than the brutal outdoors. She knew the suffering in the city was terrible. She walked the last hundred feet rapidly, drawn by what she knew awaited.

She gasped when she opened the door to Abby's beautiful home and felt warmth pour out toward her. "Heat!" she cried joyfully.

"Shut that door!" a voice called. "It's taken us all afternoon to get the house warm."

Janie laughed as a wave of delicious aromas flowed to her on the warm air. "Gladly! Especially if I really am smelling barley soup and bread. Please tell me I'm not having hallucinations."

Elizabeth Gilbert, her round face smudged with flour, appeared from the kitchen with a broad smile on her lips. "You're not having hallucinations," she answered. "You're smelling bread and soup—just not barley soup. Alice and I got out of class early today because our professor was called into an emergency. We decided to use it to surprise you and Florence." Her eyes held a question as she looked beyond Janie.

"Florence will be here in a just a little while," Janie assured her. "Doctor Anderson wanted her to stay after class a little while today. I offered to wait, but she insisted I come ahead. I believe Dr. Anderson is going to have her driver bring her home."

Elizabeth relaxed. "Good. I hate to think of her walking the streets alone after dark."

"I wouldn't have let that happen," Janie said. She lifted her nose and sniffed. "If it's not barley soup, what is that remarkable smell?"

"Mulligatawny soup," Elizabeth answered promptly.

Janie stared at her. "*What* kind of soup?"

Elizabeth grinned. "Our Southern belle hasn't ever heard of Mulligatawny soup?"

"Is it meant to be eaten?" Janie asked. "It sounds rather like a strange disease."

Elizabeth laughed loudly, her Massachusetts accent even more pronounced when she called over her shoulder. "Alice, our little Southern belle has never heard of our famous soup!"

Alice Humphries appeared moments later, her blond hair creating a stark contrast to Elizabeth's dark Italian features. "I told you she would be surprised!" She grabbed Janie's hand. "Come on. The soup will be a little while longer, but we have hot tea brewing on the stove."

Janie sighed and followed willingly, the torture of walking home forgotten now that she was warm again. "Please tell me about Mulligatawny soup."

Alice laughed and pointed her to the recipe box on the counter. "This soup is my grandma's specialty. My brothers and I grew up on it."

Janie picked up the recipe card as she settled down at the table. She took a moment to gaze around the light blue kitchen with white cabinets and counters. Even after three months of being here, she hadn't lost her sense of awe that Abby had so generously offered her Philadelphia house to live in while she was in medical school. The first few weeks had been rather lonely. The loneliness had disappeared when her fellow medical students, Elizabeth, Alice and Florence, moved in with her. They had been here little more than a week, but they already felt like family. The situation suited everyone.

Janie accepted the hot cup of tea Elizabeth held out to her, pushing her soft brown hair absently back from her face. Pulling off the thick winter hat always undid her half-hearted attempts to keep it tamed into a bun. She focused her light blue eyes on the recipe card.

MULLIGATAWNY SOUP

Ingredients: 2 tablespoons of curry powder, 6 onions, 1 clove of garlic, 1 ounce of pounded almonds, a little lemon-pickle or mango juice to taste; 1 fowl or rabbit, 4 slices of lean bacon, 2 quarts of medium stock or, if wanted, very good, best stock.

Mode: Slice and fry the onions a nice color; line the stew pan with the bacon. Cut up the rabbit or fowl into small joints and slightly brown them; put in the fried onions, the garlic, and stock, and simmer gently until the meat is tender; skim very carefully, and when the meat is done, rub the curry powder to a smooth batter. Add it to the soup along with the almonds, which must be first pounded with a little of the stock. Put in seasoning and lemon-pickle or mango juice to taste, and serve it with boiled rice.

Time: 2 hours.

"This looks like Indian cuisine," she said with surprise as she looked at Alice's blond hair with a raised brow.

Alice smiled. "My grandma had a good friend from India when she lived in England. She came over to America when I was about five years old. She brought the recipe with her. My brothers and I made her cook it for us every time we went to visit. When she learned I was going to medical school, she wrote up the recipe so I could make it here." She gazed around the kitchen. "I couldn't imagine I would have a place to cook," she said in wonder. "I thought surely I would be stuffed into some tiny, drab, freezing room." She waved her arm. "Instead I am living in the home of one of the wealthiest women in Philadelphia in absolute splendor."

The odors wafting from the pot grew more wonderful by the moment. Janie patted her growling stomach and looked at the stove yearningly. "The recipe says two hours. How much longer?"

"You have time to go up and get into more comfortable clothes," Elizabeth said. "The soup is done. We're just waiting on the bread. It should be ready when you get back."

Janie closed her eyes with a happy sigh. "I think I've died and gone to heaven."

"Yes," Alice said, pushing her from the chair, "but you can do that in your room. We're going to start eating when the bread comes out, whether you are here or not," she warned.

Janie laughed, gave both Alice and Elizabeth a quick kiss on their cheeks, and spun from the room, laughing even harder at their surprised looks. "I love you both!" she called over her shoulder. Her wonderful new Yankee friends were warm and loving, but they hadn't yet learned to deal with what they called her unique brand of Southern hospitality.

Janie gazed longingly at the closed door to what would be Carrie's room when she arrived. She loved her new friends and had been completely accepted, but there were times she wearied of being the only Southern woman at the medical school. The original plan was that she would wait for Carrie to arrive in the spring before she started classes. Dr. Anderson convinced her there was no reason to wait, and that her years at Chimborazo gave her enough practical experience and knowledge. Carrie had been so excited about Janie's news in the letter she had sent before Christmas.

Janie smiled as she envisioned the beauty of crisp, clean snow at Cromwell Plantation. She wondered if everyone had left the plantation after the holidays and gone back to their busy lives.

When she entered her room—chillier than downstairs, but still warm because of the constant flow of warm air from the oil heaters—she felt the quick tug in her heart that constantly reminded her of how much she had to be grateful for. The nightmares of Clifford coming for her had almost disappeared, but she had not yet stopped looking for him when she walked home from school, anticipating every man would have his angry face and eyes. Looking into the mirror, she raised a hand to her face. She never wanted to forget the yellow and purple bruises that had covered it after Clifford hit her. The memory of the pain and humiliation kept her focused on doing whatever it took to stay in complete control of her life so no one could ever have the power to hurt her again.

A call from downstairs made her turn away from the mirror and quickly change into a more comfortable dress. She had a brief vision of Carrie in the riding breeches she had become so fond of. Janie thought longingly of how much warmer they would be on the streets of Philadelphia and then shook her head with a laugh. She was becoming stronger and more independent, but she was not quite the rebel Carrie was. She raised enough eyebrows and ire simply by choosing to study medicine. There were some female protocols she was content to live with, even if she wished it were different.

Florence pushed in through the front door just as Janie hurried down the stairs, drawn by the smells of dinner that were even stronger than before. She laughed as Florence staggered in and closed the door behind her, her red curls spilling out when she pulled off her hat.

Tall and angular, Florence was not necessarily pretty, but her commanding presence pulled attention to her everywhere she went. She shrugged her coat off as she slipped out of her boots. "We're breaking records tonight," she announced.

"Records?" Alice asked, peering out from the kitchen.

"It's minus eighteen degrees outside," Florence muttered, her voice strengthening as she lifted her face to smell the air. "Is that dinner?" Her face split in a grin. "Have I really come home to a prepared, hot dinner?"

"Don't get used to it," Elizabeth called, breezing into the room. "I will admit it's a welcome break from cold sandwiches while we study, though." She rubbed her hands in anticipation. "I'm glad you made it in time. I just filled your bowl and plate. Do you need to change?"

"Forget changing," Florence stated. "Lead me to the food!"

Laughing, the four women filed into the kitchen.

Florence looked at the bowls of soup on the table, her grin growing even wider. "Mulligatawny soup!" she cried. "I haven't had it in years."

Janie shook her head. "Yankees," she said lightly, her eyes bright with laughter. "I'm quite sure this soup has never made it past the Mason-Dixon Line. I can't imagine that a single friend of mine would have any idea what this is."

"Which explains why you Rebels aren't as bright as we are," Florence retorted, knowing her comment would be taken with the humor it was meant to carry.

Janie shrugged. "Bright enough to make an 'A' on my first physiology exam," she said playfully, immediately regretting her words when she saw her friend's expression.

Florence scowled. "Oh sure, rub it in my face." Her eyes showed discouragement. "I studied my heart out, and I still struggled," she admitted. Then she grinned as she ate a spoonful of soup, followed by a chunk of bread slathered with butter. "Not that it seems important right this minute."

Janie felt a tug of sympathy. She knew how hard Florence studied. She also knew Florence envied how easily Janie's grades came to her. "Don't feel badly," she said quickly, her voice thick with remorse.

Florence waved her hand casually. "I don't. I may have difficulty taking tests, but I stayed later today because I've been asked to assist Dr. Anderson with some of her patients in the clinic. It seems my natural abilities are outshining my dismal academic record."

"That's wonderful!" the three women cried in unison.

Florence shrugged, only her eyes showing how excited she was. "I can't believe I'm going to say this, but I almost miss the war. No one seemed to care about my credentials when I was out on the battlefield." Instead of serving in the city hospital, Florence had gone out onto the battlefields, treating wounded soldiers until they were carried back to the hospital. There was no telling how many lives she had saved. She had wanted to be a doctor since she was old enough to understand what they did.

Janie understood. "I know just what you mean. Carrie and I worked as a team at Chimborazo. She got to do more than I did, but none of the soldiers questioned our abilities. They were simply glad we were there to help them. At the beginning of the war, people were horrified that we were practicing medicine. By the end of the war, we were almost viewed as heroes."

Elizabeth stood abruptly. "That reminds me. A letter came for you today. I think it's from Carrie, the mystery lady we hear about all the time." She walked over to the counter, filling her bowl with more soup before she returned with the letter.

Janie eyed it with anticipation but merely stuffed it in her pocket.

"You're not going to read it now?" Elizabeth asked, disappointment obvious in her voice.

Janie shook her head. "I like to read them slowly and savor them," she replied, not trying to explain that each letter felt like a hand reaching out from home. Carrie was the closest thing to a sister she had ever had. She missed her every single day and could hardly wait until she arrived in the spring. Right now, with cold wind whistling at the windows, it seemed a lifetime away. She knew they were in for more months of brutal cold.

"What is the plantation like in the winter?" Alice asked.

Janie smiled. Plantation life was something all of them were curious about. None of them had ever been to the South. They had sat mesmerized when Janie described the unique relationship Carrie, Rose, and Moses had. All of them had served in the abolition movement and truly believed all slaves were treated badly. Janie was careful not to downplay the horrible conditions many slaves had lived under, but she also wanted them to understand all Southerners didn't feel the same way.

"I don't have a lot of firsthand experience," Janie admitted. "I only visited once in the winter. The rest of my time there was in the summer and fall, but Carrie has told me about it. Things move more slowly, but there is so much to be done to be ready for the spring. The year I was there, we had a deep snowfall." Her eyes softened with the memories. "It was the most beautiful thing I had ever seen. I grew up in the city and had never seen undisturbed snow like that."

The other three women nodded their understanding. Elizabeth had grown up in Boston, Alice in New York, and Florence in Philadelphia, though her parents had moved away several years earlier to a small town in Illinois where her father practiced medicine.

"Doesn't all snow turn gray?" Alice teased.

"Not on Cromwell Plantation," Janie assured her. "It stays pure and white, reflecting back a million diamonds when the sun hits it." She smiled as she remembered. "It seems to swallow sound..." Her voice trailed off. "It makes you feel"—she searched for the right word—"safe," she finally said. "I know that sounds odd, but that's how it made me feel. Like the snow created a barrier from the rest of the world, and especially the war. They were the most peaceful days I spent during the war."

The kitchen fell silent all of the women filled with their own thoughts and memories of the war. Alice stood to fill her bowl with more soup, but not before Janie caught the bright sheen of tears in her eyes. "Alice?"

Alice stiffened as she faced the stove, remaining silent while she dished up her soup. "I got a letter from my parents today," she admitted. She turned slowly, her face tight with pain. "My brother is not doing well."

Janie frowned. "The morphine?"

Alice hesitated and then nodded. "He was caught breaking into the local dispensary to steal some." Her voice caught. "My parents say they don't know how to help him. His doctors say he doesn't need it anymore, but he'll do anything to get it."

Elizabeth nodded. "I'm hearing that story from all over the North," she said.

"And the South," Janie said quickly. "We don't have quite as big of a problem because the blockade stopped the flow of drugs long before the war was over, but there is still a large addiction problem. Morphine and opium may have been hard to come by, but moonshine is easily available in the South."

"They're blocking out memories," Florence said quickly. "All of them have so many horrible memories of what happened to them. Not to mention pain they will suffer for the rest of their lives from their injuries. Addiction is a very real thing," she said angrily. "Dr. Anderson told me today that there are hundreds of thousands of war veterans suffering from addiction. I know our doctors thought they were doing the right thing when they continued to give morphine for the pain, but the long-term results are disastrous." She scowled. "Forget what I said earlier about almost wishing the war wasn't over. I'll be happy if I never have to walk onto another battlefield covered with dead and dying men," she said fiercely. "So many are going to live with the consequences for the rest of their lives."

"The people around them will suffer as well," Alice said quietly, her blue eyes dark with worry. "My parents have tried everything to help my brother. He was only sixteen when he went to war. My parents tried to stop him, but he snuck off one night with some friends because he didn't want to miss the adventure," she said bitterly.

The three women remained silent, knowing her brother's *adventure* had sent him home minus a leg below the knee and with an addiction that was destroying him. He had just turned twenty.

"He got married during a leave from the war," she revealed for the first time, "but his wife left him a few months ago because of his rages."

Janie flinched, knowing all too well what that was like. "Is it easier up here?" she asked impulsively.

"Easier?"

"To leave your husband?" Janie asked, knowing she was off topic, but all the talk had reactivated her memories. She gripped her napkin tightly to conceal her shaking hands.

Florence looked at her closely and then reached under the table to take hold of one of her hands. "What haven't you told us?" she asked perceptively.

Janie shook her head. "I'm sorry," she said. "We aren't talking about me."

"We are now," Alice responded, her eyes warm with compassion. "Janie?"

Janie stared at the three women, swallowing back her tears at the looks of compassion and kindness on all their faces. She had not wanted to talk about Clifford. Starting a new life meant leaving him in the past. Most days she could do it, but then something would happen to trigger her memories, and she would be right back in the swirl of anger and fear that almost destroyed her.

"I was married," she began, smiling slightly at the looks of surprise. "Clifford was one of my patients. He lost an arm during a battle outside Richmond. We fell in love and got married." She paused, gathering her thoughts. "The war changed him. Or maybe it was losing the war," she clarified, the pain rising up in her again.

"Take your time," Elizabeth said softly, reaching over to put a hand on her shoulder.

Janie took strength from the kindness in her eyes. "He became angry and bitter," she continued. "He wasn't the same man I married. It got worse every day." She saw the understanding on Alice's face and knew she was thinking of her brother who had gone off to war a happy-go-lucky teenager and returned a broken, bitter man. "When we returned to North Carolina after the war, he kept me hostage in the house, not wanting my liberal feelings about blacks and the war to impact his law practice and his political ambitions."

"Janie!" Alice gasped.

Janie plunged ahead, wanting to get it over with. "Most of his abuse was verbal. He convinced me I was nothing but a worthless woman who deserved what he was dishing out." She smiled softly. "My housekeeper convinced me differently. She gave me courage to search for a way out, so I began to put aside little bits of money so I could escape."

She swallowed back tears again as she told the rest of the story. "Clifford hit me the last night I ever saw him." She flinched as she relived his fist exploding in her face, the pain and humiliation as fresh as the night it happened. "I escaped that night," she said softly. "I had just enough money to catch a train to Richmond."

"He didn't come after you?" Alice asked breathlessly.

"He did," Janie admitted. "Carrie's husband, Robert, convinced him it wouldn't be wise for him to come again."

"He beat him up," Florence said bluntly.

Janie smiled. "Yes." The smile widened to a grin when the women cheered. "Robert helped me find a judge who would grant me a divorce."

"Not easy in Richmond, I bet," Elizabeth said.

"It helped that Carrie's father worked in the Virginia government," Janie added. "He was able to point Robert in the right direction."

"Pays to know the right people," Florence murmured.

"But you're still afraid," Elizabeth observed.

Janie saw no reason to deny what they obviously saw. "Most of the nightmares have stopped, but I'm still afraid he will show up one day."

"Let him try," Florence said, the look of battle in her eyes. "He's never faced four angry women before."

"That's right," Alice said staunchly. "If we can put up with all the abuse people have dished out on us for becoming doctors, a weakling one-armed lawyer can't do a thing!"

Janie laughed now, the fear ebbing away as the support and warmth of her new friends surrounded her. "Y'all are the best!" she exclaimed. "Do you know that?"

Florence raised her eyebrows. "I still can't believe I'm sharing a house with someone who says *y'all*," she said playfully. "And of course, we know we're the best."

"And modest, too," Elizabeth said.

Florence shrugged. "My grandmother always told me I shouldn't bother to hide my light under a bushel basket. If Janie wants to believe we are the best, who am I to refute her?"

Laughter rang around the table, pushing aside all sadness and fear.

Alice grinned. "We're not done with dinner yet," she said.

Elizabeth cocked a brow. "I helped you cook dinner," she reminded her. "There's nothing else."

Alice looked coy. "Did I say anything about cooking it?" She stood and walked over to the pantry. "I barely got this hidden before you came in," she teased Elizabeth. She smiled broadly as she reached into the pantry, pulled out a dish covered in a towel, placed it on the table, and whipped the towel off.

"Pie!" the women cried in unison.

"Not just *any* pie," Alice said proudly. "This is—"

"Opal's apple pie! She always puts a little apple shape on the crust on one edge as her signature," Janie said in awe. "How did you...?"

Alice tried to look nonchalant. "I got out of class a little before the rest of you, so I decided to swing by Eddie and Opal's restaurant. I've been thinking about this pie ever since you took me there last week. She had some coming out of the oven just as I got there." She grinned again. "It helped keep my hands warm on the way home."

Elizabeth jumped up to get a knife. "I'll cut it," she offered.

"Into four pieces," Florence instructed.

"Four?" Alice asked doubtfully. "We always cut pies into eight slices."

"That's because you didn't grow up with three brothers," Florence answered. "Mama always let us cut the pie into four pieces." She rubbed her hands in anticipation. "That way we always got a quarter of a pie." She smacked her lips. "I'm tall, but my brothers are much bigger than me. It took a lot to fill us up. What's the point of a tiny piece of pie? We have no one to impress with our feminine sensibilities. I say we eat enough to count!"

"Sounds great to me," Janie said enthusiastically, as she laughed and eyed the pie. "We'll need the extra calories to stay warm in all this cold weather."

Alice still looked doubtful.

Elizabeth, a big smile on her face, carefully cut the pie into four slices. "Alice, really?" she asked. "You are going against every convention of proper society to become a woman doctor, and you're struggling with cutting a pie into quarters?"

Alice finally laughed and reached for her plate. "You're absolutely right," she admitted. "It's amazing to me how someone's beliefs can become your own even when there is no justification for it. I had a man call me a pitiful excuse for a woman today when I started into class."

The three women nodded with sympathetic understanding. All of them had experienced it.

"If I can stand against that, what will keep me from eating a quarter of a pie? In fact, I might buy another one and eat the whole thing myself," Alice finished defiantly. She dug into the pie, took a bite, and rolled her eyes. "Opal makes the best apple pie in the world," she declared. She closed her eyes for a long moment and opened them to look at Janie. "Opal and Eddie asked about you. Opal said to tell you she had a sweet potato casserole with your name on it."

Janie pretended to swoon as she finished chewing a big bite. "Next to her apple pie, Opal's sweet potato casserole is the best thing in the world." She brought another bite to her lips. "How are they doing?"

Alice hesitated.

Janie put her fork back down. "Alice?"

Alice shook her head. "They didn't say anything," she said quickly. "It was just something in Opal's eyes. She didn't seem as happy as she did when we were there before."

"She's probably freezing to death," Florence observed. "Isn't this her first Northern winter?"

"Yes," Alice agreed. "That might be all it was. They had their woodstove blazing in the middle of the restaurant, but I know that place is hard to keep warm. If they're not home all day long, I imagine they go back to a very cold home."

Janie nodded, knowing Opal and Eddie lived in little more than a shack so they could pour all their money into the restaurant. She could imagine the strain was adding up, but she made a mental note to go by the restaurant on the way home from school the next day so she could see for herself. She had gotten closer to them since moving to Philadelphia, counting on Opal to feed her before her housemates had joined her. She'd spent her whole life with housekeepers cooking for her. Even during the war, she had eaten most of her meals at Carrie's house, with May doing all the cooking. She knew pitiful little about feeding herself. She felt no real motivation for that to change, not when there were people in the world like Opal to cook for her.

The women laughed and talked as they finished their pie, but Janie couldn't rid herself of the worry niggling at the back of her mind. She was suddenly eager for tomorrow to arrive so she could visit Opal and Eddie.

Chapter Four

The weak sun did little to warm the frigid air as Janie made her way toward the restaurant. Clanging bells from streetcars, shouts from wagon drivers, and the steady clap of carriages filled the air. Record-breaking low temperatures seemed to have done little to slow activity in the city.

Janie huddled deeper into her coat. She kept her thoughts busy with what she learned that day in class as she joined the flow of people on the sidewalk. It was easy to be preoccupied with the information she had received in class that morning.

After seventeen years, cholera had returned to the United States.

Dr. Anderson had delivered the news that morning. The *Atalanta*, an English mail steamer, had sailed for New York from London on the tenth of October. She docked at Le Havre on the eleventh, and took aboard twenty-four cabin and five hundred forty steerage passengers. When she dropped anchor in New York's lower bay in December, her master reported sixty cases of cholera and fifteen deaths.

The news was devastating. In spite of the fact that ships had increased in size and their passenger lists had doubled, they still did not provide quarantine. Medical and political considerations demanded the passengers be denied entrance to America. A hospital ship was hastily fitted out in the harbor. As soon as it was possible, all the passengers were transferred to it. She could only imagine the misery of the hundreds of people confined to what they surely knew was a death trap.

Dr. Anderson reported that new cases were occurring aboard the hospital ship, but the bitter cold had so far kept the disease from spreading to the city. New York was safe for the moment, but she stressed it was only a respite—for the rest of the nation, as well as for New York. History had made it clear that when the first cases of cholera had spread to the mainland, the disease had not been content until it continued far into the Midwest, seeking out high population areas.

Janie's mind spun as she thought about the results of the horrible disease. The last major outbreak in the United States had been in 1849. Fifty-two thousand people had died in England and Wales where it began. It moved on to Ireland and killed many of the Great Famine survivors already weakened by starvation and fever. Irish immigrants, fleeing the misery in their country, brought it to the United States.

Cholera took the life of former president James K. Polk. The disease killed thousands in New York, where it was first brought by the immigrant ships, but it wasn't content to remain there. It spread throughout the Midwest, decimating one-tenth of the populations of St. Louis, Cincinnati, and New Orleans. The horror intensified when it was transmitted along the California, Mormon, and Oregon Trails. Close to twelve thousand people died in the wagon trains as they attempted to find a better life out west.

Before the cholera died out, it had killed more than one hundred fifty thousand Americans and also dipped south to claim two hundred thousand victims in Mexico.

Janie shuddered as a cold blast of wind swept under her coat, but she was sure the shudder was equally due to the realization the dreaded disease was once more perched off the New York shoreline. Was there to be no end to the suffering America would endure during this decade?

"Watch out lady!"

Janie jerked her head up when a nearby man hollered. She stepped back onto the sidewalk just in time to miss a collision with a wagon. The driver scowled at her and shook his head. She turned to thank the man who had yelled at her, but he was already hurrying down the sidewalk, his head bowed against the cold. Shaken, she scolded herself to pay more attention. Thoughts of cholera would have to wait until she got home. Forcing her eyes and her thoughts to focus, she walked faster.

The next voice she heard was more familiar. "Janie!"

Janie raised her head, realizing she was almost to the restaurant. A broad smile lit her face. "Sadie Lou!" Eddie's seventeen-year-old daughter was becoming a beautiful young woman. When she became best friends with Moses' sister Sadie, their shared names caused quite a bit of confusion, so now everyone called her Sadie Lou. "It's wonderful to see you!"

"You, too. Let's go inside and get out of this cold," Sadie Lou said quickly.

Janie frowned when she realized how thin Sadie Lou's coat was. Her gloves and hat didn't seem to be much better. "You should have more clothes on," she admonished.

Sadie Lou only shrugged. "I'm younger than you are. I don't get cold as easily," she said impishly, though the glazed look in her eyes refuted her casual words.

"Right." Janie took her arm and pulled her into the warmth of the restaurant, both of them gasping in relief when the heat from the woodstove reached out to them. Janie stood still, allowing the heat to thaw her face, aware of sensational aromas pouring into the room from the kitchen.

"Janie!"

"Opal! I understand there is a sweet potato casserole with my name on it," Janie said, taking Opal's hands and squeezing them tightly, using the opportunity to stare into her eyes. Alice was right. Opal's round face had a warm smile on it, but her eyes were heavy and burdened.

"There always be a sweet potato casserole with your name on it, Miss Janie." Opal responded. "You girls enjoy that apple pie last night?"

Janie rolled her eyes and patted her stomach. "It was like manna from heaven," she murmured. "Opal, have you ever heard of Mulligatawny soup? I had it for the first time last night."

Opal sniffed. "I've heard of it." Her eyes showed her disdain. "I've even had a bowl, but there's just nothing like good ole Southern cooking. I know people from all over the world got to eat, but they need to come south if they want to learn how to cook!"

Janie laughed and allowed Sadie Lou to lead her to a table in the back corner. Her eyes lit with pleasure when she recognized the two sitting at the table. "Susie! Zeke! It's wonderful to see you both." This was the first time she had gotten to see Eddie's eldest daughter and her husband since she'd arrived in town.

Susie patted the chair next to her. "Sit yourself down, Janie. Amber and Carl will have your sweet potato casserole out in a few minutes."

Sadie Lou pulled off her coat as she turned away. "I'm going back into the kitchen to help Opal. Enjoy your lunch, Janie."

"Impossible not to," Janie replied. "I'll see you soon, Sadie Lou." Pulling off her winter clothing, she sank onto the rustic chair with gratitude. She looked around and realized the restaurant was full of people talking, laughing and eating. Most of them were black, but there were a few whites who came because the word was spreading about Opal's cooking. "The restaurant is doing so well," she murmured.

Susie nodded. "Daddy and Opal have worked hard." She paused briefly, her eyes bright with memories. "Mama would be so proud."

"That she would," Janie assured her. She had not had a chance to meet Opal's cousin Fannie before she was killed in an explosion at the Tredegar Iron Works on the very same day Eddie was arrested for espionage and sentenced to prison. Carrie had helped Opal return to the plantation with the couple's four children, where Opal cared for them until after the war.

Susie's eyes followed Opal as she bustled around in the kitchen. "She's good for my daddy. I'm glad they fell in love after the war. They both needed a new beginning."

Janie nodded. "Carl and Amber seem happy as well."

Susie grinned. "My brother and sister are amazing. Being in school has been wonderful for them, and they actually love working here at the restaurant. They say they are warmer than any of their friends."

Janie frowned. "Your home?"

Susie tried to shrug off the question, but Janie saw the truth in her eyes.

Zeke reached over to squeeze his wife's hand. "We've been through worse," he assured Janie. "It will take a couple years to get the restaurant really making good money, but Eddie is already making plans to build a better house. Being free to make our own decisions is worth whatever it takes."

Janie nodded again. "You're right," she said immediately, but she couldn't help feeling guilty that she lived in such splendor while they struggled to stay warm. If there had been room, she would have asked them all to move in.

"Get that look off your face," Susie said sternly.

"Look?" Janie murmured in confusion.

"Yes. The look that says you should be able to change our situation. I know you would have us all move in with you if you could, but Daddy and Opal wouldn't do it anyway. They are determined to make it on their own. Daddy may have technically been free while he was in Richmond, but he never had a chance to truly live that way. His years in prison made him even hungrier for freedom. Opal has dreamed of this since she was a young girl on the plantation." Susie gazed around at the simple tables covered with red and white checkered cloths, at the glowing candles on every table, at the woodstove shooting out warmth. "This is their dream. They want to live close to it, and they want it to create a life they can be proud of. They know suffering. At least now they have control of their lives."

Janie considered her words. She knew Susie was right. She also knew that as much as she tried to understand, her years of privilege as a white woman from a wealthy background made true understanding impossible. She would have to settle for compassion.

Susie covered her hand. "You just keep coming down to buy food. Keep sending your friends. That will give them the life you want them to have."

Janie peered at her more closely, seeing something in her eyes. "And you and Zeke?"

Zeke sat up straighter in his chair. "When I was a slave down in North Carolina, I heard about people going west. I've been wantin' to join them ever since."

"West?" Janie echoed.

"The Oregon Territory. Folks don't care so much about color out there, and I hear it be real beautiful along the Pacific coast."

Janie looked into his bright eyes full of excitement before she turned to Susie. "And you want to go?"

Susie nodded. "I do. I don't think being black won't matter, but everything I've heard says it won't matter *as much*. Zeke and I want to have kids now that the war is over." She took a deep breath. "I don't want them growing up in the South. Philadelphia is better, but I'm already sick of being so cold. Daddy and Opal don't need me. Amber and Carl don't need me. I'll miss them like crazy, but Zeke and I want to start a new life." She reached over to take Zeke's hand, continuing as she interpreted the look in Janie's eyes. "We already know it will be tough. It will be tough getting out there, and it will be tough getting started."

"But it ain't gonna be no tougher than what we already lived," Zeke finished.

"Do Opal and Eddie know?" Janie asked, trying to absorb it and wondering how much to tell them about the cholera.

Susie nodded. "They know. They're sad to see us go, but they understand we want to have a new start." She smiled slightly. "I think Opal would go with us if she could. She loves the restaurant, but this cold seems to be eating right through her."

"When are you planning on leaving?" Janie asked.

"This spring," Zeke said promptly. "We're saving up money for our wagon train fare." He stopped when he saw the quick look of alarm on Janie's face. "What's wrong?" His eyes darkened with concern.

Janie searched for words. "Do either of you know anything about cholera?"

"It's a disease," Susie responded, confusion showing in her eyes. "Does this have something to do with us?"

"I'm afraid it could," Janie said. She explained what she had learned in school that morning. "Close to twelve thousand people died on the wagon trains back in 1849," she finished.

Zeke spoke into the silence. "I don't know anything about cholera. What's it like?"

Janie knew she couldn't soften the news. They deserved to know the truth. "It's horrible. The primary symptoms are profuse diarrhea and vomiting of clear fluid. People with cholera are known to produce three to five gallons of diarrhea a day. About half of them die," she finished grimly.

Zeke grimaced as he exchanged a long look with Susie. "You said it's still on that boat in the New York harbor. How's it gonna get on our wagon train?"

"They're still trying to understand exactly how it spreads," Janie admitted. "There are a lot of different opinions."

"But because no one is really sure, they don't know how to stop it," Susie added.

"I'm afraid that's true," Janie agreed. "All they know for sure is that it spreads. It started in New York seventeen years ago and then spread all across the country."

Zeke thought hard. "So that means we be as likely to get it here in Philadelphia?"

Susie eyed her husband and then turned back to Janie. "How many people died in Philadelphia back in 1849?"

"A little over a thousand," Janie responded. "Philadelphia wasn't as hard hit as New York and other cities."

"Why?" Zeke asked.

Janie hesitated. "I'm just learning all this. They're not positive, but they think it mostly has to do with cleanliness. Philadelphia's water system is better. Cholera always hits hardest in the areas that have a lot of filth."

"Like the really poor areas in New York," Susie said. She smiled at Janie's look of surprise. "You don't have to go somewhere to read about it in books."

Janie flushed. "Sorry. You're absolutely right. Yes. Although it spread into most of the areas of New York, the poor areas were the hardest hit."

A long silence fell on the table as Susie and Zeke absorbed the news.

Zeke was the first to break it. "I reckon I had a better chance of getting killed during the war than I have of getting cholera. I didn't let fear stop me then. It don't seem right to let it stop me now."

Janie understood his thought processes, even if she didn't agree with the conclusion. "You were fighting for your freedom during the war. You didn't have a choice of when the war happened or when you had to fight in the battles. You have a choice of when you go out west. I'm just suggesting it might be better to wait until next year."

"They'll have it under control by then?" Susie asked. "Are you certain of that?"

"No one is certain of anything," Janie admitted. "But it always seems to run its course and go away."

Zeke shook his head. "So they don't know where it comes from, and they don't know why it leaves?"

Janie shrugged. "So much of medicine is still unknown," she murmured. "Advances are being made every day, but I don't know that we'll ever have all the answers."

Zeke took Susie's hand. "Me and Susie got to talk and think about it," he said, managing a weak smile. "We sure appreciate your telling us about it, though."

"Janie!" Amber's voice broke into their conversation.

Janie pushed aside her heavy thoughts and summoned up a bright smile for the excited little girl. "Hello, Amber!" She waited until Amber put down the plate she was carrying and then pulled her forward into a tight hug. "Are you sure you're only thirteen? I declare, you get bigger every time I see you."

Amber giggled. "And smarter, too," she proclaimed. "I'm the best reader in my class," she said proudly. "And I'm even making sense of arithmetic."

Janie lifted up the little girl's chin so she could gaze into her eyes. "That's wonderful. I'm so proud of you."

Amber nodded. "Daddy and Opal are, too," she said. "I like making them happy. And I really like going to my Quaker school. Everybody be so nice."

"Everybody *is* so nice," Susie corrected gently.

"Right. Everybody *is* so nice," Amber said, her grin spreading across her face. "Pretty soon, I will be able to speak just like you and Carrie and Rose, Miss Janie."

"And *me*?" Susie asked, pretending offense.

"Well, of course, *you*," Amber retorted. "But you don't count, 'cause you're just my sister."

Susie chuckled as she shook her head. "I get absolutely no respect here."

Janie laughed as she pulled the plate of sweet potato casserole close to her, leaning down to take a long sniff. "No one makes sweet potato casserole like Opal," she said happily. She took a bite, savoring the explosion of flavors as she chewed. "Will you ask Opal to fix a whole casserole for me to take home? I know my housemates will love this."

"You bet!" Amber responded. "Sadie just got here from school. She and my sister are working on more of them right now. I'll tell her to make one for you special."

"Tell her she doesn't have to cook it," Janie added quickly. "I'll put it in the oven when I get home."

Amber gave a quick grin and dashed toward the kitchen. She was only halfway there when the front door flung open.

"Fire! The roof is on fire! *Fire!*"

There was a moment of horrified, stunned disbelief that held everyone in place. It quickly dissolved as yelling and high-pitched screams filled the air. Everyone jumped from their tables and pushed toward the door.

Janie remained frozen in place. A loud crackling sound brought her gaze upward. Sparks from the woodstove had ignited the roof. She stared, fascinated at the orange flames beginning to lick through the wooden roof.

"Janie!" Zeke hollered, reaching over to yank her out of her chair. "Get your coat. We have to get out of here!"

Zeke's voice pulled Janie from her fascinated trance. She had heard about the terrible fires down in this part of the city, but she had never dreamed she would see one first hand. Another glance at the ceiling told her the fire was spreading quickly. She reached for her coat, but Zeke had already yanked it from the hook beside the table.

He grabbed her hand and began to pull her through the restaurant. Many of the patrons had already spilled out into the road. Gusts of cold air blowing in through the door fed the flames. They roared more angrily as they consumed the roof and began to work down the back wall. Angry crackling mixed with the hiss of the flames.

Janie gasped as the cold air hit her. It was suddenly all real. She turned toward the door and realized how many coats were still hanging on hooks. She had a quick vision of terrified people freezing on the sidewalk. She jerked away from Zeke's hand and began to grab coats as quickly as she could. "Help me," she cried. "Those people out there will need these!"

Zeke's eyes were wide with fright as he stared at her and then glanced back at the gaping door leading to safety.

"We have enough time," Susie yelled. "Help her. I'll go in the back to make sure Daddy, Opal, and the kids get out. Hurry!" she yelled over her shoulder.

Screams and calls continued from outside as the last people pushed through the front door.

Janie flashed through the restaurant, horrified as she watched pictures on the back wall being devoured by flames, their bright images dissolved in an instant. When her arms wouldn't hold any more, she turned and rushed through the front door. She dashed far enough away from the building to safely dump her load, and then looked around frantically.

Opal, Eddie, and the kids were nowhere to be seen. Janie and Zeke exchanged a terrified glance and then turned as one to dash back into the building, ignoring the screams of the patrons telling them to stop.

As they stepped into the building, they saw Eddie and Opal run from the kitchen, their hands full of pots and pans. Susie was right behind them, pulling Amber and Carl with her.

"Sadie and Sadie Lou?" Zeke hollered over the flames as the back wall caved in on itself and began to devour the wall behind the kitchen.

"They were right behind me," Susie cried. She whipped back around, pushing Amber and Carl toward Janie. "Get them out of here!"

Janie grabbed the terrified children's hands and pulled them toward the door. She knew there were only minutes before the flames would reach the huge vats of frying oil. What was already a nightmare was about to get worse.

Zeke plunged into the kitchen with Susie.

Janie plowed into Eddie and Opal just outside the door as she emerged with the children.

"I have to go back inside," Eddie hollered. "The Sadies are in there!" His eyes bulged with terror.

Janie blocked his way, pushing him and Opal away from the building as she pulled Amber and Carl with her. "You will do no such thing," she said, trying to swallow her own terror. "Zeke and Susie will get them out of there." She could only pray she was right.

Two men ran forward and wrapped a coat around the children. Another man grabbed Eddie's arm and pulled him further from the building. Two women, tears pouring down their cheeks, took Opal's arm and hauled her away from the flames.

Opal's screams could be heard over the flames. "Sadie! Sadie Lou!"

Janie gulped back tears as she stared at the door, willing the four of them to appear. She could hear the clanging bells of the fire wagon in the distance but already knew they wouldn't arrive in time to save any part of the restaurant.

"Get out!" Eddie hollered. "Get out!" He struggled to break free from the two men holding him, but they held him tight, knowing he could do nothing to help.

Carl and Amber cowered between the two men, their eyes wide with fright.

"Sadie!" Susie yelled.

"Sadie Lou!" Zeke hollered, their voices devoured by the roar of the fire.

Susie covered her hand with her mouth, trying desperately to penetrate the wall of smoke pouring from the kitchen. "Sadie!" she screamed. "Where are you?"

"Get down on the floor!" Zeke yelled. "The smoke won't be as bad!"

Susie dropped immediately, able to see enough to push through the kitchen opening. She crawled forward, searching for the girls. They had been right behind her. What could have happened?

"Susie..."

Susie spun around as the whimper reached her. "Sadie Lou!" she gasped, reaching out for her sister. "We've got to get out of here."

Sadie Lou nodded toward her leg crushed beneath a section of the kitchen wall that had fallen. "I can't move," she whimpered, her eyes wide with terror and pain.

"Where is Sadie?" Susie asked as she began to tug at the timber, ignoring the pain from the flaming wood.

Zeke rushed forward to help her, looking frantically for something to pry the timber from Sadie Lou's leg.

"She fell," Sadie Lou cried. "She fell right in front of the stove. I tried to go back to get her, but the wall fell on my leg." She gazed up at Zeke, tears pouring down her face as she gasped for air. "You have to get her!" she cried. She screamed with pain as the flaming timber caught her dress on fire.

Zeke looked at Susie. The look in her eyes told him she had seen it, too.

The flames were licking at the vats of cooking oil.

Zeke knelt down and grabbed her hand, reaching for Sadie Lou at the same time. "I love you!" he shouted.

Susie gripped his hand tightly, never looking away. "I love you, too."

An explosion rocked the ground and sent flames shooting high into the air.

"No!" Opal screamed. "No!"

"My children!" Eddie hollered, suddenly going slack against the men holding him. "My children!" His voice trailed away to an agonized whimper.

Janie stared in disbelief as flames and thick black smoke clouded the frozen air. A sick bile rose in her throat as a silence fell on everyone watching. They all knew no one could have lived through the explosion.

Opal squirmed free of the women holding her and raced toward the inferno. "Susie! Sadie! Sadie Lou! Zeke!" She stumbled and almost fell. "I'm coming! Hold on. I'm coming!"

Janie reached her just before Opal ran into the flames. "Opal, no!" She grabbed the sobbing woman's arm and pulled her back. Two men added their strength and hauled her back from the roaring fire.

"My children!" Opal screamed. "My children!"

Janie, tears pouring down her face, pulled Opal close into her arms and held her tight. "I'm so sorry," she groaned. "I'm so very sorry."

Janie stepped back when Eddie approached, letting him take Opal into his arms. "They're gone, Opal," he croaked, his eyes red with agony. "Our children be gone."

As they rocked in each other's arms, Janie looked around frantically for Carl and Amber. She finally saw them, safe in a circle of customers who had pulled them to safety. She ran to them, completely understanding the looks of shocked disbelief on their faces.

Amber raced to Janie. "Where are they?" she cried. "Where is Sadie? And Sadie Lou?" She stared at the building, now fully engulfed in flames, as the fire wagons arrived and began to water down the buildings on either side in an attempt to save them. "Where is Susie? And Zeke?" she whimpered.

"Where are they Janie? Why ain't they come out?" Carl asked.

Janie kneeled down so she could pull them both close. "They didn't make it out," she said gently.

"They're dead?" Amber asked. "You be tellin' me they be dead?"

Janie had no words. She held the children close as their disbelief turned into heart-wrenching sobs.

Janie didn't know how long she held them before Eddie and Opal pushed through. Eddie pulled Carl close in his arms. Opal encircled Amber hungrily.

Janie stepped back, giving them space. The horror of what happened was starting to penetrate her shock. She was trembling uncontrollably when one of the women stepped forward and wrapped a coat around her. She nodded her thanks, but she couldn't stop watching the destroyed family. They had been through so much. They were fighting to create new lives with everything they had. How could this have happened?

Eddie stood up and exchanged a long look with Janie. "I'm taking my family home," he said hoarsely.

"Please come to Abby's. You've all been through too much. You need a warm place to go." She saw the refusal in Eddie's eyes. While she understood the desire to be in their own home, she knew Amber and Carl needed more than a frozen shack. "The children need a warm bed," she pressed, breathing a sigh of relief when she saw the surrender in his eyes.

Only then did he and Opal turn to gaze at their destroyed restaurant. Long minutes passed as they stood, hands clasped, staring at the obliterated dream that had become a red-hot tomb.

Janie turned to the crowd of people still huddled close. "I'll take good care of them," she promised.

"You knows Eddie and Opal from back in Richmond, ain't that right?" one woman asked, her eyes soft with compassion as she gazed at the shattered couple.

Janie nodded. "Yes. I live here now. I'm taking them home tonight."

Eddie turned. "We're coming back in the morning," he said, only his eyes revealing he was still in shock.

A group of the men stepped forward. "We'll be here to help you go through everything," one of them promised.

No one bothered to voice the words that nothing could have possibly survived the inferno caused by the explosion of the oil vats. There was an unspoken agreement that Eddie would not be alone when he discovered the remains of his family.

Janie felt the bile rise in her throat again when the image rose to taunt her, but she forced it down as she began to walk with Amber and Carl away from the rubble. She was relieved when Eddie put his arm around Opal and turned to follow her.

Chapter Five

Janie felt like she hadn't slept at all when she finally crawled out of bed. When she glanced at the clock, she knew she was right. She had drifted off around three o'clock. It was now six o'clock. She yawned and stretched, reaching for her robe and slippers. She doubted she had enough brain cells to absorb anything in class this morning, but she was determined not to miss a single session. Splashing cold water on her face helped, although she thought longingly of a hot bath. There was certainly not time for that.

Suddenly, it all came rushing back. She gasped as she sank back down on the bed and covered her face with her hands. *Sadie...Sadie Lou...Susie...Zeke.* She choked back a groan as visions of their bright, happy faces filled her mind. She saw Zeke's determined eyes when he spoke of heading west, and saw Susie's warm love as she gazed at her husband. Sadie Lou's bright eyes laughed at her, as Sadie's courage to push beyond her crippled leg pulled at her. The groan ripped from her throat. All of them had endured so much. For them tdie in a senseless fire, killed by a searing explosion, was more than she could fathom. She thought of Eddie and Opal's loss. She had heard the murmur of their voices long into the night before she finally fell asleep.

Janie huddled for long moments on the bed before she could force herself to stand. Mindlessly, she reached for a dress and threw it on. She wanted nothing more than a hot cup of coffee, hoping it would take the edge off her pain.

Carl and Amber, still in a state of shock, had fallen asleep quickly when they were tucked into the warm bed in Florence's room. Florence shared a room with Alice, while Eddie and Opal took the room that would be Carrie's. Stunned by the tragedy, all the housemates insisted they could stay for as long as needed and offered to do whatever they could to help.

Janie opened the door to her room. She stopped and raised her head, wondering at the aroma that struck her senses. Overcome with curiosity, she followed her nose to the kitchen. She knew Alice, Elizabeth, and Florence all had to be at class by eight o'clock. None of them would have time to cook a breakfast, but there was no mistaking the smell of frying bacon and biscuits.

Janie jolted to a stop when she reached the kitchen. "Opal?"

Opal turned from the stove and gave her a solemn look. "I couldn't sleep. I didn't see no reason to lie there when I knew none of you would eat more than cold biscuits for breakfast." Her eyes were swollen from a night of crying, but her face was a mask of determination.

"We're used to cold biscuits," Janie replied, not knowing what else to say. She wished she knew how to dissolve Opal's pain, but nothing but time could do that.

"Not when I'm living here," Opal retorted, a spark of life flaring in her eyes before she turned back to the stove. "Get yourself some coffee, Janie. You look like you need it."

Janie wordlessly obeyed, sighing when the first hot swallow began to warm her insides and bring them to life. She sat down at the table, pointing at the coffee pot when her housemates joined her. All of them stared at Opal's stiff back but said nothing when Janie shook her head in warning. She had told them all the night before how Eddie had lost his wife, Opal's cousin, in an explosion in Richmond. It was simply impossible to comprehend that another explosion had ripped more family away from them.

Opal placed full plates in front of them. "Don't be thinking you got to come up with something to say. There ain't nothing." She laid a hand on Janie's shoulder. "Just eat."

Janie blinked back tears as she stared down at the bacon, eggs, and hot biscuits on her plate.

"Ain't breakfast without grits," Opal said, trying to cover the hoarseness in her voice. "I know this is a houseful of mostly Yankees, but," she glared at Janie, "I thought one Southern girl would be enough to have grits."

Janie fought to respond naturally, knowing Opal needed her to. "I'll fix that on the way home," she promised.

Janie could feel the tension in the house as soon as she opened the door. Amber and Carl were curled up on the sofa with books, but she could tell they weren't reading a word. Their swollen eyes told her how they had spent the morning.

Once again, delicious smells wafted from the kitchen. She walked in and plunked down her bag. "Grits as ordered."

Opal turned from where she was flipping chicken. There was a platter of warm sweet potatoes on the counter, and the steam was still rising from the biscuits she had pulled out of the oven. "Thank you," she said gruffly, placing her hands on her ample hips as she stared at Janie. "We got something to tell you," she said.

Janie nodded and sat down at the table as Eddie walked in. His tall, lean body was stooped with pain, his shoulders sagging under the weight of his loss.

"You tell her?" Eddie said.

"Nope. I was waiting for you."

Eddie settled down at the table. "We went to the restaurant while you be in class," he began.

Janie waited quietly, knowing how hard it was for him to talk.

Eddie swallowed as his hands began to shake. Opal moved from the stove to stand beside him. Her presence gave him the courage to continue. "We found our children," he managed.

Janie's eyes burned as she listened, wishing once again that there was something to say that would alleviate some of their pain. She reached forward and took one of his rough hands. It was so little, but she knew he simply needed to know she cared.

"We ain't been here long enough to have a church yet. One of the men who helped us talked with his minister yesterday. They sent a wagon to carry them back to the church..." Eddie's voice caught. He took a deep breath. A long silence fell on the kitchen before he gazed up at Opal with pleading eyes.

"They's gonna bury them," Opal said huskily. "All of them," she added. "Sadie be just like one of our children. She and Sadie Lou hardly been apart an hour since we've been here."

Janie smiled slightly, knowing how close the two teenage girls had been. They had both dreamed of being teachers. Her smile faded as pain twisted her face. She closed her eyes briefly, the flash of the explosion searing her mind as if it were happening again.

"We're going home," Eddie said, finding his voice again.

"But you're welcome to stay here as long as you want," Janie argued. She hated the thought of them going back to their cold shack, especially since they couldn't go to the restaurant to stay warm.

"Not home here," Opal corrected. "We're going back to Richmond. Just as soon as we have a service and bury our children."

Janie stared at her. "Richmond?" she finally managed. "You're going back to Richmond?"

Opal nodded. "This cold place ain't our home. While we had the restaurant, we were managing to endure it, but with the restaurant gone, our children gone, and us having no money..."

"We got friends and family back in Richmond," Eddie finished for her.

Janie searched for words. "You know Richmond is a hard place for blacks right now."

They both nodded. "We know."

"It can't be harder than what we been dealing with here," Opal said. "Amber and Carl need to be with family."

"But..."

Eddie interpreted what Janie was about to say. "I got a letter from my brother a few weeks back. He done moved his family to Richmond. He's got kids Amber and Carl's ages. He had no idea I would need to take him up on it, but he said that if we ever decided to move back to Richmond, that we had a place with them."

"It will take us a while to get back on our feet," Opal said, "but we'll find jobs and..."

"And someday Opal will have herself another restaurant," Eddie vowed.

"Are you sure?" Janie asked, her mind spinning as she thought about the Black Codes Carrie told her about in her latest letter. "The South is not a great place for blacks right now."

Opal nodded. "I be knowing about them Black Codes," she told Janie. "Rose sent me a letter. She wanted me to know. Told me how glad I should be that I was living in the North now."

"Then you know what a risk you're taking," Janie said urgently. "There are bad things happening."

"There be bad things happening everywhere," Eddie said. "Life has been full of lots of bad things for a long time. But there be lots of good things that done happened, too."

Opal laid her hand on his shoulder. "We lost our children, but at least they died free. Sadie and Sadie Lou died with dreams of becoming teachers. Zeke and Susie died with plans to go out west. Their lives were cut way too short, but they didn't die as slaves." She cleared her throat before she continued. "I reckon Fannie was real happy to see them. I imagine she don't feel quite so alone now."

"We got two kids left," Eddie said. "There's bad things about taking them back to the South, but there be good things, too." He pulled a well-read letter out of his pocket. "I been staying in touch with some of my friends back in Richmond—at least the ones that know how to write." He managed a small smile. "Things ain't great in Richmond, but folks are coming together into a real community. Opal and I have felt alone since we got here to Philadelphia. We don't want that anymore."

Janie knew they had made up their minds. "When are you going back?"

"The funeral is in three days," Opal replied. "We'd like to stay here until then."

"Of course," Janie answered. "You're welcome as long as you need a place."

"We'll leave right after the funeral," Eddie said. "We got enough money for our train tickets. I reckon God will take care of the rest when we get there. At least I know we'll have a place to live until we get back on our feet."

"The first thing we're gonna do is go out to the plantation," Opal added. "We want to tell Annie, Moses, and June what happened to their Sadie. We want them to know she was real happy here." She leaned forward to take Janie's hand. "Miss Janie, we all gonna lose someone we can't live without. Me and Eddie's hearts be broken, and we ain't never going to get over losing those children." She took a deep breath. "I reckon that's a good thing, though. They are gonna live forever in our broken hearts."

Eddie nodded. "I broke a leg a while back. It didn't heal just right. It hurts like the dickens when it gets cold, but I learned how to dance with it again. Grief be like that. We ain't never gonna quit hurting for our children, but I learned a long time ago that I have to keep going and keep my eyes open for the good things in life."

Janie smiled at both of them warmly, in awe of their strength and courage. "Let me know if there is anything I can do to help."

She already knew one thing she was going to do.

Janie pushed through the crowd to reach the telegraph office, relieved when the operator handed her the envelope she had been waiting for. A bright smile broke out on her face when she read the contents.

Turning, she made her way back through the crowd and hurried toward the train station. She just had time to make it.

The air had warmed up some, but it was still below freezing. After the subzero temperatures during the last two weeks, however, it felt almost balmy.

As Janie strode toward the station, she felt a moment of jealousy. Last night she dreamed of Richmond—the rolling hills, the church spires penetrating the sky, the rumbling rapids of the James River. Then her dream shifted to the plantation. When she finally awakened, she laid there for long minutes thinking of how much she would love to go riding with Carrie, help at the clinic, talk to the children in the school, and sit by the fire for long chats with Rose, Moses, and Robert.

In spite of how much she loved school and her housemates, she was dreadfully homesick. She had struggled with loneliness when she first moved to Richmond during the war, but at least she had been in her beloved South. In spite of the fact that everyone accepted her in Philadelphia—even so soon after the war—she couldn't help feeling like a stranger in a foreign land. When she was young, Janie always imagined that living in a big city like Philadelphia would be so exciting. She had not expected to feel confined and trapped.

Even during the years of the war in Richmond she could stand on the bluffs where Chimborazo Hospital was situated, staring out into the distance over the James River with the wind blowing in her face. It helped her endure the crowded conditions of a city under siege. In Philadelphia, she couldn't escape the rumbling trolley cars, endless brick buildings, and the throngs of people always hurrying to get somewhere.

"Oh, for pity's sake!" Janie muttered, shaking her head as she crossed a busy intersection a block from the train station. She was in school, living a dream she wouldn't have thought possible even two months ago. She had so much to be thankful for, she should be dancing in the streets, not wallowing in self-pity. Scolding herself, she glanced at her watch and pressed forward faster.

"Janie!"

Janie smiled broadly when she saw Amber's wildly waving arm. She rushed forward to scoop the little girl into a big hug and then caught Carl close. "I'm going to miss both of you so much," she said. She loved every minute of their being in the house for the last week. Having them there, keeping them busy when she wasn't in class, helped her deal with her own grief.

"We gonna miss you, too, Miss Janie," Carl said. His face was a mixture of excitement, uncertainty and grief when he stepped back. "You sure you can't come with us?"

Janie smiled. "That sounds wonderful, Carl, but my place is here in Philadelphia for now."

Carl frowned. "I guess I'm glad you gonna be here, Miss Janie. I think Susie and Sadie Lou would be real lonely here if you wasn't staying."

Janie caught Opal's eyes over Carl's head. The funeral had been two days earlier. Every minute of it was agonizing. Having to bury four young people at the same time was more than Janie could comprehend. The cold wind did nothing more than intensify the numbness as the four coffins holding Susie, Sadie Lou, Zeke, and Sadie were lowered into the ground.

There was a large crowd of restaurant patrons in attendance, their faces somber and full of compassion, but there was no one who knew Opal and Eddie well enough to give them the comfort they sorely needed. Janie did all she could, but in spite of her reservations about them moving back to the South, she knew they needed to be with family and friends.

"I promise to visit them," Janie assured Carl, pulling him close in another hug before turning to Eddie and handing him the envelope she had gripped all the way from the telegraph office. "This is for you."

Eddie stared at her and then at the envelope. "What is it?" His eyes seemed to have lost all life since the fire. He moved through the days doing everything that was needed for them to leave, but the determination that had carried him through losing Fannie, his years in prison, and starting a restaurant from scratch had fled before the searing grief that consumed him from the moment of the explosion.

"Read it," she urged.

Eddie began to open it slowly, moving almost as if in a trance. The funeral had sucked everything from him. He'd hardly spoken since the four pine boxes were lowered.

Opal reached for the envelope and opened it quickly. She had carried the entire family since the tragedy. Her eyes were shadowed with the same searing grief, but caring for her family seemed to pull strength from her that even she didn't know she had. Janie had watched with growing admiration as her strength grew with each passing day.

Opal scanned the brief telegram and then gazed up at Janie with stunned eyes. "You the reason for this?" she asked huskily.

Janie shrugged. "You have a lot of people who love you. All I did was let them know there was a need."

Opal stared into her eyes, gratitude erasing the grief for a moment.

She turned to Eddie. "You have a job waiting for you," she told him, not waiting to see if her husband would respond. "Miss Janie sent a telegram to Mr. Cromwell telling him what happened. She told him we were coming back. He says you have a job in the factory if you want it."

Opal glanced at Janie. "I got a letter from a friend saying the new factory gonna be paying real good wages. That true?"

"Yes," Janie assured her. "Blacks and whites are being paid the same thing."

A spark appeared in Eddie's eyes. "We gonna get the same kind of pay as white men?" he murmured, doubt warring with hope.

Janie nodded. "Thomas and Abby believe people should be paid the same for the same work," she said simply. "Jeremy is managing the factory. He's making sure everyone is treated fairly."

Eddie absorbed her words. "And I got a job waiting for me?" he asked, disbelief filling his voice.

"That's right. But you ain't the only one. I got me a job, too," Opal said, her eyes still glued to the few sentences on the telegram, excitement popping in her voice. "We *both* got jobs, Eddie. We can start whenever we want."

Eddie sagged with relief and then seemed to stand taller. "We got a chance to start over," he said, his voice stronger than it had been for days. The shadow remained in his eyes, but for the first time, there was a spark of hope when he turned to Janie. "Thank you, Miss Janie," he said, letting the expression in his eyes convey the message in his heart.

"You're so welcome," Janie whispered, giving him a warm hug.

Opal eyed her keenly. "You gonna be okay, Miss Janie?"

Janie started to respond casually, but then looked Opal squarely in the eyes. "I'll miss all of you," she said honestly.

"We the only ties you got to home," Opal said.

Janie nodded, realizing just how difficult it would be to see them go. "Who else is going to make me sweet potato casserole?" she asked, forcing herself to speak lightly. "Or Opal's apple pie?"

"I left four pies in your cellar," Opal revealed with a smile. "They'll hold you for a little while."

Janie blinked back tears. "Thank you." If possible, the revelation made saying goodbye even harder.

Opal stepped forward and grasped her hands. "You're gonna be fine, Miss Janie. You got more courage than most people ever *think* of having."

Janie stared at her. "Me?"

"You," Opal said firmly. "Lots of women would have shriveled up and died after what Clifford did. You came up here to start a new life. And not just any old life—you decided to become a doctor. That done nothing but open you up to more abuse from people. You gonna have lots of people telling you you're wrong. You gonna have lots of people trying to throw up obstacles to stop you."

"Let them try," Janie growled, thinking of the man who spat on the sidewalk in front of her when she turned into the school that morning. She had been appalled, but refused to acknowledge his presence.

Opal chuckled. "Exactly. You got the courage to live the life you want for yourself. You gonna have days when you're so lonely you'll wish you could leave and come home," she predicted. "But you won't."

Janie wished she could be as sure.

"You won't come home," Opal continued, "because your dream is bigger than you are. No dream is ever easy. Miss Carrie taught me that." She took a deep breath. "I ain't lost my dream of owning a restaurant. The fire took this one, but me and Eddie gonna work until we can have another. This ain't the way I would have wanted things to happen, but I don't reckon I can tell God how to do his work. We done learned a lot of lessons, and I reckon we gonna learn a lot more. I know them children would want us to have another one."

Janie realized the challenges she had faced were nothing compared to what Eddie and Opal suffered. "You're right," she said softly. "Aunt Abby told me it takes courage to grow up and turn out to be who you really are."

It was Opal's turn to absorb the words. She squeezed Janie's hands a little more tightly. "I reckon she knows what she's talking about. You're meant to be a doctor. I'm meant to be a cook. As long as we keep our eyes on what we are meant to be, I figure we'll get there."

"Speaking of Aunt Abby," Janie said, "I got a letter from her before I got to the telegraph office. I almost forgot. She wanted me to tell you that she is heartbroken over the children, but not to waste one moment feeling bad about the restaurant. She had it insured."

Opal eyed her sharply. "Insured?"

"Yes. Fire has always been a hazard in Philadelphia. Benjamin Franklin formed the first fire insurance company back in 1752. Aunt Abby has a policy on every building she owns. She understands your need to come home, but the building that housed the restaurant will be rebuilt."

Opal bowed her head and then looked up with shining eyes. "I be real glad about that. Miss Abby been real good to us—giving us the money to get started and letting us have that building for free for a while. I hated to think of being the cause of her losing more." Relief was thick in her voice.

"I be real glad about that, too," Eddie added, his voice stronger than Janie had heard it since the fire.

A shrill whistle blast caused all of them to jump.

Eddie peered at his watch. "This be our train," he said somberly. "I reckon it's time for us to go."

Janie and Opal held each other in a long hug before they finally stepped back.

"Thomas will have a wagon there for you when the train arrives," Janie said. "The driver will take you to your brother's place."

"Thank you for everything, Miss Janie," Opal whispered, not trying to hold back the tears. "You come see us when you get back to Richmond. I'll have a sweet potato casserole waiting for you."

"I will," Janie promised. "And you give Carrie and all of them a big hug for me when you get to the plantation."

There was nothing else to be said. Janie watched as the family climbed on the train, their grief-shadowed faces filled with determination. They turned to wave one final time before the passenger car swallowed them.

Jeremy watched from his office above the floor of the factory as workers streamed in. He turned to Thomas and Abby with a broad smile. "We did it," he said. The solid brick walls rose high above the operations, large windows letting in life and allowing for air circulation.

One side of the building, dedicated to producing fabric, held machinery powered by steam engines fed by the mountains of coal housed behind the building. The other half of the building, where the clothing would be made, had long tables full of sewing machines.

Abby returned his smile, but her eyes were serious as she watched the new employees arrive. "Now the real work begins."

Jeremy wanted to refute her statement by saying nothing could be harder than the months of building a factory from the burned-out rubble, but he knew she was right. He turned back to look at the flow of workers, both white and black, entering the factory. Already, there seemed to be a line down the middle of the cavernous building full of machines. One side for the whites; the other side for the blacks.

From a business perspective, he knew things looked promising. They had already received many orders for clothing, and Abby's investment insured they had the most technically advanced machinery available from the North. It would take time to train the new employees, but within a month, things should be running smoothly.

Nine months after the end of the war, Richmond was struggling to return to its former dominance. Before the destruction and devastation of the war, Virginia's capital had represented the most advanced economic development in the South. By the 1850s, canal and rail connections with the rest of the South created new markets for all of Richmond's iron, flour, and tobacco industries. Determined to maintain its prominence, business leaders embarked on a frenzied campaign of internal improvements to promote industry.

It worked.

Between 1850 and 1860, Richmond's factory force grew by 581 percent. Richmond became the terminus of the South's major railroad network, its leading port, and an industrial pacesetter. It also became the home of a solid group of bourgeoisie who firmly believed whites were superior to blacks—that it was meant to be that way, and that it would always stay that way.

The Civil War changed things for all time. Richmond was destroyed and slavery abolished. Like it or not, a new day had dawned that demanded everything be done differently.

Thomas stared down at the divided group shuffling their feet and looking around. "They've never worked together," he murmured.

Jeremy took a deep breath. They had talked about this for hours. Before the war, few blacks and whites had worked together. Most slaves and freedmen were employed in tobacco factories or in domestic service. Most whites worked in skilled trades not practiced by blacks. On rare occasions, they would have a black helper.

The whites didn't work with the blacks, and they also didn't mingle with them outside the workplace. Their worlds were completely separate. All that was about to change.

Jeremy watched as the last workers filed into the building. "Looks like it's time," he said. He flashed a confident grin at Thomas and Abby that he hoped hid his nervousness, walked down the stairs, and climbed up to the small platform in the middle of the room.

The tension in the room reached out to him from every face. Anger and fear swirled to the rafters as one hundred sets of eyes settled on him. "Good morning, everyone," he called.

Chapter Six

Jeremy waited a moment until the silence in the room was complete. He kept both his face and his stance casual and relaxed. He wasn't going to reveal just how momentous this occasion was, nor the fact that he was well aware they were breaking all precedents and making history with the opening of the factory. "Welcome to Cromwell Clothing Factory," he said warmly. "We believe we have hired one hundred very qualified people to work here."

Jeremy was aware of the suspicious looks coming from both sides of the room. While everyone looked suspicious, the looks coming from the white side were full of anger and derision, while the veiled looks from the black side contained more confusion and fear. Jeremy understood. Since the war ended and President Johnson's policies gained momentum, racism had increased in Richmond.

He decided to hit it straight on. "We realize Cromwell Factory is breaking the mold on how things happen," he began. "In the past, whites and blacks didn't work together." He held up a hand and directed a hard look at a small group of whites who began to mutter among themselves. They quieted, but their angry looks didn't dissipate.

"Things have changed," he said. "There is one objective here at Cromwell Clothing Factory. That objective is to create the finest quality garments possible, while making the highest profit possible. We believe that will be done by hiring the best workers and treating them all with the same respect and consideration." He spoke slowly so that his words were heard clearly. "With that in mind, I'm going to erase the need for rumor by telling you straight out that every worker at our factory will be paid the same. Race doesn't matter. Gender doesn't matter. Only your ability to do your job with excellence will matter. Every person will be paid the same."

Jeremy waited a long moment for everyone to absorb his words. They had been careful to communicate this during the hiring, but he was quite sure the words were not believed. The whites were simply not able to comprehend that blacks, whom they considered inferior, would receive equal pay. The blacks were not able to comprehend that they would be compensated based on their ability, not on the color of their skin.

He ignored the restless movements and shuffling of feet. "Your ability to do your job with excellence will depend not only on the task you are trained to do, but also on how you get along with fellow employees. When you are outside the doors of this factory, I can't keep you from seeing yourself as different races. But when you walk inside these doors, part of your job description will be the requirement to treat every other employee with respect and consideration. You may never become friends, but you *will* work together."

He could see outrage growing on many of the faces—blacks included. While the whites may consider them inferior, the end of the war and emancipation had changed black attitudes. They resented white people who had owned slaves. Before the end of the war, more than half of the white male heads of household owned slaves. This was double the amount of whites that owned homes. Whites of all economic levels had kept blacks from entering skilled trades. Resentment ran high in the black community.

Jeremy glanced up at the glassed-in office. Thomas and Abby nodded their encouragement, the looks on their faces saying he was doing well. He looked back at the group of employees.

"I fully realize there are many feelings about what I've said—most of them negative. I don't believe the feelings both sides of this issue have are going to disappear overnight. It will take time." He stood taller as his voice grew even firmer. "I want to make sure all of you understand one thing, however. I said already that part of your job description will be to treat every employee with respect and consideration. I meant it. *Anyone* who causes trouble will be let go immediately."

He let his eyes sweep the crowd. "Jobs are hard to come by," he reminded them. Indeed they were. "We had over a thousand people apply for these positions. We chose the one hundred of you standing here. We're going to give you every chance to create a good income for your families while we create a factory that will help Richmond get back on its feet, but that condition is one we will not bend on. If you cause trouble, you will be fired."

He let his words settle as he caught the eyes of everyone looking up at him. "Are we clear?"

Heads nodded all over the room. Faces portrayed a mixture of reluctant admiration, uncertainty and stifled anger. It was the most Jeremy could hope for. He had no illusions that what they were doing would be easy, but they were committed to their course of action.

A sudden rustle in the back of the room caught his attention. He waited as one man surged forward, his narrow face red with fury.

"It ain't right," the man yelled. "It ain't right that some nigger gonna make as much money as I am. That ain't how things are done around here! Can't nobody tell me a nigger is as good as I am!" he hollered, seeming to pick up energy as he moved to stand below the platform.

Jeremy watched quietly as a small group of men from where the protestor emerged tensed their bodies and began to move forward. "It's how they are done now," Jeremy said. "You're fired," he said sharply.

The men surging forward stopped in their tracks, their eyes darting around to see what action they should take next. The protestor shot angry looks at them, but they didn't move. Instead, they kept their eyes locked on Jeremy.

"There are nine hundred men waiting to take your place," Jeremy said, willing his heart to beat slowly so that his voice wouldn't betray the nervousness he felt. That simple reminder was enough to make the other men look away. "You're fired," he repeated. "You may leave."

"You can't fire me!" the man sputtered, his angry look fading into one of desperation. "I got kids to feed."

"I made the conditions clear," Jeremy reminded him. "Leave the building now." He tensed as the man considered whether an attack was warranted, but he saw the moment when the man realized not one other person was going to stand with him. He was on his own. Jeremy felt a surge of pity when the man's shoulders slumped in defeat, knowing he had just thrown away the best opportunity in Richmond. Jeremy kept his face neutral as he gazed around the room. "Does anyone want to leave with him? I can have your replacement here in the morning."

No one moved.

Jeremy fastened his eyes on the man, waiting until he had stalked from the building before he swept his gaze over the room again. "There is no place for hatred at Cromwell Clothing Factory," he said. "I realize we are doing something that has never been done in Richmond, but it is also something that is long past due. I am not so naïve as to believe it will be easy, but the owners of the factory, Thomas and Abigail Cromwell, along with myself, believe it can be done."

Jeremy hoped he was right. Most of the white faces staring at him had only months ago laid down arms after years of fighting for a doomed Confederacy. The black faces staring at him were either recently freed slaves or Union soldiers who decided to stay in the South now that freedom was won.

He searched for words to begin the process of opening minds. "Prejudice is a burden that confuses the past," he began, thinking of all the things he talked about with his father before he passed away. "Prejudice threatens the future we all hope to build for the South and for ourselves. What's equally important is that it makes the present inaccessible." He paused for a long moment. "Prejudice is held by both black and white. We have all formed opinions without bothering to truly understand the facts. It takes great courage to keep an open mind and be willing to see things differently than you always have, but I believe the rebirth of the South depends on it."

Tension vibrated through the room, but it was not as intense. Jeremy decided he had said enough. To keep speaking would only turn his words into a sermon that he knew would be ineffective. Everyone standing before him was clear about the consequences if they caused trouble. Only time and the daily reality of working together would change their beliefs and actions. He knew that relieving their financial pressure through good wages would go a long way toward opening minds to think differently.

"Carlton." He nodded to a man standing to the side. "You will begin to train the machine operators." His gaze moved on to the other side of the room. "Noah, you will begin training the material cutters." The women they had hired to sew the clothing would begin training in two weeks.

No one said a word as groups of men, black and white in each one, moved to their assigned areas. Jeremy watched for several minutes before he left the platform and climbed back to the office. He was going to spend most of his time on the floor getting to know his employees and letting them know how closely he would be involved, but it was time to give them some space.

"Well done!" Thomas said the moment Jeremy stepped into the office and closed the door.

Jeremy shrugged. "Thanks, but I hated losing that man. Not because we need him, but because he needs *us*. Firing him was necessary, but it's only going to make him more bitter."

"You didn't have a choice," Abby said. "If you hedged over his attack, the factory would have operated in chaos from the very beginning." Her eyes softened. "It may make him bitter, but there is also a chance it will force him to rethink his actions and change his beliefs."

Jeremy stared down at the men working below, wishing he could believe her words, but too well aware of what wounded pride and hatred could do inside a man. He forced his voice to remain casual when he responded. "I hope so," was all he said.

Jeremy was downstairs checking one of the machines when the day ended and the workers began to leave. Tension had been high for the entire day, but there were no confrontations. Evidently, they had all received the message that anyone who began trouble would be fired immediately. He rubbed a hand across his eyes, the long day suddenly catching up with him. Abby was right as usual. The real work had only just begun. He wished working with people was as straight forward as the equipment he was fixing.

He worked steadily, his thoughts moving forward to the next day. He stiffened when a scuffling sound came from behind him. He thought the building had emptied out long before. "Who's there?" he called sharply, wondering if he had been foolish to leave his pistol in the office.

"Marcus," came the immediate reply.

Jeremy waited while a black man, muscular and powerful, moved forward from the shadows. He watched him carefully, seeing nothing in his eyes to cause alarm. He forced himself to relax. "Why are you still here, Marcus?"

"I be wanting to talk to you, Mr. Anthony," Marcus said nervously, looking around to see if anyone else was still in the building.

"About?"

Marcus cleared his throat, but his gaze didn't waver. "Me and some of the others want to know why you be paying everyone the same."

"Does it matter?"

Marcus hesitated but then nodded firmly. "Yes."

Jeremy eyed him with curiosity, liking the clear shine of intelligence he saw in his eyes. He remembered hiring him. "You served with the Union Army," he said.

"Yes."

"Before the war you were a free man. You were a blacksmith."

"You have a good memory," Marcus observed, watching him. "You remember everyone that good?"

"No," Jeremy admitted. "Do you remember Pastor Marcus Anthony?"

"Of course," Marcus said, his eyes brightening. "He was a good man." Suddenly his eyes opened wider. "Jeremy Anthony. You be Pastor Anthony's son?"

Jeremy nodded. "Yes. I remembered you from my father's congregation."

"He was a real good man. He helped my mama out a lot during the war," Marcus replied. "I'm sorry for your loss."

"Thank you," Jeremy murmured. He would always miss the man who had been his father for his whole life. "Now, why does it matter how we pay people? Isn't it enough that you'll be paid the same?"

"I got my reasons," Marcus said cryptically.

Jeremy saw the caution in his eyes and knew he wasn't going to say more. At least not yet. "It's not very complicated, Marcus. The Cromwells and I believe in equal rights for all people. We don't think people should be paid differently based on the color of their skin or on their gender."

"Most people down here—especially white people—don't think the same way."

Jeremy shrugged. "I don't care what other people think. My father taught me to stand on my own feet a long time ago." He saw Marcus open and close his mouth, fear flickering in his eyes. "What do you really want to know?" he asked bluntly.

Marcus opened his mouth again, and his eyes darted through the dark shadows.

Jeremy understood he was afraid of being overheard. "Let's go up to my office," he said. His gut told him he was safe with Marcus, but he was also aware that the pistol in his drawer would even things out if Marcus had another intent besides just talking. He moved over to the stairs and climbed them quickly. Marcus followed him, stepping to the side while he closed the door. "Now, what is really on your mind?"

"Well, I done heard a few things..." Marcus began, his voice revealing his discomfort.

Jeremy felt for his nervousness, but fatigue was pressing on him, and he knew May had a wonderful dinner waiting for him. "I've found saying things straight out usually works best," he said. "Just say what you need to say."

Marcus nodded. "I know that be best, but I don't know how to say what I got to say." He took a deep breath. "There be rumors around town."

Jeremy struggled with his impatience. "I imagine there are rumors about a lot of things. Could you be more specific?" For a brief moment, he wondered if the truth had come out about his heritage but dismissed that as paranoia.

Marcus stared at him. "You're right that straight out is best," he muttered. He straightened his shoulders and held Jeremy's gaze. "You got a black sister, Mr. Anthony?"

Jeremy stiffened, rigid with disbelief for a long moment. His voice was under control when he answered. "Where did you hear that, Marcus?" He stopped before he added the question about why he figured it was any of his business. He wanted to learn what was being said.

"Like I said, there be rumors."

Jeremy wasn't comfortable with either the truth *or* a lie. He fought to keep his thoughts clear and his face neutral, and decided to go back to his earlier question when Marcus had wanted to know about pay. "Would it matter?"

"Yes."

"Why?" Jeremy asked sharply.

Marcus took a long breath. "Look, I ain't trying to mess in your business, Mr. Anthony."

Jeremy looked at him, not willing to say anything.

Marcus looked away uncomfortably. "Me and some of the others figured if it was true, then you might be a good ally." He paused. "Now that I know who your daddy was, I figure that might be *more* true."

"Ally?" Jeremy pressed, liking everything he was feeling about Marcus but still not willing to trust him. It could all be a setup to hurt the factory or to create trouble for him as a mulatto.

Marcus shook his head and heaved a heavy sigh. "It be okay if I sit down?" he asked.

Jeremy nodded toward a chair and waited for him to continue, still standing behind his desk.

"Things ain't going so good for blacks right now," Marcus said. "You hear about the Black Codes?"

"Yes," Jeremy admitted, still not sure how much to reveal. "They're not in Virginia."

"Yet," Marcus said. "You and I both know they are coming."

Jeremy said nothing, knowing he couldn't refute the statement. His brain raced hard to figure out what to do with the knowledge that the black community knew about his heritage.

"Even without them, life ain't so good for us right now," Marcus continued. "We be free on paper, but the white folks doing all they can to rip away that freedom so it don't mean anything."

Jeremy listened and continued to wait, hoping he would hear something that would give him an indication of how to respond.

"We need help."

"And you think I can help?" Jeremy asked.

Marcus shrugged his powerful shoulders. "You're carrying an awful big burden," he said. "I figure the rumors be true, or you would have denied them outright. Instead, you're trying to figure out how much I know." He leaned forward in his chair. "I ain't got no reason to cause trouble for you, Mr. Anthony. I be taking a risk talking to you like this. I know you could fire me, but I told everyone I would do it."

Jeremy tensed. "Everyone?"

"There are a group of us who are trying to make things better. We already figured out that ain't nobody but the blacks really care about what happens to us. We's fighting in every way we can, but we ain't too proud to ask for help."

Jeremy relaxed. He had been looking for a way to help. Here it was being dumped in his lap, and he was dodging it like he was escaping an angry hornet. He managed a chuckle as he sank down in his chair. "I'm sorry, Marcus. You caught me by surprise."

"I reckon I did," Marcus agreed easily.

"The rumors are true," Jeremy revealed. "My twin sister is one of the most amazing women I know. And, yes, she is black. She grew up as a slave on Cromwell Plantation."

Marcus' eyes widened. "Mr. and Mrs...."

"Yes," Jeremy said, feeling relief to finally let it out. "Thomas Cromwell is my half-brother. My father and mother adopted me after I was sold to keep Thomas' father's reputation intact. I only found out a couple years ago."

"Your sister?"

"She is a teacher," Jeremy responded. "She escaped the plantation with the help of Thomas' daughter after the war started. She taught at the Grand Contraband Camp until last year. Her husband, Moses, fought as a Union soldier. He is now half owner of Cromwell Plantation."

Marcus leaned forward even more. "Half owner?" he sputtered.

Jeremy smiled. "Mr. Cromwell did a lot of changing during the war."

"That be for sure," Marcus muttered. "That be quite a story..."

Jeremy chuckled again. "I know about the Black Codes. I also know that as a mulatto, I am at risk, as well."

"Ain't nobody gonna guess about you," Marcus protested. "You look so white ain't nobody gonna guess you got black blood."

"You did," Jeremy reminded him.

It was Marcus' turn to chuckle. "There wasn't any guessing involved," he said. "The black grapevine works real well. It's had to ever since the beginning of slavery. It also keeps its secrets real well. Ain't no black man that knows about you gonna say anything. We just trying to stay on top of things that can help us."

"And you think I can help?" Jeremy asked again, leaning on his desk. "How?"

A wave of relief washed over Marcus' face. "We had to fight last year to get the pass restrictions taken off us. The one good thing that come from that was all of us banding together. Used to be, freed men and slaves didn't really have much to do with each other. Now that all of us be free, we's got to work together." He paused, his eyes serious. "We be doing that."

"How?"

"The way we're being treated is making folks real angry. John Oliver is helping us come together."

"John Oliver?"

"John Oliver ain't even from the South," Marcus explained. "He be from up in Boston where he worked as a carpenter. He was real active in the American Missionary Society and fought hard for all of us to be free. When the war was over, he came down here to see how things were. He found out real quick."

Jeremy raised his eyebrows at the anger that filled Marcus' voice with the last statement, but he continued to listen quietly.

"John Oliver was walking down the street last year when he caught sight of the Black Bull Pen."

Jeremy grimaced. "The old Rebel hospital," he said with disgust. He had heard about what they decided to use it for after the war.

"Yes. That's where they were putting all the blacks they were rounding up who didn't have passes from white people saying we can do our jobs. Anyway, John Oliver caught sight of it one day when he was out walking around." Marcus shook his head. "The provost guard caught sight of him at the same time. They demanded a pass. John Oliver showed them his pass from Massachusetts, figuring it would protect him."

"It didn't," Jeremy said heavily.

"No. They shoved him into the Bull Pen. He stayed there until he found someone who would write a pass for him." Marcus smiled slightly. "The good thing is that

John Oliver decided the blacks down here need him real bad, so he decided to stay. He says we all gots to become activists." His expression became serious. "He's right."

"The Bull Pen was closed and Mayor Mayo replaced after the protests last year," Jeremy said, thinking what a sacrifice John Oliver had made. Surely life was much easier for him in Boston.

Marcus nodded. "We been doing a lot since last summer. We been holding mass meetings and putting together committees. Once we got everything in place, we be going to the right public officials to present our case. Last July, there was even some of us who went up to Alexandria to the Convention of the Colored People of Virginia." His eyes glowed with pride. "I gots to go. It was really something seeing all those black people in one place willing to fight for our rights."

Jeremy listened closely. "The black community seems to be doing all the right things," he observed. "What do you need me for?"

"We're figuring it all out," Marcus admitted, "but John Oliver says it be real important to have some white people on our side. He says there gonna be times when we need the white voice to make our point."

"He knows I'm mulatto?" Jeremy asked.

"Yes, but the white people don't," Marcus replied.

Jeremy took a deep breath. "I was fired from my job last year because word got around."

Marcus frowned. "I wasn't aware of that." His brow creased with thought. "How many people knew?"

Jeremy shrugged. "I don't really know. Things were rather chaotic. I was called in one day and told my kind didn't have a place in the Richmond government anymore."

Marcus considered his words. "Them people that fired you still here?"

Jeremy stared at him as his mind raced. "No," he finally said. "They all went home to other states..." His voice trailed off as he thought of the ramifications of his own words.

"They likely didn't tell many people," Marcus observed. "Like you said, things be kinda wild back then.

Anybody said anything since you been working on the factory?"

"No," Jeremy admitted.

"I think you would have heard if that kind of rumor was still going around," Marcus said. "People know you're Thomas' brother?" He smiled when Jeremy shook his head. "I think your secret is safe, at least for a while," he concluded. "You'll help us a whole heap more if you keep on being white."

Jeremy had heard nothing else about his racial heritage in the months since he had been let go. He'd been consumed with building the factory, but it was still likely that word of any rumors would have reached him, or at least Thomas. "That could be true," he murmured. "So how can I help?" he asked with a grin.

Marcus laughed. "I'd like you to meet the rest of the committee." He paused. "I reckon you know most of them already."

Jeremy eyed him. "How...?" He stopped and chuckled. "They work here?"

Marcus smiled. "You pay the best wages in town," he said. "You do know the other white folks ain't gonna be happy with you, don't you? It ain't just about the whites you got working here. And it ain't about you having a black mama. Just the factory gonna cause you a lot of trouble. Helping us gonna make things worse for you," he warned. "Them Black Codes ain't here yet, but they be coming. They's gonna make things harder for all of us."

Jeremy nodded. "We know," he replied. "We decided doing the right thing was more important than worrying about how people might react to it."

Evidently satisfied, Marcus sat back in his chair and looked at him. "So you'll meet with everyone?"

"Absolutely," Jeremy said. "Where and when?"

"We meet at the Second African Baptist Church every Wednesday night at seven o'clock."

"I'll be there on Wednesday," Jeremy promised.

"You can't come down there all by yourself!" Marcus exclaimed.

"Will I be in danger?"

Marcus hesitated. "Resentment ain't only on the white side," he said. "Most folks down in the black quarters ain't gonna do nothing, but there be some that are angry at anything white."

"Just like there are whites angry at anything that's black," Jeremy observed, realizing Marcus spoke the truth.

Marcus nodded. "I'll be waiting for you on the corner of Broad Street in front of the hardware store. Have Spencer stop to pick me up."

Jeremy smiled. "I should probably be surprised you know Spencer, but I have a feeling you know far more about me than I suspect."

Marcus remained silent, but his eyes sparkled with humor.

Jeremy suddenly barked a laugh. "Let me guess. Spencer is part of the committee."

Marcus merely smiled. "You'll know more on Wednesday night. We learned a long time ago to keep some things hidden."

"The secret societies," Jeremy responded.

Marcus frowned. "What you be knowing about that?"

"Not much," Jeremy replied. "Some of the men from Cromwell Plantation have family here in Richmond. They brought news back to Moses about secret societies being formed to make sure the blacks are taken care of. We talked about it over Christmas."

Marcus relaxed. "I may know more about you than you suspect, but obviously you know more about the black community than *I* suspected. I reckon both of them are good things."

"I reckon you're right," Jeremy said, confident he had found a new friend in Marcus. He stood and reached out a hand. "Thank you for trusting me."

Marcus stood and grasped his hand tightly. "You may not look like your daddy, but you sure enough act like Pastor Anthony."

Jeremy felt a sting in his eyes. "Thank you. You couldn't have paid me a higher compliment."

Jeremy sat at his desk, staring down at the factory floor long after Marcus had left. So it had begun. And his decision had been made for him.

He would live as a white man so he could most effectively help the blacks fighting for their rights. The truth could come out at any time, but he would do everything within his power to make sure Rose, Moses, little John, Hope, and the rest could grow up in a better world.

He had watched his father pay a huge price for pastoring a black church. Now it was his turn to do the right thing. As he pushed away from his desk and gathered his coat, he wondered what price he would be asked to pay.

Chapter Seven

"How old did you say you are?"

Carrie grinned at Robert and stuck out her tongue. "You should know shaming me won't keep me from acting like a child," she teased as she bounced on the carriage seat. "It's been months since we've been to Richmond. I love being on the plantation, but I was beginning to feel trapped by all the snow. I'm so glad it's warmed up enough to escape!"

"Are you excited about going to Richmond, or about going to a dance with your dashing husband?"

Carrie grinned, but the surge of emotion that swamped her told her just how momentous an occasion this was. She and Robert had visited Richmond only once since the end of the war—the time she had prevailed upon Dr. Wild for supplies for the medical clinic and then made a trip to Oak Meadows to finalize the sale of Robert's family plantation. Robert had still been regaining his strength and fighting regular nightmares of battle and death. Feelings of gratitude surged through her as she gazed into Robert's sparkling eyes. "That does make the trip more exciting," she murmured. "It's been a while since I've danced with the most handsome man in Virginia."

"We danced at your father and Abby's wedding," Robert protested.

"It doesn't count," Carrie retorted. "There wasn't anyone there I could show you off to."

"Do I hear pride?"

"Absolutely," Carrie assured him. "I want every single woman there to wish they were me, and I want to see their jealous expressions."

Robert threw his head back with a loud laugh. "Who would have guessed your ulterior motives, Mrs. Borden?"

"You would," Carrie replied calmly. "It's why you love me."

Robert laughed again and reached for her hand to give it a tight squeeze. "The list of reasons I love you is far too long for the rest of this trip."

"Oh, I don't know," Carrie said, shivering at the strong love in her husband's eyes. "I think we have time."

"Not if that thing sticking up in the air is the spire of St. Paul's Church," Robert responded, tilting his head toward the horizon.

Carrie whipped her head around and bounced on the carriage seat again. "We're here!" she squealed. She sat back and breathed in the cold, February air. Bright sunshine battled with the frigid temperature and sparkled on the banks of snow that remained. The stark outlines of oak, maple and poplar created the winter woods she so loved.

"This will be the first time we'll see the factory completed," she said, still jouncing on the seat.

"I think you're more of a city girl than you let on," Robert observed. "You're going to love Philadelphia."

Carrie sobered instantly. In less than two months, she would be leaving for medical school.

Robert reached for her hand. "I'm sorry," he said. "I shouldn't have said that."

"It's the truth," Carrie murmured.

Robert let her hand go, took hold of her chin, and turned her head so he could meet her eyes. "You don't have to go," he reminded her. "You have a choice."

"Do I?" Carrie asked. "Oh, I know I can say I won't go, but what then? What will I do with my life? How will I feel if I walk away from the thing I believe I'm supposed to do? How could I live with myself?" She sighed when Robert continued to gaze at her. "We both know I'm going, but does that mean I have to be excited about it?"

"I think it does," Robert said gently. "Do you honestly believe you're meant to do this?"

"Yes, but..."

"There is no but," Robert continued. "I will miss you. You will miss *me*. You will miss the plantation and everyone you love, but being excited about moving forward in a new direction is not a bad thing."

"I never said it was a bad thing!" Carrie protested.

"Haven't you?" Robert asked, his voice still gentle. "Every time you talk about it, you say you dread going, dread leaving the plantation. Is that because you feel guilty about your excitement?"

Carrie stared at him. "Guilty?"

"Carrie, it's perfectly all right to be excited about the opportunity to make your dream come true. I don't think it means you don't love me or don't want to be with me. No one feels that way. You're carrying a burden of guilt because *you* think you should feel that way."

Carrie opened her mouth to refute his statement and then closed it slowly as the truth swept over her. "Oh my God," she whispered. "You're right." Her mind raced with the realization. "I've allowed my guilt over leaving you—in spite of your encouragement—to steal the joy of the opportunity." She looked away from him and watched as the outskirts of Richmond appeared around the bend in the road. "I *will* miss you terribly," she murmured.

"Of course you will," Robert responded. "That doesn't mean you have to feel guilty about leaving. You are being given an opportunity to do something so amazing. Why waste even one moment of that joy by choosing to feel bad?"

Carrie whipped her head back to stare at him. "How did you become so wise?"

Robert chuckled. "It's amazing what you can learn when you lie in bed for months on end trying to give up on life." His eyes grew serious. "I almost gave up everything I cared about because I felt guilty."

"Guilty?" Carrie echoed. This was the first time he had broached this subject. She had spoken with so many veterans at the clinic who struggled with guilt, but Robert had never spoken about it.

"Yes," Robert replied. "I've only just realized how much guilt I've carried. I couldn't understand why I lived and so many died. I couldn't understand why I had both arms and legs, while so many men lost one or both. I allowed the memories and the guilt to swallow me for so long. Even when I started to get better, it continued to haunt me. I felt guilty for having a wife, for being on the plantation, for the opportunity to raise horses again." He took a deep breath. "I don't know why I lived. I don't know why I wasn't maimed. I *do* know I've been given another chance to do what I love more than anything. I *do* know I have an amazing wife who needs to learn everything she can so she can help more people." He paused. "Mostly, I've realized I can hang on to the guilt, or I can choose joy."

Carrie smiled softly.

"Annie caught me out on the porch a few days ago," Robert began. She told me I was wasting good time wallowing around in my guilt. She told me there wasn't a thing to be guilty about, that God decides *who gonna live and who gonna die.*" He imitated her perfectly. "She told me I should let go of useless guilt and choose to live every single day with joy."

"Choose joy," Carrie murmured, remembering her mantra from earlier in the war. "You're right. I didn't realize it, but I *have* been feeling guilty. No more," she vowed. "I'll miss you every day I'm gone, but I'm going to choose joy that I can truly become a doctor after dreaming about it for so long." She straightened her shoulders, stared out over the horizon, and leaned over to kiss him. "Thank you," she murmured.

Carrie held her breath as they turned onto her father's street. She smiled when she saw the three-story brick home come into view. It held so many memories for her, but she didn't miss living there. Though the plantation would always be what she considered home, she was thrilled for the chance to visit. She jumped out of the carriage before it had even come to a complete stop. "Father! Abby!" She raced for the porch and, laughing, fell into her father's arms. "I've missed you so much!"

Thomas laughed and held her back. "I missed you, too, daughter, but it's only been a few weeks since we left the plantation. You clearly are ready for some city excitement."

Carrie spun away to pull Abby into a hug. "You have no idea," she murmured, exchanging a glance with her stepmother. "I'm going to leave you to talk man stuff with Robert after he puts the carriage away. Abby and I have more important things to discuss."

"Dances are more important than politics?" Thomas teased.

"In more ways than we could possibly go into right now," Abby assured him as she led Carrie into the house.

Carrie did a twirl when she entered the foyer, enjoying the sparkles dancing on the floor from the chandelier crystals catching the sun.

"Getting some practice in, Miss Carrie?"

Carrie laughed as May poked her head out of the kitchen. "I feel like I haven't danced in ages, May. I can hardly wait!" She ran forward to give her father's housekeeper a warm hug. "It's so good to see you again." She lifted her nose and sniffed. "Is that...?"

"You think I would let you come without fixing you some of my molasses cookies?" May asked, her face wreathed with a smile when she stepped back.

Carrie eyed the door to the kitchen, realizing how famished she was after the long ride. Right on the heels of realizing how hungry she was came the cold stiffness from hours in the wagon.

May waved her hand. "Go on in there, Miss Carrie. Just leave Robert some," she scolded.

"Maybe one or two," Carrie said merrily.

"Micah is taking you up a hot bath," May informed her. "I thought you would be ready for it after that long, cold ride."

"Bless you!" Carrie said. Then she turned to Abby. "Were you—"

"—able to get you a new dress?" Abby cocked her eyebrow. "Did you doubt me for even a minute?"

"No," Carrie said. "It's just been so long since I had a new dress." She shook her head. "It probably sounds silly."

"Not at all," Abby assured her. "You wouldn't spend the money during the war, and then there was nothing to be had. You haven't needed one on the plantation, but a dance is the perfect occasion for a new dress. Thalhimers had a new shipment come in last week."

Carrie sighed. "Thank you for understanding," she murmured. She looked around expectantly. "Do I get to see it?" she finally asked after a long silence.

"You want to *see* it?" Abby teased.

Just then Micah walked down the sweeping staircase that led to the next floor. "You got a hot bath all ready, Miss Carrie. I be doing Robert's next."

"Thank you, Micah," Carrie said as she gave him a quick hug. "It's good to see you."

"You, too, Miss Carrie," he said quietly, only his dark eyes expressing his pleasure. He exchanged a look with Abby. "I put what you wanted me to on the hook on Miss Carrie's door," he added.

"My dress!" Carrie gasped, laughing as she ran up the stairs. "The next time you see me, I will not be a rumpled, frozen piece of humanity."

Carrie sighed with delight as she settled back into the deep clawfoot tub. She closed her eyes and allowed the warm water to envelop her, enjoying the sound of the wind whistling through the magnolia tree stationed outside the window. Now that she was warm, she didn't care how cold it was outside. It simply made her feel cozy and safe.

She allowed her thoughts to travel back to her and Robert's conversation. How right he had been. Releasing the guilt had lifted such a heavy burden from her heart. In two months, she would be a medical student, but she would *still* be the wife of the most wonderful man she knew. Happiness soared through her heart as she let the bath completely rejuvenate her. She smiled when she heard a groan come from the next room. "It feels wonderful, doesn't it?" she called.

The next groan was louder. "The only thing that would make it more perfect would be for you to share it," Robert called.

"As soon as you make us wealthy from the horses, we'll buy a fabulously big tub," Carrie replied, a broad smile on her face.

"You might make us wealthy first, *Doctor* Borden."

Carrie laughed. "Not likely. Women doctors are considered an oddity, not a source of secure income."

"You're going to be famous one day," Robert predicted. "Whether it's because you're rich or odd, I really don't care. It will be enough to tell everyone you're my wife. And now, if you don't mind, I need to close my eyes and thaw out my body."

"My feelings exactly," Carrie agreed, closing her eyes. They flew open suddenly. "There's one more thing, Mr. Borden."

"Hmm..."

"I hope my father bought you a dashing suit for tonight, because you're going to have a difficult time looking as good as I will."

Carrie heard the smile in his voice when Robert responded. "You like the dress Abby picked out."

"It's splendid!" Carrie cried. "Now, quit talking. You have to be rested so you can keep up with me tonight. You don't want anyone to accuse you of being an old man at just twenty-six."

"We'll see who can keep up with whom, Mrs. Borden," Robert replied smugly. "Now, just because you are far more childish than me does not give you justification to disturb my bath any longer.

Carrie laughed with delight, closed her eyes, and forgot everything else but the luxury of her bath.

Dressed warmly against the chill of the house, pervasive in spite of the fires roaring in every fireplace, Carrie followed her nose toward the kitchen. She could tell Annie had just brought out another tray of molasses cookies. She stopped short when she heard a familiar laugh, and then rushed forward. "Matthew! What are you doing here? I thought you weren't arriving until tomorrow."

Matthew smiled as he embraced her. "I was able to leave Washington a day early," he explained.

Carrie eyed him. "You were eager to leave?" Matthew nodded, but there was more in his eyes. "Why?" she asked. "I've learned you don't say most of what you know. I have no desire to be protected from the truth." She thought about what he had told them on New Year's Day. "Wasn't there to be a vote this month on renewing the Freedmen's Bureau bill?"

Matthew nodded and reached for a cookie.

Carrie stepped forward to block his hand. "Those are *my* cookies, Matthew Justin."

Matthew looked to May for sympathy, but she merely chuckled and shrugged her shoulders. "So you're holding them ransom?"

Carrie shrugged, too. "A little information is not much to ask for in return for some of these cookies." She picked one up and bit into it, closing her eyes with delight. She shot May a brilliant smile. "Wonderful!"

"Not fair," Matthew whined.

Carrie reached for another cookie. "It's also not fair to hide what is happening in our country." She waved a cookie under his nose. "It will take so little to get one," she taunted.

Matthew eyed the cookie longingly and then sat down with a laugh. "I was going to wait until dinner tonight so I only had to tell it once."

Carrie tilted her head. "Your choice. The cookies will still be wonderful after dinner." She picked up the plate and winked at May. "I'll keep these safe," she promised.

Matthew shook his head. "You're a hard woman, Carrie Borden."

"Just one used to getting her way," came another voice from the doorway. Robert stepped forward to clap Matthew on the shoulder. "I'm glad you got here in time for the dance, my friend."

Thomas and Abby appeared in the door then, having returned from a trip into town. More greetings were exchanged. Abby finally looked at Carrie's hand. "Are you taking those cookies somewhere?" she asked with amusement.

"That depends," Carrie replied, merely smiling when Abby raised an eyebrow.

"She's holding them hostage," Matthew replied. "She won't let anyone have one until I tell her the news from Washington."

"Not true," Carrie said demurely, holding the plate out to her father and Abby. "Everyone in the room is welcome to these delicious cookies. With the exception of you, of course."

Abby laughed with delight. "Women do know how to get their way." She reached forward and bit into a cookie. "You really should just talk, Matthew."

Matthew chuckled and held up his hands in surrender. "I was going to. I'm glad everyone is here so that I don't have to repeat myself at dinner tonight."

Carrie, relieved to see some of the somberness leave Matthew's face, smiled and handed him a cookie. She knew how heavy a burden he was carrying. If a silly game could reduce some of the stress, it was more than worth it. "There will be more as you reveal what happened," she murmured, pleased when his eyes lit with genuine amusement.

Matthew sighed with contentment when he took his first bite, but when he opened his eyes the trouble was back. "The new Freedmen's Bureau Bill passed both the House and the Senate."

"Isn't that good news?" Carrie asked.

"It would be if President Johnson hadn't vetoed it."

"On what basis?" Abby asked. "I heard from friends that even the Republicans were assuming Johnson would sign the bill."

"*Everyone* was," Matthew agreed. "The veto came as a complete surprise. Seward, his own secretary of state, had written a conciliatory speech that criticized the bill's particulars but acknowledged a federal responsibility for the freedmen. Seward hoped to take the edge off the veto."

"He didn't use the speech," Robert guessed.

Matthew shook his head. "President Johnson's message repudiated the Bureau entirely. He said it was unwarranted by the Constitution and unaffordable given the condition of our fiscal affairs." His voice tightened. "He pointed out that Congress had never felt called upon to provide economic relief, establish schools, or purchase land for *our own people*, as he put it. He then went on to say that offering further aid to the freedmen would only injure their character and prospects by implying they didn't have to work for a living."

Silence filled the kitchen.

"Our president went on to say these decisions shouldn't be made while eleven states remain unrepresented."

"For the very reasons we need the Freedmen's Bureau renewed," Abby sputtered. "The eleven states are the problem!"

Matthew took a deep breath and continued. "President Johnson told Congress he had been chosen by the people of *all* the states, and that he had a broader view of the national interest than members of the Congress who were merely elected from a single district."

Robert whistled. "I can imagine how that went over. Not to mention that *all* the states didn't include the South."

Matthew nodded. "I overheard one Republican say that Johnson was rather modest for a man who was made president by an assassin," he said wryly, his eyes flashing with anger.

"So everything will be a fight from now on," Thomas said slowly.

"Everything to do with Reconstruction," Matthew agreed. "The battle lines have been drawn. Johnson has made it clear he will veto every bill having to do with it.

He will block any federal attempts to help the freedmen."
He shook his head. "As far as he was concerned, he believed he didn't have a good choice. However much I disagree with him, I think he honestly believes he made the better of two bad choices."

"Now that he has vetoed, he is going to have to fight the radicals," Thomas observed. "If he had signed the bill, the Democratic support he has garnered in the South would have gone away."

Carrie shook her head in disgust. "Continuing evidence that politics is more important than simple human rights. To say we've not offered aid to other people is preposterous. Other people were not stolen from their own country and enslaved for more than one hundred years! Does he seriously think the black population can emerge from that without any help at all?"

Matthew's expression made it clear he agreed with her.

"Will Congress override the veto?" Abby asked.

Matthew scowled. "They tried...the very next day. The attempt fell short by two votes of the necessary two-thirds."

Thomas whistled. "That should have made him nervous. How many Republicans voted to override it?" He smiled when Matthew looked at him with surprise. "Abby and I have been catching up with politics since your announcement at Christmas."

"We're not going to be so ignorant again," Abby added. "How many Republicans voted to override it, Matthew?"

"Thirty of thirty-eight."

Abby nodded. "That's good. Johnson has been thinking it was only the Radical Republicans he would have a problem with."

Thomas nodded. "He thought the moderate Republicans would go his way."

"He has misconstrued the lines of division within the Republican Party," Matthew agreed. "I talked to a friend before I left. President Johnson's plan was to provoke the Radicals into opposing him so they could be isolated and destroyed. He hoped the Republican mainstream would form a new party with him."

Abby gasped. "A new party? He couldn't possibly have been serious! It's been less than a year since the war ended. Did he really think all the Republicans would forget the price that was paid and simply go along with him?"

"Evidently," Matthew replied. "He had his wakeup call when the override vote almost passed. Only eight Republicans voted for him." He frowned. "It gets worse."

"Worse?" Carrie asked. "How is that possible? Our country is being run by a man who is clearly out of touch with reality."

"The day before I left, Johnson gave a speech to honor Washington's birthday. He equated Senators Stevens, Sumner, and Wendell Phillips with Confederate leaders. He said they all were opposed to the fundamental principles of this government. He even implied they were plotting his assassination."

"Oh, for pity's sake," Abby muttered. "President Lincoln would be horrified if he could see what is happening in the country."

"I agree that President Johnson is out of touch with reality," Matthew stated, "but unfortunately he has support. I listened to his speech. It certainly displayed him at his worst. He referred to himself over two hundred times in one hour, and the speech revealed just how intolerant he is of criticism."

"But...?" Thomas asked grimly.

"The Democrats loved it," he replied. "They admitted much of the speech was done in questionable taste, but they agreed with everything he said and applauded him for having the courage to say it. He also has tremendous support among Northern bankers and merchants who believe the Bureau is interfering with the plantation discipline necessary to get cotton production back on track." Matthew made no attempt to hide his disgust.

May snorted. "That's what all them Black Codes be about. We sure enough getting tired of hearing about how we don't want to work. I don't know *anybody* that don't want to work. We just want the freedom to decide what we gonna do!"

Abby reached over and took May's hand before she looked back at Matthew. "What is going to happen?"

"Many Republicans consider the veto a declaration of war against the Republican Party and the freedmen. I believe the elections in the fall are going to be a battleground."

"But what about *now*? The veto is certainly going to inflame the Black Code sentiments even more," Carrie said angrily. "They're going to believe they can get away with anything because of President Johnson's attitude."

Matthew nodded heavily. "I'm afraid you're right."

"So what will happen?" Abby repeated.

"The Radical Republicans will continue to fight."

"But...?" Abby pressed. "No more hiding things you don't think we'll want to hear. Try that again and you may never eat another one of May's cookies," she said sternly.

Matthew managed a smile before he grew even more serious. "I'm afraid it's going to take something major to force everyone's hand."

"Like?" Carrie asked anxiously, her mind conjuring up horrible images of vigilante justice.

Matthew exchanged a long look with her. "I don't know, but I don't think any of us are going to like the answer to that question."

Carrie was dressing when she heard a light tap on the door. "As long as you're not Robert you can come in," she called. She had made him go into the other room to dress so that she could surprise him.

Abby opened the door and slipped in, her eyes glowing with pride when she saw Carrie. "You're beautiful," she said softly.

"Only because you picked the most beautiful gown in the world," Carrie cried, rushing forward to wrap Abby in a hug. "Thank you."

Abby held her close for a long moment and stepped back, her eyes misty with emotion. "I've always dreamed of having a daughter to buy clothes for," she murmured. "That it is you is a joy I can never be grateful enough for. I love you, Carrie."

"And I love you, Abby," Carrie whispered. "During the long years of the war I was so afraid I would never see you again. To have you become my mother is more than I could have ever hoped for."

Abby held her close again and then waved her hand. "Spin," she commanded.

Carrie obeyed, knowing the emerald gown with soft yellow piping fit her perfectly. She laughed as she twirled, watching the wide folds of the dress catch the gleaming light of the lanterns.

"You'll be the most beautiful woman there," Abby announced, her eyes once again glittering.

Carrie swallowed back her emotion. "Only if you don't make me cry so that my eyes are red and swollen," she scolded. "Where is *your* dress? Did you buy a new one?"

"When I have a closet full of gowns?" Abby asked. She smiled brilliantly. "Of course I did!"

Carrie laughed with delight. She had loved her mother, but she had never imagined it could be so wonderful to have a woman who understood her so completely, and who was so much fun to be with. "Father won't be able to take his eyes off you."

"That's the plan," Abby murmured. Her eyes grew serious. "I have something else to talk about. I wasn't going to tell you until tomorrow morning, but I decided having secrets does nothing but show disrespect."

Carrie settled down on her dressing bench. "What is it?" she asked, slightly alarmed by the sudden shadows in Abby's eyes. "Is something wrong with Father?" He had seemed perfectly healthy when she had arrived, but...

"No," Abby said quickly. "Your father is fine."

"Then what?" Carrie asked.

Abby took a deep breath. "It's about Eddie and Opal," she began. "There was a fire..."

Carrie caught her breath but waited quietly.

"The restaurant caught fire on a terribly cold day." Abby hesitated. "There was an explosion," she finally revealed, her eyes deep with pain.

"Eddie and Opal?" Carrie gasped.

Abby shook her head. "They're fine, but not everyone made it out."

Carrie went rigid. "Who?" she managed.

"Sadie and Sadie Lou." Abby took another deep breath. "And Susie and Zeke," she managed. "They are dead."

Carrie stared at her, unable to comprehend what she was saying. "Dead?" she repeated, the word swirling through the room. "*All* of them?"

Abby nodded.

"Carl and Amber?" Carrie asked, trying to absorb the news and aware her hands were trembling.

"They're fine," Abby said. "Janie got them out in time."

"Janie?" Carrie cried. "*Janie* was there?"

"She had gone there for a meal after class. Zeke got her out before he and Susie ran back in for everyone else."

Carrie shuddered as images of searing flames leapt into her mind.

"Janie helped Carl, Amber, Eddie, and Opal out, while Zeke and Susie went in for the Sadies." Abby's voice shook. "The flames must have reached the oil vats then."

Carrie closed her eyes tightly, tears making the image of flames waver behind her eyelids. "The explosion," she whispered, vivid memories of the explosion at the Tredegar factory surging to the front of her mind. She could still hear the screams and cries of the children she had worked to save. "How they must have suffered," she said through gritted teeth.

"I don't think so," Abby said quickly. "I'm sure the explosion killed them instantly."

"That is better," Carrie said quietly. "The burns would have been horrible." The reality of Abby's news swept through her. "But all four of them!" she cried.

Memories of Eddie and Opal's children roared into her mind, and then another reality hit home. "Moses! And Annie...and June..." Her voice trailed off. "They don't know." She couldn't stop the tears from coming when she thought of Moses' little sister, Sadie, dead in the fire. "Why?" she whispered. She opened agonized eyes and stared at Abby. "Why?"

Abby shook her head and pulled her close. "It was a horrible accident."

Carrie allowed the tears to flow for several minutes before she pulled back. "Opal and Eddie? They must be devastated."

"They are back in Richmond," Abby said. "They couldn't bear the thought of not being with family and friends after what happened. Eddie's brother is in Richmond, and the whole family moved in with them last week. Eddie is working at the factory. Opal starts as a seamstress there in a few weeks."

Carrie shook her head. "So much loss," she whispered. "Fannie...and now the kids. And Zeke. He and Susie had just found each other again." She stared into the lantern on her table as wind whipped the branches of the magnolia tree against her window. She welcomed the tendrils of cold air that seeped in around the window frame. "It never ends, does it?"

Abby didn't pretend not to know what she meant. "Pain? Loss? Death?" She shook her head. "No. It never ends." She gripped Carrie's hands. "But neither does life," she said. "Neither does joy. Or hope. They all exist together."

"Choose joy," Carrie murmured. She brushed at her tears and managed a small smile. "Robert and I talked about that today." She shared their earlier conversation.

"Robert is a wise man," Abby replied. "And Annie is a wise woman. All of them will grieve over losing Sadie and the rest, but they will move forward."

"I'm so glad she had a chance to be free," Carrie said. "So glad she had a chance to travel, to go to school." Her eyes filled with tears again. "All of them were so remarkable," she said sadly. "I'm so glad I had the chance to know them."

Silence filled the room for many long minutes.

Abby was the one to break it. "I'm sorry if I picked the wrong time to tell you. I was going to wait until after the dance..."

Carrie shook her head. "I'm glad you told me," she replied. "There is never a good time for news like that." She took a deep breath. "If the war taught me one thing, it is that we all have to choose life in the midst of death and suffering. Any of us could die in an explosion at any moment. We have to hold tight to joy and life every way we can." She stood and looked at her reflection in the mirror. "I will go to the dance. I will have a good time." She looked back at Abby. "Do you know where Opal and Eddie are living? I would like to visit."

Abby smiled. "I was sure you would. Spencer will be here at nine o'clock tomorrow morning to take you and Robert there. Since it is Sunday, Eddie will not be working."

Carrie nodded her appreciation. "I'll tell Moses, June, and Annie when I get home." She knew she didn't have to tell Abby how much she dreaded it.

"That won't be necessary," Abby responded. "Eddie and Opal want to break the news themselves. Though it wasn't anyone's fault, they feel responsible for what happened. Since Sadie was in their care, they want to be the ones to tell them. Thomas and I have made arrangements for Spencer to take the family out there on Monday. They'll be back in a week. It will be good for all of them to have some time on the plantation."

Carrie smiled. "You're a good woman."

"Yes," Abby agreed, smiling when Carrie laughed. "I've never seen the sense of false modesty. We are both amazing women." She turned serious. "We are going to have to be to make it through all that is going to happen."

Carrie refused to think about all that Matthew had said that day. Abby's shocking news of the fire was all she could handle. "That may be true," she agreed, "but right now all we have to handle is being escorted by two dashing men to a dance. And *you*, my darling mother, are not ready. I'd say that is your biggest concern right now."

Chapter Eight

Carrie forced thoughts of the deaths from her mind as the carriage pulled up to a brightly lit house. All she was going to focus on tonight was the joy of being with Robert, her father, Abby, Jeremy and Matthew. She planned on dancing until her feet could no longer move. She smiled as Robert helped her from the carriage, relishing the look of pride on his face as he offered her his arm to walk up the stairs.

"You are absolutely ravishing, Mrs. Borden," he said, his eyes never leaving her face.

"And you are the most handsome man here, Mr. Borden," Carrie replied. "I do believe I was right that every woman here tonight will wish she were me." She tucked her hand into the crook of his arm. "They'll simply have to be disappointed."

"One will not be." Abby's amused voice sounded behind her. "Robert is quite handsome, but I'm afraid Thomas is the only man I want to be with tonight."

Carrie smiled with delight as she looked back at her father and Abby. She could hardly remember the grief-stricken man who had fled the plantation after her mother died. Her father's eyes sparkled with life and love as he gazed down at Abby. "I don't believe you have attended a dance with my father, have you?" Carrie asked.

"We've been too busy with the factory," Abby admitted. "I've only danced with him at the wedding."

"Prepare to be swept off your feet," Carrie warned her. "My father is a fabulous dancer. You may have a hard time keeping up with him."

Abby fluttered her eyelashes. "I'll do my best," she said coyly.

Matthew barked a laugh. "Abigail Livingston Cromwell could out-dance any woman in Philadelphia," he announced. "People made the mistake of thinking she was only a successful businesswoman. She had no trouble setting them straight."

Thomas' smile grew wider. "You continue to be a surprise," he murmured.

Abby's smile turned into a grin. "You have no idea, Mr. Cromwell. *No idea...*"

Laughter rang through the air as they climbed the stairs and entered the warm house.

Carrie gazed around with delight. Richmond was still struggling to recover from the war; much of the downtown area was not yet rebuilt after the fire that had almost destroyed the city, but one would never guess it from the home they were in. Dances during the war had been simple—and called "starvation dances" for a reason. The music had always been plentiful, but the only refreshments had been water.

She tried to remember what she knew about the owner of the home they were in but couldn't even pull forth a name. A glance in the dining room revealed a long table full of delicious food. Mounds of country ham towered over platters full of sweet potatoes, carrots and butternut squash. Fluffy biscuits and cornbread rested beside fresh pies and plates of cookies. If there wasn't as much as could be found before the war, no one was complaining. It was more than had been seen at a social function for years.

Music flowed from the front room as lanterns and candles filled the house with light. Most women wore new, brightly colored gowns, yet more evidence that Richmond's economy was slowly rebounding. Carrie was relieved that not one man was dressed in uniform. She had seen enough military uniforms for a lifetime. She prayed there would never be another war.

"The house belongs to Mrs. Penelope Mason," Abby leaned over to whisper. "She lost her husband and one of her three sons in the war. Her remaining two sons are merchants here in the city."

Carrie nodded. That explained the relative opulence she was seeing. Richmonders were strapped for cash, but they were also hungry for goods. During the war, the stores had either been empty or the prices too exorbitant for most to afford. Money was still tight, but when people had it available, they were eager to spend it. Merchants were slowly filling their stores again. Profits were being made.

"Should I be surprised we were all invited?" Carrie asked, keeping her voice low enough for the music to cover it. "I thought people were angry about the factory."

"People *are* angry, but they are also desperate for money to build back the economy. We are one of the largest employers in Richmond now. They can't afford to ignore us."

"I'm sure it doesn't hurt that you're one of the investors in the bank," Carrie murmured with amusement.

Abby's eyes twinkled. "That, too. Though I don't have any control over loans, neither am I making an effort to be sure people know that."

Carrie reached for the glass of lemonade Robert held out to her as the small orchestra struck up a lively waltz.

Robert grinned. "Drink your lemonade. You're going to need it to keep up with me tonight."

Carrie laughed and drank willingly. The cold air during the carriage ride had dried her throat terribly.

Abby smiled her thanks as Thomas handed her a glass, her foot tapping time with the music. "Do you know the history of the waltz?" she asked, continuing when no one responded. "It was created in Vienna just past the turn of this century. It was condemned as wildly immoral in England."

"The *waltz*?" Robert asked. "Am I missing something?"

"It is quite different from the way people used to dance," Abby replied, watching as the first wave of dancers moved onto the floor. "Dancing used to be very stately, slow and distant. The minuet and the allemande were very courtly and elegant dances. They were subdued, characterized by stern attitudes and slow, complex patterns. They were performed at arm's length. Dancers wore gloves so there would be no fleshly contact even at that distance."

"And they called that *dancing*?" Carrie gasped.

"It was a different time," Abby responded. "When the waltz was first created, people were appalled by the close dance position, the rapid tempo, and the constant twirling and turning."

"The very thing that makes it so enjoyable," Thomas stated. He placed his and Abby's lemonade on the table. "Care to see if you can keep up with this old man?"

Abby smiled up at him. "First you'll have to show me the old man," she said affectionately, moving into his arms. Moments later, they were sweeping across the floor, Abby's light blue gown swirling around her.

"They look wonderful," Carrie breathed, correctly interpreting the look in Robert's eyes as she moved into his arms. He pulled her close as the music soared around them.

And just like that, the magic returned. The strong, virulent man holding her close wiped away all memories of how close to death he had come. All that mattered was the music and the feel of his arms around her. They moved as one, completely oblivious to anyone else in the room.

Jeremy watched the dancers swirling and then turned to speak with several businessmen he knew, content to enjoy the music and the conversation. He knew there was a lot of resentment in town about the wages they were paying their black employees, as well as the fact that they were hiring blacks instead of hiring only white war veterans, but evidently everyone had decided to be on their best behavior tonight. Jeremy was glad. The last weeks had been exhausting as they brought the factory up to full speed, but their first orders would be going out the following week. It was a heady feeling.

He was chatting easily with the owner of Thalhimers when his eyes caught a woman sitting on a sofa against the wall, her dark blue dress setting off her porcelain skin and striking red hair. She appeared relaxed and confident as she watched the dancers, her free hand keeping time with the music as she sipped apple cider. He couldn't take his eyes off her.

"Excuse me," he finally murmured, walking over to where she was sitting. "Good evening," he said.

The woman looked up, her brilliant blue eyes open and relaxed. "Good evening," she replied with a warm smile.

She wasn't a classic beauty, but Jeremy had never been quite so taken with someone before. "My name is Jeremy Anthony. I don't believe we've had the pleasure of meeting."

"I am Marietta Anderson. You don't know me, but I know who *you* are, Mr. Anthony."

Jeremy stared at her, bemused. "You do? How is that possible?"

"You manage the Cromwell Clothing Factory that your brother and sister-in-law own," she replied, smiling at his look of surprise. "Many of my students work there," she explained.

"Your students?" Jeremy asked, and then smiled. "You are a teacher."

Marietta nodded. "I am. I teach classes down at the Second African Church."

Jeremy tried to hide his surprise but knew he was unsuccessful when she continued on with a question.

"So just what am I doing at a dance for staunch Confederate women who resent my efforts to help the blacks?" she asked with amusement.

Jeremy laughed. "I apologize that my surprise was so obvious." He indicated the spot next to her on the couch. "May I join you?"

"Certainly," Marietta replied. She lowered her voice a little. "Mrs. Mason, our hostess for the night, is rather appalled at my being a teacher, but she and my mother were very close friends before my mother moved to the North and married an abolitionist." She laughed with delight at the look on Jeremy's face. "Mrs. Mason may be appalled at what I do, but Southern hospitality demanded I be invited. In truth, she is a wonderful woman. We don't agree on politics, and we don't agree on what should be done with the freed slaves, but she has many redeeming qualities."

"So you're as open-minded as you are beautiful," Jeremy murmured, flushing when he realized he had spoken the words out loud. Since he couldn't take them back, and he saw no offense in her eyes, he decided to press his luck. "Would you like to dance?"

"I would love to," Marietta replied with a bright smile. "I thought I might sit here all night watching. Every other male in the room seems to know what I do. They have been unfailingly polite but very distant."

Jeremy smiled. "I'm glad. I shouldn't have to worry about competition."

Marietta laughed and moved into the arms he held out to her as another waltz began.

Jeremy breathed in her scent as they danced. The last several years had left him no time for relationships. Working, caring for his father, and starting the factory had taken up every spare moment. In truth, he had not met a single woman who attracted him or who could make him consider veering from his course of hard work. He suddenly knew he was holding that woman in his arms.

Matthew turned his back on the dancers as he talked to a fellow journalist from the *Richmond Examiner*, a weekly newspaper that rankled him on a regular basis, but also never failed to offer amusement. He needed the distraction tonight. When Carrie had floated down the stairs in her exquisite gown, all he could do to hide the expression in his eyes was busy himself adding wood to the fire. As much as he relished their easy friendship, at times it was nothing short of agony to hide his true feelings. There were times he cursed his love for her, but mostly he was thankful she was still a part of his life. His friendship with Robert was too strong for there to be resentment.

"How is your book coming?" Paul Sawyers asked.

Matthew pulled his thoughts back. It was easier now that he couldn't see Carrie smiling into Robert's eyes as they danced. "It's going well," he replied. "I just returned from Washington, DC. It's still far from being finished, but writing it is a series of continual revelations as I explore life in the South now that the war is over."

Paul nodded. "Do you know Edward Pollard?"

"One of the *Examiner* editors?" Matthew asked. "I don't know him well, but we met a time or two during the war."

"He's just finished a book," Paul revealed. "*The Lost Cause: A New Southern History of the War of the Confederates.*"

Matthew raised his eyebrows. "Really? I've not heard of it."

"It will be released next month," Paul revealed, watching Matthew carefully. "He sets the record straight on what really happened with the war."

Matthew smiled. "Is that right?" He decided to play along since he was a guest in a staunchly Southern home. "I look forward to reading it." He almost laughed at Paul's disappointed expression. Obviously, he expected much more of a reaction. The brief flash of amusement faded quickly, however. The memory of President Johnson's speech days before was sobering. There was nothing funny about what was happening in the country so soon after the end of four years of death and destruction. Having read Pollard's editorials, he could well imagine what his book contained.

Paul looked at him. "You won't like it," he said bluntly.

"Probably not," Matthew agreed. He had found he agreed with little printed on the pages of the *Examiner*. He watched over Paul's shoulder as Jeremy carried lemonade to an attractive woman whom he had just led from the dance floor. He was much more curious about her identity than he was about what drivel Edward Pollard had published.

"He sets things straight on the real reason the war happened," Paul asserted.

Matthew turned his eyes back. "That right?"

Paul nodded. "He makes it clear that the cause of the war was secession, not slavery."

Matthew felt a surge of anger. "Really?" he replied, his voice deliberately calm.

Paul seemed satisfied he had his attention. "Yes. He does a masterful job in communicating that squabbles over secession and the primacy of states' rights were the real cause of the war. If it had not been for Northern abolitionists who overdramatized the slavery issue, it surely would have died on its own accord, as Pollard reveals the truth that the vast majority of slaves were happy on the plantations and had no desire to leave."

Matthew stared at him. He reminded himself he was a guest in a southern home, but it was impossible to not respond. "Does Pollard mention that it was actually the dispute over slavery that caused secession?" he asked sharply. "Does he reveal that most of the southern politicians who led the way in secession believed slavery was the foundation and cornerstone of the Confederacy, and that the South couldn't exist without it?"

Paul opened his mouth to protest, but Matthew wasn't done. President Johnson's veto of the Freedmen's Bureau Bill, and the growing strength of the Black Codes, wiped away any feelings of constraint. "Does he reveal how many slaves escaped long before the war? Does he talk about the vast number who used the Underground Railroad to flee their *happy lives* on the plantation?" he asked sarcastically. "Does Pollard's entire book attempt to rewrite history to satisfy his belief of what *should* have happened?"

Matthew became aware other people were listening. Angry eyes glittered at him as he finished speaking. "Never mind," he said shortly. "I'm all too familiar with journalists and writers who use words to create whatever reality they want to." He held up his hand as Paul, his eyes glittering with angry satisfaction, attempted to say something. "I'm sorry to bring discord into tonight's party, but I find I have had my fill of fiction disguised as journalism," he said grimly. Matthew looked down as he felt a warm hand on his arm.

"And I find I have worn out my husband," Abby said lightly. "Can I talk you into dancing with an old woman while he recovers?"

Matthew managed a smile, recognizing her offer to remove him from the conversation. He grasped it eagerly. "I would be delighted, Mrs. Cromwell." He turned back to Paul. "You'll have to excuse me," he said cordially, only his eyes still flashing anger.

He led Abby onto the floor. "Thank you," he said quietly.

Abby smiled up at him. "I have no idea what you were talking about, but since I know Paul Sawyers works for the *Richmond Examiner*, I was quite sure the conversation would do nothing but make you angry. I read the *Examiner* occasionally just to see what nonsense they are publishing now. I would like to ignore it, but I find knowledge, no matter how distasteful it is, is better than ignorance."

Matthew wanted to lose himself in the music, but the anger was still burning too hot. "You've heard of Edward Pollard's new book?"

"*The Lost Cause: A New Southern History of the War of the Confederates*. Yes, I've heard about it," Abby replied calmly, only her eyes showing her disgust. "It hasn't come out yet, but I've heard conversations around it."

"They're attempting to rewrite history," Matthew said grimly.

"Yes. Things didn't end well for the South. They are attempting to save face."

"With lies."

"Yes, with lies," Abby agreed. "But there is just enough truth to confuse people and make them believe what he has written."

Matthew ground his teeth. "It's wrong." He stared down at Abby. "How can you remain so calm?"

"Who says I am?" Abby smiled gently. "Right now your emotions are strong enough for both of us. I can put a cap on mine to make sure we don't get thrown out on the streets." Her eyes twinkled. "I'm not done dancing."

Matthew laughed and spun Abby in a tight circle before he dipped her almost to the floor. "Is this better?" he teased.

"Much!"

Abby's bright laughter erased the remnants of Matthew's anger. Tonight was a night for dancing.

When the song ended, Abby glanced over at the drink table. "Who is the lovely woman Jeremy is with?"

Matthew shook his head. "I was going to ask you. You usually know everything." He frowned playfully. "You disappoint me, Mrs. Cromwell. Is marriage keeping you too occupied?"

Abby smiled demurely. "It *is* rather splendid," she admitted, her eyes locked on Jeremy. "Let's go find out," she said suddenly, steering Matthew toward the corner.

Jeremy smiled when he saw Abby and Matthew headed their way. He had wondered how long it would take before curiosity got the best of his sister-in-law. Carrie was far too absorbed in dancing with Robert to notice anything else, or she would have already approached him.

"Hello, Abby. Matthew. I'd like you to meet Marietta Anderson."

"A pleasure," Abby said warmly. Matthew echoed her greeting. "I don't believe I've seen you around town, Miss Anderson."

"Probably not," Marietta agreed. "I keep rather busy teaching your employees when they're not working."

Abby's eyes widened. "You're a teacher from the Missionary Society!" she exclaimed. "That's wonderful."

"So says the only other Yankee woman in the room," Marietta said with wry amusement.

Abby laughed with delight. "We are definitely the minority here tonight, which only makes us more special."

"My sentiments exactly," Marietta replied. Her expression grew more serious. "It is quite an honor to meet you, Mrs. Cromwell. I tried to meet you in Philadelphia but never had the opportunity."

"You're from Philadelphia?" Abby asked. "I'm so sorry we didn't meet before."

Jeremy listened closely, wanting to learn as much about Marietta as he could.

"I imagine you stayed quite busy running all your factories and coordinating activities for both abolitionism and women's rights." Marietta laughed at Abby's expression. "I never met you, but you have been a mentor to me for several years."

Abby grasped her hand warmly. "Then I'm so glad to finally have a chance to get to know you." She smiled over at Jeremy. "I see you have met my brother-in-law."

"Who is relieved to find Marietta is a fan of yours, Abby," Jeremy replied. "I'll take any help I can get."

"Help?" Marietta asked.

"Well, yes," Jeremy said easily, his blue eyes filled with warm humor under his thick thatch of blond hair. "Since I was just going to ask you if I could see you again, it's good to know you approve of my family."

Marietta laughed heartily. "Anyone who dances like you doesn't need family approval," she assured him.

"Then that is a yes?" Jeremy pressed.

Marietta smiled demurely, though her eyes flashed with amusement. "That's a yes, Mr. Anthony." She turned to Matthew when the music started again. "Jeremy mentioned wanting to dance with Mrs. Cromwell. Can I convince you to dance?"

"No convincing needed," Matthew assured her. "How else will I get to press you for information?"

"Ah," Marietta eyed him. "You must be the journalist Jeremy said was with him tonight."

"Guilty as charged," Matthew said as he swept her onto the dance floor.

Abby smiled up at Jeremy. "She's lovely."

Jeremy watched her dance away. "Very."

Abby laughed. "You look quite smitten, my boy."

Jeremy continued to watch Marietta for a long moment and then looked back at Abby, his smile rather puzzled. "I do believe I am," he murmured.

Carrie was gasping for breath after a rousing Virginia reel with her father. "I thought you were supposed to slow down when you got older," she said. "I could barely keep up with you out there!"

Thomas smiled smugly. "Forty-five is not old, my dear daughter. I prefer to think of myself as mature and wise."

"And a fabulous dancer," Abby added, sliding up to his side before she tucked her arm into his. "Did you happen to mention to Carrie that you sat out for three dances to get some rest?" she asked, batting her eyes at him.

Thomas scowled. "I thought a good wife was supposed to keep her husband's secrets."

"Then you should have chosen a wife who is not a Yankee women's rights activist," she retorted.

Carrie laughed as her father rolled his eyes. As much as he had loved her mother, she had never seen him have such unbridled fun. "Sat out for three dances?" she asked. She held out her hand as the orchestra broke into another reel. "Ready for an encore?" she asked sweetly.

Thomas groaned and shook his head. "Food. I need food."

Carrie nodded her head, her eyes bright with amusement. "Whatever you say, my mature and wise father. When you've had enough *rest*, you'll know where to find me."

"Which is with me on the dance floor," Robert said as he finished a dance with Mrs. Mason and returned to claim Carrie. He nodded his head toward Jeremy. "Who is Jeremy with?"

Carrie turned in surprise and eyed the attractive redhead. "I don't know," she admitted.

"Her name is Marietta Anderson," Abby informed them. "She's a teacher down in the black quarter."

"She's very pretty," Carrie murmured, somewhat amused by the expression on Jeremy's face. "My uncle seems rather smitten."

"He says he is," Abby agreed. "I just met Marietta, but she seems quite lovely."

Carrie kept her eyes on Jeremy as Robert led her out onto the dance floor. "I like the idea of Jeremy being smitten," she said quietly. She decided not to say the rest of what she was thinking.

Carrie was starving when she and Robert finally left the dance floor. "I need food," she moaned.

"You should after four hours of dancing," Robert replied.

Carrie's eyes flew to the ornate grandfather clock in the corner. "Four hours? No wonder I'm so hungry." She bit back a groan. "That could also explain why my feet are hurting so badly."

Robert frowned when he looked down at her feet. "It could have something to do with the shoes you are wearing."

"They are ghastly," Carrie admitted, "but they are the height of fashion. I considered tossing them aside so I could dance in my stocking feet, but I was afraid people would be appalled."

"Not that you seem to be bothered by what society thinks!"

Carrie turned as the snide voice broke into their conversation. She blinked in surprise. "Excuse me?"

Staring back at her with cold brown eyes was an elegantly dressed woman, a censoring expression on her lined face. "I said you seem not to care what society thinks, Mrs. Borden," the woman snapped boldly.

"Do I know you?" Carrie asked carefully, glancing longingly at the table full of food.

"I don't imagine so," the lady sniffed. "You seem to have no interest in proper southern women. You certainly have no interest in *being* one."

Carrie bit back a giggle. She could certainly not argue with the truth of the woman's statement. She was also certain a giggle would not be appreciated. Obviously, the woman was deeply offended.

"Do you have a problem with my wife, Mrs....?" Robert asked, stepping closer to Carrie's side.

"Mrs. Phoebe Wallington," the older lady said primly. "I would say *you* should be the one with a problem with your wife."

"I have no idea what you're talking about," Robert said calmly, only his eyes showing his irritation.

"Surely you're not pleased that your *wife* is leaving you to go north to attend medical school." Mrs. Wallington snapped. "I suppose her service during the war was admirable, but the war is over. The South will only survive and return to its former glory if Southern wives take their proper place in society."

Carrie fought back another desire to giggle. She was opening her mouth to respond, but Robert answered first.

"My wife's service during the war was not admirable," he said smoothly. "It was blatantly heroic. She saved hundreds, perhaps thousands of lives by being willing to go against proper society and use the skills and talents she has been given. As far as how I feel about her going to Philadelphia to medical school, I could not be more proud of her." His voice tightened. "If you feel you are being a proper southern woman by being cruel and judgmental, then I am completely relieved my wife is choosing something different."

Mrs. Wallington was rendered speechless for a long moment, her slack mouth gaping open with astonishment. Add in her bulging eyes, and she looked rather like a fish out of water.

Carrie decided there was really nothing she needed to add to Robert's statement. "If you'll excuse us," she said graciously. "We are quite famished after a long evening of dancing." She smiled up at Robert. "Shall we go now, my darling?"

Robert grinned down at her, his eyes shining with satisfaction. "Lead the way, Mrs. Borden."

"Well...I never!" Mrs. Wallington finally managed as they turned away.

Carrie made no effort to hide her giggle this time. "That was quite impressive, Mr. Borden."

Robert smiled broadly. "She should have known better than to mess with a hungry man's wife."

Abby was standing by the table, holding out plates to them when they arrived. "Well done, Robert," she stated, her eyes warm with approval.

Robert reached for the plate eagerly. "Doing battle with arrogance has increased my appetite," he said.

"I'm sorry," Abby murmured to Carrie.

"Don't be," Carrie replied. "I'd best get used to it."

"It won't be so bad in Philadelphia," Abby replied.

"It's every bit as bad," Carrie replied casually. "I get letters from Janie once a week. She and her housemates deal with much worse than rude women. They have been spit on and mocked in the streets. People harangue them when they go into class, and male doctors treat them like they don't exist."

"Carrie!" Abby cried.

"It doesn't matter," Carrie said earnestly. "I've never thought it was going to be easy. You once told me that being a pioneer never is. Wasn't it you that got spat on outside of an abolition meeting?"

"Yes, but—"

"But nothing," Carrie said firmly. "Women all over the country are going to have to endure treatment like this to bring about change. I'm just one of many." She smiled. "At least I'm not alone."

Abby gazed at her for a moment and returned her smile, linking their arms firmly. "No, my dear, you are not alone."

"And I find I have even more to admire about this family."

Carrie turned to identify the strange voice. She smiled at the redhead standing behind her with a plate of food, Jeremy close to her side. "You're Marietta," she said warmly. "I'm so happy to meet you."

Marietta laughed. "News travels fast around here."

"You're in the South," Carrie replied. "We're known for being nosey and intrusive."

"As well as strong and resilient," Marietta added. "You're going to be a doctor?"

Carrie nodded. "I start medical school in Philadelphia this April."

"I have two friends in school there," Marietta revealed. "You're going to love it."

Carrie laughed and linked arms with her. She smiled up at Jeremy. "I'm going to steal Marietta for a few minutes," she informed him. "I have some questions."

Jeremy shook his head sadly. "And just like that I lose my dinner date."

"Robert and Matthew will keep you company," Carrie said blithely, without a hint of remorse in her voice. "Come with me, Marietta. It's time you got to know the women in this family."

Chapter Nine

"Are you sure you want to walk home?" Jeremy asked. "There is enough room in the carriage."

"Too frigid out here for a Southern boy?" Marietta teased. "This is hardly cold compared to a Philadelphia winter."

Jeremy laughed and held out his arm. The thought of walking back afterwards presented no problem at all. He would do anything to have more time with her.

Lantern light flickered on the sidewalk as they headed south toward Marietta's boarding house. The wind had died away completely, rendering the surrounding trees into mute statues frozen in place. Candles flickered in a few windows, but the late hour assured most of the dwellings were completely dark and the streets were deserted. Fragrant smoke from fireplaces created a swirling fog for the stars gleaming through.

"It's such a beautiful night," Marietta murmured.

"That it is," Jeremy agreed, his eyes never leaving her face. "Tell me more about yourself."

"Let me think what I should admit to," Marietta replied, her eyes dancing. "I am the youngest of five children. The only girl with four brothers."

Jeremy lifted his eyebrows. "Which means you are either horribly spoiled or very independent." He cocked his head as he appraised her. "I'm going to go with very independent."

"Definitely," she confirmed. "My brothers were good to me, but we grew up out in the country. They had no desire to take care of the weaker sex, so they made sure I wasn't weaker. I did everything they did. It was expected. I have no patience with women who believe they must have a man to take care of them." She lifted her chin. "I have been a member of the women's rights movement since I was eighteen."

"Is that a warning?" Jeremy asked with amusement.

"Does it *need* to be one?"

Jeremy laughed loudly. "I imagine you and Carrie got along well during dinner. The two of you are very much alike."

"Does that bother you?" Marietta asked, watching him closely.

Jeremy stopped and turned Marietta to face him. "Let's get this out of the way, Miss Anderson. I grew up in the South, but I've never been what you would call a traditional Southerner. My father made sure of that. I believe women can do anything men can do, and I believe they should have the right to vote. I will continue to fight for civil rights for blacks, and for the freedom for them to have the vote." He paused, not free to reveal his activities with the secret societies. "Does that cover the most important things for the moment?"

Marietta smiled at him warmly. "I believe it does, Mr. Anthony."

Jeremy opened his mouth again but then hesitated.

"Mr. Anthony?"

Jeremy stared over her head into the deep shadows beyond the cast of the lanterns, feeling that he was moving into an area of conversation he had no light to navigate. He had just met Marietta. There was no need to tell her any more than he already had.

"Is something wrong?" Marietta pressed.

Jeremy's thoughts raced as he pondered how much to reveal. On the one hand, they barely knew each other. On the other hand, he was already sure Marietta could be very special to him. Was it fair to move forward without full disclosure?

"Why did you choose to be a teacher?" he asked, hoping her answer would give him time to decide what he was willing to say.

Marietta gazed at him. Her expression said she knew he was stalling, but she played along. "I've wanted to be a teacher since I was a child," she revealed. "My mother pushed me to learn as much as I could. She didn't have the opportunity for education until she came north with my father. She had been taught how to read, but the rest of her education had been on the things considered essential to being a gracious southern woman," she said wryly. "When she was exposed to my father's library, she couldn't get enough of knowledge. She taught me from a very early age to treasure knowledge and learning. I became a teacher four years ago, as soon as I finished school." She paused. "My father became an abolitionist at the beginning of the movement in the thirties. He fought for years for the slaves to be freed. When the war ended, he supported my desire to teach in the South. The Missionary Society asked me if I would come to Richmond to teach. Here I am."

Jeremy gazed into her kind, expressive eyes for a long moment. He made his decision. "My twin sister is a teacher," he said quietly.

"You have a twin sister? And she is a teacher?" Marietta asked with surprise. "Where?"

"She started a school out at Cromwell Plantation for the black children in the area," Jeremy said, trying to feel his way. He hated that he felt the need to speak so carefully, but he was aware of prejudices that even open-minded people still grappled with.

"That's wonderful!" Marietta exclaimed. Then she looked at him sharply. "You seemed hesitant to tell me about her. Why?"

"My twin is black," Jeremy replied. Marietta stared at him blankly as his words hung in the cold air. The quiet, deserted streets captured the announcement and flung it back at him.

"Perhaps you should explain," Marietta finally replied.

Jeremy saw no censure or judgment in her eyes, only curiosity. He could find no fault in that. His announcement of a black twin sister would certainly create curiosity and a desire to know the whole story. He found it rather odd that his history was being revealed on the streets of Richmond on a frigidly raw, dark night, but he was suddenly eager to have the truth known. He already knew Marietta was too important to play games with. He was certain the attraction between them was mutual. It was not fair to let it go further if his heritage was going to be a problem.

"My mother was a slave on Cromwell Plantation. My biological father was Thomas Cromwell's father..." Jeremy began, telling her the entire story.

Marietta listened quietly.

"I found out the truth after I had already become friends with Thomas. Carrie had already discovered the existence of Rose's twin, but then she unearthed an image of her grandfather that looked just like me. She had only met me once, when she was working at the hospital, but the resemblance hit her immediately. My father admitted the truth when she confronted him, but begged her to keep the secret."

"That must have been so difficult," Marietta murmured.

"It was," Jeremy agreed. "I met Rose just two weeks after Richmond fell." He smiled. "She is an astonishing woman. I could not be more proud of her."

Marietta stared at him for a long moment. "This is a very personal story," she finally said. "We have just met. Why are you choosing to tell me?"

Jeremy opted for honesty. He saw no reason to stop now. "Because I believe our relationship could turn into something much more than an acquaintance," he replied promptly. "I knew I wanted to know you the moment I saw you. I don't believe I'm imagining that our attraction is mutual." He looked to her for confirmation.

"You're not," she agreed, her eyes steady. "But..."

"I don't want to begin a relationship that has no chance of moving forward," Jeremy said bluntly.

"And you believe your heritage could be a problem for me?" Marietta asked. "Even with all you know about me?"

Jeremy took a deep breath. "I look white, but I am mulatto. Though the chances are not high, if I have children they have a chance of being black, or at least looking much more colored than I do."

Marietta managed a smile. "This is truly an odd conversation to be having with a man I just met, but I find the candor—especially from a Southern gentleman— quite refreshing."

Jeremy watched different feelings and emotions flicker through Marietta's eyes. He knew what he had revealed was a lot for anyone to comprehend and absorb. "You need time to think about this," he finally said. "I simply needed for you to know the truth."

Marietta nodded. "The best way to show appreciation for your candor is to be equally candid in return," she finally said. "While my life is devoted to black children, I've never imagined the possibility of me having one of my own. And I will admit I had not yet gotten to the point where I had considered having children with you," she said frankly.

Jeremy's lips twitched, but he remained silent.

"I like you, Mr. Anthony. You did not imagine the mutual attraction. In all honesty, I cannot give you a response as to my thoughts about having a mulatto baby, but I am quite certain I would like to spend more time with you and get to know you better. Can that be enough?"

"More than enough," Jeremy replied quickly, relief almost making him breathless. He knew their relationship could still end, but at least not because the truth had been hidden.

"Thank you," Marietta said.

Jeremy lifted his eyebrows.

"Thank you for trusting me with your story. I can assure you it will not go beyond this conversation. I am well aware of the Black Codes and their meaning for mulattoes. Whatever comes from our relationship, I will do nothing that might cause harm to you or to your family."

Jeremy smiled, suddenly aware he had been certain of that before he began to speak. "Thank you," he replied, reaching down to take one of her hands.

"Will I get the chance to meet your sister?" Marietta asked. "I would love to talk with her about her experiences in the contraband camp."

Jeremy grinned, his heart light. "I'm sure your opportunity will come," he assured her. "But for right now, I need to get you home before your reputation is destroyed by being out so late with a strange man."

Marietta laughed gaily as she tucked her hand into his arm. "I'm quite sure you have figured out by now that I don't give a fig what people think about me!"

"Another one of the things I like about you," Jeremy agreed. "Abby pulled me aside before we left and asked me to invite you for dinner on Wednesday. Are you free to join us? I can come by from the factory to pick you up."

"Absolutely. I shall look forward to it."

"We're almost there!" Amber cried, bouncing on the carriage seat. Suddenly she frowned. "I need a new name."

"A new name?" Opal asked, forcing herself to breathe evenly as the plantation grew closer. She knew it had to be done, but she couldn't imagine looking into Annie's eyes and telling her that her baby was gone.

"Yes," Amber insisted. "Sadie Lou got a new name so everyone wouldn't confuse her with Sadie. I bet Amber and Clint are still there with their mama and daddy. So I need a new name, too."

This was as good a distraction as anything. Opal managed a smile. "You got one in mind?"

"Do you *have* one in mind," Amber corrected.

Opal blinked at her.

"Susie said education is real important," Amber said earnestly. "She told me I would have more opportunities in the world if I spoke correctly."

"So that's why you've been working so hard in school?" Eddie asked.

Amber nodded. "I'm thirteen, just about to turn fourteen. I'm your only daughter now." Tears filled her eyes. "I want you to be proud of me."

Eddie pulled her close. "Honey, I'm already so proud of you I could burst. I'm real happy you be learning to speak right, but it won't make me any more proud of you."

Amber sat a little straighter as her lips trembled into a smile.

"We called you Sunny to tell you apart from little Amber before we left," Opal said. "Do you like that?"

"Not really," Amber said seriously. "It sounds like a little girl's name."

"Amber Lou," Carl blurted out. "Then you'll think of Sadie every time someone says your name. That way you can't never forget her."

Opal caught Eddie's eyes. She wasn't sure it was a good thing to force Amber to remember her sister every time someone called her name, but she was also quite sure Sadie would never be far from Amber's thoughts anyway. Their years on the plantation after their mother's death had knit them closer together than sisters. It was almost as if their souls had entwined as they walked together through those dark, sorrowful years. There had not been one night that Amber hadn't cried herself to sleep since Sadie's death, either Opal or Eddie holding her until she finally drifted off.

"What do you think of Amber Lou?" Opal asked gently.

Amber considered it and then nodded slowly. "Amber Lou." She let the name roll off her tongue, tilting her head as she considered. "I like it," she announced. "But not just for here on the plantation. I want to be Amber Lou forever."

"Amber Lou it is then," Eddie agreed. "It's a fine name."

The wagon rolled forward in silence for a while. They had talked with Spencer for the first several hours, but now that the plantation was growing closer, the tension closed down all idle conversation. The roads were still hard from frost, but the tight grip of winter had been released. There might be another snowfall, but the cold would not return with such a brutal vengeance. In less than a month, the grass would begin to green and the trees would begin to bud.

"You scared, Daddy?" Carl asked.

Eddie stared down at his little boy looking up at him with eyes wise beyond his age. At ten years old, he had experienced far more than he should have. Eddie didn't pretend not to know what Carl was talking about, and he didn't attempt to gloss it over. "I reckon I am, son. It's going to be real hard to tell Moses and his mama and sister about Sadie."

Carl nodded. "They's gonna be real sad," he agreed. "They also gonna be real sad about Sadie Lou and Susie and Zeke. I reckon they loved them a whole bunch, too."

"They sure did," Opal agreed. She sat straighter in the seat as they turned in through the brick-pillared entrance to the plantation. It had been their choice to deliver the news in person. She was glad they had come. She knew the telling would be hard, and she knew the grief would be strong, but she also knew being on the plantation for a week would be good for all of them. In spite of her dread of what was coming, there was nowhere she would rather be right now.

Moses was coming in from the barn where the men were repairing equipment when he heard the rattle of carriage wheels. He stiffened, wondering if they were about to receive another visit from the men who had come on New Year's Day. He relaxed almost immediately, however, doubting they would come in a carriage—they would arrive on horseback so they could disappear quickly. Curious now, he lengthened his stride.

Rose stepped out on the porch, bundled warmly in a thick coat, just as he reached the house. "Do I hear a carriage?"

Moses nodded. "Done with school?"

"Yes. I just got home. I let the children out a little early today because it is still so cold. June and Polly were treating their last patients when I left. They won't be far behind me. Hardly anyone came to the clinic today, but about an hour ago, two women came in complaining of stomach pain. June was mixing up an herbal remedy for them when I left. They have drugs for stomach pain, but Carrie says the herbal remedy works best." Rose fell silent as the carriage appeared in the distance.

"Were you expecting someone?" Moses asked, even though he knew Rose would have told him. Her questioning eyes gave him his answer.

"Who that be?" Annie asked, stepping out onto the porch.

Moses shook his head. "I have no idea, Mama, but I reckon we're about to find out."

The three of them stood quietly as the carriage grew closer. The horses stopped grazing and lifted their heads.

"Moses! Rose! Miss Annie!"

Moses' eyes narrowed as the cries rose into the air. "Carl?" he muttered. "Is that Carl?"

Rose stepped to the edge of the porch and shaded her eyes with her hand. "It is," she muttered. "What in the world are Opal, Eddie, and the kids doing here?"

"They done gone to Philadelphia," Annie said. "What they be doing here?"

"We'll get our answers soon," Moses said reassuringly. He tried to ignore the clench in his stomach but saw the same trouble he was feeling reflected in his mama's eyes.

All of them hurried off the porch when the carriage rolled to a stop.

"Hello! Hello!" Amber cried as she clambered out of the carriage. "We've come to visit!"

Rose caught the girl close in her arms for a warm hug. "It's wonderful to see you!" Her eyes met Opal's, her heart sinking at the pain she saw etched on her face. She caught Amber's hand and reached for Carl's. "Let's go inside where you can get some hot chocolate and cookies." She knew instinctively that Opal and Eddie had not come just for a visit. The agony in Eddie's eyes as he looked at Annie said the news was for Moses and his mama to hear first.

"Cookies!" Carl cried as he jumped from the carriage. He stopped and looked up into Annie's eyes. "I be real sorry, Miss Annie," he said gravely, and then turned to dash up the stairs.

Annie waited until he had disappeared into the house with Rose and Amber before she turned to Opal and Eddie, her eyes questioning.

Moses helped Opal down from the carriage, shook hands with Eddie and Spencer, and then took a deep breath. "What happened?" Then he remembered how cold it was. "I'm sorry. We should go in the house first."

Eddie stayed where he was standing. "I'd rather the kids not hear us talk about it again. They lived it. I don't want them to keep hearing about it."

Annie stiffened. "Lived what? What happened, Eddie? Where be Sadie and Sadie Lou?"

Opal reached down to take Annie's hands. "We wanted to tell you ourselves," she said, her voice trembling. "There was a real bad fire at the restaurant. There was an explosion..." Her voice ground to a halt as she looked at Eddie helplessly.

"Sadie and Sadie Lou are dead," Eddie finished for her, his voice and face twisted with pain. "Susie and Zeke, too," he managed, his voice barely louder than a whisper.

Moses froze, denial exploding in his head. "*Dead?* All of them? All *four* of them are dead?"

Annie stared at Eddie, her eyes wide with shock. "My Sadie be dead? And the rest? Dead?"

Opal gripped her hands more tightly. "It was a horrible accident," she said. "The roof caught fire when it was so cold. Zeke and Janie got Amber and Carl out, and then Zeke went back in to help Susie get Sadie and Sadie Lou." She shook her head, her eyes bright with pain. "The girls were right behind me when we got out. I don't know what happened," she whispered. She continued, her voice wavering. "The fire reached the oil vats..."

Moses closed his eyes, trying to block the image of the explosion. "After all the years surviving slavery," he muttered, "and she is killed by a fire?" Grief blurred his eyes as his brain tried to make sense of what he was hearing.

Rose slipped out to stand by his side, her own eyes filled with grief. Susie had been like a sister to her after the year of living together in the contraband camp. She reached down and gripped Moses' hand. He gazed down at her, but she wasn't sure he was aware she was there.

"I'm glad she was free..."

Moses looked at his mama, overwhelmed to see a measure of peace mixed with the torment etched on her face. "What, Mama?"

"I'm glad she was free," Annie repeated softly. "She gone far too soon, but I be real glad she didn't die as a slave. She died free." Her eyes sought Opal's for reassurance.

"She loved being free," Opal agreed. "She and Sadie Lou were in school, doing real well. They had both decided to be teachers." She locked eyes with Rose. "They wanted to be just like you," she said. Then she looked back at Annie. "Your Sadie was real happy."

"The explosion?" Moses asked. He wasn't sure he wanted to know, but he had to ask.

"It happened so fast," Eddie said, evidently knowing exactly what he was thinking. "I don't believe any of them felt a thing."

"They were together?" Annie asked.

Eddie nodded. "They were together," he confirmed, his voice catching as he remembered finding their burned bodies close together.

"I'm glad she weren't alone," Annie whispered.

"I'm so sorry," Opal said. "So very sorry..."

Annie shook her head. "You didn't start that fire, Opal." She heaved a heavy sigh. "There ain't no making sense of death. It didn't make sense that my Sam died when they hung him from that tree." She fixed her eyes on Eddie. "It don't make no sense how your Fannie died. And now it don't make no sense how all these fine children died."

Moses stared at his mama, wondering where her strength was coming from. Sadie had been her life for so long, the one child she had left after Moses and June had been sold off into slavery. *June...*

Rose thought it at the same time. "June," she whispered.

Annie looked off into the distance where they could see the plantation carriage rounding the bend. "Y'all go on inside where it be warm. I'll tell June about her baby sister."

"Mama," Moses protested.

Annie held up her hand. "It be my baby that died in that fire. We all gonna grieve, but it be my job to tell June she lost her little sister." She managed a small smile. "I'm just real glad they had time together after all them years apart before my Sadie died." She stood straighter as she took Moses' hand. "You go in and get ever'body settled." Then she turned to Opal. "I don't figure you're here just for the night."

"We're here for a week," Opal answered.

"Good. This where you need to be," Annie said firmly. "Now y'all go inside. I got to talk to June." Her voice wavered before she forced a smile. "I gonna be wanting to hear all about my Sadie's last months up in Philadelphia. And I wanting to hear about all the rest of them, too. When my Sadie girl decided to move north with you, I reckon all of you become my family. I be real sorry about your loss."

Moses went into the kitchen after dinner to help Annie with the slices of pie she was dishing up for everyone. She had refused help in the kitchen, saying she needed some time to move what she had learned from her head into her heart. More than a little awed by his mama's strength, Moses had tried to be strong for June, barely able to comprehend what had happened himself. He had seen plenty of death in the war, but it had never worn the face of his crippled little sister. He gritted his teeth when he thought about how little time they had together after years of being separated by the slave auction.

"You got every right to be angry," Annie said as Moses stared into the flames. "I had Sadie all them years. You did so much to make sure we all be together again, and then she got snatched away so quick."

It was only then that Moses realized his anger matched his grief. He looked down at his mama, realizing that her stout, short body housed a heart much larger than his. "I hope I'll be like you one day, Mama."

"You already be like me, Moses. You be a fine man with a powerful lot of love in your heart. You did what you promised to do all them years ago. You set June free from slavery and allowed her little boy to be born in freedom. Then you came after me and Sadie. I don't reckon we would still be hiding out on that empty plantation, but I sho 'nuff don't know what we be doing if you hadn't come. We for sure wouldn't have been in such a fine place as this, and Sadie wouldn't have had no chance to go to school up north." Annie pressed Moses' hand tightly. "You done real good, son."

Moses tried to let her words penetrate his heart. "I don't feel like I did good," he admitted.

"Course not. The grief still be swallowing you up," Annie agreed.

"How come you are so much stronger than I am?" Moses implored. "I feel like I'm drowning inside."

Annie smiled tenderly. "I don't reckon I'm any stronger. It's just that I lived longer than you and borne more death and more grief. It don't get no easier, but you do learn it ain't gonna kill you. When your daddy got killed, I didn't think I could never feel joy again, but I was wrong. It came back. It will come back this time, too." She reached up and laid a hand on his cheek. "Your joy will come back, Moses. June's joy will come back. It will take some time, but it will come back," she said firmly. "We gonna miss all those we done lost for the rest of our lives. That don't go away. But neither does the remembering. You gonna remember all the reasons you loved Sadie."

Moses took a deep breath, hoping she was right, feeling better as her love flowed into him from her touch. "I love you, Mama," he said roughly.

"And I love you, son," Annie replied, turning to pick up the tray of pie plates. "Now, let's go hear about all them fine children. I want my last memories to be of the good life they were building for themselves up there in Philadelphia."

Chapter Ten

Matthew leaned back against the bench and stared up at the Capitol Building, with its almost three hundred-foot cast iron dome standing out with grandeur against Washington, DC's, azure blue sky. He closed his eyes and relished the feel of the soft spring breeze on his face. The end of March had ushered in the end of a brutal winter. Branches that had been snow-covered weeks before were now alive with bursting buds and the fresh green of tiny new leaves. Thick winter coats had been stored away, replaced by elegant jackets, colorful dresses, and relieved expressions.

Matthew watched as members of Congress climbed the steps to the Capitol. The somber looks on their faces marked the importance of the occasion.

"What do you think will happen today?" Peter Wilcher asked.

Matthew shrugged, not responding to his colleague's question. He didn't want to think about it right now. More accurately, he didn't want to talk about it right now. He knew their strong friendship would survive his not answering the question. "Did you know the Capitol Dome was finally finished this year?"

Peter played along. "The final cost was a little over a million dollars."

Matthew looked at him with surprise. "One million dollars? I thought the original estimate was a hundred thousand?"

"It was," Peter agreed. "How many buildings are you aware of that cost what their designers say they are going to cost?"

Matthew chuckled. "You have a point." He continued to stare up at the dome, his brain trying to work through all that happened in the last few weeks.

"Did you know the Capitol Dome was constructed with nearly nine million pounds of ironwork bolted together?" Peter asked.

Bemused, Matthew glanced at him. "And you know this how?"

Peter chuckled. "I like numbers, and since you don't seem interested in talking about the vote today, I thought I would share them with you."

"I like the way it *looks*," Matthew replied, still not ready to discuss anything else. "Look at all those columns, pilasters, and windows. I love the statue best, though." He tilted his head back further as he gazed at the *Statue of Freedom* designed by Thomas Crawford. He never tired of looking at the classical female figure standing guard over the Capitol. Her long, flowing hair was encased by a helmet with a crest composed of an eagle's head and feathers, and encircled with nine stars. Her dress was secured with a brooch inscribed with "US" and then draped with a heavy, flowing, toga-like robe fringed with fur and decorative balls. Her right hand rested upon the hilt of a sheathed sword wrapped in a scarf. Her left hand held a laurel wreath of victory and the shield of the United States with thirteen stripes.

Peter nodded. "I love the ten bronze points tipped with platinum that are attached to her headdress, shoulders, and shield to protect her from lightning."

Matthew smiled but didn't look away. "The dome is a masterpiece of American will and ingenuity."

"And you're staring at it because you're hoping that what happens inside there today will reflect that," Peter said astutely.

Matthew lowered his eyes and shifted his stare to his friend. "Yes," he admitted, "but I won't admit to having any great hope of that."

"You believe President Johnson will veto the Civil Rights Bill."

"Don't you?" Matthew asked.

Peter sighed heavily. "Yes. I was overjoyed when it passed the Senate in February and passed the House of Representatives two weeks ago on March thirteenth, but I've heard nothing from our president that indicates he won't follow the same course of action he took with the Freedmen's Bureau Bill."

"He'll veto it today," Matthew predicted.

"You don't seem to be bothered by that idea," Peter observed.

Matthew turned his attention back to the Capitol Dome, enjoying how the light played against the *Statue of Freedom*'s helmet and shield, but he realized the protection it communicated was not enjoyed by everyone. "I'm not. The president will veto the bill because I believe he has gravely miscalculated the Republican stand on civil rights for blacks. They are not yet ready to give blacks the vote, but they at least believe everyone should have the right to work as free laborers and have federal protection while they do it."

"And that's a good thing?" Peter pressed.

Matthew turned back to him. "I've been in Washington most of the month. You just got here. It's been interesting, if nothing else, to watch how this has played out. I was in the Capitol recently and overheard an Ohio senator. He said all Republicans feel that the most important interests are at stake. He went on to say, *'If the president vetoes the Civil Rights Bill, I believe we shall be obliged to draw our swords for a fight and throw away the scabbards.'* " Matthew glanced up at the statue, watching as a fluffy white cloud seemed to perch on her head. "The only way we will truly be free in this country is if everyone is free. It took tremendous passion to go to war. It is going to take the same passion to ensure equal rights for everyone." He smiled grimly. "President Johnson's attitudes and actions are making sure the passion remains."

Peter inclined his head, his gaze lifted to watch the play of the clouds against the statue. "So you believe this bill is the answer?"

Matthew hesitated. "I believe it is a *part* of the answer. It was written by Senator Trumbull, a moderate Republican who honestly believed he was proposing actions our president would endorse. Of course, he also believed Johnson would sign the Freedmen's Bureau Bill. I believe they are steps in the right direction, but I don't believe they go far enough." He smiled grimly. "I believe Johnson's bullheaded position to refuse even basic rights will ignite the passion to do more. There is going to be a huge fight."

"But why would Johnson veto it if he knows how the Republicans feel? He has to know it won't go over well," Peter protested.

Matthew shook his head. "Why does our president do most of what he does? I wish I knew, but I'm confident it will backfire this time. He moved forward in reconstructing the South the way he believed it should be done, regardless of what anyone thought or told him." Matthew fought to be fair. "I think Johnson honestly believes states' rights are sacrosanct to anything else, and he fears the results of too much federal power. Unfortunately, he is also a racist who allows his own prejudices to mar his perceptions and decisions. He's miscalculating not only the Republican members of Congress but also the strength of public sentiment."

"If he vetoes it, do you believe Congress will override it?"

Matthew nodded with somber satisfaction. "I do. I believe that, for the first time in American history, Congress will enact a major piece of legislation over a president's veto."

Rose waited until every student had found a place in the schoolhouse. The windows were all open, allowing the soft spring air to flow into the building.

Crocuses carpeted the woods, and bright green ferns poked their tightly furled heads out of the ground. Winter, once it decided to leave, had rushed off in a hurry. Streams gurgled with melted snow as trees burst forth with new life, the redbud trees creating clouds of purple in the surrounding woods.

Rose stood quietly as all the children and all the adults crowded into the school. On such a momentous occasion, she had insisted everyone be present. For that very reason, she had waited until after dinner so all the men and women working hard in the fields would be done for the day. The sun was just beginning to lower toward the horizon, the air taking on the chill of an early spring evening. Moses had made sure the woodstove was stuffed full of wood and blazing brightly before he had taken a place against the back wall.

When everyone outside had found a place, Rose smiled brightly. "I have something to read to all of you," she began. "I received this today from Matthew Justin."

"He's that journalist fellow, ain't he?" a woman called.

"*Isn't* he," Rose corrected. "But, yes, Matthew is a journalist and writer. He has spent the month of March in Washington, DC, so to stay current on the information in this letter. It's a week old, so I'm sure more things have happened, but it's the most current news I have. It's something all of you need to hear."

"Be it good news?" Justine, a fifteen-year-old student, called out.

Rose eyed her quietly, her brow lifted.

Justine grinned with embarrassment. "I meant to say, *is* it good news?"

Rose smiled. "Yes, I think it's very good news, Justine." Her eyes swept over her students, some only five years old. "I realize many of you are not going to be able to understand what I'm reading, but I believe it is important for you to be here because it is a momentous day in the history of our race. Your parents will help you understand it when you get home, but you'll always be able to say you were here to hear about it." She lifted the letter and began to read the part of the letter she had marked.

I have news about the Civil Rights bill that is formally titled "An Act to protect all Persons in the United States in their Civil Rights, and furnish the Means of their vindication." The act declares that people born in the United States and not subject to any foreign powers are entitled to be citizens, without regard to race, color, or previous condition of slavery or involuntary servitude.

Rose paused to let the gasps and murmurs quiet down before she continued.

The Civil Rights Bill also says that any citizen has the same right that a white citizen has to make and enforce contracts, sue and be sued, give evidence in court, and inherit, purchase, lease, sell, hold, and convey real and personal property. Additionally, the act guarantees to all citizens the full and equal benefit of all laws and proceedings for the security of person and property, as is enjoyed by white citizens, along with punishment, pains, and penalties.

Persons denying these rights on account of race or previous enslavement are guilty of a misdemeanor. Upon conviction, they face a fine not exceeding $1000, or imprisonment not exceeding one year, or both.

Rose finished reading and looked up, knowing there would be questions.

"Does that mean black men are going to get the right to vote?" Polly asked. "I didn't hear nothing—I mean, *anything* in there about that."

Rose frowned. "No," she admitted. "The bill certainly doesn't do everything we would like it to do, but it's a big step in the right direction."

"Will it stop them Black Codes?"

Rose raised her eyebrows. It was an ironclad rule in her schoolroom that everyone speak correctly.

"Will it stop the Black Codes?" the question came again.

"I hope so," Rose said. She had made sure all her students knew about the Black Codes. They could only be extra vigilant to protect their families if they knew the risks. "Virginia has just enacted a vagrancy law. This bill will change that."

Gabe, from his place next to Polly, raised the next question. "Has that bill become law yet?"

Rose shook her head. "Not that I know. I do know it passed both the Senate and the House of Representatives, but President Johnson had not yet signed it into law when Matthew sent this letter."

"What if he doesn't sign it?" another woman called.

"That's a good question," Rose responded. Let me read what Matthew said about that."

> *You can tell your students the bill will certainly become law. Republican sentiment to ensure equal rights for blacks is quite determined. They may have to override the president's veto, but they have the votes necessary to do it.*

Silence fell on the room for a moment as they absorbed her words. A slightly built man, stooped from years in the cotton fields, stepped forward. "All that sounds real good, but how they gonna enforce it? Seems to me the white men down here ain't gonna care about a piece of paper telling them what they supposed to do. They done pulled out most of the troops down here. Didn't you tell us President Johnson done allowed all the states to form their own governments again? I don't see them making that kind of thing stick."

Rose sighed. She had been wondering the same thing. She made no attempt to correct Abner's language. He had just started school two weeks earlier and had not yet conquered reading. It was too much to ask for proper speaking yet. "I don't know those answers," she said honestly. "I've been having the same questions."

Abby raised her hand. "Could I say something about that?"

Rose had seen her slip into the back of the room shortly after the meeting started. "Please," she said with relief, and then turned back to everyone. "Most of you know Abigail Cromwell. She delivered this letter to me yesterday from Richmond because she knows how important it is."

All eyes turned toward the only white person in the room.

"Making any kind of change is a difficult thing," she began. "I became part of the abolition movement early. I truly believed slavery would be over quickly because it was simply the right thing. I soon found out that reality was different from what I expected." She smiled wryly and then added, "It took much longer than I thought it should, but it *did* happen. Equal rights for all of you is going to be the same way. It seems obvious to me that blacks and women should have the right to vote, but I suspect it is going to be a battle. There will be some steps forward, there will be some steps back, and then there will be times when you're convinced everything is simply standing in place, not moving anywhere."

Every eye was fixed on her.

"This bill is just a step," Abby continued. "But it's an important step. It was written when moderate Republicans still believed President Johnson was a reasonable man with the best interests of the freed slaves at heart. They no longer believe that. In a way, that's a good thing."

"A good thing that our president don't—I mean, *doesn't* think we deserve equal rights?" Gabe asked.

"No, of course not," Abby said quickly. "That's not what I meant. It's a horrible thing that he feels that way, but now everyone sees him for who he is. They realize he's not a man of reason, and that he doesn't have the best interests of the freed slaves at heart. They will pass this bill, but the next one that follows will be even stronger. It will demand more rights."

"How they gonna enforce it?" Abner asked again, his eyes fixed defiantly on Abby.

Abby shook her head heavily. "I don't know the answers to all these questions," she replied. "I don't know that anyone does. The country is still reeling from losing President Lincoln's leadership. Many things happened under President Johnson last year that I don't believe should have happened."

"Even with this law in place, things could get real bad, couldn't they?" Polly asked.

Abby exchanged a look with Rose before she turned back to everyone. "Yes," she admitted. "I wish I could tell you differently, but I can't. I'm sorry."

"We're used to bad times," Gabe said bluntly. He stood and turned to look at everyone in the room. "This bill is a good thing, but it doesn't mean we can let down our guard. It's still up to us to protect our families. It's still up to us to know what is going on."

Carrie could hear the rumble of voices as she finished up with her last patient, an elderly man recovering from pneumonia. When he had first come in several weeks earlier, he had been gasping for air and coughing up yellowish phlegm tinged with blood. She had been alarmed by his high fever and chills.

She had sent him home immediately, surrounded by blankets from the clinic to keep him warm. His daughter, frightened by her father's illness, left with a recipe for broth and stern instructions to keep him warm and dry.

"My daddy be doing a whole lot better," Bea said gratefully. "I thought you were a little crazy when you told me to make that soup from garlic, radishes, carrots and celery, but his breathing eased up pretty quick."

"I thought she was tryin' to drown me with that soup. Eber time I opened my eyes she was shoving that soup down me." Dalton rolled his eyes. "My daughter did just what you told her, Miss Carrie."

"You took good care of him," Carrie said approvingly.

"That she did," her father agreed. "I think it was that tea you had her make me out of milkweed that really made me better. It didn't taste so good, but it sure cleared things up."

"The pleurisy root," Carrie acknowledged with a smile. "I haven't found anything that works better, Dalton. It works on a lot of things. I've mashed it into a salve for cuts and sores. I used it once to heal someone who had burned their eyes."

Bea eyed her. "Did you learn all that when you was working at the hospital during the war?"

Carrie grinned. "Definitely not. There are still doctors who practice what is called bloodletting. They withdraw blood from a patient to cure pneumonia."

Bea looked horrified. "Why would they do that?"

"It is based on an ancient system of medicine. Blood and other bodily fluids are regarded as humors that have to remain in proper balance to maintain health," Carrie explained, knowing her words probably made little sense.

"You think they be right?" Bea asked skeptically.

Carrie shook her head firmly. "No."

Bea was silent for a moment. "Ain't you going to a fancy medical school up north, Miss Carrie? What you gonna do when they teach you about this?"

Carrie grinned again. "I'm going to listen. I'm going to learn it well enough to pass my tests. And then I'm going to do what is best for my patients."

"You gonna teach them all this stuff Old Sarah taught you?"

Carrie's expression softened as she thought of the months she had spent tromping through the woods with Old Sarah, learning the magic of the plants. "I'm going to try," she promised. "I already know traditional medicine turns its nose up at some of the herbal medicines. I probably would have, too, before Old Sarah taught me everything. She gave me a gift I can never repay."

"Then why you going?" Dalton asked.

"Because I can learn a lot from them," Carrie said. "There is so much I need to learn about surgical procedures that I don't know yet. And new discoveries are being made every day. I will always use the herbal remedies in my practice, but I'm sure other things will be developed that can help people. I want to know it all. I want to use whatever will make my patients better."

Carrie walked out to Dalton's wagon with them, waving as they rolled down the road and around the bend. They had wanted to stay for Rose's meeting, but she was concerned the ride home when the air was even cooler would be too hard on his still-recovering lungs.

June appeared at her side as the wagon disappeared. "You notice anything different about today?"

Carrie frowned. She had hoped only she noticed it. "We didn't have any white patients," she said.

"That happens when you're not here," June observed, "but there has never been a day when you're here that white people don't come."

"I know," Carrie agreed.

"You got any ideas why?" June pressed.

Carrie kept her eyes on the road, not able to escape the sense of dread that had filled her all day. Now that all her patients were gone, there was nothing to keep her mind off it. There was something in the air that prickled at her skin. "No," she finally said, "but things don't feel right."

"I agree," June said. "I've been feeling uneasy all day. I tried telling myself I'm making it up, but my mama always told me to trust when something don't feel right."

Carrie took a deep breath. "I think Annie is right," she said. She had a sudden urge to be back on the plantation. "How much longer is the meeting going to last?"

"I don't think much longer. Rose told me she wanted everyone to get home before it gets dark."

Carrie looked at her sharply. Rose almost always had night classes. "Since when?"

"Since this morning when Rose told me she felt something in the air."

The door to the schoolhouse opened. Greetings filled the air, but the schoolyard emptied quickly. Moments later, they were all in the carriage headed for the plantation. When the house appeared in the distance, smoke wafting from the chimneys, Carrie felt herself relax for the first time that day. Nothing seemed to be wrong. She saw the same relief mirrored in Rose and June's eyes.

Robert opened the door for them, a broad smile on his face. "You're home. Annie almost has dinner ready."

Carrie became acutely aware of her hunger as the aroma of fried chicken, collard greens, and cornbread rolled over them. "We'll wash up quickly and be back down," she said, heading for the staircase.

"What's that sound?" Moses asked. His hand paused on the doorknob before he could pull it closed.

Robert frowned. "Hoofbeats." He reached for the rifle that now had a permanent place by the front door and stepped back out on the porch.

Carrie tensed and turned back, exchanging a long look with Rose and June.

Within moments, a horse galloped around the curve. They heard a vague cry but couldn't identify what was being said.

"It's only one person," Robert said. He continued to hold the rifle, but he pointed it down. "I think someone is in trouble."

The rider finally got close enough for them to hear the words. "Fire! Fire!"

Clint skidded to a stop, his gelding's sides heaving and caked with sweat. "The schoolhouse," he yelled again. "It's on fire!"

Chapter Eleven

Rose gripped the seat of the carriage as the horses galloped down the driveway. Robert slowed them only slightly when they reached the turn to the main road, but the amber glow in the distance told her it was already too late. The wooden structure would burn quickly, and there was not a water supply to put it out. The single well would be almost useless against a serious blaze.

No one said a word as the carriage stopped far enough away to protect the horses from the heat. They all jumped out, watching grimly as a portion of the roof collapsed. They could see books and desks burning from the open window, but there was no way to save anything.

Carrie realized the medical clinic had not yet caught fire. "The medical supplies!" she yelled, dashing for the door. "We have to save what we can!" She covered her mouth with her hand and ran inside, horrified by the sound of the flames devouring the school.

Robert and Moses appeared beside her, heaving things out the door while Rose, June and Aunt Abby grabbed them and pulled them away from the building. All of them worked frantically to save what they could.

A sudden whoosh and crackling sound told Carrie they had run out of time. "We have to get out!" she cried. She grabbed a final box that held medical records. Coughing, she pulled Robert and Moses from the building, recognizing the determined looks on their faces.

"I can get some more," Robert wheezed.

"There is not one thing in there worth your life." Carrie watched as the roof exploded into flames. She had a vision of the terror Sadie, Sadie Lou, Susie, and Zeke must have felt as the fire consumed them. Shuddering, she stepped closer to Rose and wrapped an arm around her.

"How did this happen?" Rose whispered. "Moses banked the fire down before we left."

"It was no stray spark that ignited this fire," Aunt Abby said. "Someone set it."

Just then Clint rode up on a fresh horse. He vaulted off and ran to where they were standing. "I saw them!" he yelled over the crackle of the flames. "I tried to stop it, but it was too late."

"What are you talking about?" Robert asked, reaching for Clint's hand but releasing it quickly when Clint gave a cry. "What...?"

Carrie stepped forward. "Your hands are badly burned!" She motioned June to get some of the supplies they had saved and then turned back to him. "What happened, Clint?"

Clint's breathing was shallow. "I saw them, Miss Carrie. I was out riding Scottie through the woods when I heard voices. Something didn't feel right, so I tied Scottie to a tree and snuck up close so I could see." His voice tightened. "There was a whole bunch of white men that had horses. They went up to the school, broke all the windows, and tossed a bunch of burning branches into the schoolhouse. They was cheering when they got back on their horses and rode off." He lifted his eyes to Robert. "I'm real sorry I didn't stop them," he said hoarsely.

Robert put his hand on the boy's shoulder. "You were wise not to try to stop them. They would have hurt you. But you must have tried to put the fire out," he said with a grim look at Clint's hands.

"Weren't no use," Clint mumbled. "I ran inside and threw some of the branches out but there were too many. I couldn't get them all. The walls had already caught on fire..." He cast his eyes down. "I'm real sorry..."

Rose walked over and took his face in her hands. "What you did was so brave," she said, her own eyes glazed with grief. "Thank you for trying. I'm just so glad you weren't hurt any worse. Did you burn anything other than your hands?"

Clint shook his head. "No. They're okay. They don't hurt so bad," he said stoically.

Carrie took over, recognizing the strained look in his eyes that negated his words. There was nothing any of them could do to stop the fire. "Come with me," she commanded. "Your hands need to be taken care of."

"Here is some cloth, Carrie," June said quickly. "What else do you need?"

Carrie realized her supply of herbs and salves had not made it out of the fire. She pushed aside thoughts of the loss. "There is enough light to gather some plantain. Will you recognize it?"

June nodded. "I'll get it. I saw a brand new patch growing this morning."

"I'll help," Abby said. "Just show me what it is."

Robert stayed with Clint while Carrie went through the supplies they had saved. She breathed a sigh of relief when she found a jar of honey. She grabbed it and carried it back to Clint. Robert had pushed him down against a tree far enough away from the fire to be safe, but close enough to benefit from the light the flames produced.

"Here you go, Carrie," June said, holding out several handfuls of plantain weed. "What are you going to do with it? You don't have anything here to create a salve."

Carrie took a handful and shoved it in her mouth, waving her hand to tell everyone to do the same thing. "We missed dinner," she said lightly, trying to add humor to a tragedy. "It's perfectly safe to eat, but it's a little bitter. Just do me a favor and don't swallow. When you have it well chewed, let me know."

Everyone followed her direction. Carrie chewed determinedly until the weeds had broken down into a paste inside her mouth and then spit it out in her hand. Clint watched her quietly, but she was concerned by the glazed look in his eyes. She knew shock was a danger, especially with the temperature dropping. In spite of his casual attitude, the boy's burns were serious. "Did we save any blankets?"

Robert appeared by her side with several blankets. "Lean forward," he ordered Clint.

Silently, Clint leaned forward so Robert could wrap the blankets around his shoulders, leaving only his hands exposed.

Carrie took one hand gently, wincing at the red, inflamed skin. She spread the plantain over the wounds, accepting everyone's offering until both hands were covered. Then she carefully spread honey on the wrapping cloths June had given her and swaddled his hands. "They're going to be very painful," she said, "but they will heal completely."

Relief washed over Clint's face. "That's good," he mumbled. "I was worried I wouldn't be able to ride again if I messed my hands up."

"You will ride again just fine," Carrie said tenderly, laying her hand on his forehead. She could only imagine the pain he had endured when he rode over to tell them what he'd seen. "But not tonight," she added. "You'll join us in the carriage."

Clint nodded weakly. "Yes, ma'am."

Carrie met Robert's eyes over the boy's head. "Stay here with him," she said.

Standing, she walked over to where Rose and Moses stood staring at the still-raging fire. Moses held a sheet of paper tightly in his hand, a look of fury in his eyes. "What is that?"

Moses stared down at her. "I found this on the tree by the road."

Carrie reached for the paper, her fury matching his as she read.

> *We warned you no good would come from helping the niggers. Since words had no effect, we thought you would pay attention to action. Be warned. We are watching every moment. We will not let our beloved South be taken from us.*

Carrie snorted as she balled up the paper. "Cowards!" she snapped. She turned toward the woods across the road and lifted her fist defiantly. "If you're watching," she yelled, "know that you are all nothing but cowards. You can burn it down, but we will simply rebuild. The day will come when cowards like you will no longer have the ability to ruin our *beloved South!*" Her words rose against the crackle of the flames, hanging in the air triumphantly.

Abby joined her, raising her own fist. Moments later, June joined her. The three women stood as a determined unit against the specter of danger.

Carrie finally turned to see where Rose was and moaned when she saw the anguished look in her friend's eyes. Rose stared at the burning building, fear radiating from her face. Before Carrie could move to comfort her friend, she heard shouts coming from down the road. Stiffening, she waited to see if there was to be another attack.

Robert was by her side instantly, his rifle held ready.

Moses scowled. "One rifle won't do much against a band of men."

"No," Robert admitted, "but it's all we've got."

"Miss Rose! Miss Rose!"

Moments later, emerging from the darkness like vengeful ghosts, a large group assembled at the edge of the fire.

Justine slipped to Rose's side. "Who set our school on fire?" she cried. "Why would they do that?"

"Who did this?" another woman yelled.

"They burned our school!" a wide-eyed little girl screamed, running forward to huddle against Rose. "I'm scared, Miss Rose. They gonna come to our house next?"

Her question set off a torrent of tears from the children who had accompanied their parents. "They gonna burn us next, Miss Rose?"

A little boy named Wallace walked up to Rose and peered into her eyes. "You scared, Miss Rose?"

A quiet settled down over the clearing. The only sound was the crackling of the flames as they devoured the remaining walls. The light from the fire illuminated all the way to the edge of the woods on the far side of the road, stopping short of what might be lurking within.

Rose shuddered, wanting to scream out her fear and uncertainty. Her students were looking to her for strength, but she had none to offer. She stared over Wallace's head as the last remaining wall burned down to where shelves of books had waited for eager children. She fought to breathe as the books caught fire, their pages burning bright as sparks in the raging inferno.

Carrie, knowing Rose was incapable of speech, stepped forward. "I am so sorry," she called. "It was white men who did this." She held up the sheet of paper Moses had ripped from the tree. "This was done by cowardly men who are attempting to control by fear."

"They hate us that bad?" Wallace asked. "How come white people hate us so bad?"

Carrie knelt down to gaze into his eyes, battling a deep sense of shame. Fury rose in her to match the shame she felt over members of her race doing this terrible thing. "They don't hate *you*, Wallace."

"They just hate everything that be black," he said, the dull knowledge in his eyes revealing he had seen far more than any ten-year-old boy should see.

Carrie had a sudden wild desire to dash into the woods and pull out any cowardly men watching the results of their destructive act. She pushed the surge of emotion down, speaking calmly as she looked into the boy's eyes. Only the truth would matter on a night like this. "People hate what they are afraid of," she admitted.

"They be afraid of *me*?" Wallace asked, his eyes showing his confusion.

The children all crowded closer to hear her answer.

"They are afraid because they have lost control," Carrie replied. "Slavery was a horrible, wrong, thing, but it made whites feel in control. They've lost the control now, so they are afraid." She could hear more of the walls collapsing behind her. "They are trying to regain control by making all of *us* afraid."

"I be afraid," Wallace admitted in a small voice.

The murmur of voices from the other children and the fright shining from the adults' eyes said they were all feeling the same thing.

Carrie allowed the fury she had tamped down to rise upward, obliterating any feeling of shame or fear. She stood and gazed at the remnants of the schoolhouse and clinic for several long moments. Just as all of the men and their families from Cromwell Plantation ran up, Carrie raised her voice again.

"It takes a coward to burn something down," she called loudly for the benefit of everyone listening, seen and unseen. "It takes courage to build it again." She waved her hand toward the flames. "The fire will go out. We will rebuild." Carrie let her eyes sweep over the group, watching, as very slowly, fear began to ebb from their faces. "We will rebuild!" she said again. "We worked together to build it before. We will build it again."

Carrie motioned to Robert to join her. "Robert and I will leave in the morning to get more wood. While we are gone, all of you will clear away the rubble and prepare the foundation. We'll be able to bring enough to frame everything. You can also start cutting down the trees you'll need to finish it." She took a deep breath. "Any time someone attacks you, it is normal to feel fear, but you have to push it aside and keep moving forward. All of you will be back in school as soon as possible."

Carrie felt Rose beside her before she heard her voice.

"All of you will be back in school *tomorrow*," Rose said firmly, all fear gone from her voice. "I used to teach a secret school on Cromwell Plantation when I was a slave," she revealed. "Every time my students went to school they risked being beaten. They came anyway because they wanted to learn. We don't have to hide in the woods, because we are *free*." Her voice rose with the flames, defiance and courage pressing against the darkness. "No one can take away our freedom. They may fight it, but they can't take it away. It's up to us to push past the fear and create the life we want."

Abby stepped forward, joining hands with Carrie and Rose. "I will make sure a wagonload of books returns with the lumber," she promised. Her eyes glistened with emotion. "Please know that while it was white men who destroyed your school, there are plenty of white people who want to see you living freely with equal rights. We will continue to fight *with* you until things are better."

Gradually, fear faded from the faces surrounding them.

Gabe stepped forward. "I'll be here early tomorrow morning to start clearing the rubble," he called. His eyes swept the crowd. "Who is with me?" Twenty men stepped forward quickly. "We'll work early every morning until we have to start work in the fields. It won't take us long to get it ready."

Polly stepped forward next. "I'm going to need help making sure there is food here every morning to keep these men working. Who will help?" Another large crowd of women stepped forward, their faces determined.

Justine stepped forward next, her eyes shining with courage. "Me and the other students want to help. We'll be here in the morning, too." She raised a hand when she saw Rose open her mouth to protest. "This is *our* school, Miss Rose. We'll still come to school after we help, but we're not going to sit back and do nothing."

"Yes! It's our school, too," Amber called, her eyes fixed on her brother leaning against the tree, his face tight with pain. "Clint tried to save the school. We want to be a part of rebuilding it. My mama will feed us, too."

Justine looked at Polly. "Do you think there will be enough food for us, ma'am?"

"I'll make sure of it," Polly vowed, her eyes shining with pride.

Moses and Robert stepped up to stand beside the four women. They turned as one unit to face the darkness. The entire crowd turned in the same direction.

"We will rebuild," Moses called, his deep voice ringing through the night. "If you burn it down again, we will build it again. And again. And again. You cannot destroy us. You cannot take away our freedom."

There was a shift in the air as Moses spoke. Rose watched in awe as everyone turned to look at him, their eyes fixed on his strong face. It was as if the last remaining fears had taken wing and flown over the treetops with the billowing smoke.

"Freedom has to be fought for," Moses continued. "We spent all our years in slavery wishing to be free. Now we are. We hoped it would be easy, but it is *never* going to be easy." He reached down and picked up Wallace, holding the slight boy easily in his arms. "We're going to fight for ourselves, but mostly we are going to fight for our children. We'll fight for all those who will come after us. We already know there are people out there who will fight to take away our freedom. We won't let them." He paused, straightening even more as he turned to gaze at the fire. "Whatever they destroy... *we will build it again.*"

"We will build it again," the crowd echoed, their voices and faces resolute.

Moses wasn't done. "The men who burned down the school believe they can control us with fear. That's how they controlled us through all the years of slavery. They took away our rights to choose, they stole our families, and they beat us into submission." He paused for a long moment. "Never again," he roared. "Never again."

"Never again!" the crowd echoed defiantly. "Never again!"

Rose cuddled up against Moses after the long night finally ended and they were back home in their bedroom. "I am so proud of you," she whispered.

"I'm proud of *you*," Moses responded. "You didn't let fear get the best of you tonight."

Rose winced. "I came close." She forced her eyes to stay open, knowing that if she closed them she would see the flames destroying the schoolhouse.

"All of us came close," Moses insisted. "There is a lot going on in this world that is scary. We would be less than human if we didn't feel fear, but we can't let it beat us. You didn't let it beat you tonight," he said tenderly. "That's why I'm proud of you."

"You're doing it again," Rose said quietly.

Moses hesitated, not understanding the expression on her face. "Why are you looking at me like that?"

"Because I saw you become someone else tonight," Rose said, her eyes fixed on him. "I've always known you're a leader, but something happened to you tonight."

Moses stared at her. He wanted to refute her words, but he was afraid she was right.

"What happened to you out there?" Rose asked. "What were you feeling?"

Moses turned to gaze out the window, seeing nothing but dark shadows. "I'm not sure," he said. "At first I felt so angry and helpless. I couldn't believe the school was on fire. When I found the note, I realized this is probably just the beginning of their attempts to scare and intimidate us."

Rose shuddered but continued to listen.

"I was really scared for a minute, but then I realized that was giving them what they wanted." His voice deepened. "I refuse to give them what they want."

"There!" Rose exclaimed, sitting up against the headboard as she stared at him. "You're doing it again."

Moses shook his head. "You're going to have to help me out here. I don't know what you're talking about."

"When I was in Philadelphia, I got to hear a lot of people speak. Many of them were very important people. I listened because I knew they had something worthwhile to say, but there were only a few of them who captured my heart and mind." Rose spoke more slowly. "I knew those few people were real leaders because they had the ability to make people feel more than they were feeling. They could make people better than they were." She grabbed one of Moses' hands. "You did that tonight," she whispered. "You made every person there choose to be better than they are."

"Or maybe choose to be as great as they truly are," Moses argued. "I didn't change anyone tonight."

"If all they did was choose to be as great as they truly are, then you changed them," Rose insisted. "So many of those people were cowering in fear until you started talking. I watched their faces. I saw the change. Did you do that in the army, too?"

Moses shrugged, uncomfortable with the whole discussion. "I don't know."

"You did," Rose replied. "I listened to Captain Jones enough to know what kind of leader you were."

Moses shifted, not wanting to continue the conversation. "I'm a farmer now. A farmer who is going to be very tired in the morning if I don't get some sleep."

Roses smiled and raised her hand to lay it on his cheek. "You're not a farmer, Moses."

Moses felt a flash of alarm, mixed with a spark of anger. "What are you talking about?"

Rose didn't flinch. "Oh, you're a great farmer, and you're doing a fine job running the plantation, but you're so much more than a farmer. Every person there tonight saw you as a leader. You replaced their fear with determination. That's a gift, Moses."

Moses gritted his teeth. "It's not a gift I want," he said stubbornly. "I did what I had to tonight. I will help rebuild the school, and then I will go back to running the plantation."

Rose settled back against the headboard and smiled.

Moses shook his head. "This isn't funny, Rose."

"No, I suppose it's not. It's never funny when you don't want to be what you are."

Moses bit back his angry reply, questioning why he was so upset. He thought of all the years of abuse as a slave. His mind filled with images of men slaughtered in battle, their bloated corpses staring up at him. He had fought for freedom. He had paid the price. Now he just wanted to run the plantation, be with Rose, and raise his children.

Rose looked at him tenderly. "You've been a leader from the day I met you, but I never saw it quite as clearly as I saw it tonight." Her voice grew firmer, her eyes more direct. "Our people need you, Moses."

Moses stared at her. "I don't want to be needed," he said, cringing inwardly at his words, but meaning them completely.

"I know."

Moses heaved a heavy sigh. "You look just like your mama right now."

Rose's eyes widened. "Really?" She sounded pleased.

"Your mama used to look at me like that—like she was giving me time to come around to her way of thinking."

Rose smiled. "I know that look. She used to look at me like that all the time. She never pushed anything. She just looked at me until I quit fighting whatever it was I knew I needed to do."

Moses scowled again. "What makes you think I know what I need to do?" He bit back a laugh when Rose gave him that same look, and pulled her down beside him. "Whether you're right or wrong, I'm not making a decision about anything tonight. I'm going to get some sleep and then get up early so I can have the school ready for the wood and supplies Carrie and Robert will bring back. I know you and your students will be fine outside for a few days, but we have a school to rebuild."

Rose snuggled into him again, her warmth offering him a comfort he desperately needed, though he couldn't quite identify why he needed it.

His head was a swirl of contradictory feelings and thoughts as he finally drifted off to sleep.

Chapter Twelve

Opal breathed in the fresh air as she knelt in the newly tilled soil. The first thing she had done when she arrived at the home of Eddie's brother, Clark, was offer to plant a garden. Now the entire backyard looked just like Fannie's had when Opal first arrived in Richmond. There were little paths, but with that exception, everything else was planted. Most seeds were still germinating beneath the dark soil, but three weeks of warm weather had produced the bright green beginnings of carrots, onions, radishes, peas, and lettuces. The okra, corn, peppers, tomatoes, and watermelons would follow shortly. There was a separate bed for the potatoes that were already coming up. In a few weeks, they would be eating luscious new potatoes. With everyone in the house working, there was money for fresh butter to put on them.

Jewel found her cooing over the carrots. "I declare. You look like a mother with her babies."

Opal grinned. She and Clark's wife had struck up an easy friendship. Close quarters could create tense situations, but there had been none in the month or so since they had arrived. Clark and Jewel seemed genuinely glad to have them there.

Eddie and Clark had been separated by the auction block when they were young children. Eddie had bought his freedom when he was in his early twenties. Clark had remained a slave until the end of the war. He'd been one of the few who had been so sequestered on his plantation deep in the cotton fields of Alabama that he'd not even heard of the Emancipation Proclamation, and no Union troops had arrived to tell him of his freedom. He knew there was a war being fought, but he just continued to work the fields. It wasn't until a few months after the end of the war that the news reached his plantation. He and Jewel left the next day with their children, working their way slowly toward Richmond. He was looking for his brother. When he had discovered Eddie was in Philadelphia, he got a missionary teacher to write a letter. The two brothers were thrilled to be together again.

Amber Lou had become fast friends with their twelve-year-old, Cindy, and Carl was inseparable from his cousin George, who was the same age as him.

Opal smiled at the plants. "They *are* my babies," she agreed. "Just wait until every meal has food we pick right out of the backyard."

Jewel nodded. She was almost as tall as her husband, who stood an inch shorter than his tall, skinny brother. There was not a spare ounce of flesh on her body, but she didn't look skinny. She simply looked elegant. Her face was calm as she gazed out over the garden.

"How do you do it?" Opal asked enviously.

"Do it?"

"You've got your everyday dress on, and still you manage to look regal. I swear you look like a queen surveying her kingdom. I, on the other hand, look like a frumpy, overweight black woman."

Jewel laughed. "Nonsense. You look like a carin', lovin' mother who will do anythin' to take care of them she loves. You be strong, sensitive, and kind. That's what *I* see when I look at you." She waved her hand over the plants. "I never would have thought to do this. Our owner didn't let us have our own gardens. I sho 'nuff love bein' free, but I'm still learnin' how to live this way," she said regretfully. "I'm not sure I'm doing it very good."

Opal snorted. "You're doing fine, Jewel. You have a home, your kids are in school, and your husband has a good job."

"Because of Eddie," Jewel observed. "Clark tried for a job at Cromwell Factory before, but he got turned down. As soon as Eddie got here and went to work, somethin' came open for him. Eddie never said nothin' when we asked, but I knows it be because of him."

Opal merely smiled, pleased the arrangement was working for everyone. She herself had started at the factory two weeks earlier. She couldn't say sewing was something she enjoyed, but she was getting the hang of it. Even helping with household expenses, she and Eddie were able to put some money aside toward the new restaurant they dreamed of. Jewel stayed home to watch the kids to make sure they stayed out of trouble and went to school.

"Marcus is coming for dinner tonight," Jewel announced.

"That's good," Opal murmured, pulling tiny weeds from around the fledgling onion shoots. "He and Eddie been friends for a right long time. I'm glad he was still here in Richmond."

"He says he hopes there will be sweet potato casserole."

Opal chuckled. "At least I'll have one customer when we open our new restaurant." She pulled the last weeds and stood, brushing the dirt off her dress. "It's already in the oven." She glanced at the pile of wood next to the back door. "Did Carl and George fill the wood box in the kitchen?"

Jewel nodded but her thoughts were on something else. "I can hardly wait for the Emancipation Parade tomorrow."

Opal nodded, her thoughts full of memories. "I can hardly believe it's been a year since Richmond fell." Her lips twitched. "I imagine the white folks are still mad we're celebrating it now, instead of back in January when the Emancipation Proclamation was signed."

Jewel shrugged. "We're free now. Folks didn't for real *feel* free until Richmond fell and all them black soldiers came pouring into town. Me and Clark didn't know nothin' about it back then, but we done heard all the stories. It's *our* day to celebrate." Her face glowed with excitement. "Tomorrow is gonna be a fine day."

"What time are the men going to be here tonight?" Opal asked.

"About an hour, I reckon. They had a meeting to go to at the church."

"Jeremy going to be there?" Opal asked, still astonished at Jeremy's involvement to help everyone. He had become a fixture at the Second African Baptist Church, showing up at least two nights a week after working at the factory. His business acumen was helping many of the men, and he was also helping them understand the political system.

"Not tonight," Jewel answered. "Clark was here long enough to tell me some machines went down at the factory today. He's staying late tonight to help fix them."

Abby was tired after an achingly long day. She had seen Robert and Carrie off with two wagons loaded down with framing lumber and as many school supplies as she could round up on such short notice. She would send another wagon full of books the next week when the Missionary Society delivered them. A telegraph to a good friend in Philadelphia apprising her of the situation had resulted in a promise of all the books Abby requested.

The factory was doing well, working at full speed to fill the orders pouring in. There was still tension, but there had been no outright violence. She knew Jeremy was largely responsible for that. He insisted on being involved with every part of the manufacturing process, spending every minute of the day working alongside the men— both black and white. His presence kept violence from brewing, but she hoped his open-minded fairness was working to gradually change attitudes. Nothing would truly change until people changed the way they thought.

"Long day, Mrs. Cromwell?" Spencer asked sympathetically.

"A long day," she agreed with a smile, "but a good day." She had told him about the fire at the plantation. "I sent Carrie and Robert home today with everything they need. With everyone working hard, I don't think it will take time to rebuild the school."

"Like folks say, lots of hands make easy labor," Spencer responded. "I reckon they's right."

Abby nodded and laid her head back against the carriage seat, staring up into the new leaves exploding all over the city. Even with all the destruction from the war,

Richmond was a beautiful city. There was still a lot of work to be done, but so much had already been accomplished. Mountains of rubble had been moved outside the city limits, and new buildings were going up everywhere. She smiled as the last rays of the sun kissed the Capitol Building with a pink haze, and admired the dogwood trees that were bursting into bloom with white blossoms that stood out starkly in the waning light.

She was jolted out of her thoughts when the carriage slammed to a stop, the horses throwing up their heads and neighing in protest as a group of men stepped in front of them to form a barricade across the road. Abby sighed in irritation, too tired to feel alarm. "Why have you gentlemen stopped us?" she called crisply.

"We've stopped you because we have something to say," one man called back.

Abby looked him over carefully. He was dressed well, and his dark hair was carefully groomed. "You look like someone who should have the manners to know there is a better way to start a conversation," she replied, only her eyes flashing her irritation.

The man scowled, anger twisting his features into something quite unpleasant. Abby felt her first twinge of alarm.

"And you look like a woman who would know there is a better way to run a factory than the way you and your husband are running it now," he shot back.

Abby stiffened when she saw fury settle on the faces of the seven men standing with him, but she couldn't resist taunting him. "So it takes eight of you to have a conversation with one woman? You could have come to the factory if you have something to say."

The self-elected leader took a step forward. "I would suggest you not try any smart talk," he growled. "We already know you and your husband think you can do things any way you want to. We're here to tell you things don't work down here the way they worked in Philadelphia."

"Is that right?" Abby asked, angry enough to be bold, but all too aware she was at a disadvantage.

"That's right," the man snapped. "You have to lower the wages for the blacks at the factory. It's not right that they're being paid the same as white workers. We don't do things that way here in Richmond."

Abby knew it was useless to try reason. There was not a man staring at her who would be open to answers and reasoning. She slowly slid her hand beneath her lap blanket. "And if we don't?"

Anger flared into fury the moment the words left her mouth. Three of the men surged forward and grabbed Spencer by the arm, trying to haul him off the wagon seat. Spencer said nothing, but his tight grip on the seat held him in place.

Abby stood, pulling a pistol from beneath the blanket. Knowing the threat alone wouldn't get their attention, she fired a shot into the air, hoping the noise would alert help, but not having any confidence that it would get here in time. Richmond was still far too crowded for the police to have control. "Take your hands off my driver!"

The three men cursed and fell back but stayed within easy reach of the wagon. Spencer remained silent, his face set and stoic.

The leader laughed harshly. "One woman with a pistol? Do you think you can stop all of us?"

Abby fought to keep her voice calm. "Probably not, but which ones of you are willing to find out whom I can stop? I have five bullets left in this pistol." She reached under the blanket and pulled out another one. "I have six more in this one. At such close range, I imagine I could do a lot of damage."

The leader swore but still snickered and waved his men forward, his face set in cold, harsh lines. They exchanged reluctant looks but did his bidding, grabbing Spencer by the arm and pulling him roughly.

Breathing a quiet prayer, Abby fought to control her pounding heart, then aimed and fired, shooting the front man in the leg. She felt sick when she saw the rapidly expanding blood stain on his pants.

"She shot me," he yelled. "She shot me!"

The other two men jumped back, looking wildly between their leader and Abby's pistol.

"And that's just the first of you if you don't all step back," Abby said, cocking the hammer again. When the men retreated a few paces, she turned and aimed the pistol straight at the leader's heart. "I shot your man in the leg because I think he's a fool for following your lead. I'll have no such compassion for you. If you are not out of our way in five seconds, this next bullet is going straight through your heart," she said. "What I do with my business is *my* business. I will not allow some cowardly man to dictate my actions." The image of the burning schoolhouse added fuel to her anger. "Get out of our way!" she demanded, raising her other pistol to aim it at the rest of the men. "I'm not quite as good a shot with my left hand," she admitted, "so I'm not sure which one of you I will shoot, but I guess that is your problem, not mine."

The other men fell back into the shadows. Only the leader held his position, his eyes glazed with hatred.

Abby took a deep breath, wondering if she could really shoot a man in the heart, but a quick glance at Spencer's rigid shoulders assured her she could do whatever it took to protect them.

"We're not finished," the man growled. As he stepped back, he stared her in the eyes. "There just may be a repeat of what happened to that schoolhouse," he snapped. "Fire can be very destructive, don't you think?"

Abby fought back a sudden urge to pull the trigger and relieve the world of this man. She held her hand steady, not looking away from the burning animosity in his eyes. "So can cowardice," she said quietly. "Your attempts to save your beloved South are doing nothing but causing further destruction." She leaned forward slightly. "I think now would be a good time to leave," she whispered into Spencer's ear. "Just don't be in a hurry," she said more loudly. "I'll be happy to shoot anything that moves."

Spencer lifted the reins with steady hands and moved the horses forward.

Abby didn't take her eyes off the men until they had rounded a bend and gone a few blocks. As traffic increased in the busier part of town, she breathed her first deep breath. "Well..."

"It sure ain't never boring driving you people around."

Abby laughed, sagging back against the seat. "I'd heard Carrie got you in some bad situations."

Spencer nodded. "Yes, ma'am. She's pretty good with a rifle, though. And then Hobbs started going with us."

"Did you ever think of driving for someone else?"

"And miss out on all the fun?" Spencer protested. "Not a chance."

Abby smiled but felt a sudden surge of fear. "We have to go back to the factory."

"We can't be going back there," Spencer protested. "They might still be there, Mrs. Cromwell. Mr. Cromwell won't never forgive me if I let something happen to you."

"And I could never forgive myself if something happens to Thomas and Jeremy on the way home," Abby replied, her heart pounding again as she imagined the group of men accosting her husband and brother-in-law outside the factory. "We have to warn them. Besides, there will be less danger with all of us together. Those men are too cowardly to come after all of us."

Spencer sighed heavily and shook his head, but he turned the carriage around.

Abby sat at attention the entire way, her pistol ready and her eyes scanning the shadows for any movement. She knew the almost-dark roads increased their danger. The thought of Thomas and Jeremy facing those men without warning kept her pressing forward.

Thomas and Jeremy were just leaving the factory when they arrived.

"Abby!" Thomas cried, whitening when he saw the look on her face. "What is it? What's wrong?"

Abby quickly told him what had happened, her anger growing as she talked. "It was infuriating!" she finished.

Thomas grabbed her arm. "You could have been killed," he whispered.

The same thought had occurred to Abby, but she pushed it aside. "So could one or more of them," she replied calmly, annoyed when she felt her insides begin to tremble now that the danger had passed.

Jeremy was standing at attention beside the carriage, his eyes never still as he watched every movement. "I'd suggest we get home," he said steadily. "I think Abby is right that they won't come after all of us, but a man with wounded pride can be very dangerous. I say we finish this conversation at home."

Abby was happy to stay close to Thomas, her hand firmly in his as Spencer drove them through the darkened streets. She only relaxed when they turned down their street. She could hardly wait to sit down to a hot meal and talk with Thomas after dinner.

"Spencer! Stop!" Jeremy yelled.

Abby's mind froze as her eyes searched the street for signs of danger.

Jeremy stood tall in the carriage, staring down at the city spread below them from their vantage point on the hill. "There is a fire," he said. "Down in the black quarter."

"Not another one," Abby whispered, fatigue pressing down on her like a blanket. "Is there to be no end?"

"I've got to get down there," Jeremy said urgently.

"Of course you do," Thomas said. Jeremy had already told him what he could about his activities. He knew his brother was leaving things out, but he trusted Jeremy was revealing all he could. "Spencer?"

"Yessir," Spencer responded. "We'll get there a lot faster in the carriage. It's the Second African Church," he said. "I know right where that church be from up here."

"We should come help," Abby gasped, her thoughts flying to Marietta, already knowing Jeremy's thoughts were centered on the lovely young woman who had shared dinner with them several times.

"No, ma'am," Spencer replied firmly. "Ain't no telling what is going on down there. You done been in enough danger for one night."

"He's right, Abby," Thomas agreed. He grasped Jeremy's hand. "We'll wait up until you get home with the news."

Abby and Thomas climbed quickly from the carriage when Spencer brought it to a standstill. "Be careful!" they called as the horses returned the way they had come. They stood on the porch until the quiet of the night had swallowed all sounds, and then they went inside.

Jeremy wanted to yell at Spencer to go faster, but he knew the horses were going as swiftly as they could on the dark streets.

"You know we ain't gonna get there in time to save anythin'," Spencer said grimly.

Jeremy scowled, knowing he was right. "I doubt it was an accident."

"Don't reckon it was." He looked over at Jeremy. "How many people know you been comin' down to the church to help us?"

"Only Thomas and Abby," Jeremy replied, looking at Spencer sharply. "You think someone did this because of me?" His thoughts flew to Marietta. Would she come to harm because of him? He prayed she had left the church right after school. The thought of something happening to her had his throat closing like a vise. He struggled to breathe evenly.

Spencer shrugged. "Them men who came after Abby tonight seemed bent on destruction, but if they was the ones who done it, it weren't because of you. It was because of us. Them men might not like what you're doing, but it weren't *your* church they burned."

Jeremy gritted his teeth. "I should stop coming if I'm putting anyone in danger."

"I don't think so," Spencer responded. "That would be giving them what they want. They knows you helpin' us. They for sure don't want that."

"Then they should come after me," Jeremy snapped. Again, his thoughts flew to Marietta. He would see what he could do for the church, and then he would go to her boarding house to make sure she was safe.

"Be careful what you wish for, Mr. Jeremy," Spencer warned. "You might just get it."

"Tell me more about what happened tonight," Jeremy asked, trying to shake his helpless feeling. "I have a feeling Abby left out some things."

"She sho 'nuff did," Spencer agreed. He spoke quickly as they drew closer to the black quarter, telling Jeremy everything that had happened. "That one man was real bad news. I didn't recognize him from around town. You got to keep a close eye on Mrs. Cromwell."

"We will, but I'm also concerned about you. They would have killed you if they had gotten you down from the wagon," Jeremy growled.

Spencer remained silent, focused on his driving, but the expression on his face said he knew that was true.

"I'm going to get you a pistol, Spencer. You'll be able to protect yourself, and you can also help protect whomever you're driving."

Spencer nodded. "I reckon that be a good thing, but you might oughta teach me how to shoot it once you give it to me. Not many black people, other than them soldiers during the war, ever had a gun. I ain't never held a gun before. No telling what might get shot. "

Jeremy gave a brief chuckle before they rounded the last corner. Spencer had been right—it was impossible to save anything. There was a huge crowd of people standing outside the ring of heat, but no one was doing anything but staring and crying as the two-story, old wooden building went up like kindling. The roof had already collapsed. The burning walls were sending columns of fire and smoke high into the air.

Spencer pulled the wagon to a stop. Both of them stared at the burning church with a sick feeling. The fire was bad enough, but the malice they were certain was behind it hung in the air like a dark shroud.

Jeremy thought about the simple pews that seated the congregation each Sunday. He could clearly see the rooms set aside for students during the day and then for Secret Society meetings at night. He remembered the picnic he had attended a few weeks earlier. Good food, laughing faces, and friendship had resonated throughout the sunny spring day. It was all gone.

"Jeremy!"

Jeremy swiveled his head until he saw Eddie's wildly waving arm. He jumped down from the carriage and hurried over. "How did this happen?"

Eddie frowned, his eyes a mixture of pain and fury. "It was set. Me and Opal and Marcus was coming over for a meeting. We got here a little early because Opal had made cookies for everyone. She wanted it to be a surprise. Just as we got here, we saw a gang of white men running away from the church." He turned to stare at the inferno. "They started the fires in the back. It done took only a few minutes for it to all go up."

"Was anyone in there?" Jeremy asked, trying to speak steadily. Not many people knew about his relationship with Marietta.

"I don't think so. Classes were over for the day, and the meetings hadn't started yet. The pastor is right over there, so I know he's okay."

Jeremy nodded with relief—a relief that was short-lived when he turned back to stare at the building. He only had one other question. "Marietta? Is she okay? Are you absolutely positive she wasn't in there?"

As if summoned by his thoughts, she appeared from the darkness. "I'm fine, Jeremy." She smiled at him, but her eyes were dark with concern and anger.

This time Jeremy's relief almost swallowed him. "Thank God!" he said fervently. He grabbed both her hands and stared into her face. "Are you sure you're okay? No burns from heroic efforts to save anything?" He had vivid memories of Carrie's description of Clint's burned hands.

"No heroic measures," Marietta assured him. "By the time I got back here, it was too late to do anything." Her voice trembled slightly. "I stayed after school late today because I was grading papers. I had just arrived home when one of my students came running to tell me about the fire."

Jeremy gripped her hands tighter, knowing she probably wouldn't have had a chance to escape the building if she had been in there when the fires were set. The arsonists had done a thorough job for the building to burn so quickly. "You're sure no one else was in there?"

"Fairly certain," Marietta responded. "I called goodbye when I left the building. No one responded. I believe it was empty."

Jeremy nodded, continuing to stare down into her eyes. Their relationship was progressing, but there had been nothing else said about his feelings for her. He heard the popping sound of exploding timbers. As a more intense wave of heat rolled toward them, he pulled Marietta close into his arms, shielding her body. He buried his face in her hair for a long moment, pleased when she didn't pull away. "I was so afraid something had happened to you," he murmured.

Marietta stood quietly and wrapped her arms around him. Jeremy felt the trembles rippling through her body. He pulled her even closer. "It's going to be all right," he said softly.

Only then did she pull back. "Really? This church was one of the centers of the community. What will everyone do now?" she demanded, anger replacing her fear.

"We'll build it back, Miss Marietta," Eddie assured her. "It may take us a while, but we'll build it back."

"And until then?" Marietta asked. "What will everyone do? Where am I supposed to teach my students?"

Jeremy had a sudden idea. "Come with me." He turned to Spencer. "Can you take us to the old hospital?"

Spencer nodded, a grin spreading across his face. "Sho 'nuff can, Mr. Jeremy. Can't do nothing here anyway. Thank God the buildings around here weren't close enough to the church to catch fire. There are plenty of men to watch things through the night."

Marietta stared up at him. "The old hospital? Jeremy, I think I should be here."

Jeremy smiled, glad to have a solution to some of the problems created by the loss of the church. "I thought you wanted a place to teach your students?"

"I do, but..."

"Come with me," Jeremy insisted, tipping her face up so their eyes met. "I have your answer."

"You go," Eddie urged. "I know my kids gonna be badgerin' me about school the minute I get home. Sho would be nice to have an answer."

"You just tell them they have a school," Jeremy promised. He helped Marietta into the carriage and settled down next to her.

Marietta reconciled herself to the fact Jeremy wasn't going to say anything else. The glow remained in the sky, but the further they pulled away from the church, the quieter the night became. Hundreds of people were crowded around the fire, but there were still curious faces peering out at them as they drove through the streets.

Spencer finally pulled the horses to a stop. "Here you go, Mr. Jeremy."

Jeremy took a deep breath. He hadn't been back here since his father's death. He had stayed away because he feared the memories would be too painful. Now, two years later, the memories produced a warm pride.

"What is this?" Marietta asked.

"My father's old church. I gave it to the congregation when he passed away, but there weren't enough of them to keep it going. It's been sitting empty since the end of the war. I haven't known what to do with it."

Marietta stepped out from the carriage, but darkness shrouded the building. "How big is it?"

"Big enough," Jeremy promised. "The right side of the building was used as the church. The left side was converted into a hospital during the war. Carrie and Janie used to come down here and care for the people."

"Carrie and Janie were the doctors?" she gasped. "I didn't know! I'd heard about the hospital, but I didn't know where it was."

"You're looking at it," Jeremy replied, a fierce pride sweeping through him. His father had seen needs and filled them. Now it was his turn. "It's plenty big enough for your school, and the groups can meet here at night. The church portion isn't large enough for the congregation, but I'll let the pastor decide what he wants to do about that." He paused. "The hospital portion has dirt floors. I'm not sure what condition it is in," he said apologetically, suddenly having second thoughts about offering it. He was having a hard time seeing Marietta working in these conditions, but he understood her commitment.

"It ain't bad," Spencer assured him. "I drive by here sometimes. It ain't real clean, but the ceiling ain't leaking. I always check on it for your daddy. He sure gave a lot of himself here."

"Yes, he did," Jeremy said. "He would be pleased to know it was being used again."

Marietta turned and grabbed him in a fierce hug. "Thank you!" she cried. "It will be perfect!"

"But..."

Marietta pressed a finger to Jeremy's lips. "It will be perfect," she said, her eyes shining up into his. "I'll have the students clean everything. The parents will build some simple desks. It's not important *where* the students learn—what is important is their understanding that the act of destruction that took their school can't take away their opportunity for education. The church will be rebuilt. In the meantime, this will be perfect."

Jeremy grinned. "I'm quite sure Abby already has a plan to replace the books and school supplies. Her supply line from the North hasn't failed her yet. I know she has books coming for the plantation school next week. We'll divide them up and then get more."

"Thank you," Marietta murmured. "I can't wait to see it in the light. I'll bring people tomorrow after the Emancipation Parade to begin work. I can't think of a single thing better to do after celebrating freedom for the slaves. There is plenty I can do with the children, even without books and supplies."

"I reckon ever'body gonna agree with you, Miss Marietta," Spencer said solemnly. He looked around into the shadows and then over at Jeremy. "We been here long enough," he drawled.

Jeremy heard the words he didn't say. There was no way of knowing where the arsonists had gone or where they would strike next. He nodded quickly. "You're right. I'll drop you off at the church. You can walk the few blocks home from there. I'll take Marietta back to her boarding house."

Jeremy jumped down from the carriage and held out his hand for Marietta to step down. "You're tired," he said gently.

"It's been a long day," she agreed. "The most important thing, though, is that no lives were lost and no one was hurt."

"I'll second that," Jeremy responded. He had been so afraid Marietta had been caught in the fire. The moment Spencer had confirmed his fear that the blaze he had spotted was the Second African Baptist Church, his most pressing concern had been her safety. He cupped his hands around her face and gazed down into her eyes. "I was so worried about you."

Marietta was always so strong and resilient, but this time her eyes reflected her fatigue and vulnerability. "Thank you," she whispered. "It's nice to have someone worry about me."

With that single sentence, Jeremy understood how lonely she must sometimes feel. She lived alone in a boarding house, so far from the family and friends she grew up with. She was a passionate teacher and a strong woman, but Jeremy knew from watching Carrie and Rose that even the strongest of women needed a shoulder to lean on. "I'm here for you," he promised, his eyes never leaving her face.

Marietta swayed toward him slightly, her eyes revealing her need.

Jeremy groaned and pulled her close, kissing her gently at first and then more firmly. Her soft lips responded eagerly. Long minutes passed before he finally released her and stepped back, his pulse pounding.

"I'm not going to apologize."

Marietta continued to stare into his eyes. "I don't want you to. It would rather take away from the joy of our first kiss."

"You're not upset I kissed you?"

Marietta smiled. "Certainly not. I was wondering if you ever would."

Jeremy pulled her close again and kissed her warmly. "Go inside," he ordered. "It's been a very long day for both of us, but I could change my mind and keep you outside all night. While I'm quite certain I would enjoy every minute, I'm also quite certain we would raise questions I'm not sure you're ready to answer."

Marietta grinned. "Ah...that infamous Southern protocol. Don't you find it boring?"

Jeremy grinned back, happiness surging through him. "Very. Yet I'm not sure I can quite entirely embrace Yankee liberalism."

Marietta laughed. "Me either," she admitted, "but I've often dreamed of what it would be like to be a loose woman. I think it would be rather entertaining."

Jeremy chuckled. "I suspect you're right, but I find my wishes for our relationship go far beyond entertainment." His humor faded away as he held her back and gazed at her, devouring her clear skin and bright blue eyes. "I love you, you know."

Marietta's smile faded, but her eyes remained steady. "And I love you, Jeremy, but I don't yet know the answer to your question the first night we met." Her voice faltered. "I'm sorry."

Jeremy felt the sting but didn't look away. "Take your time. It's a big question."

Marietta frowned. "It shouldn't be," she said fiercely. "It shouldn't matter even one tiny bit what your heritage is."

"But it matters quite a bit what life would be like for a child who carried the burden of being mulatto." Jeremy saw no reason not to hit the issue head on.

"I don't know if I have the right to let my love for you dictate the life of an innocent child," Marietta said helplessly. "I realize the odds are that if we were to have children, they would be white, but I can't be certain."

"That's true," Jeremy agreed, wishing with all his heart he could be certain their child would be white.

"This is such a cruel world for black children," Marietta said sadly.

"And for mulatto," Jeremy added. "My situation is different because I don't look black."

"But your activities down in the black quarter may make people look deeper into your background," Marietta said, fear shining in her eyes.

"You think I shouldn't help?"

"No. I just hate that it even has to be considered. If we were in the North…"

"Prejudice exists there, as well," Jeremy reminded her.

"True," she agreed, "but there is also more tolerance."

Jeremy regarded her quietly, thinking before he spoke. "So if we were to move north, we could be married?" He felt the hesitation more than he saw it. The reality of it was like a kick in the stomach. He stepped back, releasing her arms.

"It's too soon for me to know the answer to that question," Marietta said desperately. "Please, Jeremy! I need more time. Can we please move slowly?"

Jeremy pushed down his sick feeling and nodded. "Of course."

"Would it seriously not matter to you if we had a black child?"

"I've thought about it a great deal," he admitted. "I see how difficult life is for Rose. For Moses. For all of them. It's why I choose to help in every way I can."

"And for a child of your own?" Marietta asked, her heart in her eyes.

"I can't know the future," Jeremy said. "I don't know why I was born white and Rose was born black. I don't know why my mother was raped. I can't know what a child from us would look like." His voice deepened. "I do know that I love you. I have asked myself whether I should walk away from you because of things I can't possibly know. The answer I keep coming up with is 'no.' Now that I know you love me too, the answer is even stronger. The only thing I know for certain is that a child who comes from our love will be greatly loved."

Marietta searched his eyes before her gaze fell away. "But will our love be enough?" she cried. "Will it be enough when society shuns our child? Will it be enough when our child loses opportunity because we chose to let our own love rule our hearts and decisions?"

Jeremy understood her agony all too well. "Like I may lose our love because I am mulatto?"

Marietta looked away. When she looked back, tears were brimming in her eyes. "I'm sorry, Jeremy."

"I know." Jeremy stepped forward and grasped her arms again. "I will not give you up so easily. You asked for time. I will give it to you." He pulled her close again and kissed her warmly. "I love you, Marietta."

He stepped back, climbed into the carriage, and drove away before she had a chance to respond.

Chapter Thirteen

Carrie and Rose were silent as they moved through woods bursting with new life. Mid-April had blown in with warm winds and brilliant sunshine. Delicate bluestar flowers mingled with the bobbing heads of red columbine. Catalpa contributed a brilliant white that contrasted nicely with the bright yellow blooms of chinkapin. Ferns were completely unfurled as they burst forth from the forest floor. The leafy arms of maple and oak trees towered over the dogwood trees bursting with both pink and white blooms.

Carrie took a deep breath. "It is so very beautiful," she said softly.

Rose eyed her. "You're going to miss this."

"Every day," Carrie agreed. The path opened into a small clearing that held Old Sarah's grave. She turned to Rose and gripped her hands. "But not as much as I'm going to miss you."

Rose nodded, fighting the envy threatening to choke her. "I'll miss you, too," she murmured.

Carrie pulled her down on a log. Silently, they watched butterflies and dragonflies flit around the clearing, the chatter of squirrels the only sound. She finally broke the quiet. "Are you going to tell me what is bothering you before I leave?"

Rose sighed. "Sometimes I wish you didn't know me so well." Here, with her mother's presence so palpable, Rose could do nothing but tell the truth. "I'm so jealous I could scream," she admitted. "I tell myself every day that caring for my family and teaching at the school should be enough for anyone..."

"But it's not," Carrie finished. "I've seen the restlessness growing."

Rose sighed again. "Why can't I be content? Why can't I focus on blooming where I'm planted?" She stared at her mama's grave. "My mama used to tell me I could choose joy right where I am."

"And she was right," Carrie replied. "But you didn't have a choice about being a slave. You really didn't have a choice about staying here on the plantation when your mama was still alive. You had to bloom where you were planted because you couldn't leave. Now you're free. You have a choice."

Rose shook her head. "Do I? I have a husband and two small children. I have a school that was just rebuilt, full of eager students who count on me." She turned helpless eyes on Carrie. "Why can't I let that be enough?"

"Because you're bigger than all of it," Carrie replied steadily.

Silence filled the clearing for several minutes. "You've felt all this," Rose murmured.

"Yes. I told myself it should be enough to be here with Robert and all of you. I told myself it should be enough to meet the needs here in the clinic." She reached down to pick a clover from the patch beneath her feet. She examined it as the sun turned it a brilliant emerald green before she continued. "It wasn't enough," she said bluntly. "I felt guilty because I felt that way, but Robert helped me see I was choosing guilt because I was actually afraid."

Rose frowned. "You think I'm afraid to do something more?"

"No," Carrie answered. "I don't think we're in the same situation. I don't have children to consider. You do."

"But I *am* afraid," Rose said. "I'm afraid I will never get my chance."

"You'll get your chance," Carrie vowed.

"How do you know?" Rose asked desperately. "How *can* you know? I want you to be right, but I can't keep living off wishful thinking. I'm afraid hope will do nothing but make me more restless, and then more resentful if it doesn't happen. Perhaps it is best if I find acceptance in what is."

"Like Moses is trying to find acceptance in being a farmer?"

Rose whipped her head around to stare into her eyes. "What are you talking about?"

Carrie regarded her steadily. "I saw what happened the night the school and clinic burned. I saw how Moses stepped up. More importantly, I saw how the people responded to him. I've also seen how they have treated him since then. Without being aware of it, or even trying to, Moses has become their leader."

"I know," Rose agreed as she shifted to stare at her mama's grave. "He doesn't want it."

"I know. Moses is trying to ignore it all," Carrie observed. "He doesn't want to be a leader because he's comfortable being here on the plantation. After everything he's been through, I don't blame him." She turned and gazed at Rose. "But you're not doing that. You've dreamed of being so much more than a teacher. You want to be a leader for your people in education. You can't do that from the plantation. You can't do that without more education. Of course you're restless. The only way you could not be is if you choose to simply accept what is and decide to be comfortable."

"I can't," Rose whispered brokenly. "I've tried. I can't do it."

"I know," Carrie replied. She stood and walked over to Sarah's grave, staring down at the rock and wooden cross that marked her final resting place. "You won't be here forever, Rose. Moses may think he can ignore being a leader, but something is going to happen that will ignite the flame inside him. *Your* flame is already burning. All you can do right now is be the best teacher you can be and learn as much as possible." Carrie smiled tenderly. "I remember your mama scolding me when she thought I wasn't studying my medical books enough. I had lost hope of ever going to medical school. She told me I had to prepare every single day so I would be ready when the time came. Little did I know it would be five years after that conversation..."

"You've been studying every day," Rose acknowledged as she walked over to join Carrie. She reached down and pulled a few weeds from the grave. "And now you're going off to school."

Silence filled the clearing again for a long moment.

"Will you send me books from Philadelphia?" Rose finally asked, knowing that with that simple statement she was refusing to accept her situation. She was going to prepare for the day when her opportunity arrived.

"Everything I can get my hands on," Carrie promised. Fighting to keep her emotions under control, she walked over and caressed the wisteria just beginning to open, the heady fragrance already strong but nothing like what it would be when it was in full bloom. Vines full of purple flowers would soon fill the woods with their perfume. "I'm going to miss the wisteria this year," she said regretfully.

"You don't think there will be any on the streets of Philadelphia?" Rose teased.

Carrie tried to smile but failed. "Remember all the days we spent in this very clearing when we were growing up?"

Rose smiled. "How could I forget? It was my favorite place in the world. It's why I buried Mama here." She gazed around. "When it was just the two of us playing in this clearing, I used to pretend I wasn't a slave and that I could make decisions like you did."

Carrie grabbed her hand. "And now you can."

Now it was Rose's smile that fell short. "Is it okay to wish it were easier?"

"It is. I wish you and Moses didn't have to fight so hard for everything. I wish life was going to be easier for John and Hope." She shook her head firmly. "It's getting better, Rose. Congress overrode President Johnson's veto. The Civil Rights Act passed. Congress is working hard to make things better. New schools are opening for blacks. Even colleges are being founded. The first Southern black college was founded in Raleigh, North Carolina last year."

Rose chuckled. "I bet Clifford loved that."

Carrie grinned and then sobered. "There are people fighting for black rights everywhere." She paused. "Janie told me something in her last letter that I didn't know about. Did you know there is a black university in Philadelphia?"

Rose nodded. "I learned a little about it when I was at the Quaker School."

"They train teachers," Carrie added.

"I know." Rose smiled, reading her thoughts. "You're thinking it would be perfect if we could both be in school at the same time in Philadelphia."

"The thought crossed my mind," Carrie admitted.

Rose sighed. "I've thought about it every day since you got accepted into medical school. Moses isn't ready." She fought the surge of resentment and restlessness that surged up in her. "I have to be patient," she whispered.

"Something neither one of us is very good at."

"I'm not very good at it, but I love my husband. I love my children. I love my school." Her voice grew stronger as she stared at the still tightly furled wisteria blooms, smelling the fragrance already filling the air. "It may not be time for me to go to college, but it doesn't mean I can't be happy right here. I just have to choose to be." She heard the desperation in her voice. She whirled around and grabbed Carrie in a big hug. "I refuse to be unhappy. I refuse to be jealous. I can't choose when I go to school, but I can choose everything else."

Carrie held her tightly. "I'll send you every book I can get my hands on. And I'll write you every week." Her voice broke slightly. "I love you, Rose Samuels."

"And I love you, Carrie Borden," Rose responded. She stepped back. "We've already broken our promise to Robert about coming back quickly. We'd better get back to the house so you two can leave. It's not safe to be on the road to Richmond in the dark."

The two women walked back through the woods in silence. Everything that needed to be said had been said.

Abby slid her arm around Carrie's waist as the train moved slowly away from the Richmond station. "Are you okay?"

Carrie blinked back her tears as Robert waved his hand one last time. She lifted hers in return until the train rounded the bend, and then she slowly lowered it. After years of dreaming and hoping, and after months of preparing, she was actually on her way to medical school. To have Abby with her was more than she could have hoped for. "I still can't believe you're with me."

Abby smiled. "I'm so looking forward to going to the Women's Rights Convention in New York City. It will be wonderful to be with my friends the Stratfords again."

"You haven't been back since the riots three years ago, have you?"

Abby shook her head. "The war kept me too busy, and we put all women's rights issues on hold. This will be the first official meeting since the war ended. Mostly, I'm glad to get away from the factory for a little while. All the extra guards are driving me crazy. I can't move without someone watching me or going with me."

"Father is worried about you," Carrie responded. "As he should be. Jeremy told me about what happened."

"I told you what happened," Abby protested.

Carrie lifted a brow. "You told me the cleaned up version. I knew Jeremy would tell me the truth...which he got straight from Spencer."

Abby shrugged as her lips twitched. "I wasn't harmed."

"This time," Carrie scolded.

Abby stared at her. "You're hardly one to speak, daughter dearest," she said. "Just who was it that tempted bands of men by going to the black hospital?"

Carrie chuckled. "So you talk to Spencer, too. I guess we both have our stories."

"And we both are determined to do what we have to do, regardless of how other people respond to it."

"But surely you understand why Father has posted extra guards around the factory," Carrie protested.

"Certainly," Abby said calmly. "But that doesn't mean I have to like it. Any more than you liked having Hobbs accompany you everywhere you went during the war once Robert discovered what had happened."

"Point made," Carrie said with a laugh. "But it's all moot right now. Right this moment, we are two independent women on their way to Philadelphia. I'm so pleased you'll be there for five days before you head to New York." Memories assailed her suddenly, causing her smile to fade.

"Carrie?" Abby's voice was concerned.

"Do you realize it's been five years since we were together in Philadelphia for the first time?" Her mind rolled back to the first day she had met the slender, gray-eyed woman who was now her stepmother.

"We've lived a lifetime in those five years," Abby said softly. "We think we have the future all figured out, and then life takes over. All any of us can really do is go from one day to the next, trying to do the best we can. I still make plans, but I've gotten better about going with the flow when everything I've planned completely shifts."

"That's the secret isn't it?" Carrie asked.

Abby smiled. "The secret to peace? Yes," she agreed. "The older I've gotten, the more I realize every day, every single moment is simply a piece to a puzzle. I look for where something fits, but I have no idea of the entire picture. I just keep trying to fit pieces. When I insist on seeing the whole picture, I end up frustrated."

The train picked up speed, swaying as it chugged down the track. Deer stood poised at the edge of the woods, watching them with wide eyes before springing away. Fluffy cumulus clouds decorated the sky with shifting shapes.

"I can't wait to see Janie," Carrie said, her thoughts spinning forward to her new life in Philadelphia.

"And I'm sure she's counting the minutes," Abby assured her. "Now, my dear, you didn't answer my question back there," she said gently.

"Which one was that?" Carrie pretended ignorance, but she knew what Abby was referring to. She just had no clue how to respond.

The look in Abby's eyes said she recognized the pretense. "I asked you if you're okay with leaving Robert."

Carrie frowned when tears filled her eyes. "Don't you get tired of me crying?"

"Why would I get tired of you crying?" Abby asked in astonishment.

"I'm supposed to be a strong, independent woman," Carrie responded. "Shouldn't that bring with it a certain toughness that would preclude crying so much?"

"Do you think it should?" Abby asked carefully.

Carrie laughed suddenly. "I feel like it's five years ago and I'm eighteen again. You always asked me questions then, too."

Abby smiled, but her gaze was steady. "I really want to know. Do you think being strong and independent means you shouldn't cry? Do you want to be tough?"

Carrie considered the question. Finally she shook her head. "I know tough women," she said. "I don't really want to be like them."

"Do you think the tough women you know don't have feelings?"

Carrie thought carefully, sensing this was an important discussion. "I think everyone has feelings," she said. "I think they've just learned how to not show them."

"Why do you suppose that is?"

Carrie shook her head, impatient with the questions. "Does it matter?"

Abby narrowed her eyes. "I think it does."

Now it was Carrie's turn to ask the questions. "Why?"

Abby chuckled. "Turning the tables on me, are you?" Her expression turned serious. "I *do* think it matters. I've watched so many women become tough and hard. At first, I thought it was a necessary part of being strong and independent, or just an expected result of going through horrible times, but the more time I spent with those women, the more I realized I didn't want to live that way. I didn't want to shut down my emotions, and I didn't want to carry the guilt that tears are a sign of weakness."

"So you don't think they are?" Carrie was suddenly relieved.

"I think they're a sign of strength," Abby declared, laughing at Carrie's astonished expression. "Women have always cried more easily than men. I prefer to think it's because we are tenderer inside. Being strong and independent doesn't change that tenderness unless we let it. I want to live my life freely as a *woman*, not try to become a man in order to make my life easier. I believe that is the whole point of fighting for women's rights. It's not just about getting the vote," she said, staring out over the countryside. "It's about the right to live as a woman the way I want to live."

"You've thought about this a great deal," Carrie realized.

"I have," Abby agreed. "I love the fact that your heart feels deeply enough to shed tears. You and Rose have both kept that ability, even after all the horror you went through in the war. So many others have shut down their emotions because they believe it will protect them from pain."

"But it doesn't," Carrie murmured.

"No, it doesn't," Abby said softly. "You are getting ready to live your dream, but it is also going to carry pain. You're going to miss Robert every day. You're going to miss Rose and Moses. You're going to miss the plantation. You're going to miss the freedom to run Granite down the roads. You're going to miss driving into Richmond to visit your father and me."

Carrie blinked tears again, but this time she didn't brush them away. "I will miss it all," she said softly.

"It's okay to feel it," Abby said. "I already know you'll push through the pain to make the most of this new time in your life. There is no need to harden yourself. You may cry yourself to sleep a lot, but that's okay—even for a woman *doctor.*"

Carrie sighed and tightened her arm around Abby. "I am so grateful for you, you know."

"No more grateful than I am for you," Abby assured her. "You can be certain I'll find every possible excuse to visit Philadelphia so I can see you."

Philadelphia had suffered a brutal winter, but spring had erased all evidence. Carrie and Abby peered out the windows as they neared the Philadelphia station. Flowers bloomed in wild profusion from the window boxes on multi-storied brick homes. Oak limbs, clothed in bright green leaves, waved in the light breeze. Cherry trees sporting clumps of lustrous white blooms decorated the roadways and yards. Horses, delighted to be rid of the icy snow, pranced lightly as they pulled their carriages. Smiles were on almost every face.

Carrie's excitement dimmed as she thought of the restaurant explosion that had taken Sadie, Sadie Lou, Susie, and Zeke. She had seen Opal, Eddie, Amber Lou, and Carl for a short time before she left. She knew they were doing well and thriving, but she could still see the shadow of sadness lurking in their eyes. She knew it would be there for a long time.

She sat back for the last minutes of the train ride, watching as the residential area faded away into an industrial area belching black smoke into the clear air. When the station appeared, there was a large crowd waiting for the passengers. Carrie peered through the crowd, searching for Janie.

"Carrie! Abby!" Janie jumped up and down, waving her arms frantically, a big smile on her face.

"Janie!" Carrie cried, leaning out the window to return the wave. Everything slipped away as she recognized the beginning of a brand new life. She waited impatiently for the train to grind to a halt and then leapt off the steps. Moments later, she was in Janie's arms, happy tears streaming down both their faces.

"You're here! You're finally here!" Janie laughed through her tears. "It seems like forever since I saw you in December." She broke away from Carrie to give Abby a huge hug and then tugged them toward three women watching the reunion with broad smiles. "Come meet your housemates."

Carrie was delighted to meet Elizabeth, Alice, and Florence, and found herself immediately attracted to the strength and compassion she saw shining in all their eyes.

Florence tucked Carrie's hand in her arm and led the group toward the baggage platform. "I'm quite glad to see you're a mere mortal like the rest of us. Janie extols your virtues so often I think we were all a little afraid to meet you," she said mischievously, her blue eyes sparkling with fun.

"You may be quite appalled to find out how human I am," Carrie said cheerfully. A feeling of joy surged up in her so strongly it made her gasp.

"Carrie?" Janie asked, her face concerned. "Are you all right?"

Carrie stared at her, the joy pulsing in her heart. In spite of the fact that she was in the middle of a busy train station in sophisticated Philadelphia, she dropped her small suitcase and did a twirl on the platform, her arms raised to the sky. "I am so very happy to be here," she sang, laughing at the startled looks on the faces around her. Passing women stared at her as men cast baleful glares, aghast she was ignoring the protocols of proper female behavior. Carrie laughed even harder. Nothing mattered except the overwhelming feeling that after so many years of dreaming, hoping, and continual disappointment, she was actually about to start medical school.

After a moment of shocked silence, Florence added her own laughter, grabbed Carrie's hands, and did another twirl with her. "Come dance with us," she called to the other women. "We've already destroyed every societal norm by being in medical school. What's one more?"

Carrie watched in stunned disbelief as Abby, Janie, Elizabeth, and Alice grabbed hands and spun in a circle around them, laughter ringing through the air.

Abby smiled with appreciation as she entered her home, lifting her nose to sniff. "Do I smell soup?"

"Beef vegetable," Alice responded.

"And bread?" Carrie asked hopefully, her stomach growling with hunger.

"Four loaves put on the counter just before we left," Florence assured her.

Carrie pretended to swoon.

Janie laughed and carried one of her bags toward the stairs. "Let's get you and Aunt Abby settled before we eat."

"I'll unpack after dinner or in the morning. I tried not to bring too much."

Florence eyed the stack of suitcases. "If that's not too much, I would hate to see what too much *is!*"

Janie waved her hand. "I saw the look on the carriage driver's face when he picked them up." She turned to look at Carrie. "If I'm not mistaken, most of those suitcases are full of books."

"Guilty," Carrie responded lightly.

Florence groaned. "Janie was right then. You really *are* a paragon of virtue." She stared at the stack of suitcases, a look of dramatic dismay on her face. "You seriously have spent the last five years studying medicine?"

Carrie smiled and shrugged. "I find I'm rather passionate," she admitted.

"And you actually did surgery and served as a doctor during the war?" Elizabeth asked. "Janie didn't make that up?"

Carrie flushed with embarrassment. "I was an assistant."

"An assistant who actually assisted in surgeries and did work on her own when Dr. Wild wasn't around? An assistant who helped thousands of men that would have been without medication if you hadn't known herbal medicine that you learned from a slave on the plantation where you let all the slaves escape?" Alice demanded.

Carrie laughed helplessly. "I'm not sure how to answer."

"Honestly," Abby said firmly, stepping forward to put an arm around her waist. "You did *all* those things, Carrie. To try to pretend your experience was less than it was does nothing to promote the equality of women in this country. False modesty is a pointless virtue in my opinion."

Astonished silence fell on the room.

Abby smiled calmly. "I'm sorry to shock you, but I won't apologize for speaking the truth. I'm afraid my time in the South has made me even more impatient with women who refuse to do anything more than be what people expect them to be."

Florence found her voice first. "You mean what *men* expect them to be," she said. "You didn't shock us, Mrs. Cromwell, you awed us. We sometimes forget there are other women fighting the same battle we are. The struggle is sometimes very tiresome."

"You must call me Abby," Abby said quickly, and then grabbed one of Florence's hands. "And you wouldn't believe how many women are fighting this battle with you. You are most certainly not alone. The fight for women's equality took a back seat during the war, but it is coming front and center again. That's why I'm here. After a few days in Philadelphia, I'm headed to New York for the Eleventh National Women's Rights Convention."

"We know," Elizabeth said excitedly, exchanging a glance with her housemates. She winked at Carrie. "We'll get back to you later," she warned before she turned back to Abby. "We were hoping we could all go together."

Abby stared at her. "The convention? What about school?"

"Dean Preston believes we shouldn't miss it," Elizabeth responded.

"Dr. Ann Preston?" Carrie asked, her eyes wide. She wanted to hear more about the convention, but she wanted to know who was running her medical school even more. "I thought the dean was Dr. Fussell? He re-opened the hospital last year once the war ended."

"*Was* is the operative word there," Alice said, anger sparking in her eyes. "Our Dr. Fussell refused a medical degree to Mary Putnam Jacobi, even though she met the required qualifications. This caused quite a rift in the faculty because they disagreed with him."

"Quite dramatically," Elizabeth added.

"As they should have," Florence threw in indignantly.

"Anyway," Alice continued, "Dr. Fussell resigned after the beginning of the year. Dr. Preston has become the dean."

Abby smiled brilliantly. "Well done, Ann! That makes her the first woman dean of a medical school. How appropriate that it is a *women's* medical college. That's as it should be."

Carrie turned wondering eyes to her stepmother. "You know Dr. Preston?"

"Indeed I do," Abby agreed. "We worked in the Anti-Slavery Society together. She was privately educated in medicine by Nathaniel Moseley for two years. Of course, she couldn't get into a male medical school," she said, "so she entered the Female Medical College of Pennsylvania when it first opened."

"Dr. Preston was one of eight women awarded their MD in the first graduating class of 1852," Florence added. "How wonderful that you know her!"

"Ann went through so much during the war," Abby murmured.

Alice hesitated. "We heard Dean Preston got rheumatic fever during the war. We've been told she was so exhausted and sick that she was confined to a hospital for three months to recuperate."

"That's true," Abby confirmed. "Ann was determined your college would succeed. The male physicians here in the city barred women from their clinics and medical societies. Ann organized a board of lady managers to fund and run a teaching hospital so her students could gain clinical experience. Trying to come up with the money was quite a challenge, but Ann wasn't going to admit defeat. She walked door to door soliciting funds."

Carrie winced. "She must have endured horrible abuse and humiliation."

"That she did, but she raised a lot of money in spite of it. Her efforts took a toll on her. That's when she became ill with rheumatic fever." Abby paused. "You all know your school closed during the war. What you might not know is that Ann had raised enough money to send her friend and colleague, Dr. Emmeline Horton Cleveland, to

Paris to study obstetrics so she could be the resident physician at the new hospital."

"Dean Preston is amazing," Florence whispered. "So is Dr. Cleveland. I didn't know their stories. Thank you for telling us all that."

"I told you because I don't want you to feel alone," Abby replied. "There are so many women who have forged the path you are on right now. We've only begun, though. It is going to be up to all of you to widen the path and make it easier for everyone who will follow. Women in this country are going to be fighting for a very long time for equal rights."

A thoughtful silence fell among them as the shadows of women fighting for equality seemed to fill the room, marching down the corridors of time with determination and courage. Carrie breathed it all in, her sense of commitment and purpose growing along with her excitement.

"Now," Abby said briskly. "What is this about all of you going to the convention?"

Florence grinned. "Dean Preston says going to the convention is as important to our education as everything we are learning about medicine. She says if we're going to fight to enter what has always been an all-male world, then we need to do it with knowledge of how to accomplish it. We're also going to spend time in New York learning about the current cholera outbreak."

"Cholera *outbreak*?" Carrie whispered, sinking down onto the sofa. "I thought it was confined on the boat in the harbor? That was the last I heard."

"It was," Janie confirmed. "Once winter lifted, it was only a matter of time before it came on shore."

Carrie shook her head with dismay. "Cholera took so many lives the last time there was an outbreak in 1849." Her mind whirled with questions as she opened her mouth to ask them.

Florence stepped forward to grab one of Carrie's suitcases. "I realize we could all talk for hours, but I would much rather do it over soup and bread, not standing here in the foyer." She groaned as she lifted one of the suitcases. "Everyone grab a bag and we'll be done in one trip. Except you, Abby. Will you please go dish up the soup and slice some bread?"

Abby raised a brow. "Are you suggesting I'm too old to carry a suitcase up my own stairs?"

Florence grinned easily. "I would never do such a thing. What I'm suggesting is that any wise woman surrounded by women twenty years younger should take advantage of their years of experience and let *them* do the hard work."

Abby threw back her head in a hearty laugh. "I like you, Florence."

Carrie echoed her sentiments, knowing she had found a kindred spirit in the tall redhead.

"Since I'm wise enough not to admit to not being wise, I'm happy to let all you minions do the heavy lifting," Abby said smugly.

"Minions?" Alice cried. "Did you call us *minions*?" she demanded with a laugh.

Abby merely chuckled and disappeared into the kitchen.

Chapter Fourteen

Moses gazed around as the carriage rolled up to the Broad Street train station. Raindrops dripped from the eves of the building and glimmered on the street. It had rained all morning, but the sun had peeked out just before they left Thomas' house. Remnants of azaleas and dogwood trees still decorated the city. Their blooms were tired looking but still provided vivid splashes of color. Oak and maple trees were still clothed in the bright green of spring, but it wouldn't be long before they settled into the deep green of summer. Fresh coats of paint were going on some of the houses, but the majority still wore the stark poverty of the war years. This was his first time back in the city since early last summer. Progress was being made, but there was a long way to go.

"What do you think?" Robert asked.

"Of the city?" Moses responded. "I prefer the plantation." He thought of the endless green rows of tobacco poking their heads up from the earth, stretching as far as the eye could see. He could almost smell the rich soil. After years lying fallow during the war, every tillable acre on Cromwell Plantation was sporting new growth.

Robert nodded. "Me, too," he admitted. "It means a lot to Matthew that we're going to Memphis with him." He watched as Matthew entered the train station to buy their tickets.

"I know," Moses said. "I don't regret joining the two of you. I just find that, especially after the war, I prefer the quiet and beauty of the plantation."

"Who wouldn't?" Robert asked. "I'm glad you're going."

Moses watched the door to the station that Matthew had disappeared through. He had seen the haunted look in Matthew's eyes deepen as the anniversary of the *Sultana* disaster drew nearer. Just as all of them carried the horrors of the war, so did Matthew. The sinking of the *Sultana* and the senseless loss of so many lives had affected the tall journalist even more than his months in Libby Prison. When Matthew received a letter from Peter and Crandall suggesting they acknowledge the anniversary with a trip to Memphis, he had first resisted and then relented enough to consider it. Robert's urging, and his promise that both he and Moses would accompany him, had made Matthew decide to go. It was going to become a new chapter in his book.

"I'm glad, too," Moses said quietly. It was true, but it was also true that being back in Richmond had stirred a restless discontent inside him. He wanted to pretend he didn't see the tight tension on almost every black person's face. He tried to ignore the frustration and anger, and the faces of children. He tried to block out the disdain and hatred on white faces as black people walked the sidewalks, but the reality was rising in him like bile.

Matthew emerged from the building, three tickets held aloft. "We're all set," he called. "I have three first-class tickets for us."

Spencer swiveled on the carriage seat and stared back at Moses. "First class?" he asked. His expression was inscrutable.

"Will there be a problem?" Moses asked carefully.

Spencer hesitated and shrugged. "Maybe not," was all he said. His eyes said something different.

Moses stared at him hard and tried to prepare himself for whatever was going to happen.

"There won't be a problem," Matthew said, although he looked a bit uneasy.

The three men grabbed their luggage and walked over to the train platform. Moses held himself erect, his head lifted high as they climbed the steps to the loading platform. He was aware of eyes following him as he walked with Robert and Matthew.

Matthew stepped forward with the tickets. "Three first-class accommodations."

The conductor's eyes swept the three of them. His first response was evident discomfort, but it quickly hardened into disdain. "I'm afraid that's not possible," he said.

Matthew started to open his mouth, but Moses stepped forward. He didn't want someone else to speak for him. "I have a ticket for first-class accommodations," he said evenly.

The conductor seemed a little intimidated by his towering height, but his eyes glittered with something much too close to hatred when he stared up at him. "Blacks don't ride in first class."

Moses felt a flash of fury. "I have a ticket that says I do."

The conductor sneered. "Only because the ticket clerk didn't realize you're a nig...that you're black," he quickly corrected. "I saw you waiting in the carriage. Did you think you could sneak your way on, *boy*?"

Moses fought to control his temper, wanting nothing more than to smash his fist into the little man's face.

Matthew had heard enough. "Moses Samuels is a free man," he snapped. "He has a first-class ticket. He will ride with us in first class."

"Not unless you plan on changing the law in time to catch the train," the conductor responded smugly.

"The law?" Robert responded as he stepped forward, his eyes flashing. "What law? What are you talking about?"

"The blacks may all be free, but that doesn't mean they can socialize with proper white people," the conductor replied. "You ever heard of the Black Codes? Virginia may not have caught up with all the codes further south where people have more sense, but they make sure niggers don't ride on our trains." His voice was hard with contempt.

Moses' anger deflated beneath the harsh reality. He managed to keep himself erect, his face impassive, but his heart pounded with defeat...and something else he couldn't quite identify. It was something that churned and burned, demanding to be heard, but he couldn't discern what it was trying to say. It took every bit of his self-control not to turn around and stride off the platform, but he reminded himself the trip to Memphis wasn't about him—it was about his friend. He managed to keep his voice calm when he reached out to touch

Matthew's arm. "It's okay. Let's just get on the train so we can get to Memphis." He turned to the conductor. "What car do I ride in?" He refused to look down or away as he stared at the conductor.

"It's not okay," Matthew said angrily. He stepped in front of the conductor. "We will all ride in whatever car Moses will be in...*after* I get a refund for my first-class tickets."

The conductor jerked his thumb toward the back car. "Suit yourself. The train leaves in ten minutes."

Moses felt a flash of gratitude, but hard on the heels of the gratitude was a knowing of what he had to do. He strode after Matthew and Robert toward the ticket counter but stopped them before they walked inside. "Don't," he said quietly. He held up his hand when Matthew opened his mouth to protest. "I appreciate your willingness to ride with me, but your being there will make it impossible for me to talk to the other passengers."

"What?" Robert asked, confusion evident in his eyes.

Moses became more certain of what he needed to do as he thought about it. "I want to talk to *my people*," he said. "They won't talk as freely if there are two white men in the midst of them. I need to know what they are dealing with. I need to hear their stories." He wasn't sure why he needed to do it, but he felt more certain with every word that came out of his mouth.

"But—" Matthew protested.

Robert laid a hand on his arm to stop him. "Moses knows what he wants."

Moses flashed him a smile, grateful for the closeness they had developed since Robert had healed from his illness. "We'll be together as soon as we get to Memphis."

"Then at least let me apologize that there are such bigoted idiots in the white race," Matthew said, deliberately raising his voice so he would be heard. "You're a better man than anyone else on this platform."

Moses saw the conductor flush, but he also saw his eyes glitter with greater hatred as they settled on him. While he appreciated Matthew's support, he doubted it would do anything but create more trouble for him. He fought back a sigh as he picked up his bag and walked to the back of the train. He forced himself not to think of the relative comfort Matthew and Robert would experience during the long trip. He was already sure the car reserved for blacks would have little to offer in way of comfort, but perhaps it was going to offer something he hadn't expected.

Moses bit back his bitterness as the train pulled out of the station, black smoke blending with the dark gray clouds hovering overhead until it disappeared. He forced himself to relax, reminding himself he had suffered far greater humiliations when he enlisted in the Union Army as their first black spy. This was nothing in comparison.

"Who them white men you was with?"

Moses jerked his head around when the man in the narrow, cramped seat behind him spoke. "What?"

"Who them white men you was with?" the man repeated. His narrow face, creased with wrinkles, belied the bright sparkle in his eyes.

"They are friends," Moses replied. "We're on our way to Memphis." He had come back here so he could talk with other blacks. There was something about this man he liked. "My name is Moses."

"Name is Charlie," the old man said easily. "Them men really be friends?" he asked skeptically.

"Yes," Moses assured him, not sure he should go into details. He didn't have a need to talk; he wanted to listen. "Where are you headed, Charlie?"

"Nashville," Charlie responded. "Going to look for my wife."

"How long have you been separated?" Moses asked. He'd heard stories like this from so many.

"Twenty years," Charlie replied, the pain in his eyes contrasting with the smile on his face. "We were together on a plantation down in eastern Virginia for eighteen years. Our owner came up on hard times and had to sell most his slaves. He kept me, but he sold my wife and chilun. My chilun done all be grown by now. I ain't got no idea where they be. "

Moses winced, anger mixed with the pain that shot through him. "How did you find your wife?"

"Took me a lot of lookin'," Charlie admitted. He hesitated, a deep look of suspicion on his face. "You don't talk like no black man I know," he muttered.

"No," Moses agreed.

"Why not?"

Moses knew he would have to earn the man's trust. "I was a slave all my life. I was sold to a plantation outside of Richmond the year before the war started. My wife grew up as a slave there. She taught me how to read in a secret school out in the woods. She also taught me how to talk correctly. She told me it would make it easier to exist in a white world."

Charlie stared at him for a long moment. "You reckon it's done helped?"

"I reckon it has," Moses responded. "I was a spy for the Union Army for a few years before I headed up a battalion of soldiers."

"Do tell," Charlie said with a whistle, admiration shining in his eyes. "I sho 'nuff wanted to fight, but they done tole me I was too old. Sho was hard to sit it out. You got hurt?"

"Only if you consider a crater in my chest from a cannonball being hurt," Moses said casually, anxious to earn this man's trust so he would talk openly.

"And you lived to tell about it?"

"One of my closest friends was a doctor at Chimborazo Hospital. She saved my life. My unit brought me in right after Richmond fell." Moses held back his chuckle, knowing he was certain to get Charlie's attention with his statement.

"*She? Chimborazo Hospital?* That be a white hospital." Charlie's expression went from amazement to complete suspicion and then wavered back. He clearly had no idea what to think of what Moses was saying.

"Yep." Moses smiled. "Carrie Borden's father owned the plantation where I was a slave. He went into

Richmond before the war and left Carrie to run the plantation. Carrie helped me and my wife, Rose, escape through the Underground Railroad. Carrie became a doctor at the hospital during the war. She was there when my unit brought me in. I would have died without her."

A long silence stretched between them as Charlie stared into his eyes. "I do believe you be tellin' the truth, but that sho 'nuff be some kind of crazy story."

Moses smiled. "I can't disagree with that."

"What you doing now, Moses?" Charlie asked.

Moses decided that attempting to explain his relationship with Thomas Cromwell and the fact that he was half-owner of the plantation would be completely unbelievable. He didn't want to shatter the rapport he felt building. "I'm headed to Memphis with my friends."

Charlie nodded, not seeming to care if he knew more of the story. He was suddenly eager to tell his own. "My kids be all grown up now. I ain't sure where they be, but I found out through somebody in Richmond that my wife be out in Nashville. As far as I know, she ain't with no other man."

"Does she know you're coming?"

Charlie shook his head, his eyes revealing his hesitation. "I don't know nothin' 'bout sendin' no letter," he admitted. "I don't know how to read. I don't reckon my wife do either. What good be a letter?"

"Do you know where she lives?" Moses asked. He knew Nashville wasn't a small town.

"Done heard she lives with a sister down in the black part of town. I'm gonna look till I find her." Charlie's face twisted with emotion. "I sho 'nuff didn't figure I would ever see her again. I don't know for sho that I find her, but I sho 'nuff gonna try."

Moses had more information he wanted. "Have you lived in Richmond since the end of the war?"

"Pretty much. I came in from the master's place right before all them men got rounded up last summer and shipped back out to the country. I guess they left me alone 'cause I be so old. They didn't figur' I'd do them much good workin' in the fields again."

"How have you been living?" Moses asked.

Charlie shrugged. "I been stayin' here and there with folks. I been tryin' to get a job, but nobody wants me 'cause I'm so old. Folks been takin' pretty good care of me, though. Ever'body be stickin' together pretty good. I don't see many people full, but I don't see many starvin' either. We all knows we be in the same boat." He stared out the windows for a moment. "I left me some good friends in Richmond, but I want to see my wife again before I die. I done seen lots of families gettin' back together over the last year. I reckon I wouldn't mind none if it were me that had the smile on my face."

Moses put a hand on his shoulder. "I hope you find her, Charlie."

He looked around at the other people on the train. One in particular caught his attention. The piercing eyes focused on him indicated he had caught the other man's attention as well. He stood, gripping the seatbacks to steady himself against the swaying of the train, and walked back. "Mind if I sit down?"

"Nope."

Moses sat, studying the man who was eying him so intently. He liked the man's lean muscles, steady eyes, and calm expression. "I'm Moses."

"I'm Dillon."

Moses waited for him to say more, but he was met with only silence. "I'm heading out to Memphis," he prompted, hoping Dillon would give him more information. "Have you ever heard about the boat that went down outside of Memphis last year?"

Dillon's face twisted. "The *Sultana*."

"Yes. I'm heading out there with a friend who almost died when the boat exploded."

"One of the men you tried to board first class with?" Dillon asked bluntly.

Moses smiled. Dillon was obviously a careful observer. That meant he had heard everything he told Charlie. His gut told him Dillon also had a good reason to be so careful. "Yes. Matthew Justin is a journalist. He was traveling up the river with the returning soldiers from the prison camps."

"Andersonville," Dillon said bitterly.

"That's right," Moses said, sensing that the surface calm hid a churning cauldron. "You spend time there?"

Dillon sighed and seemed to relax some. "No. A bunch of men from my battalion were captured the last year of the war. They got sent to Andersonville." His face stiffened. "They all died."

Moses grimaced. "Over thirteen thousand men died there," he said. "Did you know the man who ran Andersonville, Henry Wirz, was found guilty of war crimes and hanged last November?"

Dillon nodded. "I heard. Seems to me he's about the only one that didn't get away with what he did. The rest of them highfalutin Confederate men seem to have gone back to their cushy lives." His eyes flashed angrily and took on a haunted look that quickly faded into blankness.

Moses watched him. "Where are you headed, Dillon?"

"North." Dillon's voice was now as emotionless as his eyes.

Moses had seen this before. Talk of Andersonville had triggered painful memories for Dillon. "Where in the North?" he probed, trying to bring his new friend back from the darkness.

"As far as I can go," Dillon said after a long silence. His eyes met Moses'. "I was stupid enough to think things would be better after the war. I thought if I helped win our freedom, that life would be better."

Moses waited quietly. He understood what the man was feeling all too well.

Dillon's eyes took on a new level of raw pain. "They came for us."

Moses waited, but Dillon seemed to have turned inward. "Came for you? What do you mean?"

Dillon eyes turned wild and feral. He clenched his fists as his face seemed to melt with agony. "A bunch of white men," he ground out. "Last month, I was down in North Carolina with my family. I had walked into town through the woods to get some supplies. When I was almost home, I heard a bunch of horses coming from the direction of my house..." His eyes glazed over as his voice faltered.

Moses felt sick. He knew what was coming.

"I jumped into the woods," Dillon continued. "A group of white men galloped by. They was laughing and talking like they ain't just done something horrible." He shook his head. "I knew even before I got there. My wife and kids..." His voice faltered again. "They'd been beat to death." His shoulders shook with silent sobs. "They done left me a note saying I best get out of the South or they would come back for me."

Moses' heart ached and filled with a fury so intense it almost choked him. "I'm sorry," he managed. Right on the heels of his words was a fear of what could happen to Rose and the rest of his family while he was gone. He tightened his fists as he battled his feelings.

"You got a family, Moses?" Dillon asked hoarsely.

"A wife and two children," Moses responded, trying to speak evenly.

"You ought to leave the South," Dillon hissed. "It ain't gonna do anything but get worse."

Moses saw the flames devouring the school and saw the fear on everyone's face. He fought to think clearly. "They passed the Civil Rights Act," he said. "Congress is fighting to make things better." He winced when he realized how little confidence he had in those facts.

Dillon watched him with something akin to pity. "Can't no law stop hatred," he said. "Me? I'm going north to look for work. There ain't nothing left to keep me down here. People in the South forced me to live as a slave most all my life. Now they done killed ever'body I loved. I wish I had been there so they could have killed me, too, but I weren't so lucky."

Moses searched for something to say, but he knew there were no words that would make any difference. He reached out and put his hand on Dillon's shoulder for a long moment. Dillon's eyes thanked him, but it did nothing to erase the pain on his face.

The two men sat quietly. Moses took deep breaths, beginning to see the shadow of an outline that was trying to give shape to his rampaging thoughts and feelings.

Matthew and Robert had passed the first hours in silence, both content to sit with their thoughts. The clouds had cleared, leaving a golden sun to kiss the tops of the mountains as they drew closer to the foothills. Rivers, swollen with melting snow and recent rains, gushed beneath the wooden bridges they crossed, newly rebuilt in the year since the war ended. They passed plenty of empty, barren fields, but they were now patch-worked with vibrant green fields bringing life back to the scorched Shenandoah Valley.

"Lots of memories," Matthew finally murmured.

Robert nodded, too buried in haunting thoughts to even attempt to communicate with words.

"Has it gotten easier?" Matthew pressed.

Robert considered the question, sensing his friend was asking for *himself* as much as he was asking about him. Both of them had suffered so much through the war. "Easier? I don't know. I live with the memories better, at least on the plantation. Being back here...remembering all the battles...all the lives lost..." His voice faltered. He stared out the window until he felt control return. "I'm alive. The nightmares aren't as bad. I chose not to die," he said thoughtfully. "I guess that means it's a little easier."

"I suppose that's all we can ask for," Matthew agreed. "Libby Prison was a hellhole, but it's one I escaped. I guess that is what makes it easier. The *Sultana*? It was a senseless destruction of lives that should never have happened. Sometimes I can't tell the difference between my grief and my anger."

Robert nodded. He understood all too well. He picked his words carefully. "I guess I have found a measure of peace in knowing there are no answers. I used to try to make sense of it. I tried to understand all the reasons for the war. I thought that would help."

"It doesn't," Matthew said. "I tried to make sense of everything for my readers every day, but in the end, I realize none of it makes sense. We are simply left to attempt to live our lives in the wake of a handful of people's decisions. I did the best I could to clarify issues, and I hoped I could compel people to take action if they disagreed with something, but in the end, I have no control of anything."

"We simply do the best we can," Robert agreed. "I love life on the plantation because there are many days I can pretend we never had a war. I don't think about battles, or being paralyzed, or almost dying." He took a deep breath. "I work with the horses, I teach Clint and Amber, and I breathe fresh air. That's all I really want."

"It's a good life," Matthew said.

"It is, except that I miss Carrie every moment of every day." His heart tightened as he thought of his beautiful wife. He missed her laughing green eyes and the way she understood what he was feeling even before he said anything. "It's been only two weeks since she left, but it seems like forever."

"Do you regret her going to medical school?" Matthew asked.

"Not even for a moment," Robert responded, "but that doesn't mean I don't miss her. It seems we've been apart more than we've been together since we married."

"It seems that way because it's true."

Robert sighed. "I remember when I first met Carrie. I fell in love with her almost immediately. I thought life would be so simple. We would get married, return to Oak Meadows, and raise a family."

"And then the war happened."

Robert shrugged. "Even if the war hadn't happened, life would never have been the way I dreamed it would be. Carrie is not a plantation wife. She has always wanted more than that. I got a letter from her right before we left. She loves being in Philadelphia. She loves her new housemates. They are all going to the Women's Rights Convention in New York." He wasn't surprised when Matthew cocked his brow at his tone. He frowned with frustration. "Is it wrong that I struggle with my wife's insistence on independence?"

"Is it?" Matthew asked, his eyes watching him keenly.

Robert shook his head. "I'll never stand in her way, because I love her too much. I can't help wishing, though, at least sometimes, that she was content with staying on the plantation. It would certainly make life simpler."

"I understand how you feel."

"Do you?" Robert asked sharply, hating the tone of his voice, but his surging emotions made it impossible to sound reasonable. "Do you really? Sometimes I think it would have been better for Carrie if she had fallen in love with you instead of me."

Matthew gazed at him steadily. "This isn't about any feelings I have for Carrie. It's about the fact that she loves you with all her heart. I know it ripped her in two to leave you on the plantation, but she is following something inside of herself that is bigger than she is. I know what women in medical school go through. It takes more than a casual desire to put up with the abuse they take on a regular basis. She's choosing to be a doctor because it's who she *is*. She would not be the woman you love if she shoved aside her own desires to stay on the plantation with you. It would make her less than she is."

Robert sighed heavily. "I know," he admitted. "I'm sorry for what I said. Can we chalk it up to a moment of weakness and forget it?"

Matthew smiled easily. "If our friendship endured a war that put us on opposite sides, I'm certain we can handle a conversation."

A sudden commotion at the front of the car grabbed both their attention.

Chapter Fifteen

"If things don't change, Memphis will be destroyed!" a man shouted angrily. He leaned over his seat and shook his fist at a man in the seat behind him, his generous girth straining against his elegant jacket as dark eyes flashed beneath iron gray hair. "And it will be your fault, John Eaton. That poor excuse of a newspaper that you publish is going to be the end of all that is good about Memphis!"

Robert stretched forward to see the man being verbally attacked, and was immediately impressed by the steady dark eyes beneath a wave of dark hair. John Eaton's face was covered by a salt and pepper mustache and a beard that hung down almost to his chest. He gazed calmly at his attacker.

"I hardly think one newspaper can destroy Memphis, Alfred."

Alfred's face grew even redder as he continued to shake his fist. "Your kind is doing all it can to destroy the city I helped found forty years ago. If it were up to you, I think you would want nothing but niggers filling the street."

"From what I can tell, it's not the blacks creating problems in Memphis," Eaton responded. "You might look to the Irish running your government and police, or to the conservatives who are trying to deny basic human rights to all those who now call Memphis home."

Robert leaned over to Matthew. "Do you know this man?"

Matthew nodded, his eyes locked on John Eaton. "He's the owner and chief editor of the *Memphis Daily Post*, one of the city's two Republican newspapers. He's not been in the city very long."

Alfred was still ranting. "All that is good about the South has been destroyed," he shouted. He pointed suddenly out the window.

Robert followed his pointing finger. Huddled by the side of the tracks, tucked against the woods, were groups of blacks gathered around campfires, laughing and talking as they ate.

"Look at them poor niggers," Alfred snapped. "Everybody knows they can't take care of themselves. They call that *freedom*? They think Yankees have come down here and done something good for them, but they're forgetting the Southern people were always their best friends."

"Friends don't make their friends slaves," Eaton said blandly.

Alfred scowled. "The niggers have always needed someone to take care of them. We were doing them a favor."

"That's a dead argument," Eaton responded, his eyes flashing but his voice calm. "The blacks are no longer slaves. They are free people who are close to getting the rights they deserve. You *are* aware the Civil Rights Act passed, aren't you?"

Alfred shook his fist again. "They can pass whatever blasted law they want to pass. Memphis is *our* city, and we're going to treat the niggers the way we want to treat them. We don't need all of them crowding our city. We certainly don't need all the Yankees cluttering our streets, and the missionaries have done nothing but create problems ever since they arrived with their ridiculous plans of educating the niggers. They're doing nothing but putting foolish ideas into their heads."

Eaton smiled. "Are you aware of how many blacks are in school? Are you aware of how many are working? They aren't *cluttering your streets*, Alfred. They're helping to create a city we can all be proud of. You would see that if you weren't so stuck in your *Old Citizen* ways. You may have helped found Memphis, but it's going to take everyone in the city to move it into the future."

Alfred's face grew bright red as his Adams apple pressed against his starched shirt. He sputtered, searching for words to continue the attack.

Matthew took advantage of the break in the action to fill Robert in on what he knew. "John Eaton is on the executive committee of the Union Republican Party of Memphis that was created just this month. They are staunch believers that all men are created equal, and they believe the federal government has a duty to protect citizens' rights."

At the front of the train car, Alfred seemed to have run out of steam, at least for the moment. He sank down in his seat, his face set in angry lines.

"Eaton was a brevet brigadier general in the Union Army during the war," Matthew continued. "He started out as a teacher and public school administrator and then went into the ministry."

"The ministry?" Robert echoed.

"When he went to war, he went as a chaplain, not a soldier. In 1862, he was appointed to oversee the care of thousands of runaway slaves who had made it to the lines of Grant's Army in west Tennessee and north Mississippi."

"A contraband camp," Robert murmured, thinking of everything Rose had told him about the Grand Contraband Camp where she taught.

"Yes. He ran the camp for the rest of the war and then joined the Freedmen's Bureau in Washington, DC. He decided he could better serve the Union by publishing a Republican newspaper here in Memphis, so he gathered enough investors to finance it. He and his wife moved here late last year."

"There are obviously people not pleased to have him," Robert observed wryly.

Matthew chuckled. "If I've learned anything during this time, it's that no matter what you believe, someone is not going to like it."

Alfred jumped up again, his face bright red. This time he waved a paper that had been passed to him by another man. "You say in your supposed newspaper that you don't believe the South deserves readmission into the Union! What kind of nonsense is that?"

"As long as there are people in the South who are being denied their rights, the South has proven they are not ready for readmission."

"Those niggers are causing us nothing but grief!" Alfred shouted.

"I'd say you're the ones who have caused the *blacks* grief," Eaton returned. "You might remember all the white predictions about the effects of emancipation. You were so certain the blacks would murder their former masters. The only murders taking place are whites murdering the blacks." His voice rose. "You predicted the blacks wouldn't work. The crops last year were less than usual, but it was the blacks, who were only partially paid and given little freedom, who brought the crops in."

"That's all they're good for," Alfred sputtered, his bluster deflating as Eaton met his statements with facts he couldn't refute.

"No," Eaton continued. "They are gifted farmers, but they're capable of so much more if given the chance to accomplish it."

Angry murmurs rose in the train car as others listening in began to voice their opinions.

"You Yankee Republicans are the cause of our problems," another man called. "You'll find we have ways of getting rid of what doesn't belong in our city."

Robert leaned over to Matthew. "Eaton doesn't seem bothered by the threat," he said quietly, watching the publisher with admiration.

Matthew shrugged. "He knew what he was getting into when he came here. I imagine he's heard much worse," he said, but his eyes were full of sympathy as he watched Eaton.

Alfred had regained his steam now that he knew he wasn't alone. "You'll find those of us who created this city still wield a great deal of influence. We may have lost our slaves, and our Confederate bonds may be worthless, but we still have our property. That counts for more than you know," he said arrogantly.

"And you still dominate the ranks of Memphis lawyers, doctors, and newspaper publishers," Eaton said agreeably. "Which begs the question: Why are you so threatened by a dissenting voice, Alfred? I find I am greatly curious why the less fortunate white people in Memphis are so eager to follow the very men who led them into a disastrous war." His eyes swept the car, resting briefly on Robert and Matthew. "I realize this is a Southern phenomenon, but I suspect time will dilute your influence. Whether you like it or not, things are changing. Right now there may just be glimmers of change, but time will fix that."

"Don't count on it!"

Robert watched as a stout, muscular man stood and glared back at Eaton. His accent easily identified him as Irish.

"Me and the boys are getting real tired of all the niggers in our city. We got plans to take care of the problem." His voice was quiet, but his eyes were dangerous.

Robert stared in fascination at the blue eyes that glittered like dark orbs.

Eaton stiffened, but his voice remained calm. "What are you and the rest of the Memphis police planning, Connor?"

"I won't be telling you nothing you can put in that paper of yours, Eaton," Connor drawled nastily. "You'll know about it once it happens."

Alfred's anger wasn't reserved just for Eaton. He turned on Connor. "It's not enough to destroy our city government with Irish incompetence?" he taunted. "You and your *boys* took office simply because we were disfranchised from the vote after the war. You Irish have made a mockery of our city. We may have a problem with the niggers, but whatever you have in mind will certainly not fix it," he added haughtily. "The Irish are hardly better than the niggers. You are inferior, disgusting, crude, and ignorant. Not to mention the fact that you're undisciplined, drunken, untrustworthy, and violent. We'd do well to get rid of all of you, as well."

Connor flushed with rage as he lifted his fists and advanced on Alfred. "You're about to find out first-hand just how violent we can be," he growled.

Alfred took a step back, his face paling as he realized he had provoked a fight he would certainly lose. He gazed wildly around the car, but no one stood to come to his aid.

Eaton was the one to restore calm. "Fighting him won't resolve anything, Connor," he said, standing to step in front of the advancing Irishman. "Better to report what he said to the authorities and let them keep an eye on him. Regardless of what he says, you're the one with power in Memphis."

Alfred opened his mouth to protest but closed it quickly when his face registered the knowledge that Eaton was saving him from a beating.

"I should beat him to a bloody pulp," Connor snapped.

"I understand the feeling," Eaton responded, a flash of humor in his eyes, "but when all is said and done, his words are nothing but hot air."

Robert chuckled as he saw the frightened rage racing across Alfred's face. "He's skewering him at the same time he is saving him," he muttered with admiration.

Matthew nodded. "I'd heard he was a brilliant man. I'm seeing evidence of it myself."

When the long trip ended, Matthew and Robert had just stepped onto the platform to go in search of Moses when Eaton approached them.

"You're the ones who tried to get your black friend on board back in Richmond."

"That's right," Matthew replied. "I was very impressed with how you handled everything with those men in the train car. If you ever decide to leave the newspaper business, you might want to try politics." He smiled as he reached out to shake Eaton's hand. "My name is Matthew Justin."

Eaton's eyes widened. "The journalist who was on board the *Sultana* when it exploded? I've read everything you wrote about it."

"Yes," Matthew admitted, surprised Eaton had any idea who he was.

"And what are you doing back in our city?"

"It's been almost a year since the explosion. I've come to write a follow-up article." Not wanting to go into detail about his need to lay some ghosts to rest, he nodded his head toward Robert. "This is Robert Borden, my best friend. He served as an officer in the Confederacy and also helped me escape Libby Prison."

Eaton grinned. "You do know how to lay the foundation for a great story." His eyes flashed between the two men. "Where are you staying?"

"We don't know yet," Matthew replied. "We're about to search for a hotel." He raised his hand and waved when he saw Moses, relieved to see he looked fine after the long trip.

"Come stay with me," Eaton offered. "All three of you," he said firmly when Moses walked up. "I have plenty of room, and I can guarantee we have a lot to talk about."

Matthew shook his head. "There aren't just three of us. I'm meeting two other colleagues coming in early tomorrow."

Eaton shrugged. "My wife and I have plenty of room. It would be an honor to have all of you stay."

Matthew saw agreement in Robert's eyes and then turned to Moses. "What do you think?"

Moses smiled easily at Eaton and reached out to shake his hand. "I appreciate the offer, but I have other plans."

Matthew stared at him. "Other plans?"

Moses nodded. "I met some fellow soldiers on the train ride. They asked me to stay in the fort with them. Most of them will be mustered out at the end of the week, but they are still living in the fort for now." The confused looks on Robert's and Matthew's faces told him he needed to explain more in depth, but he didn't know the man who had just invited them to stay. He would keep what he had learned to himself.

Eaton stepped forward, sensing his hesitation. "My name is John Eaton. I'm the publisher and chief editor of the *Memphis Post.*"

"Nice to meet you," Moses said evenly. "My name is Moses Samuels." He appreciated the warm light in the man's eyes, but he had learned too much on the train ride to talk openly with a newspaperman. He kept his face stoic while his mind raced.

Eaton stepped back with an easy smile. "None of you have any reason to trust me or talk with me, but I believe I can do a great deal to help you during your stay in Memphis." His expression grew serious. "Memphis is a powder keg right now. It's just a matter of time before it explodes." He locked eyes with Moses. "I don't know that you're safe down in the black part of town," he said bluntly.

"Probably not," Moses agreed, "but that is where I will be." He had thought carefully before saying he would stay in the fort. He was quite sure he would be safer at Eaton's home, but everything in him was telling him he was not in Memphis for safety. He didn't know what was going to happen, but he knew he needed to be in the midst of it. He longed to explain more to Robert and Matthew, who were watching him with grave concern, but now was not the time.

"Then at least let me take all of you to lunch," Eaton insisted. "It's best you know as much as possible."

Moses considered the offer. "I appreciate it." He could gather information without giving anything away. "Let me tell my new friends. I'll be back in a few minutes." He could feel Robert and Matthew's eyes on his back as he walked away.

Roy and Harry watched Moses as he walked back. "You still coming?"

Moses smiled. He understood their suspicions. "I am, but first I'm going to have lunch with my friends."

Harry frowned, his long, narrow face scarred by a whip during his years of slavery in Mississippi. He exchanged a skeptical look with Roy, a much shorter, stocky man with a ready smile and suspicious eyes. "That right?"

Moses held his gaze. "I learned a long time ago that knowledge can go a long way toward evening the scales in a fight. John Eaton, the older man, is the editor of the *Memphis Post*. You have my word I won't say anything about what we have discussed, but I may get some information that will help us."

"I know who Eaton is," Harry replied. "As far as I can tell, he be a good man. He seems to be fair, and his newspaper don't make up all the nonsense stirrin' up the trouble, but I ain't in much of a mood to trust."

Moses wasn't either, but he was also aware it would take both white and black people to fix what was going on in Memphis...as well as the rest of the country. He glanced at Robert and Matthew, who were watching him. Their friendship was the only thing giving him the ability to trust after what he had learned during the long trip. He wanted to introduce them to Roy and Harry, but he didn't want to do anything to put them in more jeopardy. "I'll be at the fort this afternoon," he promised.

"Make sure you get there before dark," Roy growled, his face tight with doubt. "Ain't no black man oughta be out on the streets after dark, especially one as big as you."

"I'll be there," Moses replied, searching for something to say that would reassure him. "You don't have a reason to trust me, but you can."

Roy scowled and then forced his mouth into a smile. "I know we can, Moses. We heard enough of your stories. You know what it like to be a black man. Go see if you can find out somethin' to help us, but be careful. Especially around them Irish police. They don't need an excuse to come after you. You going into the white part of town is like an invitation to get you."

"I'll be careful." Moses shook hands with both of them and then walked back over to the group of men waiting for him. He chose to ignore the questions in Robert and Matthew's eyes. Now was not the time for explanations.

Matthew gazed around the store they were walking through as they made their way to a restaurant tucked in the back. Large framed photos of Robert E. Lee, Stonewall Jackson, and Jefferson Davis adorned the walls of the shop. He shook his head when he saw decks of playing cards featuring the engraved portraits of fifty-two Confederate generals. He leaned closer to inspect a volume of poems and songs composed in the South during and right after the war. The store was a true testament to the Lost Cause.

Eaton followed his eyes. "Whenever a band strikes up 'Dixie' you will hear cheers."

"How about 'Yankee Doodle'?" Matthew asked sardonically.

Eaton shrugged. "Don't be surprised if you hear hisses. Yankees are less than popular around here."

"Southerners don't take defeat well," Robert observed.

"They shouldn't have started a war then."

"True," Robert agreed with a grin. "Don't think I'm going to start a fight with you. I had quite enough of that during the war. I'm simply making an observation."

"Refreshing," Eaton said, eying him thoughtfully. He led them into the restaurant, choosing a table in the back of the room beside a window overlooking the streets.

Matthew smiled. He recognized the strategy. The noises from the street would do much to cover up their conversation in the crowded, loud restaurant. His smile faded when he saw the glares aimed at Moses, who was the only black man in the restaurant. "Is this safe for Moses?"

Eaton nodded reassuringly. "As safe as any place," he said as he settled down at the table, his back to the window so he could watch the doors. "The men here in the restaurant are not the ones you need to worry about. They are all hot-headed conservatives who would like nothing better than to rid Memphis of all Republicans and blacks, but so far they seem to be content with trying to urge boycotts that never seem to take shape because everyone loves a good bargain. They turn up their noses, avert their eyes, and glare a lot, but that seems to be the extent of it."

"Yet you're worried," Matthew said. He was aware Moses was watching Eaton carefully. He wished he could get inside his friend's head, but Moses' shuttered eyes gave nothing away. Years of abuse during slavery had taught him how to shut down. He would not reveal anything until he was ready.

Eaton frowned. "Yes, I'm worried. I told you Memphis is a powder keg. Right now the explosive tension is between the Irish and the blacks."

"The Irish?" Robert asked in surprise. "Why?"

"They believe they have something to prove," Eaton responded. "About twenty percent of our population is Irish."

"Close to seven thousand residents," Matthew commented.

"Yes. The majority of them emigrated during the potato famine. Most of them were laborers with no property, or they were very marginal landholders in Ireland. When they got to America they were impoverished, poorly educated, and unskilled. Almost all of them are Catholic, meaning they stand out in an overwhelmingly evangelical Protestant society." He glanced out the window as a small group of Irish policemen strolled by. "They work hard for paltry wages, they drink hard when the workday is done, and they pray hard on Sundays."

"So why such tension with the blacks?" Robert asked.

"They retain their love for Ireland, but they are also eager to become American citizens. They have embraced their American identity as fervently as their Irishness. Most of them are rabid Democrats, and they have adopted an especially fierce strain of the racism they learned here in the South."

Eaton stopped talking when their waiter approached. "I recommend the beef stew," he advised. When everyone nodded, he placed the order all around and went back to his explanation. "There are a few well-educated and affluent Irishmen in Memphis, but most of them earn their poverty-level wages through manual work."

"The same work the blacks are doing," Matthew observed. He knew of the tension that had existed before the war, but his time in Memphis during the war was limited to his recovery in the hospital after the explosion. He pulled his thoughts back from flashing images of the explosion and bloated corpses on the waterfront and forced himself to focus.

"Exactly," Eaton replied. "Unfortunately, the Irish also hold the positions of power in Memphis. Our mayor is Irish, many of the councilmen, most of the policemen and the firemen." He answered Matthew's next question before he could ask it. "By state law, anyone who aided the Southern rebellion could not vote in the municipal general election last year. Most of the Irishmen in Memphis declined to fight in the war, and by the time Confederate conscription was in place, Memphis was already in the hands of the Union. When the war ended, most of the native Memphians couldn't vote. The twenty-five hundred voters were predominantly Irish."

"They voted the Irish into office," Matthew stated, the picture becoming clearer as the pieces fit into place.

"Yes. And then those elected officials appointed many more to municipal positions," Eaton added.

"Like the police," Moses said, speaking for the first time since they left the station. His eyes shone intensely as the picture of what he and his new friends had talked about began to form in his mind.

"Like the police," Eaton agreed, turning his attention to Moses. "The police chief is a native Southerner and longtime Memphian, but one hundred sixty-two of his hundred seventy-seven men are Irish."

"Is that a problem?" Matthew asked, watching Moses. He would help him get the information he was evidently after.

"Yes," Eaton responded bluntly. "Chief Garrett has done his best to professionalize the force, but the good old boys' club is in full swing throughout his superiors. There are a large number of policemen who are really nothing but incompetents, drunkards, loafers, thugs, or crooks." He nodded his head toward a group of policemen entering a local saloon. "Many of our fine police spend more of their on-duty hours in the saloons than they do on the streets."

"The city can't do anything?" Robert asked.

"We're trying. Our woefully unprofessional police force is one of the few things both Republican and Democratic newspapers agree on. The complaints have made it to Nashville. They're close to passing a bill that would take control of the Memphis police away from the city government and vest it in a board appointed by the governor."

"The mayor doesn't care what is happening with the police force?" Matthew asked.

"Our *mayor* is a drunk," Eaton said. "I've heard that at one time he was competent, but he seems to live in the bottle now. You very rarely see him when he is not inebriated."

Matthew whistled, quickly adding up what he was hearing. "So you're afraid the Irish police are going to ignite trouble with the blacks, and you don't believe anyone will be able to stop it."

"Yes." He looked at Moses. "You need to be careful while you are here."

"I'm careful everywhere," Moses said, his eyes flashing with resentment.

Matthew peered at him, seeing something in Moses' eyes he hadn't before. He exchanged a long gaze with Robert, knowing he was seeing the same thing.

"The trouble goes back to before the war," Eaton continued. "Before the war started, the Irish had to compete with slaves whose masters hired them out for the same work they did. The Irish made no secret of their resentment, and the blacks repaid it in full. The only thing that kept the violence under control was the power of the masters. It seems they would not tolerate abuse of their slaves by anyone but themselves," he said with disgust, his eyes flashing his sentiment.

"Now that we're free, they don't worry about that," Moses said.

"True. In addition, the black population has multiplied, which has made it more of a problem to the Irish." Eaton eyed Moses. "You said back there you were a Union soldier?"

"I was," Moses said carefully, his face closing down again.

Eaton smiled. "You have nothing to worry about from me. From the way I saw those men at the station looking at you, I figured you had done something to earn their respect. They are careful men."

"With reason," Moses replied evenly.

"With reason," Eaton agreed. "The presence of black troops in Memphis has added a particularly volatile fuel to the fire. The Irish are incensed that blacks have any authority over them."

"We saw that in Richmond, too," Matthew said. Moses had experienced it firsthand, but Matthew knew he didn't want to talk about it. His concern for whatever his friend had in mind was growing.

Eaton frowned. "I suspect it would be a problem anywhere in the South, but I believe I am objective enough after my travels to say it is the worst I've ever seen here in Memphis." His frown deepened as his gaze swept the crowded street. "I believe there will be a racial explosion very soon. I can feel it in the air." He turned back to the three men. "You may have picked a very bad time to come to Memphis."

As he looked out on the streets, Matthew could sense danger in the air. He suspected any newsman could, but he had developed a sense for it that, unfortunately, was never wrong. As he glanced toward the horizon, the river glistening below, he had the grim realization that this trip wasn't going to be about the sinking of the *Sultana*. His skin prickled as the sense of foreboding deepened.

Chapter Sixteen

Carrie trembled with excitement when their train pulled into New York City. When she left home two weeks earlier, she had never dreamed she would be coming to America's largest city. The plantation, and her life there, felt a million miles away.

"Pinch me," Janie murmured as her head swiveled to catch everything.

Carrie obliged with a grin.

Janie yelped and returned her grin. "Can you believe it? New York City! And we have ten whole days before the Women's Conference convenes on May tenth."

Florence frowned. "You'll like Philadelphia even more once you've experienced New York City," she predicted.

"You don't like the city?" Abby asked. "I've been here a few times, but my experience is limited."

"It's not my favorite place," Florence admitted. "I came here with my parents when I was a child. It seemed wonderful and exciting then, but the last twenty years have changed it. The city has done a poor job of responding to its rapid growth from immigrants."

Elizabeth eyed Abby. "You were here during the draft riots three years ago, weren't you?"

"I was," Abby agreed, pain filling her eyes.

"I heard it was terrible," Alice said sympathetically.

When Abby only nodded, Carrie knew she wasn't going to tell the other girls about the terrible ordeal she had suffered. "Didn't you say Dr. Benson is joining us for dinner tonight?"

Abby glanced at her with gratitude when she changed the subject. "Yes. Dr. Benson and his lovely wife, Elsie."

"Isn't Dr. Benson on the new Metropolitan Board of Health?" Florence asked with excitement, grinning when Abby nodded. "I was so hoping we would be able to speak with someone who is working to clean up the city. To say it's beyond time would be putting it mildly."

Carrie watched Abby while the other women talked excitedly. Abby had told her the whole story about the draft riot late one night when everyone had gone to bed. The flickering flames of the fire seemed to have given her the courage to tell the harrowing tale. Abby and Dr. Benson had stayed in contact since the deaths and destruction of the riot connected them.

Abby raised her hand and waved at one of the carriage drivers lined up on the curb. The long line of conveyances ran the gamut from simple to wildly luxurious. The carefully appointed carriage that pulled away from the curb revealed the wealth of the Stratford family. "Paxton!" she called.

The carriage pulled to a stop in front of them, and a ruddy-faced man jumped down from the seat. "Mrs. Livingston!" he said. "It's a pleasure to see you again."

"And you, as well, Paxton," Abby said sincerely. "But my last name is no longer Livingston. I married last year. My last name is Cromwell now."

"Congratulations," Paxton said cheerfully. "You look wonderful, so marriage must be agreeing with you."

"I'd like you to meet my stepdaughter, Carrie Borden."

"It's a pleasure, Mrs. Borden," Paxton said formally.

Abby quickly made the rest of the introductions. Carrie watched Paxton carefully. His smile and manner were impeccably professional, but he wore grief like a cloak. She could tell by the look in Abby's eyes that she saw the same thing, but she knew Abby wouldn't question him in front of everyone.

Paxton loaded the luggage, settled everyone in the carriage, and took his seat. With a raise of his reins, the horse moved forward willingly.

Carrie appreciated the gleaming shine of the bay's coat but was equally aware of the poor condition of many of the other horses lined up along the station curb. Dull hair, exposed ribs, and listless eyes spoke of poor care. She scowled with anger when she saw how many whips were being brandished. Already, she was disenchanted with New York City.

She watched as a driver stood up in his carriage and began to mercilessly lash the poor horse standing trapped by the heavy harness. Carriages in front and behind made it impossible for him to move.

"Stop!" Carrie cried, anger and pain causing her heart to pound as she saw the miserable fear in the horse's eyes. She reached up to grab Paxton's arm. "Paxton, stop right this minute!"

Paxton shot a look at Abby and then pulled back on the reins. "Ain't nothing you can do, Mrs. Borden."

"You watch me!" Carrie vowed, jumping from the carriage and running across the road, narrowly avoiding being run over by another carriage. She reached the horse that was being beaten and raised her hands. "Stop right this minute!" she yelled, fury checking the tears that wanted to flow down her cheeks at the horse's pitiful condition.

"What's wrong with you, lady?" the driver growled, raising the whip again.

Carrie was poised to jump up into the carriage to stop him, when she felt Paxton by her side.

"Stop it, Lyle," Paxton ordered. "You done driven that horse to death."

Lyle smirked and slashed forward with the whip again.

Another lash mark scoured the horse's side. "No!" Carrie cried, searching her mind for a way to stop the man. Suddenly, Abby, Janie, Elizabeth, Alice, and Florence were all standing with her, scowling up at the brutal driver.

The watching carriage drivers began to laugh. The driver's face reddened with anger and humiliation as he stared down at the women. "Get out of my way," he snapped. "This ain't none of your business."

Carrie opened her mouth to reply when a tall man, dressed elegantly in a top hat stepped forward.

"It is most certainly her business," the man said grimly. "Not only that, you are breaking the law."

"What law?" the driver asked suspiciously. "And who are you?"

"My name is Henry Bergh. I am the president of the American Society for the Prevention of Cruelty to Animals."

"Ain't never heard of it," the driver retorted.

"It's quite new," Bergh responded. "It was created on April tenth of this year. On April nineteenth, an anti-cruelty law was passed. My society has been granted the right to enforce it." He had deliberately raised his voice so the other carriage drivers would hear him.

"Still ain't never heard of it," the driver repeated, but this time he sounded less certain.

"Your ignorance is no excuse for breaking the law," Bergh replied. "If you so much as raise that whip again, I will have you arrested."

The driver's face, if possible, got even redder, but he remained still, his eyes casting around for help. The other drivers, now that they had heard mention of the police, turned their attention elsewhere.

Bergh moved forward to release the horse from the harness cutting into his flesh.

"What are you doing?" the driver exclaimed.

"I am freeing this horse from your violent care."

"How am I supposed to drive my carriage?" the man asked angrily.

"That is hardly my problem," Bergh replied.

Carrie moved forward to help him, her hands moving gently over the horse's body as she pulled the harness away. Fear faded in the horse's eyes as he realized he was being rescued, but nothing could erase the misery caused by years of obvious abuse. Carrie felt sick, wanting nothing more than to put the horse on a train and send it back to the plantation. Bile rose in her throat as raw, oozing sores emerged from beneath the harness.

While the driver sputtered and cursed, she and Bergh finished freeing the horse. Bergh stroked its face gently and walked him away from the carriage. The horse moved slowly, his head bowed, relief radiating from his eyes.

"Where will you take him?" Carrie asked, one hand resting protectively on the horse's neck while she caressed his side, careful to avoid the lashes and sores. She was certain the horse had experienced no kind human contact.

"I have secured a stable in Manhattan," Bergh replied. "I will take him there until I can find a place in the country. This horse will never pull another carriage. I can assure you he will be well cared for."

"Thank you," Carrie said gratefully, tears filling her eyes now that the horse was safe. She glared back over her shoulder. "That man should be shot."

"Agreed," Bergh replied. "Since that option is not legal, I will continue to try to save the animals."

Carrie peered up at him, drawn by the kindness etched on his narrow face. "I've never heard of your society."

"Not a surprise. It is the first in America, designed after England's Royal Society, which was founded in 1840. We've only begun to fight for animals' rights here in America, but we will continue to fight until things change."

Carrie shuddered. "It's inconceivable to me that someone would treat a horse this way."

Bergh eyed her. "You're experienced with horses."

"My family owns a plantation in Virginia. We raise horses."

"And what are you doing in New York City?"

Carrie saw no reason not to be honest. "I'm here with the rest of my friends to attend the Women's Rights Conference, but also to meet with doctors on the Metropolitan Board of Health."

Bergh raised his eyebrows as he looked around. "All of you?"

Carrie nodded. "With the exception of this wonderful woman who is a very successful business owner"—she nodded toward Abby—"we are all students at the Women's Medical College of Philadelphia."

Bergh smiled. "It is indeed a pleasure to meet all of you. I will think of you fighting ignorant people for the right to be doctors as I fight ignorant people who believe they can abuse animals."

He bowed to all of them and then led the horse slowly down the street.

Carrie glanced over at the driver, now sitting on a carriage seat that had no horse to pull it.

"See what you done now?" the driver called, his eyes sparkling dangerously.

"I do," Carrie said calmly. "I have saved a wonderful animal from an ignorant man who should never have another one." She spun on her heel and marched back to the carriage.

Paxton waited for everyone to get back into the carriage and then climbed into his seat. "You sure she's just a stepdaughter?" he murmured to Abby. "She's just as independent and hard-headed as you are."

Laughter rang merrily through the air as the carriage pulled away from the station.

Abby waited until Paxton had unloaded everyone's luggage and carried it up onto the porch. The house butler took over, showing Carrie and her friends to their rooms. She had known the Stratfords would not be home when they arrived, but Nancy should be returning within the hour. Nancy hated not to be there for their arrival, but she was involved in final plans for the Women's Rights Conference.

When everyone left the porch, Abby turned to Paxton. "Is something wrong?" she asked gently.

"Excuse me?" Paxton mumbled.

"I know I don't have the right to ask, Paxton, yet I can't help but see the grief in your eyes."

Paxton stared at her, his green eyes numb under his reddish thatch of hair. "It's a bad time to be alive," he said. "Actually, it's a bad time to be dead." His eyes flashed with desperate grief.

"What happened?" Abby asked. She sensed Paxton had no one to share his grief with, and she could tell it was eating him up from the inside.

Paxton remained silent for so long, Abby doubted he was going to say anything, but finally he let out a heavy sigh. "Have you heard of the *Monarch of the Seas*?"

"I'm sorry, no. I'm assuming it is a boat?"

Paxton nodded, grief turning his eyes into molten emeralds. "My two sisters sailed from Liverpool on March nineteenth. They were coming from Ireland to start a new life." His voice twisted and he fell silent.

Abby suspected she knew the ending of the story.

"It's gone," Paxton finally said.

"Gone?" Abby echoed. "Do you mean it sunk?"

"Just *gone*," Paxton ground out through gritted teeth. "It completely disappeared. Everyone figures it has sunk, but no one is positive. It has simply been given up as lost."

Abby gasped, raising her hand to her mouth. "I'm so sorry!"

Paxton continued as if he hadn't heard her. "Six hundred ninety-eight people on board. Five hundred nineteen of them from Ireland."

Abby reached out a hand and put it on his arm. "Paxton, that's terrible. I'm so very sorry."

Paxton gazed at her. "I went down to the docks every day for a month, hoping the ship would appear with a story about their trip." His voice faltered. "It's gone," he said hopelessly as he shook his head. "All those lives lost. My sisters..."

Abby knew there was nothing to say to alleviate his suffering. She kept her hand resting on his arm, offering what little comfort she could.

"It might be for the best," Paxton muttered, his eyes clearing slightly.

"What do you mean?"

"Things were real bad when you were here three years ago. It's worse now."

Abby thought back. "You were very concerned about the conditions your family members were living in," she remembered. She tried to recall the conditions in that part of town, but all she could see when she closed her eyes were the rampaging crowds and the cries of black people as they were beaten and murdered. She managed to control her shudder as she kept her focus on Paxton's grief.

"They're living in conditions not meant for animals," he growled. "The pigs back home in Ireland lived better than my brothers and their families." His eyes clouded over again. "I know my sisters were miserable in Ireland, but I couldn't imagine them in that squalor. I talked to Mrs. Stratford about getting them work. She had a couple of housemaid jobs lined up with some friends, but I suppose they won't be needing them now," he said sadly.

He stared down at the ground for several moments and then gazed back up at Abby beseechingly. "Is it wrong of me to be glad they're gone? Ain't nobody meant to live the way people are living down in the tenements. I've seen too many people that look worse off than if they were dead."

Abby tightened her grip on his arm. "You loved your sisters," she said softly. "You didn't want them to suffer. I'm sorry things are so bad down there."

Paxton sighed heavily. "They're trying to make things a little better. I've heard Dr. Benson talking. They've cleaned up some of the filth to try to stop the cholera, but they can't change the living conditions."

Carrie and the others spent a wonderful afternoon resting and talking with Nancy Stratford. They had been immediately charmed by the petite blonde who exuded such warmth. Her husband, Wally, arrived home shortly before darkness fell on the city. He had welcomed them all graciously, insisting they sit on the wide porch to enjoy the late spring evening. There was just enough of a nip in the air to appreciate the hot tea the maid brought, her accent revealing that she was Irish as well.

Carrie listened, but her attention was drawn to the thick bank of roses blooming along the front fence, the outskirts of the yard outlined with heavily laden lilacs, their purple and pink blossoms perfuming the air. She had not been able to take her mind off the poor, abused horse she had helped rescue. The Stratfords' home revealed their wealth, but the smells and heavy air they had ridden through on the way up the hill said there was another side to the city that wasn't nearly as pleasant. She had read enough about New York to expect it, but she sensed the reality was going to be something entirely different than even her worst expectations. As desperate as Richmond had been during the war, she suspected New York harbored horrors she had never experienced.

"Carrie?" Janie murmured, moving her chair closer to her friend.

"I'm okay," Carrie replied quietly. "It's been a very long day." She didn't know how to articulate what she was feeling, but she knew it didn't really matter. Janie always had the ability to understand what was churning inside her.

"I'm glad to be here," Janie said, her eyes resting on the bright pink roses trailing up the fence, "but I suspect the next ten days are going to be quite challenging." Her gaze settled on the polluted air resting over the city beneath them, evident even in the rapidly encroaching darkness. "The South is dealing with so much destruction, but from everything I've studied, New York seems to have brought it on to themselves."

"Some people would say the same about the South," Wally interjected. "I'm sorry, but I couldn't help but overhear your conversation."

"Yes," Janie agreed. "The South did much to cause the war that brought so much destruction, but it seems like New York has even more problems than we do. And on a much larger scale."

"Unfortunately, you are right," Wally said heavily. He glanced apologetically at his wife. "I know this isn't proper conversation to have before dinner, my dear."

"It is for *this* group," Nancy replied. "These women are here looking for answers to make our country better for everyone, but especially for women. There is not a single person on this porch who needs or wants the facts to be sugarcoated."

"We will be offended if you do that," Florence said. "I already know New York City is a mess. How bad has it gotten?"

"Bad," Wally admitted.

When he hesitated, Carrie knew he was wondering how much to say. "Tell us," she pleaded.

"Tell me about the area where Paxton's family lives," Abby asked, her eyes sharp with intensity. "No sugarcoating," she said firmly.

Carrie listened carefully. Abby had told them about her earlier conversation with their driver.

Wally scowled, his heavy brows drawn together over eyes that were both fierce and sad. "It's hard to describe it," he said after a long silence. "New York has a population of over one million people."

Florence gasped. "I knew it had grown, but I didn't realize the extent. Where are you putting everyone?"

Wally's scowl deepened. "We are still trying to figure that out. No one could have guessed our population would double in a decade. Troubles in Europe have played a huge part in that. About forty percent of our population are the Irish who have come here to escape famine and persecution. They arrive with practically nothing." He took a deep breath. "The area where Paxton's family lives is particularly troublesome. There are over a half million people living in about fifteen thousand tenement houses."

Carrie gasped, trying to envision it. "A half million people!" Richmond had seemed horribly overpopulated during the war, but this was beyond anything she could imagine.

"Immigrants are flowing in from Europe with hopes of a better life," Nancy said ruefully, her eyes heavy with dismay. "They're hardly finding it."

"What a shock New York must be to them," Alice murmured, her eyes clouded. "I've not been here since my parents brought me as a teenager. I had no idea it was this crowded."

Wally nodded. "Crowded and completely without services," he replied. "A typical tenement house that should hold perhaps a dozen people sometimes has more than two hundred. There are no inside facilities and no running water. The bathrooms, perhaps two or three for a building that size, are outside privies not connected to any kind of sewer system. The filth and squalor are unbearable," he said. He shot a glance at his wife. "You said to give it to them straight."

"I did," Nancy agreed. "You can't change something by trying to ignore it, or pretend it's not as bad as it really is."

Carrie shuddered as she absorbed the reality Wally communicated. "The disease rate must be horribly high."

"It is," Wally replied. "Typhus, typhoid, and dysentery run amok down in the tenements." He paused. "The death rate is very high." He closed his eyes for a moment and then opened them again. "We're making changes," he added. "It's still bad, but it's not as bad as it was even six weeks ago."

"The Metropolitan Board of Health," Florence said quietly. "I have so many questions about that."

The rumble of carriage wheels on the cobblestone broke the night air. Carrie shivered. The soft night air, once comforting, now seemed to wrap around her like a tight cloak, suffocating her with the secrets it held within its grasp. Even in the midst of the worst misery in Richmond during the war, it had never been like New York. The city that most of the world saw as a beacon of hope was actually a deathtrap of misery and disease.

Wally stood and peered down the street illuminated by gas lanterns. "The Bensons are here," he announced. "Dr. Benson will be able to answer all your questions about the new health board." He hurried down the steps to meet the carriage at the curb.

Carrie didn't miss the look of relief on his face. She was sure he was glad to let someone else carry the conversation of the plight of his beloved city. People coming to Richmond for the first time could not possibly envision the gracious city it had been before the war. New York, she knew, had at one time been a prosperous, exciting city—the beacon of a proud country. It must break the heart of native New Yorkers to see what it had become.

Abby, a warm smile on her face, waited on the edge of the porch as the Bensons stepped out of the carriage. She hurried down the steps, meeting them as they entered the yard. "Dr. Benson! Elsie!" She gripped Dr. Benson's hand and then embraced Elsie. "It is so wonderful to see both of you again."

"And you," Elsie said gladly, dark eyes sparkling in her lovely ebony face. "You look wonderful."

"It's such a pleasure to see you under less challenging circumstances," Dr. Benson said, his cultured voice blending well with his tall, elegant bearing. Iron gray hair made him look only more distinguished.

"How are the children?" Abby asked.

Elsie smiled brightly. "They are all doing well." Her smile faltered and she looked away. "They are no longer in the city," she whispered, her eyes pleading for understanding.

"Oh?" Abby asked carefully.

"What's this?" Wally asked. "Where are your children?"

"With my sister further out in the country," Dr. Benson replied. He shook his head. "This city is not the place for growing children." His sad look sharpened into a scowl. "I want my children to live. Where we live is better than the tenements, but disease is not stopped by neighborhood boundary lines."

"When did you move them out?" Abby asked, her eyes shining with compassion.

Carrie leaned forward in her chair to make sure she didn't miss a word. She couldn't imagine having to send one's children away.

"Right after the riot," Dr. Benson revealed.

"Shelby wouldn't have lived if she had stayed," Elsie said sadly. "The combination of disease and violence were simply too much. We realized we were putting all the children at risk if we kept them here." She shook her head and continued. "We see them every two weeks. They are all thriving."

"Stephen?" Abby asked.

"He's in college," Dr. Benson said proudly. "Oberlin College in Ohio. He's doing extremely well."

"You must be very proud," Abby said softly, laying her hand on Elsie's arm.

Elsie lifted her head, her eyes shining with gratitude. "Thank you. So many have judged us for sending our children away. They believe we should have all left the city together."

"And why didn't you?" Wally asked gently. There was no judgment in his voice, only genuine curiosity.

"Our place is here," Dr. Benson said firmly. "If everyone who can help leaves the city, it will certainly crumble beneath filth, squalor, and death. We have decided to stay and do all we can to help." His gaze swept the whole group. "New York City was not always like this. We can't walk away from these problems."

Carrie stepped forward then. "It is an honor to meet both of you," she said sincerely.

Dr. Benson smiled. "And you are?"

"This is Carrie Cromwell Borden," Abby replied. "She is my stepdaughter."

Elsie blinked in surprise. "Your stepdaughter? I remember you telling me about Carrie Cromwell when we were trapped on the roof during that long day, but..."

Abby grinned. "I married her father, Thomas Cromwell," she explained. "We met after the war ended. I fell very much in love with the open-minded Southern plantation owner."

Dr. Benson whistled and gripped Carrie's hand. "It's a pleasure to meet you, Carrie. Abby told us so much about you while we were together during the riot." His eyes swept the rest of the women, his warm gaze welcoming them all. "So many stories to be heard," he murmured.

"Which we can do once we go inside," Nancy interjected smoothly. "Dinner is almost ready. Our cook will not be happy if we don't sit down while it's hot. She has been working on it all day. When she heard you and Elsie were coming, Dr. Benson, she worked extra hard. You are somewhat of a hero in the black community."

Dr. Benson smiled slightly. "I'm just doing my part to protect our city," he said modestly.

A tall young man with curly dark hair stepped out onto the porch. "Hello, everyone," he called.

"Michael!" Nancy cried. "I wasn't expecting you home until later." She turned quickly. "This is our son, Michael."

Michael grinned and stepped forward to swoop Abby into his arms. "How is my favorite auntie?" he asked lightly.

Abby laughed and patted his cheek. "It's wonderful to see you, Michael. How are you?"

Michael's grin faltered as he directed his gaze to Dr. Benson. "I came home early because I have news for you."

Dr. Benson sighed heavily. "The first case has been reported."

Carrie's stomach clenched. The look on Dr. Benson's face could only mean one thing. "The first case of cholera?"

Chapter Seventeen

Grim determination replaced Michael's grin. "I'm afraid so. I realize it's not much of a welcome to our fair city, ladies, but it was important Dr. Benson be informed. I'm sorry to spoil everyone's dinner."

"Thank you for letting me know," Dr. Benson responded, his voice grave with concern. "We knew it was only a matter of time. Now we find out if our preparations will stop it." He frowned as he stared out over the city lights twinkling below. "We've made great progress, but there is still so much to be done."

"Must you leave right away?" Wally asked.

Dr. Benson considered the question and shook his head. "No. We have put all the protocol into place." His eyes swung to Michael. "Has the team been dispatched?"

"Yes, sir."

"Where was the first case reported?"

"Ninety-Third Street," Michael replied. He answered the question in his mother's eyes. "Paxton's family is several blocks away from there. I gave him the news when I came in. It's only fair he know."

Dr. Benson nodded. "There is nothing to be done tonight. I'll get more information in the morning." His eyes swept the group on the porch. "In the meantime, it is my honor to spend time with five women who are preparing to advance medicine in this country. Just as it was a struggle to become a doctor as a black man, you will face many challenges to have people accept women doctors." His voice was casual but his eyes intense when he continued. "If you want it badly enough, you will press through."

Carrie smiled as she slid her hand through the crook in his arm. "We want it," she said firmly. "And we have so many questions for you, but we are going to have to ask them in the dining room. You're going to need to fortify yourself to answer all our questions," she said lightly, covering up the deep sense of foreboding that had gripped her almost as soon as she stepped from the train.

Conversation flowed smoothly during dinner. By unspoken consent, everyone avoided the topic of cholera and the Board of Health. Talk of death and suffering had no place during the skillfully prepared meal.

Air flowed in through the open windows, causing the sheer curtains to sway in the breeze. Gas lanterns lit the room brightly, illuminating the heavy Chippendale furniture and the gorgeous landscape paintings that decorated the soft yellow walls with splashes of vivid color. Tall vases of fresh-cut flowers adorned the serving tables. Perfume from the lilacs outside the window mixed with the aroma of freshly baked chicken and the mountain of vegetables that had been carried out.

Carrie was content to listen during dinner. She was eager to learn as much as she could about the Stratfords, Bensons, Paxtons, and New York City. She caught Abby watching her several times, but she merely smiled and continued to eat, letting the flow of conversation soothe her anxious feelings.

Dr. Benson waited until all the dishes were whisked away before he cleared his throat and looked over at Carrie. "What do you think of our city, Carrie?"

Carrie jolted out of her thoughts. "Excuse me?"

Dr. Benson smiled. "You've not said one word since dinner began. You have merely been absorbing everything going on around you. I could almost see your brain cataloging information. Have you reached any conclusions?"

Carrie stared at him, liking the openness in his gaze. She sensed a deep sincerity in his question and could do nothing but respond with candor. "When I was growing up on the plantation, I used to dream of visiting New

York. I envisioned statues, opera houses, art galleries, and splendor for everyone."

"That's all here," Dr. Benson assured her.

"I'm sure it is," Carrie agreed, "but I no longer find the same things important. The splendor of New York City seems to have been overcome with disgusting odors, refuse, and disease. I now believe good privies are far more important than grand palaces and fine art galleries." She took a deep breath. Silence had fallen on the table, but Dr. Benson's eyes encouraged her to continue. "I believe life itself must be guaranteed to a person before one can hope to improve anything else about them."

"You've thought about this a great deal," Dr. Benson replied, his eyes shining with appreciation.

"Certainly since I arrived in your city today," Carrie replied. "I want to have nothing but glowing things to say, but—"

"—they would be lies," Dr. Benson interjected.

"Yes."

Dr. Benson glanced at Abby. "I like your Carrie." His eyes swept the table, seeing nothing but agreement on the faces of all her friends. "Now you know why I stay in the city, instead of going out to the country with my children."

"I do understand," Carrie answered. "Richmond was a terrible place to be during the war, but I found I didn't want to be anywhere else. I was needed, and I believed I could make a difference." She reached down and gripped Janie's hand beneath the table. "Janie and I had many challenges, but we're glad we stayed. Please tell us more about the Metropolitan Board of Health."

Dr. Benson took a long sip of hot coffee from the cup in front of him. "As horrible as cholera is, I find I have reason to be thankful for it right now. We have fought for years to bring reform to the so-called health board of New York City. All our efforts were blocked for political reasons and monetary gain."

Carrie bit back her groan. "Will politics and money never cease to control our destiny?" she asked. She desperately wanted Dr. Benson to tell her something different than what she believed.

Dr. Benson looked at her for a long moment. "You want me to tell you it will not always be so. I can't do that. Unfortunately, human nature has always, and I'm afraid will for all eternity, be the controlling factor in decisions. Fortunately, there always seems to come a time when the pain of continuing forward on a certain course outweighs the reluctance to change." He locked his eyes with Carrie. "And never believe, even for a moment, that enough people raising their voices cannot create change. The problem is that most people seem willing to flounder along in complacency until something jolts them awake and *makes* them take action."

Carrie got his message. "I won't lose hope," she said quietly. "My friends and I are determined to raise our voices and be heard. We have been given the legacy of a country mired in deep troubles. Turning our backs isn't an option."

"Good!" Dr. Benson exclaimed. "The Metropolitan Board of Health was finally created when people could no longer refute the facts of how bad New York has become. It can be easy to turn a blind eye to poverty and disease when it doesn't touch you. Our facts show us that ninety-three percent of New York illnesses, and ninety percent of our deaths, come from the tenements. As devastating as those statistics are, there are far too many people who have believed the people in the tenements bring it on themselves because they are poor and illiterate."

"Preposterous!" Abby snorted.

"I agree," Dr. Benson said. "I hear the same arguments about the freed slaves."

"Who simply need a chance to learn and create a new life," Janie added.

"True again," Dr. Benson agreed. "Unfortunately, the people around this table are not representative of the American population as a whole. Too many want to turn their backs on the immigrants and wish for the day when America was full of a different kind of people."

"But was it ever?" Carrie questioned. "Wasn't American populated by people desperate for a new beginning in a new land? How are the new immigrants any different?"

"Good question," Dr. Benson replied. "In spite of efforts to believe it is different, I agree with you that it is not. I don't believe it ever will be. The plight of the immigrants has pushed itself to the forefront because cholera entered our harbor last December. When it last visited America in 1849, it proved it was not controlled by typical borders. It hit the wealthy as badly as it hit the destitute. That reality helped us push through all the naysayers to create the Metropolitan Board of Health. The wealthy and powerful in New York City finally understand they can only protect themselves and their families by protecting everyone in the city."

"The Board was officially created in February," Elizabeth commented. "Is it possible to make a difference so quickly?"

"We're about to find out," Dr. Benson responded. "We've been working hard since then to change things. Now that the first case of cholera has been reported, we will discover if we've done enough. We're not finished by any means, and we're not so naïve to think we can stop it entirely in such a short time, but we have hopes the death toll won't be as high as before."

"How many died in 1849?" Alice asked.

Janie answered before Dr. Benson could speak. "Five thousand died in New York City, but they had less than half the population then, and things weren't as dire. One hundred fifty thousand died throughout the country, with another two hundred thousand dying in Mexico." She smiled briefly. "I've been studying."

"That's right, Janie," Dr. Benson said approvingly. "If cholera takes the city the way it did before, the death toll will be much, much higher this time. And it will spread much faster throughout the country."

Carrie thought about everything she had learned about cholera. "Dr. Benson, do you agree with Dr. Snow's conclusion that cholera is carried through contaminated water?"

Dr. Benson raised his eyebrows. "I thought you were just beginning medical school, Carrie. How do you know about Dr. Snow?"

Carrie smiled. "I've been reading medical books and journals for the last six years. Especially ones from Europe. My father and Abby have made sure I have them." She looked fondly at Abby. "Abby even bought them and saved them all for me during the war. I've done a lot of reading since the war ended."

"Why *especially* Europe?" Dr. Benson asked, watching her closely.

Carrie looked at him directly. "Because European medicine is far more advanced than American medicine," she replied. "I find they develop their medical protocols based more on fact than religious dogma or belief."

Dr. Benson held her gaze. "So you don't believe the people in the tenements carry most of the illnesses because they are a lower class of people or because of the sin in their lives?"

Carrie didn't try to contain her snort. "Or because they can't pay the high pew rents the churches demand? The churches deem them immoral because they don't attend mass, but yet they make it impossible for them to do so." She stared at Dr. Benson. "It makes me wonder who is the most immoral." She made no apology for her directness.

Dr. Benson nodded slowly, a smile lighting his eyes. "Are you sure you don't want to stay here in the city and work with us?" His eyes swept the table. "All of you."

Alice chuckled. "I'm quite happy in Philadelphia for now. Even though we have been in school longer than Carrie, none of us have her experience or her vast knowledge. I basically feel ignorant any time I have a conversation with her." She softened her words with a playful smirk at Carrie.

"That's not true!" Carrie laughingly protested. She turned back to Dr. Benson, questions swarming through her mind. "So you do agree with Dr. Snow?"

"I do. When Dr. Snow first entered medicine in England, it was believed cholera was caused by poisonous gases thought to arise from sewers, swamps, garbage pits, open graves, and other sites of organic decay." He paused. "Dr. Snow's careful research during the last London cholera epidemic proved that it is transported through the water supply. In spite of the fact that there are many American doctors who still believe it spreads because of sinful behavior," he said ruefully, "we believe drinking water is how cholera spreads so virulently. It can also be transferred through contamination caused by a patient."

"Through their bodily fluids," Elizabeth stated. "I heard a little about the crews you have prepared to follow up on cholera cases."

"Yes," Dr. Benson said. "It is imperative we isolate the disease. We already know there is no cure for cholera. Since we can't cure it, we have to prevent it. Which means it is important to stop in its tracks. The reason Michael knows about the first case is because we have been working closely with the police department ever since we formed the new board. We identify problem areas and then the police enforce the actions we take. Michael, will you tell them how it works?"

Michael nodded. "Each case is to be reported directly to the closest police precinct station. As soon as we heard about the case today, we telegraphed the Board's central office. They immediately dispatched a wagonload of disinfectants to the infected tenement. In less than an hour, they had a team of well-trained men disinfecting the clothing, house, and belongings of the victim."

"What do they disinfect with?" Florence asked, her blue eyes sharp with intensity.

"They were very thorough," Michael explained. "The beddings, pillows, old clothing, and utensils—basically, anything that might have been contaminated with bodily fluids—were piled in an open area and burned. Then they scattered chloride of lime through the house. After that, they distributed five barrels of coal tar and other disinfectants around the surrounding area." He paused. "The tenement house with the first case is one of the worst I've seen. It is full of waste and filth, and it reeked of alcohol."

"You were there?" Nancy asked, her eyes dark with concern.

"I had to go by and confirm the illness," Michael said soothingly. "I was very careful."

"I suppose that should make me feel better," Nancy said, "but I would much prefer you weren't anywhere near it."

Wally's eyes snapped with worry as they landed on his son. "It's time for you to go to law school, son."

Michael shrugged away the comment with an easy grin. "I'll go soon. Right now, I'm needed."

Abby rested her hand on his arm. "You're a good man, Michael."

"Yes," Nancy sighed. "Sometimes I wish he was a little more selfish, but then I suppose I wouldn't be so proud of him."

Carrie was still full of questions. "If you destroyed the patient's belongings, what are they going to do?"

"Good question," Dr. Benson replied. "Part of our plan was to stockpile clothes and household belongings so we could replace what has to be restored."

"Impressive," Carrie murmured. "I'm learning medical care is about much more than treating the patient." She paused, pulling her thoughts together. "What have you been doing the last six weeks to prepare?"

Dr. Benson scowled. "Moving waste. Quite simply, parts of our city are buried under waste created by humans and animals. Add snow, ice and dirt into the mix, and it is a huge job. We delivered our first clean-up order on March fourteenth. As of today, we have delivered close to seventy-six hundred such orders. We have been cleaning yards, emptying dirty cisterns, and disinfecting privies. We have already moved hundreds of tons of waste. It is nasty, thankless work. The men performing it are heroes."

"Where are you putting it all?" Carrie asked with horrified fascination. It was difficult to even imagine what he was describing. Her mind contained vivid images of mistreated horses pulling wagons heavily laden with waste and rotting carcasses through streets clogged with snow and ice. She controlled her shudder and forced herself to listen.

"We're hauling it out of the city and forming mountains," Dr. Benson said. "It's the best we can do for right now, but if this city is going to survive, we will have to work together to create sewers and clean water systems. It will be a huge undertaking, but people are beginning to understand that health begins with cleanliness—not just personally, but throughout all civilization."

"Have you provided a quarantine hospital?" Elizabeth asked.

Dr. Benson shook his head heavily. "No. In spite of our best efforts, we've not been able to secure a location."

Carrie searched her mind for what she had read about New York City medical establishments. "There was a quarantine hospital on Staten Island," she remembered. "What happened to it?"

"It was burned," Dr. Benson replied. "A group of thirty arsonists destroyed the entire compound in 1858 after some neighborhoods on Staten Island were infected with smallpox. The people were convinced it was because of the hospital."

"Could it have been?" Carrie asked. "If we're just now discovering the true causes of these diseases, isn't it possible the surrounding neighborhoods were in danger?"

"Unfortunately, the answer is yes," Dr. Benson admitted. "It was also unfortunate to lose such an extensive facility."

"All the patients were killed?" Abby asked with horror.

"No," Dr. Benson answered quickly. "Evidently, the administrators had been warned of the attack. When the fires started, the few staff working that night tried to rescue the patients, as well as the animals they used to feed them. No one was there."

Alice gaped. "They had evacuated everyone? Where did they take them?"

"That's a good question," Dr. Benson said. "The fires that destroyed the quarantine hospital forced the patients into areas not so well protected, but no one ever revealed where they were taken because they were afraid the same thing would happen."

"People are terrified of getting ill," Abby observed. "With good reason."

"True," Dr. Benson agreed, "but that still leaves us with no facilities in case there is another serious cholera outbreak. We find buildings that could work, but the judges block us."

"I thought the Board of Health was given unprecedented freedom," Wally protested. "How can the judges stop your efforts to move forward?"

"The joy of politics," Dr. Benson said mirthlessly. "The judges owe their seats on the bench to people with power and money. They are quite adept at blocking our efforts. When they created the board, they gave us quite broad power in dealing with outbreaks, but we have very little power when it comes to prevention. A quarantine hospital is considered preventative right now, so every move we make is blocked."

"But that's absurd!" Carrie cried. "Isn't it far better to take action before people are sick and dying?"

"Welcome to the real world. It would be so simple if logic was the criteria for decision making. Unfortunately, that is not always the case," Wally said, his eyes shining with sympathy. "I believe New York will rise above all its challenges, but it is only going to happen because there are enough of us who refuse to stop working to make things better. It seems like every time we take two steps forward we get knocked back, but we're not going to stop trying," he said firmly. "Failure is simply not an option. There is too much at stake. Too many people are counting on us."

A long silence fell on the table as everyone absorbed his words.

"How are the patients going to be treated?" Florence asked.

Dr. Benson stared into his coffee cup for a long moment, slowly shaking his head. "There is no treatment for cholera," he replied. "There are things doctors do, but we have learned they are ineffective. About half of everyone who comes down with cholera will die from the disease. The best we can do is keep them warm, give them liquids to prevent dehydration, and do everything we can to keep it from spreading."

"There are still doctors who believe bleeding them or purging the patients of fluids will help," Janie observed.

"There are also people who still believe the earth is flat, but that doesn't make them right," Carrie responded angrily. "I was appalled by how many doctors at Chimborazo used old methods that had been proven not to work."

Dr. Benson nodded. "Doctors feel they have to do *something*. Unfortunately, their methods do nothing to help the patient, and in many cases actually increase their suffering and hasten their demise. Patients who have cholera die from dehydration. Purging or bleeding them simply speeds up their death, making them more miserable in the process."

Carrie felt sick as the truth of his statement sank in. "There are good reasons that the European medical establishment looks down on American medicine."

"Why do you say that?" Dr. Benson asked.

Carrie plunged ahead, not caring if he was offended by her observation. After so many years of dreaming of becoming a doctor, she was determined to let nothing stand in her way. People were already offended by women becoming doctors. They were also offended by outspoken women who didn't observe the traditional roles expected of women. She didn't care that she fit in both categories. She didn't think Dr. Benson thought either of those things, but it wouldn't have mattered if he did. "Too many medical colleges have abysmal requirements for their students. They seem to view their schools as nothing but a business endeavor. As long as someone can pay, they are willing to give them a medical degree. Every time that happens, the respect for our profession is diminished."

Dr. Benson nodded thoughtfully. "I agree with you." He held her with his gaze. "Are you quite certain the Women's Medical College is different?"

"I am," Carrie said. "Women willing to go against the tide of societal expectations will accept nothing but the best. We expect to be challenged and pushed. Dean Preston is working hard to continually raise the standards, and she is also pushing for us to get even more clinical experience by working with the Philadelphia College of Medicine."

"And she believes the men will allow that?" Dr. Benson asked, his voice skeptical.

"It will be a fight," Carrie agreed. "But when something is important, you keep fighting until you win." She eyed Dr. Benson. "Surely you understand that. You have had to fight tremendous challenges as a black man to become a doctor and have the influence you do."

"Oh, I understand it *too* well," Dr. Benson replied with a smile. "I was just making sure you are up for the challenge." His smile deepened into a grin. "My conclusion is that anyone who attempts to stand in your way will simply be rolled over."

Carrie laughed along with everyone else, but she felt warmed by his approval. She glanced around the table. "I'm afraid I have monopolized the conversation," she said apologetically.

"Not at all, my dear," Nancy replied. "We have all learned things. I find I have a better understanding of my own city after all your questions." She turned to Dr. Benson. "I do have another question. I'm aware a colleague of yours moved to Memphis, Tennessee in the last six months. Dr. Pearlman is a longtime friend of my family. I've known him since I was a child. He used to come for dinner every Sunday. Have you heard from him?"

"I have," he answered hesitantly.

"What's wrong?" Nancy asked, concern once more darkening her eyes. "And please tell me the truth."

Dr. Benson exchanged a long look with Elsie. "I got a letter from Howard a couple days ago. He is thinking about leaving Memphis."

"Why?" Nancy pressed.

"Because Memphis is a powder keg getting ready to blow, and he's concerned for his family's safety. The racial tensions are much like the tensions that exploded into our draft riot three years ago. I have heard terrible things about the police force in Memphis. They are convinced the blacks are the reason for all their troubles. The state is trying to bring things under control, but it might not happen in time. The Irish seem to be looking for an excuse to unleash their fury on the black populations." He scowled. "We have all experienced what happens when things get out of control. I have a friend in Nashville who is trying to change things, but he fears violence is inevitable. He suspects they have plans to provoke a riot. Soon. He predicts it will be bad."

The housekeeper appeared at Carrie's side. "I'm sorry, Mrs. Borden, but I forgot to give this to you earlier. A letter came for you today."

A grin broke out on Carrie's face as she saw Robert's familiar handwriting on the envelope. She caressed the envelope briefly before sliding slid the letter into her pocket. It would be rude to read it now.

"Oh, read it," Nancy laughed. "I can tell the look of a woman who misses her husband dreadfully. If you don't read it now, you'll be wondering what it says for the rest of the night."

Carrie blushed. "You're probably right," she admitted. "No one minds?"

"Read it," Abby commanded. "I want to know what is going on at home as well."

Carrie smiled, used her knife to slit the seal of the envelope, and pulled out the single sheet. The blood drained from her face as she read it.

"Carrie?" Abby asked sharply. "What is it?"

Carrie read the few sentences again more slowly before she looked up. "Robert sent this letter a week ago. He was on his way to Memphis with Matthew and Moses. They are there right now."

Chapter Eighteen

Moses leaned against a parapet on the walls of Fort Pickering. He gazed out over the city he had already developed an intense dislike for in the past three days. He had seen very little of Robert and Matthew since their lunch, but he had spoken with them long enough to explain that he felt the need to stay at the fort. He was still trying to figure out the compulsion that had prompted him to make the decision. He liked the men he had met, but he wasn't clear exactly what he was doing at the fort.

He forced himself to relax as he stared down at the muddy waters of the Mississippi River. Fort Pickering had been built as a strategic command post for the Union Army during the war. It stretched nearly two miles along the South Memphis bluffs, commanding an amazing view of both the river and the city it protected. The fort included a hospital, a rail depot, water works, and a saw mill. Right now, the only troops occupying the fort were a detachment of the Sixteenth US Infantry Regiment, a few quartermaster troops, support personnel and remnants of the Third Colored Heavy Artillery Unit that had remained behind to enforce the Union presence after the war. Like in Richmond, the presence of the black troops fueled intense resentment among the white population.

Every man in the unit had been mustered out the day before. The city hoped the cessation of black troops would relieve the tensions. Unfortunately, the men had still not been paid. Moses, after a few days at the fort, realized the truth of the situation. The men had not received six months of pay. Most of them were destitute and unable to support their families that were housed nearby. They had also received very poor food supplies. Anger boiled in Moses as he understood the reality that the United States Army was treating the men as if they were indeed inferior. They had officially been mustered out on April 30, but most remained in uniform because they had no other clothes and were choosing to remain in the fort while they waited for their pay.

Moses knew the Third had its share of rowdies and criminals. Most of the soldiers were good men looking forward to a new life as free men, but discipline was much more lax than it should be. He had seen fights break out among the men and heard the rumors of petty theft. They were forbidden to drink, but many of them readily found alcohol. They hung out on the streets drinking, getting louder and more boisterous as time passed. More serious were the soldiers who committed burglary and theft in homes and shops. He knew most of them were propelled by desperation to provide for their families since they were not being paid, but their actions had fueled the anger of white Memphis against everyone in army clothing.

Now that they were mustered out, he suspected it was going to get worse.

Moses pulled his hat down over his eyes to block out the rain, a sense of danger growing in him as dense as the slate gray clouds hovering over the city.

"I thought I would find you here."

Moses turned and smiled briefly, moving over to make room for Roy. "My gut tells me something is going to happen today."

Roy scowled as he stared out over the city. "We ain't getting our bonus," he said bitterly.

"What bonus?"

"We was promised a bonus when we mustered out. Not only ain't we been paid, but they ain't giving us our bonus. The fellas be pretty upset."

Moses nodded. He could feel the tension building on both sides of the walls of the fort.

"Harold was brung back last night."

Moses looked up sharply. "The soldier the police beat ten days ago?"

"Yep."

Harold's story was the one that had prompted Moses to come to the fort. Five policemen had arrested the soldier for no apparent reason. His only crime had been walking down a Memphis street in broad daylight. As they led him away, he had begged for an explanation. Their answer was to club him savagely on the head until he fell. face-down into the muddy street, his body twitching spasmodically. The policemen laughed, summoned a dray, and sent him off to jail. Justifiably, the other soldiers in the area had been upset and angry. "How is he?"

"He'll live," Roy said shortly. "I guess he can be thankful for that."

"Did they ever tell him why they arrested him?"

"Nope. And he learned not to ask if he didn't want more beatings. They pulled him out of the basement jail this morning and dropped him off at the fort walls. They told him if he knew what was good for him, he wouldn't come out of the fort again." Roy clenched his fists. "It ain't right."

Anger pulsed through Moses. "No, it isn't right," he agreed, trying to think clearly through the fury burning his body.

"Why are you here, Moses?"

Moses watched a steamer plowing slowly up the flooded Mississippi. "I wish I knew," he admitted. "When I heard Harold's story, I wanted to do something to help." He shook his head. "I haven't been able to do a thing."

"There's some little girls who done think you're a hero," Roy said with a grin.

That was enough to make Moses' fury abate. He had made it a special point to visit the school nearest the fort. He knew Rose would want a report. The teacher had begged him to talk about his time as the first Union spy. Moses had regaled them with stories, enjoying the look of pride lighting their eyes. He knew how important it was to prove to them that they could be more than white society told them they could be. Four of the little girls had clamored for his attention. One of them, ten-year-old Felicia, had stolen his heart with her soft, eager eyes and her gentle smile.

"You done give some of the boys hope," Roy continued. "There's some of them still not believing you actually own half a plantation in Virginia, but me and some of the others know you ain't lying. I heard them talking about the fellas working there who have their own land now and are building houses. It makes them hope that someday somethin' like that might happen for them."

"I wish I could hire them all," Moses muttered.

"You reckon things can really change?" Roy asked, doubt mixing with the hope in his voice.

"I do, but it's going to be a long, hard road."

"Can't be as hard as slavery," Roy responded.

Moses wasn't so sure. "It might be," he said slowly. "It might be hard in a different kind of way." He thought of the school burning...of Carl being beaten...of Abby being accosted by thugs outside the factory. "Getting our freedom was the first step. Now we are going to have to fight to actually *live* free. Most of the South doesn't want us to be free. Most of the North doesn't know what to do with us now that we are."

"You figure they used us to win the war?"

Moses wanted to deny it, but he couldn't. He chose to not answer directly. "Whatever their reason, we are now free," he said firmly. "Whatever it takes, we are going to stay free." Visions of John and Hope filled his mind. He saw Rose standing in front of a class full of eager children. "It's up to us to create the life we want to live."

They sat together in silence for a long time, the wind whipping waves on the Mississippi and causing the clouds to scuttle across the sky as they deposited a soft rain. Moses struggled to find release from his agitation, but red flags were waving wildly in his mind. "Something is going to happen today."

"You hear what happened last night?" Roy asked after a long silence.

"I heard." Three of the soldiers had come back with the story of an altercation with the police when they were returning to the fort around mid-afternoon. The soldiers had given way to the policemen on the sidewalk, but words and taunts had been exchanged. By the time the incident was over, one of the soldiers had been clubbed by a pistol so viciously that the gun had broken in half. He had returned to the fort bleeding both from his head and from his nose. He had been taken immediately to the hospital. Another had been hit in the back of the head with a rock. He, too, had received medical care.

"From what I can tell," Moses said, "there was blame on both sides, but the soldiers definitely caught the worst of it." His eyes continued to scan the horizon. He didn't know what he was looking for, but he could feel it coming.

Moses was heading back to the barracks with Roy when Harry stopped them.

"Come on out with us," Harry called.

"Out where?" Moses asked cautiously.

"A bunch of us are going to Grady's saloon to let off some steam," Harry replied.

Moses glanced up at the sky as he thought about how he wanted to respond. The clouds had cleared. Sun and breeze were working hard to dry the ground.

"Come on, Moses," Harry pressed. "You've done little but stay inside the fort for the last three days. There are some fellas that want to talk to you. I'm figuring you decided to stay in the fort 'cause you got things you want to learn. You'll find the fellas talk a little easier when they got some drink in them."

Moses hesitated, quite certain the fellas were also less likely to be cautious when they were drinking. He couldn't shake the feeling of imminent trouble.

"Do what you want, Moses," Roy said. "I'm going out."

Moses stared at him, not liking the reckless look in his eyes. He made up his mind. "I'm coming," he announced. He had grave doubts about his decision, but he wanted to be where he could do some good if his new friends needed him.

Harry grinned and headed for the fort's gate. "Let's go do some celebrating. We're no longer in the army!"

Moses' tension grew as they approached a boisterous group of several dozen soldiers bunched together on a corner. They had evidently decided to leave Mary Grady's saloon. He knew their loud yelling and laughter was fueled by the whiskey in their canteens. Several of them were quite obviously drunk. He could see shop owners and residents scowling at them, but they seemed oblivious. If the soldiers felt the disapproval, they didn't care.

As they reached the soldiers, Moses saw a small group of policemen approaching.

"What are all of you doing?" one policeman called.

"Just drinkin' and goin' on," a soldier responded with a drunken laugh. He raised his canteen and guzzled some more whiskey.

Moses didn't know the man who answered, but he could see the fury in the policemen's eyes.

The same policeman stepped forward. "You must cease your carousing and get off the street," he ordered brusquely.

Moses stiffened as the entire group ignored the order, acting as if the police weren't even there. He sidled up to Roy and Harry. "We should go," he said quietly.

Roy scowled. "They ain't got no right to tell us to leave," he protested. "We ain't hurting nobody."

"Perhaps not," Moses responded, "but things are about to get bad." Everything in him was telling him to go back to the fort, but he was hesitant to leave Roy and Harry.

"Let them get bad!" Harry sneered, reaching for a canteen a fellow soldier was holding out to him. His eyes flashed with anger as he raised the canteen. "Hurrah for Abe Lincoln!" he called out.

Moses saw the policemen's eyes flash with contempt.

"Shut up!" the policeman yelled.

"Your old father, Abe Lincoln, is dead and damned!" another shouted.

Moses stepped back into the shadow of a building, watching as the altercation escalated. He could feel the tempers growing on both sides. He forced himself to remain calm and figure out what he should do. His decision to stay in the fort did not include heckling the police with a group of drunken soldiers who were doing nothing but causing trouble for every black in South Memphis. Perhaps they had the right to drink on the street corner, but everything in him said they were about to bring down a terrible wrath on innocent citizens who were trying to do nothing but live.

"Get out of here!" one of the soldiers yelled, rage twisting his face.

Moses recognized Charles Nelson, a self-proclaimed enemy of the white race. He had been imprisoned for sixty days of hard labor under ball and chain after trying to stab an Irish policeman. After he was released, days later he was arrested on a false arson charge and beaten severely.

"That's the man who beat me!" Nelson howled. He grabbed a club and lunged toward the offending policeman.

Moses looked around for an escape route as some of the soldiers grabbed Nelson and held him back. He saw the anger in the policemen's eyes fade into fear as they recognized how vastly outnumbered they were. They began to back up and retreat down the road.

Moses remained where he was, watching as a few of the soldiers followed on their heels. The rest of the soldiers stayed back further. He groaned as one of them rushed forward and shoved a policeman, but the policemen, evidently realizing they couldn't win against such a large group, kept moving.

"Stone them!" one soldier hollered.

"Let me at them with my club!" another yelled.

Moses watched helplessly, knowing he could do nothing to stop whatever was going to happen. Even if they had been his own men from his old unit, and he had the ability to command them, they were too drunk to listen to reason.

When the four policemen reached the bayou bridge, Moses began to relax a little, hoping the incident would end with yelling and shoving. He stiffened when he saw one of the soldiers in the rear of the group pull out a pistol and fire it into the air.

The one shot prompted other soldiers to pull out their own weapons and do the same.

As Moses watched, the policemen, certain they were being fired on, stopped abruptly, pulling their pistols as they turned. He bit back an oath as they leveled their guns and began to fire.

"They're firing at us!" a soldier hollered, lowering his pistol and aiming at the policemen. Within moments, twenty of the soldiers were firing at the Irish officers, cursing as they surged forward.

One of the policemen crumpled to the ground.

The shooting stopped quickly. As the whitish powder smoke began to dissipate, Moses could see two of the policemen fleeing up South Street, turning onto Causey, and continuing northward. He was quite certain they were headed to the station downtown to gather reinforcements. A few of the soldiers ran after them, but most of them, sobered by what had happened, stayed where they were.

Only one of the policemen had stayed with the downed officer. Moses couldn't help but feel admiration for the man who had not run. He could tell by the amount of blood that the wounded officer was badly hurt. The one who had stayed with him looked around frantically for help. No one made a move to help them, but neither did the soldiers seem to have any intention of hurting them.

Moses gazed at the walls of the fort longingly and then moved toward the bridge. He knew his size would make him seem menacing. The policeman, his eyes narrow with both anger and fear, watched him approach. "Let me help you get him off the bridge," Moses called as soon as he was close enough to be heard.

The policeman stared at him suspiciously but didn't move to draw his gun.

Another black man who had been watching from the sidewalk stepped forward. "Let's get him into the grocery store until the doctor can be called."

Moses stepped forward. "I'm sorry this happened. At least let us help him now."

The policeman nodded, relief mixing with his anger and fear.

Moses and the bystander stepped forward and lifted the wounded man. Moses winced when he saw bone protruding from the hole in his pants. The bullet had shattered his thighbone. "You have to get him help quickly," he snapped. "You have to stop the bleeding."

"Just get him into the grocery store," the policeman growled, his eyes widening with new fear as a crowd of black soldiers re-emerged from the street.

Moses helped lay the man down carefully and then left quickly. His thoughts were churning. Years of pent-up emotion and hatred had reached the boiling point in Memphis. He had done what he could to help, but now all he wanted to do was return to the relative safety of the fort. He thought briefly of trying to locate Robert and Matthew, but he instinctively knew it was not safe for any black man to be on the streets.

He had just started toward the fort when more of the soldiers who had followed the policemen came running around the corner.

"We done killed us a policeman!" one hollered, brandishing a police billy club covered with blood. A few howled their approval, but most of the soldiers exchanged uneasy looks.

Roy appeared at Moses' side. "We got to get out of here," he said urgently.

"We've got to get back to the fort," Moses agreed. "The police will be back with reinforcements. It's going to get bad."

Roy nodded, waving his arm and yelling. "Everyone get out of here! Head back to the fort!"

Moses was relieved when he saw one of the unit's former officers, Lieutenant B.F. Baker, appear and start calling out orders. "Everyone back to the fort," Baker called. A few of the men ignored him, but most followed him to the front gate of Fort Pickering.

Moses took his first easy breath when they were behind the closed gates, but he knew it was a matter of time before violence exploded again. The police were certain to retaliate now that one of their own had been killed. Many of the soldiers from the Third were still in the streets. His gut told him they would catch the worst of it, but he knew it would be nothing but foolishness to venture out again.

He hurried to the top of the fort walls, which were soon lined with soldiers peering over to watch the action in the streets below.

Matthew, Robert, Peter, and Crandall were eating an early dinner at about five o'clock when they saw a crush of people moving down the street toward South Memphis. They knew from the angry expressions that something bad had happened. Exchanging anxious looks, they pushed back from the table and rushed out of the restaurant.

Robert grabbed the arm of one passerby. "What has happened?"

"The niggers are rioting," the man sputtered, his eyes wild with anger.

"They shot down a policeman," another man offered as he moved with the crowd. "The policemen have sworn revenge. They are going to shoot down the damned niggers!" His eyes glittered with satisfaction. "It's about time something was done. The police aren't going on their own. We're going to help them!"

Robert and the other men remained on the sidewalk, watching with dismay as the crowd grew to hundreds of white people. With what he could tell from appearances and accents, all of them were working-class Irish. And all of them seemed to have guns.

"It's beginning," Matthew said grimly.

"Moses is down there." Robert's stomach clenched at the thought of something happening to him. The man who had once saved his life and had since become his good friend was about to be in grave danger. He shook his head. "We should have left yesterday like we planned in the beginning."

Matthew sighed regretfully. "I'm afraid you're right. I wish I hadn't agreed to Eaton's request to stay longer."

"We all agreed to it," Robert said quickly. "No one is to blame." He stared in the direction of the fort. "We can't leave Moses down there on his own."

"This crowd is waiting for the police to lead them," Matthew said urgently, his eyes scanning the street. "Perhaps we can get there first and find Moses."

"Go," Peter said. "Crandall and I will find Eaton. If anyone will know the truth of what is going on, it will be him. We'll connect at our hotel later. I'm sure Eaton won't return home tonight, so you might as well stay with us."

Robert turned and started running. He felt Matthew fall in beside him as they dodged wagons and traffic, intent on making it to South Memphis before the bloodthirsty crowd did. When they turned onto Causey Street, they encountered another large crowd of police and white citizens surging south.

"That's Chief Garrett," Matthew gasped. "Perhaps he can maintain control."

It took Robert only moments of watching the crowd to realize they were looking at anything but a cohesive, disciplined force. He shook his head, forcing himself to run faster. "They're in no mood to take orders," he snapped. "They are out of control."

Suddenly he saw two black men heading toward them, lunch pails swinging in their hands, obviously coming home from work. Robert opened his mouth to yell a warning, but it was too late. Several of the police rushed toward the men who were staring back at them with wide, frightened eyes. The men turned to run, but the crowd fell on them like wild dogs. They attacked them with their billy clubs and pistols, clubbing them until both men fell on the street.

"Kill every nigger," one of the policemen shouted. "No matter who—man or woman!"

Robert could do nothing but watch the violence. "We should help them," he muttered, feeling sick at the sight of the men's battered faces.

Matthew grabbed his arm. "Help will come. We have to reach Moses. This has turned from an angry crowd into a homicidal mob. There will be no stopping them now."

Robert took a deep breath and started running again. It was to their benefit that the crowd assumed they were part of them. Now he could only hope they would outrun them. He groaned when many of the men in the mob pulled out pistols and began firing bullets in every direction, but he kept running. "Do what I do," he hollered back to Matthew, dodging and feinting as he moved down the street, hampered by the mud, but managing to stay at the front of the crowd. He pushed back terrifying flashes of the battlefield, focusing on the need to reach Moses.

Robert slowed and looked around as the mob approached the intersection of South Street and Rayburn. The area was crowded with black people merely going about their business. Surely they had heard the guns. Why were they calmly moving down the street? He watched the expressions on their faces melt into fear and confusion when the firing resumed. Every black person in sight turned and began to run down Rayburn, many of them heading across the eastern branch of the bayou. "Run!" he whispered urgently. He turned to Matthew. "What is the fastest way to the fort? I'm hoping Moses expected trouble and has gone there."

Just as Matthew pointed west down South Street, Robert saw a man burst from the grocery store on the southwest corner of the intersection. "Isn't that the man you interviewed a couple days ago?" he asked.

Matthew nodded. "John Pendergast. He's the Irishman who owns that grocery store. He's looking for trouble," he added grimly. "He told me he's been prepared for trouble ever since some blacks tried to burgle his store. He ran them off, but now that there is a mob, he will be dangerous. He's been looking for payback for months."

Robert turned to run toward the fort, but something held him in place. He watched as Pendergast followed the crowd of rioters and the blacks who were fleeing. The grocer advanced on a man running about twenty feet in front of the rest of the mob, almost directly across from where Robert and Matthew were standing. Pendergast raised his pistol, aimed, and shot the fleeing man in the back of his head. The man pitched face forward into the street.

Pendergast rushed forward with a triumphant expression, grabbed his victim's arm, and rolled him over. "Blast it!" he muttered. "I am sorry I shot this man. I thought he was a no-good nigger man."

"Idiot!" Matthew exclaimed. "He just shot Henry Dunn. He's a fireman. I met him when I went by one of the fire stations with Eaton."

Pendergast looked up wildly. "Them niggers will pay for this," he growled.

Robert stood frozen in place as he watched Pendergast run toward the bayou, advancing on a short black man in army uniform. Evidently the grocer had decided more violence was the way to atone for his murderous mistake.

"Hey, you!" Pendergast called. "Come back here. You will not be harmed."

The soldier slowed and stopped, his eyes wide with uncertainty.

Robert exchanged a quick look with Matthew. "Is he telling the truth?" There was so much chaotic confusion that he couldn't make sense of what was happening, but the tightness in his gut told him the black man was walking into a trap. He opened his mouth to holler a warning, not caring if it opened him to suspicion. Again, he was too late.

As the soldier approached, a pleading expression on his face, Pendergast smirked and pulled the trigger, shooting him in the face. Another policeman, seeing the soldier fall, put a bullet into his side. "We got him!"

Pendergast howled, rushing forward to hammer the fallen soldier's head with his pistol.

Robert felt sick. He saw two more blacks in uniform on the ground, presumably dead. He had not seen one black fire a gun or offer any resistance at all. "This is nothing but a slaughter," he growled.

Matthew pressed his arm. "We have to get out of here," he said. "It's only going to get crazier. Right now they are only shooting blacks in uniform, but that could change. Come on!"

Robert pushed down the bile in his stomach and started running again until they broke out onto South Street.

Matthew's prophecy came true.

The mob quickly spread east and west along the street, shooting and beating any black person they came upon. Crazy yelling and pistol fire added to the chaos as black people fled, many of them screaming with terror. A young servant collapsed on the sidewalk, blood streaming from a gaping wound. A teenage boy fell in the street, lifting his hand for help as the mob ran past. One man stopped to give him a brutal kick in the head. The boy's hand dropped.

Robert and Matthew pressed up against the side of a building, watching helplessly as black people continued to fall. Soldiers were the primary target, but no one was exempt. "We have to stop this!" Robert gasped.

"Why would you want to stop it?" a voice snarled.

Robert whipped his head around, just then realizing there were many white people pressed against the buildings. Instead of the horror he was feeling, most of the faces reflected angry satisfaction. The man who had spoken to him was rotund and bald, his blue eyes glittering with something that looked like glee. Robert scowled. "It's wrong," he said angrily.

The glittering eyes flattened to a deadly cobalt as the man stared at him. "You some kind of nigger lover?"

Robert, in spite of his fury, realized he and Matthew could also be in danger if he said what he was thinking. They had come to get Moses. They would do him no good if they were hurt or killed. They had fought their way out of messes since their college days together but taking on a mob was foolish. He exchanged a glance with Matthew and moved out into the street, walking rapidly toward the fort. He breathed a sigh of relief when he saw blacks coming out to gather up the fallen, but his relief died when he acknowledged that most of them must surely be dead.

Moses felt sick to his stomach as he listened from his place on the wall. He couldn't see much of what was going on, but the fusillade of bullets and the screams told their own story. Most of the men had been called into their barracks, but Moses, not being part of the unit, had been left alone. Anger and pain warred in him, pulling up memories and depths of feeling he had been trying to tamp down since the end of the war. He tried to force himself to breathe evenly, but his chest heaved with raw emotion.

His attention was caught by a flash of movement across the street from the gate. As he watched, he saw a man in uniform peer around the corner and then dash across the road toward the fort, terror written all over his face. Moses slid off the wall and hurried down just in time to see the doors open enough for the man to slip through. Only then did he recognize him as one of the soldiers he had met his first day in Memphis. "Frank Williams?"

Frank whirled around, his lean face coated with dust. "Moses!" His face twisted with agony. "How many of the fellas are here?"

"Most of them," Moses assured him. "What's happening out there?"

"It's bad," Frank said grimly. "I was downtown when I heard rumors of a riot. I decided to check it out for myself. When I got to Main, I found a bunch of police and white people attacking blacks. Then I saw Jimmy..." His breath caught. "We done served together since they let us in the army. They shot him, Moses. I watched him fall." He shook his head. "I wanted to help him, but I saw them shoot another soldier, so I ran," he mumbled, shame mixed with the pain in his eyes.

Moses gripped his arm. "You were wise to get out of there. Your uniform makes you a target."

"That's what I figured," Frank agreed. "I got out of there as quick as I could. I knew I had to get to the fort. I ran down a cross street to Shelby, but I done found another group of people killing blacks." His voice broke off as he shuddered. "Somehow I got away and came here."

By the time he was finished with his report, many of his comrades had gathered around. Their faces were grim as they listened.

"We got to get out there!" one exclaimed. "My family be out there."

"We can't leave our families out there while we hide away like cowards!" another cried.

Colonel Kappner, once the commander of the Third, walked up from behind them. "You all have to stay in the fort," he ordered. "More black soldiers on the street will only stoke the violence. I know you're frightened for your families, but your presence could put them more in danger."

Moses, knowing he was right, watched the men's faces. He could tell Kappner's warning had gotten through to some of them but angry agitation filled most of the faces as the muttering continued. Some of the men returned to their barracks, but about one hundred of them continued to mill around in confused indecision.

It was Roy who finally stepped forward to take control. "We ain't in the army anymore," he hollered loudly. "Ain't no one can tell us what to do. Especially when they ain't paid us for six months! I ain't hiding out in this fort while my wife and children are gunned down."

Moses understood why Colonel Kappner wanted them to stay in the fort, but he also couldn't blame Roy for what he was feeling. He would never stay in the fort if he knew Rose, John, and Hope were in danger. The not knowing would kill him, and if something were to happen to them, the guilt would eat him alive.

"That's right!" another man cried, rushing toward the gate. Within moments, the one hundred men who had been milling around followed him.

"You coming, Moses?" Roy challenged.

Moses shook his head slowly. As appalled as he was by what was happening, and as certain as he was that nothing would keep him inside if Rose and his children were in Memphis, he also knew it would serve no purpose for him to join in the riot. "No."

Roy's lip curled as he stared at him. "I thought you came to help us." His voice was thick with contempt.

Moses understood his anger. There was a part of him that wanted to join in the melee. He welcomed the opportunity to release his anguish and anger with violence. Another part of him, the part that compelled him to stay in the fort, was telling him this was not the battle he was meant to fight. He didn't understand it, but he couldn't ignore the certainty he felt. "Be careful," was all he said.

Roy glared at him and ran through the gate, pulling out the pistol he had tucked in his waistband.

Moses watched him go, exchanged a long, sad look with Colonel Kappner, and walked slowly back to his scouting position on the wall. He no longer knew what he was looking for, but it felt better than hiding out in the barracks.

Robert and Matthew were close to the fort when they saw the gates burst open and discharge a large group of black soldiers. Instinctively, they ducked into a narrow opening between two buildings. They had seen no more white rioters in the past several blocks, but they didn't know what was going on behind them.

Robert peered into the group, frantic to know what was happening with Moses but hoping he was not with these soldiers obviously intent on retaliation. In spite of the fact that Moses was not in uniform, his massive size would make him an easy target. He breathed easier when he didn't see his friend, but fresh worries over whether Moses had already been wounded or killed filled him.

"Right now we're nothing but white men," Matthew observed. "I don't know how we're going to find Moses. At this very moment, we're an easy target." He glanced at the darkening sky. "We don't want to be trapped down here at night."

"And I'm not at all sure we want to follow the soldiers," Robert replied. "I don't think they would give us time to explain who we are." He managed to grin. "We've found ourselves in some interesting positions, my friend, but I'm not sure how to get out of this one."

Matthew nodded, his eyes fixed on the fort. "We take refuge in the fort."

"Peter and Crandall will be worried," Robert protested.

"Worry is better than grief," Matthew said shortly. "Moses is smart. My bet is that he's in the fort."

"And if he's not?"

"Then there is nothing else we can do tonight anyway," Matthew said. "I was the one who brought all of you to Memphis. The least I can do is try to get us out alive."

"Robert! Matthew!"

Robert jerked his head around when he heard his name. His face split into a broad grin when he saw Moses peering down at them from the fort walls.

"I do believe we found Moses," Matthew gasped with relief.

Checking to make sure no one was close by, the two men ran across the street and rapped on the fort gate.

It swung open immediately, but their way was blocked by two grim-faced soldiers. "Who are you?" one of them snapped.

"Friends of mine," came the reply as Moses stepped into the light cast by the lanterns shining down on the yard.

The two soldiers, both white men from the Sixteenth Battalion, relaxed a little but held their guns ready. "That right?" one questioned.

Robert nodded. "Moses came to Memphis with us. When we heard about the riot, we came down to find him."

The soldier who was speaking smirked. "Moses used to be your slave?" he questioned. "I heard some of the slaves aren't real anxious to leave their masters. It's good to know some of them still know their place."

"There is not a single black person in this nation who would rather be a slave," Matthew snapped. "The fact that you are ignorant enough to make that statement after serving with these men only shows how far we have to go. You're a disgrace to your uniform! I'll make sure to include your statement in my book, as well as the report I send to the government." He turned to Moses with a smile. "It's good to see you, my friend. You had us worried."

Moses turned to them as soon as they were out of range of the soldier. "This isn't over," he said urgently.

Chapter Nineteen

Peter and Crandall, standing just outside City Hall, watched as the aldermen spilled out of the building. They had seen the mayor, obviously drunk, stumble inside as the meeting was about to start twenty minutes earlier.

"They're leaving already?" Peter asked with surprise. "Certainly they had a lot to talk about since their city is being torn apart by rioters."

Crandall stepped in front of one of the aldermen. "Is there anything you can tell us, sir?"

The alderman's eyes flashed. "I can tell you our mayor is a drunken idiot," he snapped. "He tried to form us into a posse." His eyes narrowed with disgust. "His response to the peril in our city is to lead a little force of city aldermen to South Memphis to deal with the unrest. Imagine!"

"Has there been a request made to General Stoneman?" Peter asked. He knew Stoneman, a prominent cavalry commander during the war, had only taken over as the head of all military personnel a few months earlier in January. His offices on Promenade Street were a long way from the fort. His research had shown Stoneman was determined to protect the freedmen from gross abuse, but the general had little confidence in the blacks' capacity for productive citizenship, and he was far more critical of the black troops.

"He has declined to help," the alderman said briefly, his eyes sparkling with disdain.

"Declined to help?" Peter echoed. "How can he do that?" His mind raced as he considered the implications of no military assistance.

The alderman sighed. "Our relationship with the army has not been the best. We have told them repeatedly that we are capable of handling our own affairs. Now that we need them, we have been told to prove our ability to do what we say we can do." He shrugged with frustration. "Even if he was willing to help, the remaining forces under his control consist of only a hundred eighty-five men. They are barely larger than our police department."

"So what is going to be done to stop the violence?" Peter asked. He chose not to make the observation that since it was the Memphis police *causing* the violence, they could hardly be counted on to *stop* it.

The alderman stared at him for a long moment, shook his head, and walked away.

A noise in the distance caught Peter's attention. "There is more rioting on Beale Street!"

Crandall nodded. "We've done all we can do tonight," he said uneasily. "We should go back to our hotel."

Peter considered this. He knew Crandall was right, but he shook his head. "I can't report what we don't see. I'll meet you back at the hotel later." He didn't say that he was also looking for Robert and Matthew in the madness. He turned and walked toward the sound of gunfire. Crandall heaved a heavy sigh and followed him.

When they broke out onto Beale Street, they saw pockets of police and white citizens attacking black people whose only crime had been leaving their homes. Peter was sure they were simply unaware of the violence in South Memphis.

"The poor devils," Peter said between gritted teeth, as he watched a man try to run into a grocery store to flee the mob, only to be grabbed and beaten viciously. The man finally managed to break free and run into the store. Peter hoped he would escape through the back.

Moments later a black man emerged from a building's basement carrying a pan. He hurried toward him to warn him of the danger, but before he could get close enough to even holler a warning, he saw a dozen men pounce on him, beating him in the head. The man fought desperately to escape, but a club blow to the head dropped him to his knees. Another blow felled him completely. He collapsed into a gutter and lay lifeless.

Peter watched helplessly as the mob continued to beat him, egged on by a larger crowd of white men and boys who were content to merely watch. "Shoot him!" one of the watchers yelled maniacally.

Peter gaped in horror when one of the policemen pulled out his pistol and fired a bullet into the hapless man at close range. Peter heard the man groan loudly.

The policeman laughed. "Let's go find us another one, boys!"

Peter clenched his fists and began to move forward, jerking to a stop when one of the policemen walked back and casually fired another shot into the man's body, laughing gleefully as the black man emitted another loud groan.

Peter waited several minutes, making sure the crowd wasn't going to return. He was not going to leave the man in the gutter. He knew he was putting himself in danger, but he was beyond caring. If he couldn't stop the violence, at least he could do something to help the victims.

"We've got to get out of here," Crandall whispered frantically, gazing around into the shadows.

Peter hesitated, wondering if he shouldn't just go back to his hotel. Surely there was nothing that could be done to save the man lying in the gutter. A sudden movement caught his attention. He tensed himself for another attack, but all he saw was a tiny black woman run to the man's side. She looked frantically up and down the street and then knelt by the victim, who was obviously her husband. She rested her hand on his chest and leaned close to speak to him before she cradled his bloody head in her hands and bowed her head. Sobs shook her shoulders, convulsing her slight frame.

Peter moved forward with determination, hesitating again when he realized he wasn't alone on the street. Three other white men appeared from the shadows and walked up to where the woman knelt beside her husband.

"We ought to finish off this nigger," one growled.

The woman froze, not lifting her head to acknowledge them. Peter was sure at that moment that she was wishing they would kill her as well.

"Why waste a bullet?" another of the men said dismissively. "They killed him once. Why kill him again? The nigger women ain't worth our ammunition. We got other niggers waiting for our bullets."

Peter gritted his teeth, waited until they were out of range, and then moved forward before someone else appeared. The woman raised her head defiantly when he knelt down beside her. Her young face was twisted with deep anguish. "I am so sorry," he said quietly. "I'm not here to hurt you or your husband." He swiveled his head. "We have to get him off the streets." He scanned the man's body. "His wounds are severe, but he is still alive. Let's get him back into your home where he can get treatment."

The woman stared at him. "Why are you helping me?" she asked faintly.

"Because all white people are not like the idiots tearing Memphis apart tonight," Peter said. He motioned to Crandall, who ran forward, watching over his shoulder to make sure no more men were headed in their direction. Peter knew the mob wouldn't hesitate to turn on a white man with black sympathies.

Moving quickly, Peter and Crandall lifted the piteously wounded man as carefully as they could and carried him into his basement room. He was unconscious and covered with blood, but he was still breathing. They laid him down gently onto the rough mattress on the floor, noticing that the room, though simply furnished, was scrupulously clean. The smell of baking beans filled the air.

"He was on his way to get some cornmeal for me," the woman whispered. "I sent him out to his death."

"You had no way of knowing what was happening," Peter said. "Can you have someone go for a doctor?" he asked. "He needs immediate care."

The woman nodded. "My neighbor will go. He can slip out the back." She stepped forward and gripped Peter's right hand tightly. "Thank you."

Peter nodded, his heart catching at the brave courage shining through her grief. "I'm truly sorry this has happened. I tried to warn him, but it was too late."

The woman nodded. "This trouble done been brewing for a long time. It ain't nothing we're not used to. We done hoped it would be different once we was free, but trouble seems to follow black folks."

"It will change," Peter said encouragingly, not sure if he believed his own words. Violence against blacks was only escalating now that freedom had come.

The woman looked at him with eyes both wise and knowing—eyes far too old for such a young face. "Will it? It gonna take a long time for this much hatred to change. I don't reckon if change ever does come, that it gonna be in *my* lifetime." She squeezed Peter's hand and released it. "You're a good man. Now get out of here. And don't let nobody see you coming out of our home. There's still a lot of hatred out there right now. It ain't all been used up yet."

Peter nodded and eased out the door, watching carefully from the shadows for many minutes before he and Crandall stepped out into the street and hurried toward their hotel.

Matthew, Robert and Moses followed the other gate guard to an empty barrack where they would stay for the night.

"He isn't always like that," the soldier said apologetically, his brown eyes shining sincerely beneath his thick thatch of brown hair.

Matthew glanced at him. "Bigoted ignorance is not what we need in our country right now," he said bluntly. "Especially not from people who are supposed to be protecting the rights of the freedmen. It is inexcusable."

"You're right," the soldier said. "I just wanted you to know he hasn't always been like that."

"What changed him?" Moses asked. "Your name is Hopkins?"

"Yes, Larry Hopkins." He paused, obviously searching for words. "He has some cousins that ran a grocery store in Memphis. They were doing really well until they got robbed one night by some black fellows."

"Let me guess," Moses said heavily. "They were from the Third."

Hopkins nodded. "Unfortunately, yes. The thing is," he continued, "all the men took was some food…"

"To feed their families," Moses finished for him, fully aware of how much the soldiers' families were suffering because they had not been paid. "Was anyone hurt?"

"No," Hopkins admitted, "but they went out of business shortly after that. They were already struggling, but the robbery was the last straw. They closed their doors two weeks later."

"And he blames the soldiers," Moses responded.

"Yes. His cousins went bankrupt and had to leave the city."

"Did he think about blaming the United States government for not paying the soldiers for six months?"

Hopkins met Moses' eyes squarely. "It's easier to blame someone you can take it out on."

Moses nodded, a smile lighting his eyes in spite of everything he was feeling. "You're a smart man."

"I joined this fight to help free the slaves," Hopkins replied. "My parents were some of the first to join the abolition movement. I was like everyone else who thought it would be a short war." He frowned. "People change after years of death and destruction, Moses. Some think they are lucky to be alive. Others wish they had died along with their friends so that they don't have to endure what is happening in our country now. Everyone is confused, but there are a lot of soldiers who can't make sense out of what is happening right now. They thought the end of the war would be the end of our problems."

"And you?" Moses asked, watching him closely.

"I'm glad to be alive, but I know things aren't going to change very fast."

"What do you think will force change?" Moses asked, very much wanting to hear from this man with clear, thoughtful eyes.

Hopkins stared at him. "Black men who will step up to be leaders," he said. "There aren't enough of them." He paused thoughtfully. "I wouldn't want to do it if I were black, but I don't see another way."

Moses wanted to block out what he was hearing, but he knew the time had come to stop hiding.

"There are certainly a lot of blacks who helped abolition become a reality," Hopkins continued, "but those were Northern blacks. It's time for the Southern blacks to show they are not what white people think they are." His voice shifted as he looked at Moses again. "I've been watching the men of the Third, Moses. They are looking to you for answers."

"What makes you say that?"

"I heard Roy and Harry talking one day about the stories you told them on the train. The other men were eating it up. They need to believe they can be more than what they hear from everyone. The Union let them fight in the war, but now that the war is over, they are being treated as inferior. The Civil Rights Act passed, but you and I both know that is just a first step. It is going to take black men and women willing to fight against a lot of prejudice to turn things around."

"I run a plantation in Virginia," Moses said weakly. "My work is back there." Even in the midst of hearing his voice, he knew he was coming to the end of his denial. Anger battled with acceptance. He was tired of fighting for the right to live. Would it ever end?

Hopkins gazed at him for a long moment. "I been roughed up a few times because of my views about black people. There's a lot of good people all over this country, but there are still too many who want to be controlled by hatred and prejudice. I'm willing to take the consequences of my beliefs, but big change isn't going to come from what *white* people do. People won't change until they see blacks from the South destroying their white perceptions." He took a deep breath. "It's going to take a lot of courage for the freed slaves to do that. It's also going to take strong leaders who can make people believe they can do more than they believe they can do. Leaders who will give them the courage to take action.

From what I can tell, you're one of those leaders, Moses. I understand why you don't want to do it, but..." He let his voice trail off, but the message in his eyes was clear.

Moses stood in silence. He nodded slowly, recognizing the moment when he ceased fighting the battle he had been engaged in since the end of the war. He felt Matthew and Robert's eyes on him. He could see by the looks on their faces that they realized the shift that had just occurred.

"I've got to get back to the barracks," Moses said firmly. He reached out and grasped Hopkins' hand. "Thank you."

Moses watched the group of men huddled together in the corner, talking furiously but keeping their voices very low. Roy and the others had still not returned. He knew the only thing keeping the other men from joining the fray was a lack of weapons.

One man raised his voice loudly enough to be heard. "Our old weapons be stored in the fort's armory. Since they ain't paid us, I reckon them guns and the ammo belong to us."

"That's right!" another man cried.

Moses stepped forward. "They have guards around the armory," he warned. "You won't get past them."

"You watch us!" one of the men cried. "My family be out there with no protection. If the army ain't gonna go take care of them, it's up to us!"

"We must have our guns!" one man cried.

Other men took up the cry. "We must have our guns!"

Moses shook his head, following at a distance as twenty or so men rushed out to descend on the armory. It was just as he predicted. A party of troops stood guard in front of the armory with their loaded muskets and fixed bayonets. Captain Thomas Durnin of the Sixteenth

Brigade stood to the side. Moses was close enough to hear the quiet order he gave his troops.

"Fire."

Moses was relieved to see the muskets were pointed well over the heads of the raiding soldiers, but the sound of the bullets whizzing over their heads was enough. They jolted to a stop, exchanging wild looks. Moses stepped forward.

"There is another way," he called. "You won't help your families if you're shot for trying to steal government supplies, or if you're thrown in the brigade. Go back to the barracks."

Growling angrily, they turned back to the barracks. Durnin exchanged a long look with Moses and motioned for his men to lower their guns.

The gate to the fort swung open. The hundred or so soldiers who had left earlier came striding back in, boasting of all they had done.

Roy approached Moses. "They're gone," he announced. "We done run them off!"

Moses had one question. "How bad is it out there?"

Roy scowled. "It's bad. I seen dozens of people lying in the road and heard about lots more folks who were hurt before they hid inside."

"Do you think they'll be back?"

Roy shook his head. "Nah. We scared them off. I reckon the whole thing be over."

Moses nodded, but he knew Roy was wrong. His gut told him there was plenty of trouble ahead.

Peter and Crandall were approaching their hotel in the heart of downtown when rioting broke out afresh. Mobs of white people seemed to coalesce spontaneously, joining together to shoot or beat every black person they caught.

"There is not one black person resisting," Peter muttered, his heart pounding with fresh fear as he wondered if they could make it back to the hotel.

"What good would it do?" Crandall demanded. "They're so outnumbered they know it won't do any good."

Peter caught sight of United States Marshal Martin T. Ryder leaving the offices of the *Memphis Post*. He had met him the day before when he had gone by to talk to Eaton. Ryder had lived in Memphis for almost a decade, but he still was a devout Unionist and an active Republican. Eaton had warned him yesterday that he should consider himself a target if anything were to happen, but Ryder had laughed it off.

Peter moved forward to deliver another warning but was stopped when a carriage overturned in front of them. He bit back an oath as he jumped back just in time to keep from being hit.

The driver tried to halt his team, but the terrified horses bolted, pulling the carriage behind them as they plunged down the muddy road. Three white men savagely beating a black man barely escaped being hit. The distraction gave the black man the opportunity to jump up and flee. Other whites gave chase, but another one eyed Marshal Ryder and moved forward with an angry sneer on his face.

Peter, every sense alert for danger, moved close enough to listen.

"I know who you are," the man growled.

Ryder stood silently, returning his glare with a level look.

The man snarled now. "You and the rest of folks like you are responsible for stirring up the blacks. If it weren't for you and them other Yankees coming down here and making the niggers think they are better than they are, this wouldn't be happening. I reckon you ought to be killed for it. We have killed us a lot of niggers tonight, but they ain't the only ones causing trouble." He turned to the crowd of people that had formed. "You're nothing but a damned Yankee abolitionist." His voice rose to a fanatical pitch as he realized he had an audience. "You're worse than a nigger!"

Peter hoped the incident would end with name calling, but as he began to move forward he saw the man grab his pistol and slam Ryder in the head with it. Ryder staggered but managed to stay on his feet. He saw Ryder begin to reach for his gun and then withdraw his hand, afraid doing so would encourage the man to shoot him.

"Well done!" Peter called loudly, clapping his hands together in applause. "It's about time these Yankees get their due!"

He hid his smirk when the attacker turned to him with a gloating smile on his face. Ryder met Peter's eyes over the man's head. Ryder nodded his gratitude and quickly vaulted into his saddle, his horse breaking into a gallop immediately.

"Stop!" the man cried when he whipped around to find his quarry fleeing.

"Don't worry about it," Peter said soothingly. "You made your point. I reckon that Yankee will be in hiding for the rest of the night." He was quite sure Ryder was on his way to disperse more information to the government, but he didn't feel the need to point that out.

"You're right," the man said smugly. "Them Yankees ain't nothing but cowards who think they can come down here and change the way we live. We're teaching them a lesson today we should have taught them a long time ago."

Peter nodded his agreement, somehow managing to hide his disdain, and continued down the street.

Crandall regarded him with admiration. "Quick thinking."

"I met Ryder yesterday. He's a good man. He has a wife and two kids who need him to come home."

Peter and Crandall continued moving toward their hotel, slowly realizing the street was completely clear of black people. Surely the trouble would end since there was no one else to attack. There still were groups of white men milling around, but Peter hoped they would all go home soon.

"Let's get back to the hotel," Peter said wearily.

"I'm with you," Crandall responded, his face reflecting his own fatigue. "Even with the warnings that this could happen, I wasn't prepared for it to be this bad." His eyes settled on two black men sprawled in the mud, their bodies glowing oddly under the nearly full moon shining down on them. "What will happen with them?"

Peter swallowed. "I'm hoping once the streets empty, their friends and family will come out for them." Suddenly, the reality of the situation was almost more than he could bear. Worry for Matthew, Robert, and Moses erupted. He jolted to a stop and stared in the direction of the fort. "Do you think they made it back?"

Crandall shook his head. "We won't know until we get back to the hotel, but they are resourceful men."

Peter heard the uncertainty in his voice but knew he was right. "Let's go," he said. "I need to know they're okay."

They were blocks from their hotel when movement caught their attention. There was a part of Peter that wanted to ignore it. His bed was calling him, but the journalist in him couldn't let it go. "What's that?" he asked.

"I suppose we have to find out," Crandall replied reluctantly.

Peter managed a chuckle. "For someone who always seems to resist everything, you're never anywhere but in the midst of the action."

Crandall grinned. "It's part of my strategy. I keep people off guard and then slip right in for the story." His grin evaporated quickly, a look of alarm filling his face. "That's Chief Garrett with a unit of his policemen."

"They haven't done enough damage already?" Peter snapped. He was just tired enough to throw all caution to the wind. Increasing his pace, he stepped up to the chief of police. "Hello, Chief Garrett."

The chief, his eyes swinging through the night for signs of danger, blinked and then focused on him. "Hello, Peter," he said distractedly. "I can't talk right now."

"I know you're busy," Peter replied. "Where are you headed?"

"South Memphis," Garrett replied. "I will not rest until the blacks are thoroughly under control."

Peter gazed around. "You believe there is still danger? Every black downtown is off the streets." He turned his eyes on the group of policemen, trying to choose his words carefully. "I understand things got a little out of control earlier today."

Garrett scowled. "That won't happen again. These men will be under firm control. My sole agenda is to establish a police presence in South Memphis that will maintain order and suppress black unrest."

Peter had grave doubts, but he was dismissed when Garrett strode away to join his squad of men. Peter's eyes met Crandall's. By unspoken agreement, they melted into the shadows and began to follow the police. Peter pushed all thoughts of slumber out of his mind. Regardless of the chief's intent, he recognized trouble when he saw it brewing.

The streets were virtually empty as they made their way toward the fort. There were no faces peering out from windows. Every building was shrouded in darkness, the frightened residents understanding that nothing should draw attention to them. Peter could imagine people huddled inside in stark fear of what the rest of the night would bring.

Wanting to hear what the policemen were saying, Peter motioned to Crandall and picked up his pace. Just as he was rounding a corner, he approached close enough to a burly Irish policeman to hear his words. "I aim to kill every black person I can find, and then I'm going to burn down every nigger shanty I can get my hands on."

Peter exchanged an alarmed look with Crandall. "The only hope for these people is to stay off the streets."

He watched as Chief Garrett pulled the men together, exchanged a few quiet words, and waved his arm to indicate they should break into smaller squads.

"He's a fool," Crandall muttered. "It will be impossible for him to control these men now."

Peter nodded, his heart thudding in his chest. "If the people just stay off the streets..." he muttered again.

During the long day he had not seen one black person resist or fight back. The best thing they could do was simply hide.

It took only five minutes for him to realize it didn't matter. He and Crandall chose to follow a squad of four men. He watched in horror as they marched toward a shanty and kicked the door in. He could hear the frightened voice of a woman but couldn't make out what she was saying. Peter gritted his teeth with helplessness, realizing there was nothing he and Crandall could do to stop the invasion. Even if they had weapons, he knew they would be shot down for interfering. Peter's only comfort was knowing every action taken would be reported. The policemen had no idea they were being followed.

When the men finally emerged, their voices were triumphant. "I ain't never taken my way with a pregnant nigger before," one called. "She was right pretty for a nigger woman."

Peter leaned his weight against the building, bile rising in his throat.

"We got us three hundred dollars, too," another boasted.

"They're crazy," Crandall said in a fierce whisper. "Can Garrett seriously be stupid enough not to realize what is going on?"

Peter shook his head, unable to summon words to express what he was feeling. Not one resident of South Memphis was safe.

Chapter Twenty

Carrie was pacing on the Stratfords' porch. Janie and the rest had gone on a shopping expedition earlier. They had all offered to stay, but she had waved them away, insisting she would rather be alone. She wasn't sure she had meant it, but when they disappeared in the carriage, it had been too late to call them back. She had spent all morning worrying. She whirled around in relief when the door opened, but her face fell when she saw Abby step out alone. "Has there been word from Michael? When is he coming home?"

Abby shook her head. "I don't know. There was another case of cholera reported today. I don't believe he's had time to check on any news coming from Memphis."

"But he did say a wire had come through with news of violence in Memphis!" Carrie burst out, fear hammering at her chest. She knew her reaction was probably extreme, but she felt certain Robert was in danger. "It's bad, Abby," she said desperately. "I know it."

Abby stepped forward to grasp her hands. "You don't know anything," she said soothingly, only her eyes showing her deep concern.

Carrie shook her head and pulled away, moving to the edge of the porch so she could stare down upon the city. She had no idea what she was looking for, and she knew she would find no answers in the air swirling with coal dust, but she felt she would implode if she merely stood still. "All of them are in danger," she said through gritted teeth. "Why didn't they leave when they understood what was happening there?"

Abby managed a smile. "You do realize who we are talking about, don't you? Have you ever known any of those four men to ever run from anything? Especially Matthew and Peter?"

"Robert and Moses aren't journalists!" Carrie burst out, tears stinging her eyes. "If something happens to them, it will be Matthew and Peter's fault." She knew as soon as the words came out of her mouth that she wasn't being fair, but she was having trouble thinking clearly.

"Stop."

Carrie jerked at the sharp tone of Abby's voice. She swung around and stared at her. "What did you say?"

"I said stop," Abby repeated, her voice filled with compassion now. She moved forward and took Carrie's hands again, holding fast when Carrie tried to pull them away. "You are letting your fears take control of your thinking."

Carrie stared at Abby, her eyes burning with tears she refused to shed. Anger warred with fear. "It's so hard not to know anything," she said, looking away because she couldn't look into Abby's eyes any longer.

Abby continued to grip her hands. "Look at me," she commanded.

Carrie reluctantly swung her eyes back to Abby's face, her tears finally spilling when she saw the love etched there. "I'm so afraid," she whispered.

"Why?" Abby seemed genuinely perplexed. "Memphis is a large city. The odds are that they are nowhere near it."

"You know better than that," Carrie managed.

"You're right," Abby admitted. "I know better than that." She took a deep breath. "What is confusing me, however, is why you are so afraid. You had to wait while Robert went through scores of horrendous battles. You had to wait while everyone believed he was dead. You had to wait for him to return from England. You had to wait during the long months he gave up on life. Surely those things were scarier than his being in Memphis?" She placed a hand under Carrie's chin and forced her eyes up. "Why this? What is scaring you so much?"

"I've almost lost him three times," Carrie replied in a broken voice. "It's been a miracle that he came back to me." She stopped, knowing she wasn't answering Abby's question. Forcing her mind to slow down, she searched for the answer. When it came, her eyes widened.

"What is it?" Abby pressed.

"If something happens, it is my fault," Carrie cried. "I left him in Virginia." The realization almost choked her. "If I had stayed on the plantation, he wouldn't have gone to Memphis."

"And you know this how?" Abby asked.

Carrie hesitated. In some part of her mind she knew she wasn't making any sense, but that didn't stop the stream of words that rushed out. "It's foaling season. He wouldn't have left the plantation if he wasn't upset." Even as she said it, she knew Robert was certain the mares wouldn't drop their babies until late May, long after he would return. Besides, he had Clint there to handle things. None of it mattered to her churning heart.

Abby continued to watch her quietly. "Did he give you any indication he was upset with your decision to enter medical school?"

Carrie waved her hand. "No, but he wasn't being honest."

Abby heaved a sigh. "Carrie, where is this coming from?"

"It's a woman's place to stay home!" Carrie cried. Hearing the words come from her mouth was enough to shock her into silence. She stood motionless for a long moment and then sank into the rocker behind her. "Did I really just say that?"

Abby sat down next to her but remained silent.

"I really just said that, didn't I?" Another realization hit her. "Does that mean I believe it?" The very idea horrified her.

"Do you?" Abby questioned gently, nothing but love shining in her eyes.

"I said it, didn't I?" Carrie asked, confusion swarming through her.

"You did," Abby agreed. "That certainly means you have been *conditioned* to believe it, but that is different from actually *believing* it."

Carrie stared at her. "I sounded like my mother when I said that." She shook her head, trying to make sense of everything. "But I've always rebelled against the things she said."

"That doesn't mean they didn't sink deep into your being," Abby responded. "It can be very difficult to break free from beliefs ingrained in us from childhood. We can take action, but that doesn't mean we don't carry the weight...or the guilt of going against those beliefs."

Carrie stared at her, feeling an odd relief at the expression on Abby's face. "You've felt this way, too," she gasped.

Abby smiled wryly. "More times than I care to admit." She reached over to hold Carrie's hand. "It's almost impossible not to feel them. Every woman is trained from birth to believe and act in certain ways, but if you're from the South it notches up to an entirely different level."

Carrie managed a small smile. "That's putting it mildly." Memories of her mother trying to shape her into a proper Southern plantation mistress swarmed through her mind.

"Carrie, up until now you've *planned* on rebelling. You've *planned* to go to medical school." Abby continued. "Now that you have actually done it, the lessons forced on you when you were young are rising up to tell you your decision was wrong."

"Does every woman face this?" Carrie asked.

"Only the ones determined to live life on their own terms," Abby replied. "When you decide to do something against the status quo, or when you decide to be more than men tell you is possible, you will fight not only society, but what has been ingrained in you."

"Wonderful," Carrie murmured.

Abby laughed. "At least you're not alone." She sobered and turned to look in Carrie's eyes. "It takes tremendous courage to do what you are doing. Each of your housemates is being courageous, but you were the only one to leave your husband. The voices inside your head are going to be louder. Every time a man taunts you outside the medical school, you are not just going to see the face of a man. You are also going to see Robert. Part of you will wonder if you are being utterly selfish in becoming a doctor. You will feel guilt for leaving your husband."

Carrie nodded, feeling a surge of relief to have her feelings expressed so eloquently. "You don't believe I'm being selfish?" She knew the answer, but she needed to hear it again anyway. She was confident Abby wouldn't make light of her question.

"You're not being selfish at all," Abby assured her. "The dream of being a doctor has pulled you forward for a long time. More important is the fact that you have a gift many women don't have."

"Don't have, or won't use?" Carrie asked, her thoughts moving smoothly again. She couldn't believe she was one of a fortunate few who had been gifted with innate abilities.

"Good question," Abby replied with a smile. "I believe every single person—man and woman—is born with a gift and skills that are meant to be developed. There is something they are meant to do. Men are encouraged to find their skills. Women are told to simply be what men need or want them to be. Women who refuse to do that are criticized and humiliated. They are made to feel that they are somehow not truly female because they aren't following the roles men have set out for them."

Carrie gazed at her, thinking about all Abby had been through since her husband died. "You don't sound bitter," she observed. "Why is that?"

"Because it serves no purpose," Abby responded. "Oh, there have been plenty of times when I was bitter and angry. When Charles died, I felt so completely alone. I railed against every man because they were my enemy. Then I met Matthew. When he stepped in to help me, I realized I couldn't target an entire gender with my anger. Once I let go of the fury, I found more men who were open-minded. There weren't many of them," she admitted with a smile, "but there were enough to give me hope. There were enough to keep my heart open…"

"Which is why you fell in love with my father," Carrie said quietly.

"Yes. Your father is an extraordinary man, but I would never have married him if I were not completely confident he saw me as his equal."

"I'm not sure Robert sees me that way," Carrie whispered, facing another fear as the breeze swirled around the porch, lifting the tendrils of her dark hair and caressing her hot cheeks.

"What makes you feel that way?"

"We never talked about equality before we got married," Carrie admitted. "I was so in love with him. There was a war going on, and I had almost lost him. All I wanted to do was marry him before he left again."

"Has he given you any indication that you should not become a doctor? Or that he believes you are not equal?"

"No," Carrie said quickly, "but I'm not sure he would tell me even if he felt that way."

"You think he is hiding resentment and anger?" Abby pressed.

Carrie considered the question carefully. "No," she finally answered, feeling a surge of relief when she recognized the truth of her answer. "Robert genuinely wants me to become a doctor." Horror followed quickly on the heels of her relief. "So it's *me* who is not sure I should be a doctor?" she gasped.

"It's you who has been trained that it's wrong for you to be anything more than a subservient woman available for her husband's needs," Abby responded. "It takes time to get rid of those beliefs."

"How *much* time?" Carrie demanded, impatient to be completely free from the shackles of her upbringing. "There is so much I want to do. I don't want to feel this way." She laughed as a surge of joy coursed through her. She could almost feel the chains dropping away.

Abby laughed with her. "I'd say facing it today is a huge step. Now that you know it is there, it won't have the same power over you." She sobered. "Neither will it go away quickly. Generations of women being forced into acceptable roles is not easy to break out of. It would be a mistake to think it is. You have to face it every time and then make the conscious choice to set your old beliefs behind you and live in a different way."

Carrie choked back her laugh when she saw the gravity shining in Abby's eyes. She thought of her mother so carefully crafted by Southern society. She was quite sure her grandmother had been the same and somehow just as certain that it flowed through generations of women on both sides of her family. She could almost see a long line of compliant, gentle-faced women staring at her across the whispers of time. The surprising thing was that she didn't see condemnation or judgment. Rather, she saw eyes gazing at her with almost desperate hope. "Why am I different?"

Abby smiled now. "That is a good question. I have wondered the same thing about myself many times. On May tenth, you will meet hundreds of women who are different—who are willing to go against society." She stared across the yard thoughtfully. "All I can tell you is that things are changing. A large number of women have had the courage to step forward and change things. Right now it seems like there are only glimmers of change, but it is enough for me to believe things will get better." She opened her mouth to say more, but the rattle of wheels on the street distracted her.

Carrie leaned over the railing to see who was coming. "It's Michael!" She straightened her shoulders with defiance, determined to fight the fear and guilt that had consumed her earlier. She turned to Abby and embraced her warmly. "Thank you. I honestly don't know what I would do without you."

Abby pulled her close. "And I don't know what I would do without you," she whispered. Then she released Carrie and pushed her toward the walkway. "Go talk to Michael."

Carrie was standing by the gate when Michael pulled up. He smiled brightly, but he couldn't cover the worry in his eyes. "Bad news?" Carrie asked, keeping her voice level.

Michael climbed down, his gaze encompassing Abby as well. "There is no specific news about Robert, Matthew or Moses," he informed them, "but the news coming from Memphis is serious. I want to emphasize that we know very little, however. The telegraphs are brief. I don't know that anyone is completely certain what is happening."

"What do the telegraphs say?" Carrie pressed.

Michael frowned. "The blacks have been rioting since yesterday afternoon. There have been deaths." He shook his head. "I'm sorry, but I really don't know more than that. We're going to have to wait until more wires come through."

Carrie forced down her fear, knowing she had no facts to substantiate them. She forced herself to change the topic of conversation. "I understand there was a new case of cholera."

Michael frowned again. "Yes," he said heavily. "It was in another part of town."

"That's not good," Abby responded. "It means it could be very difficult to contain."

Michael nodded. "Very difficult, indeed."

Rose tried to concentrate on her teaching, but she had been distracted all day. She wanted to blame it on the clear skies and warm air that blew in through the windows with the aromas of spring, but the fear pulsing in her heart told her it was something more. Moses and Robert had been gone for almost a week. She had encouraged her husband to go because she knew Moses needed to get off the plantation, but she had been uneasy ever since.

Her fertile imagination had her jumping at almost every sound, and she was much too aware there were only women living on the plantation right now. Simon had offered for him and June to move back into the main house while the men were gone, but Rose had waved off their suggestion, insisting they would be fine. Why then were alarm bells ringing so loudly in her head?

"Get a hold of yourself," she muttered. "You're borrowing trouble that isn't here." She tried to pull up memories of her mother's calm voice, but nothing was working.

The sound of hoofbeats brought her closer to the window. She forced herself to move casually, not wanting to alarm her students. She was aware they were already watching her carefully, their young senses far too attuned to her anxiety. She made herself breathe evenly as she smiled at them. "Keep working on your reading," she called brightly. "We'll talk about it in a few minutes."

As they all turned back to their books, she peered out the window, stiffening when she saw a group of white men slowly riding by. She stood where they couldn't see her, but she didn't miss the anger on their faces, nor the hostile looks they directed toward the school and clinic. Polly had not been feeling well that day, so the clinic was closed. Rose was alone with the children.

She stood and watched until the men disappeared around a curve, not able to stop the shudder of fear that coursed through her body.

"Is everything alright, Miss Rose?"

Rose turned to find Justine by her side, her mature eyes searching the road. She didn't admonish her for leaving her desk. Just like Rose, Justine carried the memory of watching the school burn. "I don't know," she said honestly, keeping her voice low so she wouldn't alarm the other children.

"I'm feeling something in the air," Justine said quietly.

"Me, too," Rose agreed, glad to have someone, even if it was a fifteen-year-old student, to share her thoughts. She gazed at the other children and made a decision quickly. Her mama had always told her to listen to her gut. She had learned to tell the difference between unreasonable fear and a warning she should pay attention to. Her gut was telling her to send the children home early so they were all sure to be safe. She hated to rob them of even a minute of education because of fear, but common sense told her it was the wisest course of action.

She clapped her hands. "Guess what, class?" If she was going to end school early, she was not going to send them home fearful. "It's such a beautiful day that I'm going to let all of you go early!"

Everyone smiled, but many of the gazes were watchful and cautious. Rose knew the older ones could see through her subterfuge, but that was probably good.

That meant they would help the younger ones get home quickly.

Rose smiled brightly, aware of Justine's watchful eyes. "The strawberries are ripe right now!" she called. "I bet if you go home through the woods, you'll be able to pick some for your dinner tonight." She was hoping the lure of the sweet, red fruit would keep them off the main road.

"Yea! Strawberries!" several of the children called, their faces beaming with excitement.

Rose helped them all with their books, grateful she didn't have to send the youngest ones off with fear. She forced herself to breathe evenly, more sure than ever that something was wrong.

"Can I do anything, Miss Rose?" Justine asked quietly, her eyes tense with anxiety.

Rose hated that the girl had seen through her, but she was also relieved to have support. "Will you walk home through the woods with everyone?" she asked. She wasn't willing to say anything more than that, but she already knew the teenager was aware trouble was in the air.

"Yes, ma'am," Justine responded. "I'll get the other older kids to stay with them, too."

"I don't want anyone else scared," Rose protested.

"We all know something is going on," Justine said, her eyes flickering with fear for the first time. "We be getting everyone home as quick as we can," she promised.

Rose felt a surge of warmth, not bothering to correct Justine's last sentence. She was too grateful for her understanding and too anxious to get the children into the covering of the woods.

"Miss Rose?" Justine hesitated before she followed the rest of the kids into the schoolyard. "You'll be careful, too?"

"I will," Rose promised. "It's probably nothing."

"If it wasn't something, you would never have let me get away with that last sentence," Justine replied knowingly.

Rose chuckled with disbelief. "You were *testing* me?"

"I know you don't want us to worry, but one thing I've learned is that I can't be prepared for trouble if I don't know it might be coming." She smiled slightly. "Protecting us won't keep us safe, Miss Rose. There is not one student here, even the little ones, that doesn't know something could happen every single day. We choose to come to school anyway. Moses did that for us the night they burned the school down. I wanted to run and hide that night and never come back to school. He taught me that I can't give in to fear." She paused. "If something happens tonight, we'll still be back tomorrow."

Rose was speechless as she watched Justine run into the yard, calling the children with a bright smile. They all crossed the road and disappeared into the woods. Only then did she breathe a sigh of relief. With the relief, however, came the realization she was completely alone. Within moments, she was mounted on Caramel, a gentle sorrel Clint had given her to ride to school every day. Forcing herself to maintain a steady trot, instead of the wild gallop her heart was screaming for, she rode home, bypassing the road by using a trail through the woods.

Rose leaned back in her rocking chair, smiling with gratitude when Annie carried out a tray of lemonade and cookies. She nestled Hope closer in her arms, watching contentedly as John and Simon played in the yard.

The horses were all out in the pasture peacefully munching grass as they waited for Clint and Amber to bring them in for the night. A red-tailed hawk circled overhead, patiently waiting for his evening meal to appear below. A doe with twin fawns edged out of the woods, her white tail swishing as her nose sniffed the air.

Her earlier fears seemed completely unfounded, but Rose remained alert. Moses was ever present in her thoughts. She couldn't shake the belief that he was in danger.

The sudden sound of carriage wheels sent her into instant panic. "John! Simon!" Rose called sharply. She grabbed Annie's arm. "Please take the children inside," she said urgently, passing Hope into her grandmother's arms.

"Something I should know?" Annie asked keenly. "You been acting jumpy all day long."

Rose shrugged. "I don't know what I'm feeling," she admitted, "but I want to make sure the children are safe." It gave her comfort to know all of them could disappear into the tunnel at any moment, but she was afraid of what could happen to the house and all the horses. "Please go!" she pleaded as the carriage noise grew closer.

"You be careful," Annie said. She smiled brightly at the boys clambering onto the porch. "I got me some hot cookies coming out of the oven. I sure could use some tasters."

The boys grinned, their smiles just like their daddies'.

Rose reached down to give John a fierce hug and then opened the door so they could disappear inside. Alone on the porch again, she forced herself to take deep, steady breaths. Her eyes narrowed and she dashed into the house, emerging moments later with a rifle resting in her arms. Moses had insisted she learn how to shoot before he left for Memphis. He would be appalled that she had almost forgotten to get her weapon. She had to admit she felt better holding it.

Moments later a carriage rounded the curve, but in the growing dusk it was too dark to see who was driving. She forced herself to wait, vaguely aware vigilantes would probably not arrive in a carriage. They would prefer the speed of horseback. Rose stood stiffly and ordered herself to remain alert. She was the only person standing between her children and trouble.

"Rose!"

As soon as the familiar voice sounded in the evening air, Rose shuddered out a relieved gasp. She relaxed and dropped the rifle onto a nearby table. "Thomas!" she cried, dashing down into the drive. "Spencer! What are you two doing here?" She tensed when she realized

Thomas wouldn't have driven all the way out from Richmond unless there was a very serious reason. "What's wrong?" she demanded, fear once more pounding through her blood.

Thomas stepped from the carriage and reached for her hands. "It's good to see you."

Rose shook her head impatiently. "It's good to see you, too, but I have been anxious about something all day. I kept expecting something to happen here, but that's not it, is it? You have to tell me what is wrong."

Thomas nodded. "I received a telegram today from Memphis."

Rose stared at him. "Memphis?" New terror roared through her mind. "Moses? Has something happened to him?" The roaring in her head was so loud she was afraid she wouldn't hear Thomas' reply. Had he survived the war only to die in Memphis?

Thomas shook his head quickly. "I don't know anything about Moses," he assured her, "but there has been a riot in Memphis."

Rose stared at him, knowing there was more. "Tell me all of it," she commanded.

Thomas heaved a sigh. "There have been black deaths, but we don't know anything more."

Rose waited, knowing he was holding something back. "You're not telling me everything," she said levelly. "I'm a grown woman, Thomas. Tell me."

Thomas glanced at Spencer. "I told you she would see right through me."

Rose waited.

"The telegram was from Peter," Thomas continued. "When they got to Memphis, Moses insisted on staying at the fort with other soldiers."

"Not with Matthew and Robert?" Rose asked. "Why?" Her mind swirled with questions.

Thomas shook his head. "I don't know. I do know that when the rioting broke out yesterday, Robert and Matthew went to find him." He hesitated. "As of this morning, Peter had not heard from any of them."

Rose forced herself to breathe. "How bad is it?" she asked.

"It's bad," Thomas admitted after a long pause. "A lot of blacks have been killed or injured. When Peter wrote, he said things were out of control." He paused and glanced back down the road. "I wanted you to hear the news from me."

Rose considered this and shook her head decisively. "That's not why you're here," she said, her mind thinking through everything she had heard. "We would have no way of hearing this news if you had decided to stay in Richmond. You could have waited until you had solid information before you came out here." Now it was her turn to glance down the road, falling silent long enough to determine if she could hear anything in the distance. When only silence filled the night, she turned back to her brother. "You are here because you're afraid we're in danger."

Spencer grinned. "I told you she weren't gonna fall for it." His grin faded as a serious look filled his face. "We knows you be out here by yourself, Rose."

"News of the Memphis riot will spread," Thomas interjected.

"And you're afraid it will spark more violence everywhere," Rose finished, her mind filled with the image of the men who had ridden by the school earlier.

"Yes," Thomas admitted. "We decided we wanted to even the odds a little more if you needed help."

A sudden movement at the edge of the woods caught Rose's attention. She watched, open-mouthed, as Simon appeared, followed by all the plantation workers and their families.

Thomas watched the group move closer. "I wasn't willing to risk their safety, either. All black communities are considered easy targets. I believe everyone will be safer on the plantation. Vigilantes will think twice about coming onto Cromwell."

Simon held up his gun. "I reckon everyone has gotten word that we all used to be soldiers, as well." His face was set and determined. "We won't let anyone get hurt."

"They don't know Robert and Moses are gone," Rose protested, but she couldn't deny the instant feeling of comfort she felt now that everyone was together. She could read the same relief on the other women's faces as their children ran around the yard, squealing as they chased the first fireflies of the year.

"Word gets around," Thomas replied. "I wasn't willing to take a chance."

Rose felt a warm surge of love as she slid her arm around Thomas' waist. In spite of how far they had come, overt expressions of affection were still rare. "Thank you," she said softly.

The door to the plantation house flung open. John and Simon came running out, thrilled to find the yard full of other children. Their happy laughter joined that of the other children. Firefly-chasing quickly turned into a game of hide-and-seek.

Rose watched the carefree children for several minutes before she turned back to Thomas.

He read the question in her eyes before she asked it. "Jeremy is running the factory. He has agreed to send someone out with news as soon as they hear something definite."

Rose nodded. She was concerned about Moses, but something had shifted inside of her. She was certain she would feel it if something bad had happened. She had been anxious all day, but she didn't feel a sense of loss. She knew the ache in her would be a gaping, dark void if her husband was dead or wounded. She had experienced that agonized knowing when Moses had been shot during battle. She felt none of that now.

Thomas sighed as he settled back in the chair he had pulled close to the window. He had no real reason to expect trouble, but he certainly didn't have a reason *not* to.

Rose carried in cups of hot tea and settled down in the chair across from him. The house was finally quiet. The children were asleep, Annie had finished in the kitchen and gone to bed, and Spencer had been settled in a room upstairs. She was certain he was watching out the window, too. The knowledge added to her sense of warm security.

"That was a heavy sigh," she commented as she took a sip of her tea, watching fireflies create sparkles of light in the oak tree. In spite of the risk of danger, she felt safe. Six of the men were stationed outside the house. The rest of them were protecting the women and children down in the old quarters.

"I had this insane idea that things would be peaceful when the war ended," Thomas replied. He took a sip of his tea, but his eyes never quit scanning the darkness. "Our country feels like it is just as explosive as it was before the war. Perhaps more so. Before the war, the feelings in the South were toward the North. I felt them, but they weren't coming from the people around me. It was the people *out there*." He paused, gathering his thoughts. "Now the anger and hatred are focused *here*, on the more than four million freed slaves surrounding us every day." His fist clenched. "But it's not just them. It's also focused on people like Jeremy who are mulatto, and people like me who no longer hate and discriminate. We are all a threat they wish they could snuff out."

Rose listened quietly. This was the first time it had ever been just her and Thomas. She knew her half-brother accepted and loved her, but there had always been other people around when they talked. It felt good to sit quietly and listen to him, his voice blending with the crickets and frogs tuning up their orchestra.

"Are you afraid?" Thomas asked, swinging his gaze away from the window.

Rose met his gaze. "Most of the time I'm not. Today was a different matter. I could feel something in the air that scared me." She had told Thomas about the horsemen. He had agreed it had been wise to send the children home. "It is difficult to balance fear and reason," she admitted. "I don't want to give in to fear. Neither do I want to be foolish."

"I know what you mean. I've been scared for Abby ever since she was accosted on the way home from the factory. She hates being constantly watched, but I couldn't bear it if something happened to her."

Rose nodded. She had clear memories of Thomas' grief when his first wife died. She didn't want that for him again, and it would break her own heart if something happened to the woman she loved so much. "She'll have to deal with being watched," she murmured.

Thomas glanced back toward the window when an owl hooted loudly. "I was relieved when she headed for New York City and thrilled Carrie and the rest of the students could join her. I thought she would be safe there. Now I'm not sure any of them are."

Rose was alarmed when his face creased with a scowl. "Is something wrong in New York?"

Thomas shrugged. "They've had cases of cholera reported. Abby assures me they are safe, but I am worried."

Rose sucked in her breath. Carrie had told her enough of past cholera epidemics to know they were not easily controlled. "They are leaving the city?"

Thomas managed a small smile. "Do you remember who you are talking about? They went to attend the Women's Rights Conference. They refuse to, and I quote, *'let a little thing like cholera stop them from attending.'*"

Rose chuckled, but it did nothing to abate her sudden worry. New York was a massive city, but cholera was no respecter of people or wealth. The two women she loved best were both there, and both were in danger of a catching a disease she knew would most likely kill them. She was suddenly tired of it all. A wave of anger merged with her worry, threatening to overwhelm and swallow her. "Do you ever get sick of it?"

Thomas cocked an eyebrow. "Sick of it?" His expression invited more.

Rose groped for words. "Sick of the worry. Sick of the fear. Sick of not knowing what will happen next. Sick of waiting and hoping that things will get better, but having no real confidence it will ever happen. *Just sick of it!*" She finished with a heated burst, her heart pounding, but somehow feeling a little better that she had expressed it. The wave shrank back, lessening the pressure.

"Every day," Thomas assured her. "Then I remind myself I have no choice in what is happening, but I can definitely choose how I respond." He reached forward to grasp Rose's hand. "I almost lost myself during the war. I was so angry and bitter. I was sick of everything. Thank God I finally realized my bitterness was doing nothing but hurting myself. I still struggle with it," he admitted, "but I deal with it much more quickly."

Rose heard his words, but something bigger was happening in her as she stared down at their hands intertwined, her slim dark fingers nestled in his strong white ones. Hope soared through her, blotting out the fear and worry that had threatened to consume her. This man had once been her master. His father had raped her mother. He had sold her father and brother to protect his own father's reputation. Yet here they were, siblings connected by their humanity and a very genuine love.

Thomas seemed to read her thoughts. He gripped her hand more tightly. "Change will come, Rose. It will happen slowly and there will be much pain, but change will come."

Rose looked up and gazed into his eyes. "I believe you're right," she said softly. "I do believe you're right."

Chapter Twenty-One

As dawn claimed Memphis, sparse clouds in a clear sky could do nothing to lessen the horror daylight brought. Matthew and Robert, anxious to get back to the hotel to relieve Peter and Crandall's worry and find Eaton, left the fort as soon as there was enough light to leave safely.

"Be careful out there," Moses cautioned.

Robert smiled briefly. "You're the one who needs to be careful." He knew it was best for Moses to stay in the fort along with the hundreds of other black refugees who had poured through the gates during the long night, but it was difficult to leave him. If it had been safe for Moses to appear on the streets, Robert would have insisted he come with them. However, experience told him no one with dark skin was safe in Memphis right now.

"I'll be fine," Moses said. "Go."

Robert had gone less than a hundred yards before he saw a black man sagging against a building, his head cocked at an odd angle. He moved forward to offer assistance, but Matthew tugged him back.

"It's too late," Matthew said grimly. "He's dead."

Robert stopped, a closer look telling him it was indeed too late. They continued to walk, his shocked silence deepening as they passed other black bodies. Most were men in uniform, but women and young children lay unmoving as well. With the exception of the dead or wounded, there was no sign of life on the streets. "They're too scared to even come outside," Robert finally whispered through his clenched teeth. Sorrow and anger battled for control.

"As they should be," Matthew said in a clipped voice, his eyes blazing with anger, grief, and disgust. As much as he wanted to stop and help, he knew he needed to get back to the hotel and find out what was going on elsewhere in the city. He hurried through the streets, breathing a sigh of relief when he spotted Peter and

Crandall standing on the sidewalk outside the Hotel Gayoso.

"Peter!"

Peter jerked his head around, a relieved smile appearing on his face when he saw Matthew and Robert striding toward them. "It's good to see you two!"

"We were worried sick," Crandall added.

"Sorry," Matthew replied. He quickly explained what had kept them at the fort. "What is going on in this part of town?" he asked, desperate for more news.

Peter scowled. "It's bad. There were murders and beatings everywhere."

Matthew's eyes scanned the road as Peter filled in the details. He could feel fresh danger lurking in the air as a soft breeze rustled the leaves.

"Eaton?" Matthew asked. "How is he?"

"I don't know," Peter responded. "We were on our way to look for him. Right now the attacks seem to be centered on blacks, but my gut tells me this isn't over, and there is plenty of hatred to spread to black sympathizers."

Matthew nodded, knowing Peter was right. "Let's go. We need to find him." Eaton had the contacts that would allow him to understand more of the entire picture.

"Have you eaten?" Crandall asked.

Matthew shook his head impatiently. "There's not time."

"Make time," Crandall responded crisply. "It's going to be another very long day. If we're going to tell the truth about what is going on here, we have to have the energy to follow everything. Right now it's calm, but I don't think it will last long."

"He's right," Robert said. He took Matthew by the arm and led him into the hotel dining room. "It won't take long to eat some breakfast. We haven't eaten since lunch yesterday."

Matthew knew they were right, but he had his mouth opened to protest again when a broad smile lit his face instead. "Eaton!" He hurried toward the editor, who was sequestered in a back corner with a small group of men with grim expressions.

Eaton broke off whatever he was saying, watching them approach with an equally broad smile. "You're all right!" he boomed, lowering his voice when eyes turned their direction. "I was worried."

"As were we," Matthew replied, clapping Eaton on the shoulder. In the few days he and Robert had been staying with him, they had become close friends. He appreciated the editor's clear thinking, his sense of justice, and his deep love for America.

Eaton's smile faded as he waved his hand toward the empty chairs around the table and waited while they all took a seat. He made quick introductions and then picked up a paper lying on the table. "This is from the *Argus* newspaper," he said, his eyes flashing angrily as he read.

> *There can be no mistake about it. The whole blame of this most tragical and bloody riot lies with the poor, ignorant, deluded blacks who have been led into their present evil and unhappy ways by men of our own race.*

Matthew snorted. "That's preposterous!" His fists clenched as he recalled the black bodies lying in the streets. "They dare to call that news? It is nothing but lies!"

Eaton responded by picking up another paper. "This is from the *Avalanche*." He searched for where he wanted to read and began.

> *The police deserve the very highest credit for the gallant conduct they exhibited in enforcing the majesty of the law when the messengers of death were hurled at them on all sides. Our noble policemen are towers of might and purpose and courage...*

He laid the paper down, cleared his throat, and waited for comment.

Matthew stared at him, trying to find words to express his outrage.

"Are they in the same city we are in?" Robert finally asked, his voice ripe with indignation and fury.

"I'm thinking it would be a good paragraph in a fiction book," Crandall snapped, "but it has nothing to do with what is happening in this city."

"Can you prove that?" Eaton pressed.

Crandall met his eyes. "Peter and I were out most of the night watching policemen attack helpless black citizens. We never saw one black draw a weapon or even resist. These papers are making up lies and presenting them as the truth."

Matthew reached for the paper and read the passage again. When he looked up, his eyes were blazing. "They've gone too far," he said quietly. "The people who wrote and printed these lies are just as guilty of the deaths as are the ones who actually did the killing. I'm sick of the media using its power to create its own reality. The entire nation will have the truth of what is really happening here."

"Good," Eaton snapped. "They will accuse me of being too subjective because I live here. I'm sorry you have to be here, but I'm also relieved you're here to tell the story." He heaved a heavy sigh as he glanced out toward the street. "As sick as I feel, I can't say I'm surprised."

"You warned us," Matthew replied tightly.

Eaton shook his head. "I never dreamed it would get this bad," he admitted. "I'm not surprised by the violence, but even in my worst nightmares I didn't envision this." He gripped the paper in his hands and shook it toward the four men. "Go out and get the truth," he growled.

Matthew nodded but reached out to grip Eaton's arm. "You're in danger," he warned, glancing at Peter.

Peter reported what had happened last night with Ryder, but Eaton never blinked. "Let them come," he growled. "They will have to kill me to keep me from telling the truth."

Matthew hoped it wouldn't come to that. He knew they were in for another day of violence.

From his position on the fort wall, Moses watched the sun climb into a brilliantly clear sky. The streets remained quiet. He saw a few blacks venturing forth hesitantly, the first activity he had seen since the horror of the long night.

Roy joined him, watching silently for several minutes before he spoke. "We got to get out there. Most of the men they attacked are probably dead," he said, "but there might be some we can save. If nothing else, we can at least collect their bodies."

Moses nodded. "It's time," he agreed.

Roy's eyes widened. "You're going with us?"

"There doesn't seem to be any danger right now, but that could change. I don't believe this is over. If we're going to find your friends, we need to do it now." He couldn't explain his sudden compulsion to leave the fort, but he was learning to follow his feelings. "We need to keep the group small so we don't lose control."

Roy nodded, knowing the actions of the group that had emerged from the fort the day before had played a part in igniting the violence that followed. "I'll get some men you can trust," he promised.

A few minutes later, fifteen men followed Moses and Roy out of the gate. They moved quietly through the streets, nodding solemnly at the few blacks peering forth from their homes.

"Is it safe out there?" one elderly woman called, her eyes wide with fright. "Can we come out?"

"Stay inside," Moses advised. "This isn't over. You'll be safe inside."

The old woman snorted. "Tell that to the young women who were raped last night," she snapped.

Moses stiffened and walked over to the slender woman with silvery hair and wrinkled, leathery cheeks. "What are you talking about?"

"Them policemen were all back last night. They didn't leave till early this morning. They were breakin' into homes and stealin' whatever they wanted." Tears filled the old woman's eyes. "They were taking anythin' else they wanted, too." She nodded to the shanty next to her. "I heard what they done to my neighbor. And I heard her crying the rest of the night. And she have them two little children in there, too." The woman shook her head helplessly, her eyes pleading with him to do something.

Moses' blood boiled with anger. He saw renewed fury and pain erupt on the faces all around him. Every one of the men with him had family in the city. He knew exactly what they were feeling. He also knew Roy had chosen these men because their wives and children were all safely sequestered in the fort. They could be counted on to fulfill their mission.

He reached down and laid his hand on the woman's shoulder. "Stay inside," he ordered again. "We'll do what we can." As he started walking again, his mind was spinning with the new information. He knew that kind of violence wouldn't die out overnight. He could feel the black clouds of hatred forming again, heading toward South Memphis.

His attention was caught by a small group of people standing in front of the schoolhouse on the corner of South and Causey. His eyes widened when he realized they were children. He hurried forward, ready to tell them to go home. Before he could open his mouth, Horatio Rankin, a black missionary from the North who ran the school, reached the students.

"You are all incredibly brave," Rankin said gently, "but there will be no school today. I don't believe the danger is over. You must all go home immediately."

Moses bit back an oath when Felicia, the little girl he met at the school, stepped forward. "Moses Samuels told us all about the men who burned their school down back in Virginia. He said everyone was real scared there, too, but they came back for school the next day. They refused to be afraid," she said resolutely, a slight tremble in her voice as she lifted her chin with determination. "I want to be in school today."

Moses stepped forward then, exchanging a long look with Rankin. "I love that you are so brave, Felicia," he called, his heart catching at the little girl's courage, "but your teacher is right. There is a time for bravery, and there is a time when it is wise to be careful."

Felicia ran over to him and threw her arms around his waist. "Does this be one of those times, Mr. Samuels?" she asked, finally allowing a shadow of fear to appear in her eyes.

"Yes," Moses said. "This is one of those times." He knelt down to gaze into her eyes. "You go back home, Felicia. Right now. Go inside with your mama and daddy. Stay there for the rest of the day."

"What if they come to our house, Mr. Samuels?" Felicia asked, her eyes searching his for an answer.

Moses knew she must have seen horrible things the night before. "That won't happen," he murmured. He knew it might very well be a lie, but he couldn't tell a little girl the brutal truth. He hugged her gently and then gave her a gentle push. "Go home, Felicia. I'm putting you in charge of making sure everyone gets home as quickly as possible. Can I count on you?"

Felicia straightened with importance, her new mission melting the fear in her eyes. "Yes, Mr. Samuels," she said clearly, purpose ringing in her voice. She turned to the other children. "We gots to get home right now."

Moses watched her lead the small group away, praying she would be safe in her home. Then he turned to go look for the bodies of slain soldiers.

They had not advanced far when Moses saw swarms of black people around a building.

Roy followed his eyes. "That there is the Freedmen's Bureau. I reckon them people are there asking for someone to protect them."

Moses noticed an authoritative man striding down the street toward the Bureau. "Who is that?"

"That be Superintendent Runkle," Roy answered. "He's a good man. He came out of the war as a brevet brigadier general. He got himself almost killed in battle and won himself a whole bunch of medals."

"Can he stop what is going on down here?" Moses pressed.

Roy shrugged. "I doubt it. He ain't got no troops to command. I would fight for him, and I reckon the other men would too, but since we ain't got no weapons, we won't do him much good." He waved his arm impatiently. "We got to get going, Moses."

Moses watched Runkle approach, noticing the distraught look in his eyes. He stepped into his path. "Hello, Superintendent Runkle," he said.

Runkle stopped and looked up at Moses. "What can I do for you?" he asked distractedly, looking beyond Moses to the group of soldiers behind him. Their presence seemed to pull him from his thoughts. He cleared his throat and gazed at Moses expectantly.

"We need troops down here," Moses said urgently.

Runkle sighed. "I know. Unfortunately, I don't have the power to make that happen."

"These people need help," Moses insisted. "Is there someone else I can talk to?"

Runkle eyed him more closely. "Where are you from? If you're with the Third, why aren't you still in uniform?"

"I'm not with the Third," Moses replied. "I'm from Virginia. I came out here with friends of mine who are reporters. I met some of the men from the Third on the train and decided to stay in the fort with them."

"To get a story?" Runkle asked, a suspicious look in his eyes.

"No," Moses said, wishing he could fully explain what he was doing in the fort, but he had yet to fully figure it out. "I just had a feeling I could help." He knew his answer was inadequate, but it was the best he could do. "I'm one man, Superintendent Runkle. Just as you are. We need troops down here to stop the violence. Where are they?"

Runkle fixed him with a long gaze. "They aren't coming," he said. "Oh, they are going to send a small squad to protect the Freedmen's Bureau, but that was all I could get them to agree to."

"Why?" Moses asked with disbelief. "The United States government has promised to protect the freedmen."

"You're right," Runkle agreed, "but our General Stoneman seems to not be too affected by that reality. He has agreed to allow Captain Allyn to bring a squad of fifty soldiers out from the fort to patrol from Beale to South Streets, but the rest of the soldiers..." His voice trailed off as he glanced at the soldiers massed behind Moses.

"What?" Moses pressed.

Runkle shook his head wearily. "The rest of the soldiers are supposed to keep the members of the Third in the fort. Stoneman is afraid their presence on the streets will do nothing but increase the violence."

"Are they aware it's the soldiers of the Third who are being killed?"

"I don't think anyone truly knows what is going on," Runkle admitted, spreading his hands, "but I have to agree that violence will probably abate if they are in the fort."

"It didn't seem to have an effect last night," Moses snapped, telling him briefly what he had learned from the old woman.

Runkle groaned, his eyes flashing with both frustration and fury. "It's maddening not to be able to offer protection to everyone." His eyes swept the crowds still surrounding the Bureau. He looked at Moses again, lowering his voice.

Moses leaned in closer to hear what he was saying, knowing the words were meant for him alone.

"I asked Stoneman for a force of soldiers to protect the freed people, protect the Bureau, and apprehend lawless whites. The *general*," his voice sharpened with sarcasm, "informed me he didn't have enough soldiers because they were busy protecting valuable government property." His voice lowered even more. "He also told me that many of the soldiers from the Sixteenth would be less than dependable because they despise the blacks as much as the rioters do..." His voice trailed off in defeat.

Moses watched, stunned into silence, as Runkle walked away to address the crowd of people pressed around the building.

"Go home," the superintendent called. "I'm sorry, but I can offer you no protection."

Moses watched the looks of hope fade into stunned disbelief and renewed fear.

"Go home!" Runkle called again. "You will be safest in your homes." He turned, sent Moses a long apologetic look, and then disappeared into the Bureau.

Moses watched the confusion settle on the faces around him. Taking a deep breath, he stepped toward the crowd. "Listen to him," he called, relieved when every eye turned toward him. "There is no help coming right away." He couldn't bring himself to say there may not be any help at all. He had visions of thousands of slain blacks, but he pushed them away. It would do no good to let himself go there. "The best thing you can do is go back to your homes or go to the fort."

"A lot of good that did last night," one woman called, two children clutched to her side.

Moses wondered if he was looking at the woman who was raped last night, but he couldn't take time to find out. He could feel the dark clouds moving closer through the clear sky. He had to convince them to leave. "I realize I can't promise that you will be safe in your homes," he yelled, "but I can tell you that you're absolutely *not* safe on the streets. The rioters are coming back." He knew many of them had stayed in their homes instead of retreating to the fort because they didn't trust the US government any more. "The people in the fort are safe," he called out. "You will be safest there, but if you refuse to go, at least go back to your homes."

He waited, watching as the confused looks evaporated into fear as his words sank in.

"They be coming back?" an elderly man asked, his thin voice quavering.

"Yes," Moses said firmly. "All of you need to get off the streets." He breathed a sigh of relief as the old man walked away, casting one final disbelieving look at the Freedmen's Bureau that had promised him protection.

Soon, the streets were once again empty.

Matthew and Robert had split up from Peter and Crandall, agreeing to meet back at the hotel in an hour. The downtown streets had begun filling shortly after they had finished their breakfast. Clusters of angry white men appeared on every corner.

Matthew moved closer to one of the groups, hoping to find out what had them so riled up.

"It's true," a stout man with a swarthy complexion insisted. "The blacks are all getting together down there. They have vowed to resist the police to their death."

"Good!" another man shouted. "I killed me a nigger last night, but I got a lot of bullets left." He waved his pistol in the air, his eyes flashing with something akin to mania.

Matthew gritted his teeth against his scathing reply. It was his job to report the truth to the nation. Self-control was paramount. He and Robert moved on to another group.

"The blacks have taken control of Fort Pickering!" another man cried, his eyes wide with genuine terror. "I thought they were brought under control last night. Something has to happen to stop this!"

"Are you sure it's true?" Matthew asked quietly. He had left the fort less than an hour ago, but he couldn't reveal that if he wanted the men to keep talking. He also knew that revelation would put him and Robert in grave danger. He could already see the pack mentality taking over, just as it had the day before. Wild rumors were going to do nothing but stir them into a frenzy. He had seen the results of that yesterday, but he was almost certain there was no way to stop the inevitable violence.

"Of course it's true!" another man hollered. Matthew had seen him walk up to the group moments before. Hard, dark eyes flashed from beneath long blond hair. "Sheriff Winters just got word that the nigger soldiers have left the fort. They broke into the armory and seized four hundred muskets. They are killing every white person they see."

Matthew shook his head, unable to stop his protest. "That's ridiculous!" he cried, falling silent when angry eyes rested on him suspiciously.

"Let's go," Robert said urgently, gripping Matthew's arm and leading him away.

"This is crazy," Matthew sputtered.

"Everything happening in this city is crazy right now." Robert stared around at the growing number of men filling the streets. "I suggest we stay in front of this group."

"You don't have to do this," Matthew protested. "I'll find Peter and Crandall and then head down to South Memphis." He was determined to get the true story, but there was no sense in putting Robert into more danger.

"What? And miss all the fun?" Robert asked. His lips were curved into a smile, but his eyes were deadly serious. He clapped a hand on Matthew's shoulder. "We're in this together. Just like we always have been. Remember when we snuck into the building down in Charleston for that secret meeting before the war?"

"What I mostly remember is you starting a fight with the man who seemed offended by your lack of enthusiasm for the Southern cause at that time."

Robert grinned. "I remember that, too. I won."

Matthew snorted. "You knocked him down and then we ran."

Robert shrugged. "We had more important things to do," he said. He began to walk toward the hotel. "We're wasting time. You know I'm not going to let you head back into trouble without me. Let's get Peter and Crandall and get down there before this mob does."

Peter's voice sounded from behind them. "We're here. Let's go." Matthew turned to him with an explanation, but Peter held up his hand. "Crandall and I just heard Judge Thomas Leonard order Sheriff Winters to recruit a posse of five hundred men to put down the black uprising."

"The one that doesn't exist?" Matthew asked, his mind seething with what he knew was impotent rage.

"We both know that doesn't matter," Peter snapped. "They are already gathering men together. If we want the country to know the truth about what happens next, we have got to be there to report it."

Moses could tell by the sun's position that it was almost ten o'clock. The growing tension in his body told him they were running out of time. "It's time to get back to the fort," he told Roy.

Roy nodded but continued to move forward into the bayou, plunging through the shallow waters. "We already found three of our men," he said angrily. "What if there are more?"

"Then we'll come back for them," Moses said. He glanced at the rest of the men spread out around them. "It won't help anyone if we are attacked."

"What makes you think they are coming back?" Roy demanded belligerently.

Moses sighed, knowing he would feel the same way if he spent the morning finding the bodies of friends who had been gunned down or beaten to death. "They're coming back," he repeated patiently. "It's up to us to keep the rest of the men from getting hurt," he said, letting the urgency creep into his voice. "They have wives and children waiting for them in the fort."

Roy turned and stared at him, the fury in his eyes fading into anguish. Slowly, he nodded his head. "Let's go," he called. "We gotta get back. You won't do no good for your family if you get killed."

The rest of the men glared at him, but they slowly moved in his direction. Moses breathed a sigh of relief as they came together and headed back toward the fort. His relief was short-lived. He could feel the danger before he could hear it, but moments later, the sounds of horses and yelling men split the quiet streets.

Roy exchanged a wild-eyed look with Moses. "Run!" he cried.

The whole group broke into a run, but Moses knew it was too late. His mind spun as he tried to figure out what to do. He stopped abruptly, raising his hand in command. The whole group stopped, turning to him for direction. Moses looked around and dashed for a shadowed opening between two buildings.

When he had all the men huddled together, he gestured for them to listen, talking as quietly as he could. "It's too dangerous for us to all stay together. We will all be easy targets for a mob of men with guns. We have to split up. No more than two together," he ordered. He paused, knowing he may be talking to some of these men for the last time. He had hoped he left violence behind on the battlefield, but it had followed him to Memphis. "Do whatever you can to get back to the fort. It's the only place you'll be safe. Use the alleys behind buildings. Stay off the main roads," he said. He locked eyes with all of them. "Good luck."

He motioned to the first two men. "You two go out the back." He waited a couple minutes and then gestured to the next go. "Go," he urged.

Several minutes later, he was alone in the opening with Roy. "Guess it's the two of us," he said easily, swallowing his fear just as he had on the battlefield. There would be time for fear and emotion later. Right now his life depended on clear thinking. He walked between the buildings to the back alley, peering out and listening. When he heard nothing that would indicate anything in close proximity, he nodded to Roy, ducked his head and started running.

Gunfire and screaming broke out on the street behind him, but no one had entered the alley. Moses knew there was nothing he could do to save the blacks who had dared to venture out into the streets. He cursed himself for staying away from the fort so long, but he couldn't waste energy on regrets right now. He and Roy reached a corner and stopped, peering out around a building. Moses groaned at what he saw.

Two of their group were pressed up against a building, held there by four policemen. One of the police was shouting at them. "You shot one of our own yesterday!"

"I didn't!" Tony pleaded, his eyes bulging with fear.

"He weren't there!" Bernie insisted, his eyes both frightened and angry. "I tell you, he weren't there."

Moses closed his eyes for a brief moment and then forced them open again. He already knew what was coming.

"It was you!" the policeman screamed. "And if it wasn't, you still ain't nothing but a useless nigger." He sneered and fired his pistol.

Moses saw the spurt of blood erupt from Tony's leg. For a moment, he had hope they would be content with shooting him in the leg. His hopes splintered when two more of the police raised their guns, silencing both of the soldiers with a bullet to their heads.

"No!" Roy cried.

Moses clapped his hand over his mouth and pulled him back, shoving him into an opening he had spied during their run. "Be quiet!" he hissed. He prayed Roy's cry had not been heard over the melee in the street. "There is nothing we can do now."

Roy fought him briefly and then sagged into his arms, sobs shaking his shoulders. "They ain't done nothing," he muttered, his eyes wild with grief. "They ain't done nothing."

"*No one* has done anything," Moses muttered, his own eyes filling with hot tears. His mind spun as he tried to figure out a way to get back to the fort that didn't include the main streets. He knew he was at a serious disadvantage because he didn't know the area. "Roy!" He shook the sobbing soldier's shoulders. "You've got to help us get back to the fort."

Roy shuddered, trying to control his tears. "What?" he managed.

"We can't cross that street," Moses said, forcing his voice to remain calm, trying to block out his fear that he may never see Rose again. Never see John. Never see Hope. He fought to bring his thoughts under control. "You know this area. Is there another way to get back to the fort?"

Roy gasped as he tried to breathe, but the wild look in his eyes gradually faded. He stared out from the opening, his mind searching for an answer. "We can go back the way we come and then cut over a few streets. We might have a chance if we come up from behind the fort. It will take us longer—"

"Let's go," Moses snapped, not letting him finish his sentence. He edged out from between the building and waited for Roy to join him.

Roy broke into a run. Moses kept up with him easily, his eyes scanning the alley for any sign of movement. In less than two hundred yards, they ducked back into another opening, moving east away from the river. For a moment they left the horrifying noises of the riot behind.

Remaining silent, Roy worked his way east. They stopped at the edge of every building, watching to be sure it was safe to advance before sprinting forward. Roy raised his hand in a signal to stop when they reached a narrow alley cluttered with garbage from the shanties crowded onto the lots. "We turn south here," he whispered. "We'll come up behind the fort. If we're lucky, there will be someone manning the gate at the rear."

"And if not?" Moses asked quietly.

"Then we climb the wall," Roy said, his eyes once more focused and determined. "Whatever it takes, we'll get in the fort."

Moses took a deep breath and prepared to sprint forward, but the sound of a door crashing open froze him in his tracks. "Wait!" he hissed.

Roy went rigid, his eyes darting everywhere to determine where the sound had come from.

Chapter Twenty-Two

Matthew was in the midst of the mob when violence exploded again. His eyes widened when he caught sight of several uniformed men from the Third darting between buildings.

"They're trying to get back to the fort!" Robert yelled.

"I can't imagine why they are out at all. I can only hope Moses had enough sense to stay there this morning." Something was churning in Matthew's gut that warned him Moses might not have made that choice, but he decided to keep his thoughts to himself. When Robert remained silent, Matthew knew he was thinking the same thing.

"Where are *they* going?" Robert muttered.

Matthew looked in the direction Robert was gazing. He frowned as he saw four policemen separate from the mob and head east.

"Go after them," Peter urged. "Crandall and I will stay with the main mob. If we're going to report what is really happening, then we need to see everything we can.

Matthew nodded. None of them retained any hope they could stop the violence, or even help the victims. All they could do was make sure the country knew the truth about what happened when it was finally over. He clasped Peter and Crandall's hands tightly. "Be careful," he urged, before he and Robert broke away to follow the policemen.

They remained far enough back not to alert the police of their presence but made sure they didn't lose sight of them. Matthew peered around a corner and held up his hand. "They're surrounding a shanty," he whispered to Robert.

They both watched as the police approached the primitive home. Sparse clumps of grass sprang up from the tiny dirt yard. A few tomato plants struggled to survive against the rickety fence.

"Get out here!" a slightly built policeman with dark hair yelled. "It's time to pay up for being a Yankee soldier." His voice dripped with anticipation and hatred.

"You can't hide from us," another taunted, his full face red from exertion. His stomach bulged against his uniform as he settled himself in a threatening stance. "We know you're in there!"

"I hope he got out of there last night," Matthew growled. He tensed with disbelief when he saw the door open slowly. Surely whoever they were after wasn't going to walk right out to them. He opened his mouth to yell a warning, but Robert's sharp squeeze on his arm reminded him it would be futile.

"Why looky there!" another policeman jeered, his strong Irish accent evident. "We got us a nigger smart enough to know he can't be getting away."

A tall, lean man with glistening dark skin stepped out the door, but as soon as his feet hit solid ground he darted to the left and ran toward an opening between shanties a few yards away.

"Run!" Matthew breathed, watching as the policemen raised their guns and fired, the explosions shattering the early morning. The man had run barely ten feet before he fell, clutching his abdomen as his eyes rolled in agony.

"That will show you not to leave your old mistress and master," the slight policeman snapped. He kicked the man to make sure he couldn't get up, and then riffled through his pockets. "I got twenty-five dollars!" he called jubilantly, hoisting a fistful of money into the air. He raised his gun again. "We need to finish this nigger off!"

"Don't waste another bullet on him," the burly policeman answered, lifting a hand to push the pistol down. "We got him in the stomach. He ain't gonna live long." His lips curled, and his eyes shone with glee. "Let's go find us another one. I heard about another *veteran* around the block," he said contemptuously. "They think they can hide in their homes, but we're about to teach all of them that we're going to get them one way or another."

Matthew exchanged a silent look with Robert. Never had he felt such shame to be an American, or to be a white man.

"They're going to try to slaughter all of them." Robert's voice broke and his eyes blazed with fury. "I can't believe there are no troops coming out to stop this mayhem."

Matthew pushed aside his shame and disgust, moving out into the street to follow the quartet. "Come on," he said heavily. "We've got to follow them."

"I don't know that I can keep following them while they slaughter defenseless people," Robert answered slowly. "Do you really think we're going to do any good?"

Matthew shook his head. "I don't know," he admitted, "but we have to try. I've been predicting it was going to take a disaster to make people in the North realize the truth of what is happening in the South..." His voice trailed away as hopelessness flooded him. Would it really make any difference at all?

Robert grabbed his shoulder. "Lead on," he said stoutly. "You're right. All we can do is try."

Matthew flashed him a look of gratitude and turned right to follow the policemen. Two hundred yards later he stopped to peer around a building.

"Get out here!"

"They're after another one," Robert said angrily. "I hope this one has the sense to stay inside."

"It won't matter." Matthew sighed.

The red-haired policeman, evidently too impatient to wait, strode forward and kicked the door in. It gave way easily before his heavy boots.

"Mama! Daddy! They's come after us!"

A man with an average build and light caramel skin appeared at the door, obviously trying to block the soldiers from his family. His stoic look said he knew what was coming.

"There's a woman in there," the slight policeman said, gloating anticipation in his voice as he rubbed his hands together. "I been right lonely for a while. I don't mind the little ones either. A lot of the boys had their fun last night. I figure it's my turn now."

The black man's lips curled back in a growl before he launched himself at the policeman, pulling out the knife he had hidden behind his back. The other men lifted their pistols, but it was too late. The policeman, a look of utter surprise on his face, slumped to the ground. Shots rang out a second later. The man collapsed, shooting a look of apology toward the house before his eyes closed.

The only cop who had stayed silent so far looked down at the stabbed policeman with disdain. "We ain't down here to rape nigger woman," he spat. "I'm here to kill them and move on. Fool!" He stepped toward the house, raising his pistol.

"We can't leave him," the burly policeman protested.

"He isn't dead. He's just bleeding good. We'll come back for him, but I'll not be letting him stop me from what I came to do."

Matthew and Robert exchanged another look. Neither one of them could sit idly by while these man shot a woman and her child. Both of them, without saying a word, began to edge forward.

Moses crept forward when he heard the door crash in. He remained silent while the Irish police called a man outside. Moses knew he wouldn't be able to stop them. But it was when he heard the child cry out that his blood froze. "Felicia!"

He felt Roy's eyes on him. "Felicia?"

"The little girl," Moses snapped, his brain spinning as he tried to decide how to save her. "I made friends with her when I was at her school a few days ago." Keeping one eye on the house, he reached slowly for his weapon. He knew he was outnumbered, but he would stand back while something happened to the little girl he had grown to love. He could still see her eyes shining with bright courage that morning when she had come to school as usual.

"We can't stop it!" Roy whispered urgently.

"I know," Moses admitted hoarsely, "but Felicia is going to know someone tried to save her. You've got to make it back to the fort, Roy. I want you to let Rose know I tried to come home to her."

Roy stared at him wildly and then slowly reached for his pistol. "Tell her yourself," he replied. "What's the plan?"

"We'll have to kill them," Moses said, realizing exactly what kind of consequences could come down on them if they were caught. He knew they would have to move quickly.

Before he could even take a step, a woman came racing from the house, throwing herself down on the ground beside her husband. "Billy!" she sobbed.

Moses watched in stunned silence as the burly policeman, without a word, lifted his pistol and fired into the woman's head.

"Mama!" Felicia appeared at the door, her eyes wild with grief and anger. "You shot my mama!" she screamed, her lithe body taut with fury. "How come you shot my mama and daddy?"

Moses began to move forward.

Roy grabbed his arm. "Wait!" he whispered. "Moses, look! Ain't them the men who were with you in the fort?"

Moses shook his head to clear his eyes. Matthew and Robert were moving forward, their hands gripping thick pieces of wood.

"Hey!" Robert yelled. "What's going on? Did we miss all the action?" His voice was thick with frustration. "I see you got us some more niggers!"

The policemen, surprised by anyone else's presence, all turned away from Felicia.

Felicia's eyes suddenly met Moses' across the narrow alley. He was still crouched, ready to spring. When her mouth flew open, he raised his finger to his lips and shook his head once. "Be quiet," he mouthed. He wanted to tell her to run, but he knew she had little chance of outrunning their pistols.

Felicia remained still, her eyes locked on him with desperate hope.

"Who are you?" one of the policemen asked suspiciously.

Robert and Matthew continued to advance. "We missed all the fun yesterday," Matthew said gruffly. "I'm not letting all this happen without killing me a nigger."

The policemen relaxed. "There are plenty more waiting for us," they assured him, looking at each other as they laughed.

Matthew took advantage of them looking away. Moving in unison, he and Robert swung their wood with deadly accuracy, cocking their arms back to swing again before the policemen's faces even seemed to register that they were under attack.

Moses heard the thwack of wood against the men's heads, watching as they seemed to collapse simultaneously. Only then did he break from hiding and dash across the opening.

"Mr. Samuels!" Felicia cried, tears coming for the first time.

Matthew and Robert spun around, shocked looks on their faces. "Moses?" Their eyes moved past him. "Roy?"

Moses knelt down as Felicia flew into his arms, wrapping her up tightly. He gazed up at Robert and Matthew. "Thank you," he said quietly. He peered down the road. "We can all exchange stories later. I suggest we get out of here."

"I think you're right," Matthew agreed, his grieved eyes locked on Felicia.

"She's coming with us," Moses said. He held Felicia back for a moment and looked down into her face, aching at the pain he saw etched there. "Can you climb on to my back and hold on real good, honey?" he asked softly.

Felicia nodded, but her face crumpled into a new spate of tears when she looked back at her mama and daddy. "We're leaving them?" Her voice was barely audible.

Moses hugged her again, fighting to bring his emotions under control. "They're gone, sweetheart." His mind wouldn't form any more words.

"Dead?" Felicia whispered.

Moses bit back an angry curse as he held her away from him and looked into her eyes. "Yes. I'm so sorry," he said. "I'll come back and get them later, but first I have to get you to the fort where you are safe."

Felicia gazed up at him. "Okay, Mr. Samuels. I'll get on your back, and I'll hang on real good." In a cracked voice, she added, "I played this game with my daddy, too."

"And can you be real quiet, Felicia?" Matthew asked tenderly. "We don't want anyone to know where we are."

Felicia nodded somberly, courage and fear flickering in her eyes.

Moses, still kneeling, waited for her to clamber onto his back. His thoughts spun with gratitude for what Matthew and Robert had done. "Roy knows a way to come up around the back of the fort."

The sound of voices in the distance made them all run.

It took them almost an hour of ducking into darkened alleys and dodging between groups of rioters, but they finally made it back to the fort. Every time they had to stop, Moses pulled Felicia down from his back and held her close. In spite of the heat, she had not stopped trembling since she had climbed on his back but neither did she make a sound.

"She's going into shock," Robert whispered.

Moses nodded. He recognized the signs, but all he could concentrate on right now was getting her to safety. The only way he could do that was to make sure all of them stayed alive as well. When the back gate to the fort finally appeared in front of them, he sprinted the last hundred yards, grunting with relief when the gate opened without his even having to raise a hand.

"Glad you made it back," Hopkins said, pulling the gate closed firmly when all of them were inside.

"The rest of the Third that went with us?" Roy asked. "Did they make it back?"

Hopkins shook his head. "I don't know. It's complete pandemonium in here. We've got all the soldiers and hundreds of black residents who have come here for protection."

Moses looked at him sharply.

"They're getting what they came for," Hopkins assured him. "We don't have orders to go out into the streets, but any of the residents that make it here are safe."

Moses nodded and then pulled Felicia off his back and into his arms. "No one can hurt you now," he said gently.

Felicia stared at him, her dark eyes haunted and dull. "My mama and daddy really be dead?" she whispered.

Moses wished he could do more to erase the fear and pain from her face, but he knew they had been engraved there by one horror after another. Losing her parents was just one more thing. "Yes, Felicia." He stroked her hair and gazed into her eyes.

She held his gaze, the fear beginning to fade as grief filled its place. "Mama!" she cried, tears flooding her eyes and spilling down her cheeks.

Moses cradled her sobbing form close to his heart and gently rocked her. "I'm so sorry," he whispered, knowing there was nothing else to say.

"Where are the men?" Roy asked after a long silence.

"Captain Smyth got them all into the barracks," Hopkins replied.

"That's good," Roy replied after a brief hesitation.

Moses knew what that admission cost him. It was the acknowledgement that the violence was completely out of control. The soldiers couldn't save their families. Any person with black skin who was found on the street would be gunned down. Blacks in their homes were being violated, beaten, and robbed. The only safe place was the fort. He prayed that would continue. He couldn't imagine the white mob turning on the fort, but he had already seen things happen that he could never have imagined. Anything was possible.

Matthew stepped up to him. "We're going back out," he said with quiet resolution in his eyes.

"Why?" Moses asked. He wanted to insist they stay in the fort, but one look into Matthew's eyes said it would be a futile attempt.

"We have to," Matthew replied. "We came down here to make sure the country knows the truth of what is going on. We can't tell it if we're in the fort."

"What if the men you clubbed see you?" Roy pressed.

Matthew's eyes darkened as he exchanged a long look with Robert.

"Then we'll finish the job," Robert said. "Those men are nothing but cowards and murderers. I don't think they'll be waking up for a while, and I doubt they'll feel much like doing anything, but we'll deal with it if the time comes." He managed a grin. "With any luck, they won't remember what we look like."

"I'm pretty sure we scrambled their brains," Matthew said lightly.

Moses stared at both of them over Felicia's heaving shoulders. "Thank you," he said again. "Be careful," was all he added. He knew they were doing what they believed they had to do.

Robert stepped forward and rubbed his hand on Felicia's back. "Take good care of her," he whispered.

Peter was seething with frustration. "I can't believe no one is doing anything to stop this!"

"As far as I can tell," Crandall said angrily, "every white man coming down here to *supposedly* quell the unrest is simply using it as an excuse to kill as many blacks as possible."

"General Stoneman gave orders for Captain Allyn to protect the blacks with his troops," Peter burst out as he saw another black man running for his life, his bloodied face testimony to the fact he had already been beaten. "Where are they?"

"Wait!" Crandall exclaimed, pointing north toward the Beale Street market. "Here they come."

Peter moved up onto the stairs of a nearby store so he could get a better view. He breathed a sigh of relief when he saw Captain Allyn at the head of about forty heavily armed infantrymen marching toward them. Riding alongside the group was Sheriff Winters. "Nice of Winters to finally make an appearance," he snapped.

Peter understood the confused expression on the sheriff's face as he looked around from the back of his horse. "He's been hearing about black rioting all morning," he muttered. "I'm sure he wonders where it is. It's about time someone came down to learn the truth." He felt a twinge of hope, but he was still too angry at all he had witnessed for it to make him feel any better.

"Let's follow them," Crandall urged.

Peter nodded and joined Crandall in the street. He watched as the crowds of whites who had come down to experience the riot glared at the troops with angry faces. He knew they were disappointed that something was happening to stop the violence. As far as he was concerned, the onlookers were as guilty as the policemen and other citizens who had done the beating and shooting. They had cheered it on and done nothing to stop it. Their cheering had died away to indignant muttering as they watched the soldiers approach, but no one had left. He knew they were hoping the troops would pass on and leave them to their entertainment.

The first violence they encountered was when the troops turned onto South Street.

"Shoot him! Shoot him!" A crowd of whites, oblivious to the troops' existence, was calling for the death of a black man being led toward them. "Shoot him! Shoot him!" they hollered again.

Sheriff Winters rode forward quickly, his horse scattering the crowd as the soldiers followed him. "Stop!" he called, lifting his rifle as he spoke. He suddenly seemed to realize the truth of what was going on. "We are here to preserve order and protect innocent parties. We will arrest anyone, white or black, who disturbs the peace." His voice rang through the street.

The crowd fell silent but regarded him belligerently before they began to edge away.

Peter stepped closer as Sheriff Winters dismounted and took custody of the black man from the policeman.

"You are dismissed," the sheriff said curtly.

Peter read disappointed indignation on the policeman's face, but he released his prisoner's arm and moved back. The sheriff spoke briefly to the man whose bloodied face was full of frantic relief as he escorted him to a cabin fifty yards away. The terrified man cast one more desperate look at the crowd before he opened the door to his shanty and disappeared.

More armed men arrived.

Peter and Crandall exchanged a glance. Were these men here to kill more blacks?

Sheriff Winters immediately took control of them and directed them to patrol the streets. "We are here to preserve order," he barked. "Create trouble, and I will arrest you."

"Thank God," Peter said quietly. "I believe he actually means it." He caught sight of Chief Garrett and Mayor Parks talking on the sidewalk. Moving slowly so he wouldn't attract their attention and make them aware they were being listened to, Peter made his way close enough to hear the conversation.

"It's over," Garret snapped. "We have to get the policemen out of here."

"That's a good idea," Mayor Parks responded, his words slurred as he swayed slightly. "I guess we've done all the good we can."

Peter scowled and watched as Garrett rounded up the police and marched them back toward the station house. When they were out of sight, Peter hurried to catch up to Sheriff Winters and Captain Allyn, who were approaching a crowd of whites congregated at the corner of Main and South.

"Go home!" Sheriff Winters called. "It's over." Many of the crowd stared at him defiantly, but when the soldiers lifted their rifles, they began to melt away. When they had dispersed, he urged his horse onward.

Peter and Crandall continued moving forward, tensing when they reached Hernando Street and saw Winters break into a gallop. They ran forward to make sure they didn't miss anything. They reached the corner and watched as Winters surged toward a group of ten men who had surrounded four black men. They were beating one of them viciously on the head.

"Stop!" Winters ordered, pulling his horse to a stop and aiming his rifle at the group. "You will desist immediately and release those men."

The men growled and turned toward him menacingly, only gradually becoming aware of the infantrymen advancing toward them, rifles at the ready.

"Release them," Winters snapped.

"Why doesn't he arrest them?" Crandall demanded as the crowd melted back, leaving the black men staring up at Winters with wild hope in their eyes.

Peter shook his head, watching as Winters directed two of his men to escort the blacks to a tract of woods in the distance. Peter didn't look away until he watched them disappear into the woods at a run. When he turned back to see what Winters would do with the attackers, Peter was stunned to see them moving slowly up the street, some of them laughing as they talked about their exploits. "He's letting them go," he said in disbelief. "He's really letting them go."

Matthew had seen Peter and Crandall with the squad of soldiers. He had also seen Garrett and Parks depart with the policemen. He was quite certain the rioting would stop now that the police were gone. A sudden movement caught his attention as another group of armed men led by a lieutenant from the fort rounded the corner, leading two men they had obviously arrested. "Let's follow them," Matthew said urgently. "Lieutenant Clifford is from Fort Pickering."

As they followed the arresting party down the street, they saw black faces peering from windows, but all the doors stayed securely closed. They could hear crying children, but the mob of whites had melted away. The streets were empty until they reached the intersection of

Main and South and found another crowd of whites clustered around a tall man on horseback.

Matthew moved closer. "Surely Lieutenant Clifford is not handing over those men to Creighton," he muttered.

"Who's that?" Robert asked.

"He's the city recorder," Matthew said dismissively. "He records the minutes of city meetings and makes them public. He has no authority, but he tries to make people think he does. Eaton tells me he has a violent hatred for the black citizens of Memphis."

"I have prisoners," Clifford said crisply.

Creighton stared at the two men. "They are policemen."

"Do you accept custody of them?" Clifford asked. His face revealed his relief that he had found someone authoritative-looking to pass them off to.

"Certainly," Creighton responded, not bothering to hide the smirk on his face when Clifford handed them over and turned away to rejoin his troops.

Matthew watched as Creighton waved his hands, ordering the immediate release of the policemen, who sneered at Clifford's back and turned around to grin at Creighton. Matthew clenched his teeth with fury, reminding himself that no one was getting away with anything because he was going to make sure every bit of this was in his book and in the country's newspapers.

Creighton stared after Clifford with a smug expression and then rose in his stirrups to address the crowd. "Our policemen are free," he called. "I promise you that no man brought before the Memphis courts for carrying a weapon will be punished." His face settled into hard lines as he stared coldly at the soldiers watching from a distance. "It's not over," he yelled. "I'm going to kill every nigger I can find!"

Fury pulsed through Matthew's veins, but he realized Clifford's small unit of soldiers could not defend themselves against a crowd this size if they were to turn violent again.

By one o'clock, the streets were calm and completely empty. The blacks, fearing for their lives, refused to come outside.

Matthew breathed a sigh of relief, but he started at every noise, peering around the streets for renewed signs of violence.

"It's not over," Robert said bluntly, reading his thoughts.

"No," Matthew agreed. "It's not." He stared around the streets. "But it seems to be calm for now. Let's go find Eaton and tell him what we know. I also want to send out some telegrams while things are quiet." He turned toward downtown, aware of the pressing weight of hatred that continued to swirl in the air.

Moses climbed to his place on the wall and stared out over the city. Felicia had finally fallen asleep, watched over by a neighbor woman who stepped forward to care for her the minute Moses led her into the barrack housing the refugees. The petite woman with sorrowful eyes had pulled Felicia into the midst of her own four frightened children. Her husband was one of the members of the Third. He had risked his life to go out into the city to bring them back. He had been one of the lucky ones.

Everyone was more relaxed now that the gunfire had stopped, but Moses was still tense. He leaned back against the wall, staring down upon streets that were totally deserted. He could only hope the residents would stay sequestered in their homes.

Now that things were calm, at least for a while, he had time to think. His mind traveled back to the fire at the schoolhouse. He thought about all the things Rose had said afterward and how hard he had fought against her belief that he was meant to be a leader. He thought of all the years of abuse as a slave. His mind filled with images of men slaughtered in battle, their bloated corpses staring up at him. He had fought for freedom, and he had paid the price. Now he just wanted to run the plantation, be with Rose, and raise his children.

Then had come the invitation to accompany Matthew to Memphis, followed by his compulsion to stay in the fort. The last several days had given him a clear understanding of what he and every black person in the country was going to be up against now that they were free. His massive fists clenched as he realized there was not one black in the South who was truly free—every one of them was constrained by hatred and contempt. They were bound by men determined to keep them in the same condition they had endured as slaves.

Rose's words from the night of the fire haunted him.

You've been a leader from the day I met you, but I never saw it quite as clearly as I saw it tonight. Our people need you, Moses.

He also remembered his response that night. "I don't want to be needed," he whispered into the somber air, knowing somehow that it no longer mattered what he wanted. His people needed him. Equally important, he needed to know he was not merely standing idle while other people fought the battle for *his* rights. He wanted to someday look John and Hope in the eyes and assure them he had fought for them to have a better life. The war had been a series of battles, and now the rebuilding of their country was going to be another long series of battles. Somehow he knew it was going to last much longer.

It had been a lack of leadership that allowed this riot to happen. It had been a lack of leadership that denied protection to the thousands of freedmen the government had pledged to protect. It had been a lack of leadership that allowed hundreds of police and rampaging white men to take control of Memphis. It had also been a lack of leadership that resulted in scores of black people venturing forth from their homes to their own massacre. No one wanted to step forward and claim control because it meant even more risk.

You're meant for more, Moses.

Moses no longer questioned the truth he felt flowing through his soul. He simply accepted it. As he looked down on the streets here and there littered with dead bodies—people were too afraid to come out to move them—he realized he and his family might pay a heavy price for his decision to become a leader for his people, but he was no longer fighting it.

By the time he climbed down from the wall, he had made another decision as well.

The first fire began at two o'clock when a black schoolhouse was burned to the ground. An uneasy silence settled on the city for several hours after that, but violence erupted again at ten o'clock. Clusters of white men roamed the city, intent on arson and destruction. Bands of soldiers, woefully undermanned, were unable to squelch the violence.

By the end of the long night, every black church and school had been burned. Dozens of black homes and shanties had been scorched. More dead bodies joined those already beginning to bloat in the streets.

When the sun finally rose on May 3, 1866, the Memphis riot was over.

Chapter Twenty-Three

Carrie couldn't resist bouncing on her bed in excited anticipation as she waited for Janie to finish dressing. A warn breeze flowed through the window, carrying the odd mixture of coal-laden fumes drifting up from the city and perfume from the flowers that were now in full bloom around the house. She had gotten used to it, but it still made her long for the pure air of the plantation. She had been up since dawn, dressing carefully in the soft yellow gown Abby had insisted would be perfect. Ever since the telegram had arrived from Robert telling her everyone was safe, she had been able to relax. She was horrified by the riot in Memphis, but her relief that all of them were safe had erased her fears.

Their first nine days in New York had passed in what seemed to be a blur. After four cases of cholera had been reported, there had been a surprising reprieve, with no one else falling sick. While no one believed the city would get off so lightly, the Metropolitan Board of Health was taking advantage of the opportunity to continue sanitizing every area they could. The warm weather was delightful, but it would also make the spread of the disease that much easier.

Carrie and her housemates, along with the rest of the medical students who had come to New York, spent long hours accompanying students from the New York Medical College for Women as they attended classes, toured their hospital, and met with the few open-minded male physicians in the city. She knew Dr. Benson's influence had made much of that happen. Her head swam with all she had learned, but the stimulation was thrilling. Instead of ending each night exhausted, she wished for longer days so she could learn even more.

She smiled as she thought of the day Abby had arranged for her, Janie, and the rest of her new friends. They were to have a long dinner with Dr. Clemence Sophia Lozer, the charismatic woman who had founded the New York Medical College. This trip had convinced Carrie that Abby must know every woman of influence in the country.

Carrie had sat fascinated as Dr. Lozer spoke of being orphaned at age eleven, married at seventeen, and widowed at twenty-four, suddenly left on her own to care for her little family. She had opened a school for young ladies, drawing her clientele from families of the highest social standing in New York. Her passion for medicine led her to close the school and overcome many challenges to earn her doctor's degree and open the college so other women could follow in her footsteps.

As Carrie gazed out at the early morning sky, cumulus clouds piled on the horizon. She hoped her own passion would push her through any obstacle that got in her way, but she was also acutely aware of the massive sacrifices made by women over the last two decades that enabled her to be in school at all. She prayed that what she was doing would help open the doors wider for the women who would follow in her footsteps. The very idea that there were women who would follow after her was both exhilarating and terrifying. She longed to create a legacy worth following.

Swinging away from the window, she stopped bouncing and looked at Janie. "You look beautiful," she said, impatient to get on with the day. She could hardly believe she was attending the Women's Rights Convention. "Let's go!"

Janie smiled patiently and continued to position her blue, feather-festooned hat. Her matching eyes twinkled merrily. "Bouncing around won't get us to the meeting any sooner," she said. "Paxton said he would pick us up at eight o'clock. We still have almost an hour. I see no reason to hurry. Nancy said breakfast would be served in thirty minutes."

A sharp rap on the door made Carrie spring up, thrilled to have a distraction. "Florence!" she cried when she opened the door, pulling the laughing redhead into the room before she had a chance to open her mouth. "You look beautiful."

Florence raised her head and pretended to float around the room, her soft green dress rustling around her. "I prefer to think I look like a woman who deserves the right to vote," she said loftily.

Carrie waved her hand. "Every woman on the street of New York looks like that," she announced. "We just have to get these hard-headed men who think that their sex makes them superior to realize it. Surely it will happen soon."

Abby sailed in the door in time to hear her. "Don't count on it," she said matter-of-factly. "The battle for abolition was drawn out much longer than I would have ever imagined, but I believe the battle for women's rights will take even longer."

Carrie stared at Abby, her enthusiasm somewhat deflated. "It's so clearly the right thing," she argued.

"Absolutely," Abby agreed, "but the rightness of something doesn't make it so."

Janie spun away from the mirror. "It's because men have considered women inferior far longer than they have considered blacks inferior," she said. "We're going to have to fight longer."

Elizabeth and Alice walked into the room. "Which just goes to show what idiots men are," Alice said scornfully, her blue eyes snapping above her cream-colored gown.

"How dare they believe that!" Carrie added.

Alice settled down on the window seat where Carrie was perched. "You may be the medical genius, but you clearly have a lot to learn about women's place in society."

"Our *place*? You believe we have a place?"

"Well, of course not," Alice replied. "If I did, I certainly wouldn't be in medical school, but can you honestly tell me you haven't bashed into patriarchal beliefs before? The church has done a rather effective job of indoctrinating men with their self-proclaimed place in the sexual hierarchy. Most men believe women are not only inferior, they believe it is their duty to control women and help them redeem themselves from their naturally sinful being."

Carrie stared at her, her thoughts spinning. "The same way the South felt about the slaves?"

"Yes, but it goes far deeper because it's not a regional issue or an economic issue. It's not even a religious distinction. It's become much more than that. It's a belief that the vast majority of men all over the world hold."

Carrie stared at Alice and then turned her attention to Abby. "She's right, isn't she?" she asked. "Have I really been so oblivious to the battle women have to fight?" She had known things were harder for women, but she was slowly becoming aware that her understanding was startlingly limited.

"You've been rather preoccupied the last few years," Abby said gently. "And you were just eighteen when the war started. You had a father who gave you free rein on the plantation, and the circumstances of the war meant that Dr. Wild gave you freedoms you might not have received in other circumstances."

"*Might* not have received?" Janie snorted. "Dr. Wild wouldn't have even had the choice if there hadn't been a war going on."

Carrie spun around and stared at the strange light in Janie's eyes. She'd never heard such contemptuous anger in her gentle friend's voice before. She wasn't sure she recognized this woman. "Janie?"

Janie smiled, but the light of battle still burned in her eyes. "The last year has changed me," she said with a shrug. "Clifford made me wake up to the truth of how few rights I had as a woman. Coming here to school, having to fight the men that harass us daily and deal with male doctors who try to block everything we do has given me a fresh understanding of how vital equal rights are for women."

Carrie opened her mouth to respond, but was interrupted when Nancy appeared at the door holding several newspapers.

"Michael delivered these," Nancy said. "As promised, I am bringing them to you immediately."

Carrie and Florence dove for the newspapers. Florence was the first to discover what they were looking for.

"Here it is," she cried. "The article by Matthew written two days ago on the eighth."

Carrie settled back to listen, exchanging a long look with Abby. They had both received long letters from Robert and Matthew that had explained the full horror of what they had experienced. Articles had been pouring in in the last five days detailing the events of the riot. It seemed every newspaper in the country had picked them up, creating a firestorm of sentiment.

Florence smoothed back the paper and began to read.

> *Five days after the last fire was extinguished and the last black man fell before an attacker, another steamer full of blacks anxious to escape Memphis has headed north in the wake of the steamers that carried most of the Northern missionaries away from the violence. Men and women who came to Memphis intent on helping the freedmen have fled to escape the retribution that had been promised by the rioters. Thousands of the freedmen, desperate to escape the danger and memories, have followed.*

"Thousands of the blacks were hiding in Fort Pickering since the riot," Carrie interrupted. "I bet they are the ones who headed north."

The others nodded somberly and then looked back at Florence. She took a breath and continued reading.

> *Now that peace has once more settled on Memphis, attention has turned to understanding the true circumstances of the riot. I have learned that General Stoneman, now solidly in control of the city, is demanding answers from Mayor Parks. He wants to know what steps are being taken by the civil authorities to punish the rioters, and how Memphis will compensate those whose property was destroyed. He also wants to know how the authorities are going to ensure that citizens not go around armed, and how they plan to protect the freedman.*

I have also learned General Stoneman sent a letter to his commanding offer, Major General George H. Thomas in Nashville. In this letter he vows to make the city of Memphis pay the full value of all losses and expenses suffered or incurred in the riot, either by individuals or the government. He believes such a tax levy will not only secure financial restitution, but also make the city of Memphis, and through them the people of the South, feel and realize that such disgraceful proceedings cannot and will not be tolerated by the United States government.

While his boldness is admirable, I cannot help but wish General Stoneman had exhibited such boldness and initiative while forty-eight blacks were being killed and scores of others raped, beaten, and robbed. I wish bold action had been taken before hundreds of buildings and homes were burned to the ground, but I am also grateful for his dedication in the aftermath.

General Stoneman has appointed a commission to investigate the riot. This four-man commission, led by Runkle, the head of the Freedmen's Bureau in Memphis, will call witnesses, gather facts about the causes and events of the riot, identify rioters and victims, and tally the property losses. A conversation with Stoneman revealed he already has a solid idea of what the commission will find, bolstered by what he has learned since the riot.

It is very clear now that the Memphis Rebel newspapers had serious influence in provoking the riot by spurning the truth and printing fiction that would inflame the rioters and help them fulfill their own agenda of clearing Memphis of all blacks. It is also blatantly clear that the largely Irish Memphis police, instead of protecting and serving their city, were instead the ones responsible for much of the violence and killing. I and my fellow journalists saw it with our own eyes, as we have reported, but now many are stepping up to reveal the truth.

It is also important to note that the great majority of whites in the city, including former Confederate soldiers, not only had no hand in the riot, but were violently opposed to it. I myself saw many whites trying to put out the fires flaming throughout the city on the last night of the riot.

I am told by many sources that the men who have the most blood on their hands from the riot have either fled the city or are hiding out. Having seen what they are capable of, this journalist is not surprised by their cowardice.

In answer to several Rebel newspapers' assertion that the freedmen started the riots and that the whites were the primary victim, I would like to put these questions out for consideration. Has one white woman or one white child been harmed? Has a single dwelling of a white person been entered or destroyed? Has any unarmed white man been in any way injured by a freedman?

The answer to all the above questions is a resounding no. The riot in Memphis was nothing more than a massacre of unarmed and unresisting blacks. It is clear that the United States government should force the civil authorities, who failed in their duty to prevent the slaughter and destruction, to make restitution.

This will not help the children who will never again see their slain parents. It will not aid the women emotionally battered by rape. It will certainly not change reality for the scores of black men who have been so severely injured they will never be able to work again.

It will, perhaps, send a message that any new violence against the freedmen anywhere in the country will not be tolerated. Perhaps the certainty of circumstances will make people think twice before they copy the hatred and violence in Memphis.

A long silence fell on the room when Florence finished reading. The rumble of carriages on the road below the house slowly brought them back to the present.

"Impressive," Alice said softly. "I can feel his passion in his writing." She glanced at Carrie. "Will you introduce me to him when he is next in Philadelphia?" she said coquettishly.

Carrie laughed, glad to have some humor to lighten the atmosphere, but her thoughts were heavy. "I thought when the war ended that life would be easier." She felt the others' eyes on her, but the room remained quiet as they gave her time to express her feelings. "I've learned enough to know life will always be full of challenges. I wish it wasn't so, but wishing won't change reality. I'm proud of Matthew for using the riot to open people's eyes to needed change. I'm proud the city of New York has stepped forward to make life better for everyone because of the threat of cholera. I'm glad women are stepping up to fight for their rights, not allowing antiquated beliefs to mandate the future."

A bell in the distance broke into her thoughts. "And now it's time for breakfast," she proclaimed, turning toward the door. "We'll read the other articles later. Right now we have to go change the world for women!"

The room emptied quickly. Abby slid up to Carrie and slipped her arm around her waist. "I'm very proud of you," she whispered.

Carrie didn't pretend not to know what she was talking about. "I think I might be growing up."

"I'd say you are already quite grown up," Abby responded, squeezing her tightly. "Now you are simply becoming a wise woman."

Janie shivered as she entered the Church of the Puritans in Union Square. Everywhere she looked she saw women with strong faces full of purpose. Most of them were in small groups, talking animatedly as the building filled. She could feel the power reaching out to her. The energy was both encouraging and challenging.

Just standing in the same room made her proud to be a woman.

Carrie leaned in closer as they moved toward their seats. "I can feel it, too," she whispered excitedly.

Alice, Elizabeth, and Florence had stopped to talk to friends, but Janie had promised to save them a seat. Her head swiveled as she stared at all the women, wishing she could learn their stories. She wondered how many had suffered from abusive husbands, and how many had lost opportunities because men didn't believe they were capable. She wanted so much to know what had made them decide to swim against the tide of society, inviting ridicule and humiliation for their efforts.

Carrie grabbed her arm. "Abby is waving at us. I think she wants us to meet someone."

"Go ahead," Janie replied. "I'll save the seats."

"No," Carrie said firmly. "We'll put our bags and notebooks down on the seats and then go over. Whomever she wants us to meet, I want you to meet her, too."

Janie nodded slowly, realizing how far she still had to go. There was nothing she wanted more than to meet whomever Abby was talking to, but she had been so quick to decide she wasn't worthy of doing more than saving a seat for everyone. A sudden vision of Clifford's angry face rose in her mind, but she just as quickly banished it. She had taken back control of her life, and now she had to live like she had. "Let's go," she said firmly.

Moments later, she and Carrie were approaching Abby. Janie's eyes widened as they drew closer.

Abby smiled, pulling both of them forward by grabbing their hands. "Elizabeth, these are the two women I was telling you about. Carrie is my stepdaughter, and this is Janie Winthrop Saunders. Both of them are students at the Women's Medical College in Philadelphia."

Janie knew she was gaping, but she couldn't help herself. "Elizabeth Cady Stanton?" she said faintly. She had heard so much about the grandmotherly woman with plump cheeks and tight curls who was the president of the National Women's Right Committee and who had helped organize the world's first women's rights convention in 1848. When she looked into her eyes, she saw the fire and determination that had propelled her to fight for women's rights for the last two decades, all while she and her husband were raising seven children. Janie couldn't help but feel awe.

Carrie's eyes were equally as wide. "It's quite an honor to meet you, Mrs. Stanton. Thank you for all you've done for women."

Mrs. Stanton smiled graciously. "It's a pleasure to meet both of you. Abby has told me a little about you." She turned to Janie first. "I understand your husband was quite a cad, my dear. I'm so proud of you for leaving him. Quite frankly, I don't believe any woman should stay in a marriage that makes them unhappy. You have reclaimed your life and become a medical student. You make me realize everything we are fighting for is worth it!"

Janie stared at her, not able to find a single thing to say in response. She knew, though, that Mrs. Stanton's words would carry her forward for a long time.

Mrs. Stanton turned to Carrie next. "And you, my dear, have long been a rebel."

Carrie smiled. "So I'm told," she said ruefully. "I find I have no choice in the matter. It is simply who I am."

"Wonderful!" Mrs. Stanton said. "That reality is what has propelled me forth, as well. There are many people who are offended by what I believe and say, but I find I can be nothing more or less than who I am." She reached forward to grip Carrie's hands. "Our country will demand much of you, if you're willing to serve. There are many women who are quite powerful if they have someone just a bit more powerful to lead them." She paused, staring deeply into Carrie's eyes. "May I say something to you, Carrie?"

Carrie nodded, drawn into the depths of Mrs. Stanton's eyes. "Of course," she replied, somehow knowing what she was about to hear would change the course of her life. The knowledge both frightened and thrilled her.

"You are going to be a fine doctor, Carrie Borden, but that will just be the first step for you. You are one of the rare individuals who have the courage to go against everything others may believe is right if you don't believe it is right for you. Women are going to look to you. They are going to depend on you. They are going to *need* you," Mrs. Stanton said firmly. "You will perhaps pay a heavy price if you decide to be the woman they will need you to be, but I can tell you from personal experience that the rewards far outweigh the cost."

Carrie gazed at her, trying to absorb the import of her words. "I'm not sure what to say," she finally murmured.

Mrs. Stanton threw her head back with a cheerful laugh. "Of course you don't. How in the world *could* you? You just tuck what I've told you away in your heart and mind. You'll know the very moment it makes sense to you." She turned suddenly, her attention drawn by a call from the side of the room. "You'll have to excuse me now. The meeting will be starting soon. I'm needed up front." She turned and sailed away.

Carrie and Janie stared at each other for a long moment. Janie was the first to speak. "I could leave right this moment and have everything I came for."

Carrie nodded, her mind still swirling from what Mrs. Stanton had said. She supposed she should feel flattered by Mrs. Stanton's words, but instead she felt the beginning of a bubbling resentment.

Abby laughed and pulled Carrie's arm through her own. "One of the things I love about you, darling daughter, is that your face is so easy to read."

Carrie blinked. "It is?"

Abby laughed harder. "You're not at all sure you want to aspire to the things Elizabeth told you, and you're struggling with resentment."

Carrie sighed. "There truly are times I wish you didn't know me so well." Even as she said the words, she knew they weren't true.

"No, you don't," Abby said confidently, continuing on in a much gentler tone. "But don't worry, I'll not say another word about Elizabeth's rather startling prediction. What the future holds for you is for no one else to determine but you."

"It *was* quite a lot to take in," Janie said almost apologetically. "Is it all right to admit I'm glad she didn't say those things to me, oh mighty one?"

Carrie laughed, resisting the urge to stick her tongue out only because there were so many peers who would witness her childish behavior. And besides, the future was the future, and today was today. All she had to do *today* was sit in the audience and learn from the speakers. As she settled into her seat between Abby and Janie, she also admitted there was a part of her that hoped Mrs. Stanton had been right. In spite of a bubbling fear, she also felt an emerging desire to be at the forefront of a movement that would give freedom to women all across the country. Now she just had to work on becoming a woman who deserved to be listened to.

The day spun past as a parade of people she had only heard about spoke. Susan B. Anthony, Lucretia Mott, Wendell Phillips, Anna Dickinson, and others inspired and challenged every person in the room. These were the people who had first led the fight to free the slaves. Now they were turning their passion to equal rights for both blacks and women.

Abby grew more troubled as she listened to the speakers and talked to women in between sessions. This was the first convention since before the war. So much had happened, and now it must all be resolved and fit together. Most of the people in the room had been closely identified with the anti-slavery movement. The war was over and the slaves were now free, but the battle for equal rights for blacks was just as necessary as it was for women. She knew there were many people in the room who felt it was necessary to put aside the fight for women's right to vote until blacks had been franchised.

During one of the breaks, Carrie found Abby standing outside, staring into the distance. "What's wrong?" she asked quietly.

Abby struggled to find words for her feelings. "I fought so hard for blacks to be free, and I was happy to put the women's rights movement on hold during the war, but I find I'm not willing to do that any longer. I want blacks to have the right to vote, but I believe it's equally important that women get the vote." She took a deep breath. "I'm trying to decide if that makes me selfish."

"There is not a selfish bone in your body," Carrie replied.

Abby shook her head. "I wish that were true, Carrie, but I'm human. I'm doing my best to see this clearly, but it seems to be a muddy mess. The riots in Memphis make me question my own feelings around this issue. Do I have the right to insist on equality for women when blacks are in such dire straits?"

Carrie cocked her head, thinking about everything she had heard that day. "Would blacks having the right to vote really stop the violence? Would it have stopped the riot in Memphis?" she asked. Before Abby could answer, she asked another one. "Are men really so threatened by women having the right to vote that they would block the black vote to make sure we didn't get it?" Her tone was disbelieving.

Abby sighed. "I'm afraid that may be true."

"Why?" Carrie asked in astonishment.

Abby sighed again. "I wish it were a simple explanation." She gazed across the street, trying to find comfort in the bed of bright flowers swaying in the breeze, but her insides continued to churn. "To fully explain it would take all day, but at the core is the belief that a woman's place is in the home and that politics is a dirty business that soils the pristine persona of the female," she answered, not bothering to hide the disgust in her voice.

"Nonsense!" Carrie retorted. "I heard that same argument during the war when I was working at Chimborazo." Scorn rippled in her voice. "Men are such idiots."

Abby smiled slightly. "I wish it was only men," she said. "There are women who believe the same thing."

Carrie stared at her. "Excuse me?"

Abby knew Carrie needed to be aware of the truth. "There is a large number of *women* who hate what we are doing. They believe women are biologically destined to be child bearers and homemakers. They also believe we are going against the laws of nature if we enter politics and shake up the status quo."

Carrie groped for words, the silence stretching out. "You're serious," she finally murmured.

Abby nodded. "I sincerely wish I wasn't, but I am."

"I don't even know what to say," Carrie admitted. "What do they say to a woman like Mrs. Stanton who has accomplished all she has *while* raising seven children?"

"They would say she should have been content with raising her children and that any time she spent away from home or diverted from her life as a wife and mother was time ill-spent."

"So there are *women* in this country who believe my desire to be a doctor is wrong?"

Abby smiled gently. "Less than a week ago, *you* were struggling with your decision to leave Robert," she reminded her. "Carrie, don't judge other women too harshly. I completely disagree with them, but I recognize fear is a powerful force. It's also true that centuries of being programmed to be a certain way, to believe a certain way, is very difficult to cast aside. The very idea of doing so makes you afraid you'll no longer know who you are if you're not what you have always believed yourself to be. There are many women who are more than content to simply go on as they always have because they're comfortable in knowing what is expected of them. They view our efforts as a threat to what they have always known."

"The right to vote? The right to make choices for our own lives?" Carrie asked. "How can that be a bad thing?"

Their conversation was interrupted by a call from the church door. "The next speaker is starting," Abby said quickly, ashamed to realize she was relieved that she wouldn't have to answer Carrie's question. At the same time, she understood their conversation had also made her own thoughts clear. She would fight for equal rights for blacks, but it would be a fight for equal rights for *all* blacks, both male and female.

After many hours of speeches and conversation, Elizabeth Cady Stanton stepped to the podium and read from a notebook in front of her.

> *As the same persons have been identified with the Anti-slavery and Woman's Rights Societies, and as by the Proclamation of Emancipation the colored man is now a freeman, and a citizen; and as bills are pending in Congress to secure him in the right of suffrage, the same right women were demanding, it is proposed to merge the societies into one, under the name of "The American Equal Rights Association," that the same conventions, appeals, and petitions might include both classes of disfranchised citizens.*

Carrie felt a surge of excitement when she realized her presence at the convention gave her the right to have a say in the decision. She was disconcerted the proposition did not meet with unanimous approval but thrilled when it received the approval of a majority of those present. Her commitment to become a doctor was not diminished, but she also fully embraced the belief that women's voices should be heard through the vote. The new association would fight for black rights, but it would also continue to fight for women's rights.

She smiled broadly when Janie's eyes met hers and leaned in close enough to whisper, "I'm so very glad to be a woman!"

It took her a moment to realize the importance of her own words. The very act of saying them made her realize there had been so many moments in her life when she wished she had been born a man, born with all the freedoms being a male brought with it. She had railed against being a woman because it always signified a person who was *less than.* She had fought to be independent and strong because she believed those were inherently male qualities. The truth sweeping through her made her feel light-headed, while at the same time filling her with a sense of power she had never experienced.

She was a strong and independent *woman.* She was equal to any male on the planet. Her voice deserved to be heard as much as anyone's voice did.

Carrie sank back against her pew as acceptance of the truth followed the knowing. A smile played on her lips as she caught Abby's questioning eyes, but she wasn't ready to give voice to her experience yet. Suddenly, she remembered Mrs. Stanton's earlier words to her.

"You are going to be a fine doctor, Carrie Borden, but that will just be the first step for you. You are one of the rare individuals who have the courage to go against everything others may believe is right if you don't believe it is right for you. Women are going to look to you. They are going to depend on you. They are going to need you. You will perhaps pay a heavy price if you decide to be the woman they will need you to be, but I can tell you from personal experience that the rewards far outweigh the cost."

Carrie took a deep breath, remembering Mrs. Stanton had also added that she would know the moment the words made sense. This was the moment. She closed her eyes, letting the wonder of it fill her, recognizing at the same time that she had been given a heavy responsibility.

Chapter Twenty-Four

Rose pulled back on the reins, easing Caramel to a stop on the banks of the James River. She had deliberately picked a spot that would allow her to keep an eye on the road leading into the plantation, but she was sure she had some time to herself before the carriage arrived. She dismounted, tied Caramel to a low tree branch, and settled down on a nearby rock.

Spring rains and continuing snowmelt from the Appalachian Mountains had churned the river into a chocolaty ribbon stretching as far as she could see, whitecaps dancing like frothy topping. It mirrored her emotions perfectly. She was thrilled Moses and Robert were coming home today, but she was a little less clear on how she felt about his bringing Felicia home to expand their family. The fact that she had conflicting feelings made her feel horribly selfish, but she also couldn't deny that her hopes for her own future seemed to be slipping further and further away. She had come down to the river to face things before they arrived.

Moses had told her in the letter containing the news about Felicia that he had come to terms with a lot of things in his life during the riot, and that they would talk about it when he got home. She hoped that meant he was more open to becoming a leader, but that still did nothing for her own burning desire to go to college. She loved teaching her students, but the desire to continue her studies and truly become an educator for her people seemed to be increasing, not diminishing. And now she had *three* children to raise.

What was she going to do with her rampaging feelings? She didn't want them to impact a little girl who had just lost both parents in a brutal murder, but would ten-year-old Felicia feel them churning beneath the surface?

"What am I going to do?" she whispered, wishing with all her heart that her mama was still here to advise her.

"Mama?" Her heartfelt plea floated out over the river, hovering over the waves before the wind seemed to pick it up and carry it over the treetops on the far bank.

Rose watched as the breeze picked up, swirling the frothy whitecaps closer to where she perched. They seemed to be calling her. She wished she could jump into the river and ride the waves to a different future than the one that seemed to stretch out toward her. Just feeling it made her ashamed. She had a son and daughter that she loved fiercely. Why couldn't it be enough? What was wrong with her? She groaned and sank her head into her hands.

What be wrong with you, girl?

Rose's head shot up as a strong voice flowed into her mind. "Mama?" Rose knew it wasn't possible, but she also couldn't deny the sound of her mama's voice ringing through her head.

Of course it be me. I thought you done learned to not borrow trouble 'fore it be here. I thought you done learned to not let fear choke you all up inside.

Rose couldn't hold back a smile as the scolding voice resonated through her. "I know it's wrong," she said. She could see her mama shake her head, her eyes full of the compassion that had always been there for her little girl.

Ain't about being wrong, Rose girl. You got big dreams inside. Ain't nothing wrong with that. Ain't nothing wrong about you wantin' somethin' so fierce bad that it makes your insides ache.

"But I'm a mama now," Rose cried. "You were always so happy just to be my mama. Why can't that be enough for me?" She wasn't going to analyze this strange conversation—she was simply going to be grateful.

Rose girl, I didn't have no choice. I spent my whole time being your mama as a slave.

Rose sat quietly as the words flowed through her, remembering the quick shine of intelligence in her mama's eyes. She thought about how quickly she had learned to read and the pride she had taken in being able to read the Bible. "You wanted more," she said slowly. Quick understanding came with the realization.

Ain't nothin' gave me more joy than being your mama, Rose, but I had dreams, too. I don't reckon there be anyone in the world who don't have dreams. It's just that most folks ignore them or stomp down on dem until dey be dead. Me? Since I was a slave, I made up my mind to be happy with where I was planted.

"Bloom where you're planted," Rose murmured. "You've told me that so many times. I keep trying to let that be enough, Mama. I love being a teacher here at the school, and I love being a mama to John and Hope. They are so wonderful. I feel so selfish because it isn't enough!"

Of course they be wonderful! How could they not be, with you and Moses as their mama and daddy? There ain't nothin' wrong with you, Rose. You be doin' some fine bloomin'. But you ain't always gonna be here. There be more waitin' for you. It only be natural that you be wantin' to get there. You been wantin' things before it be the time to have them eber since you were born.

Rose sucked in her breath, certain she could hear Sarah's chuckle rising above the wind. "Really?" she whispered. "There is more waiting for me?"

Ain't I teached you nothin', girl? God sho 'nuff didn't give you this burnin' desire just to let it smolder out here on the plantation. You go ahead and love that Felicia child like you love your own. You ain't got no idea what a gift she is to you. You'll figure it out soon enough. Your time is coming, Rose girl. Your time be coming...

Rose stiffened. How could her mama know about Felicia? She hadn't said anything out loud.

Sarah's knowing chuckle surrounded her for a long moment and then faded away, leaving only the breeze and the waves.

Rose looked around wildly for several moments, half-expecting her mama to appear over the water, but there was nothing but frothy waves continuing their swirling dance. She finally relaxed, accepting the gift she received as she realized there would always be mysteries she couldn't possibly understand. Gratitude poured through her as the battle that had been raging inside her died away. The only thing that remained was burning impatience to have Moses and Felicia arrive.

"Thank you, Mama," she whispered. A quick glance toward the road confirmed what her heart was already telling her. A broad smile exploded on her face when she saw the carriage rounding a curve. Jumping up, she quickly untied Caramel, leapt into the saddle, and took off at a fast gallop that would have impressed even Carrie.

Moses had been counting the minutes to the plantation since they had left Thomas' house hours earlier. He had enjoyed Felicia's wide-eyed wonder as they traveled through the beautiful countryside, but now that he was almost home, he could hardly wait to see his wife again. He jumped out of the carriage before Spencer pulled it to a complete stop.

"Rose!" He pulled his beautiful wife into his arms and held her against him, reliving the moments in Memphis when he was afraid he would never see her again. When she began to push back, her laughter muffled against his massive chest, he pulled her close again, unwilling to release her warmth. He sighed when she relaxed into him and squeezed more tightly with her arms. He knew she understood. The remnants of horror and fear that he had carried home from Memphis faded away as her understanding swept through him.

When he finally released her, she looked up at him with eyes shining with tears and love. "Welcome home," Rose whispered, reaching up to lay her hand against his cheek.

Moses closed his eyes for a moment, relishing in her touch, and then opened them again. "I have someone for you to meet."

Rose moved to the side of the carriage. She saw a pair of eyes staring at her with fear and curiosity. "Hello, Felicia," she said gently, reaching over the side of the carriage to take hold of one of her hands. She smiled at Robert, who had elected to stay in the carriage. Her heart warmed at the genuine love she saw on his face as he watched the little girl. "Welcome home, Robert."

"Thank you," Robert answered, his eyes already scanning the pastures. "How is everything?"

Rose continued to hold Felicia's gaze while she told Robert what he wanted to know. "Clint took a few of the mares in from the pasture about an hour ago. He said they were acting like it was their time."

Robert sucked in his breath and jumped from the carriage. He turned back and laid a hand on Felicia's shoulder. "You're home now, honey."

Felicia looked away from Rose to stare at Robert for a long moment and then returned her gaze to Rose.

Rose smiled, recognizing Felicia's hunger for a woman. She could only imagine what it must have been like to watch both her mama and daddy be murdered. Felicia's daddy had been gone through most of the last four years during the war, but her mama had always been there for her. Now she was gone. Rose controlled her shudder and gripped the little girl's hands tighter. "I'm so glad you're here," she said softly. She understood the question in Felicia's eyes that she knew would remain unspoken. "This is your new home now. I'm so glad Moses brought you to us."

She watched while a tiny amount of the fear and pain etched on Felicia's face faded away.

"Really?" Felicia whispered, her eyes watching Rose with a wild desperation.

"Really," Rose replied. She reached out her hand. "Let's go inside and see your new room."

Only then did Felicia look up at the plantation house. "Go inside there?" she asked, obvious disbelief overriding her fear.

Rose smiled. "This is where we live. Cromwell Plantation is your home now, too."

Felicia continued to stare at the white three-story house rising above her. "We ain't gonna live in the slave quarters?" she asked.

"I told you we weren't," Moses broke in, his voice amused. "Didn't you believe me?"

Felicia shrugged, relaxing a little as she looked up him. "I figured you were trying to make me feel better about coming this far," she replied primly, a spark of humor glimmering in her wide eyes.

Rose sucked in her breath as Moses laughed easily and swung Felicia from the carriage. She had seen the flash of quick intelligence in Felicia's eyes as she parried with Moses. The little girl didn't know what to think of her yet, but she had obviously already fallen in love with her husband. She watched as Felicia walked beside Moses up the stairs to the house, her heart already filling with love for the little girl with a long braid trailing down her back.

The door to the house swung open. "Who this be?" Annie demanded, leaning down to stare into Felicia's face. She glanced up at Moses. "This be the little girl you done told me don't like molasses cookies?" she demanded.

Rose choked back a laugh.

Felicia was silent for a moment, but then reached out to touch Annie's dress. "Ma'am?"

Annie turned back to her. "Yes?"

"I like molasses cookies just fine," she murmured.

Rose's heart melted a little more as she saw Annie's face soften.

"Whew! That sho do make me feel a sight better!" Annie said dramatically, smiling. "You know who I am, Felicia?"

Felicia looked up at Moses and waited for his nod. "You are Moses' mama," she said clearly.

"That's right," Annie said with deep satisfaction. "Since you gonna be part of the family now, that makes you another one of my grandbabies." She sent Moses a warm, approving look.

Moses smiled, knowing his mama would love Felicia just like she loved John and Hope. His heart swelled with love for her.

Felicia looked confused. "I ain't never been a grandbaby," she answered hesitantly.

Rose moved forward then. She knew Felicia had grown up on a plantation, only moving to Memphis after the war ended. Like most slaves, any extended family had most likely been sold away. "Well, now you are," she said cheerfully. She took Felicia's hand, feeling a quick rush of warmth when Felicia met her eyes with gratitude. Rose knew all this had to be terribly confusing to a ten-year-old little girl. She knelt down in front of her. "You also have a little brother and sister now," she said gently.

Felicia nodded. "Moses told me about them. John and Hope."

"That's right," Rose answered. "They are both taking naps right now, but I predict they will wake up soon."

Felicia stared up at the house again. "They live here, too?"

Rose bit back a smile, knowing Felicia had no point of reference for a black family living in the big house. "That's right," she answered. "You are going to have a room right beside Moses and me. As soon as Hope is old enough, she will move in with you." The house was large enough for Felicia to have her own room, but she suspected the little girl would not want to be all alone.

Annie bent down again. "You ready for some of them cookies? They's still be warm," she said temptingly.

Felicia gazed up at her again and nodded slowly, a small smile flitting on her lips. "Yes, please."

"We'll be right in," Moses said, knowing Felicia was in good hands. As soon as the doors closed, he pulled Rose close again and claimed her lips. When he finally lifted his head, he held her tightly. "I missed you."

"I missed you, too," Rose whispered, reaching up to pull his head down again. She didn't know how she had ever survived the long months of being separated by the war. Her husband had been gone only two weeks this time, but it seemed like an eternity. After their kiss ended, she nestled close, content to let the sounds of the plantation swirl around them. She could hardly remember the angst of the morning. It had been miraculously replaced by a consuming peace that pulsed in her being.

"I have so much to tell you," Moses began.

Rose lifted her hand and placed it across his lips. "It will wait until we have made a little girl feel at home." A noise from above brought a tender smile. "And after a little boy spends time with the daddy he missed so much."

Moses looked up, grinning broadly when John's sleepy eyes peered over the window sill. He already loved his children fiercely, but seeing so many orphaned by the Memphis riot had intensified his love even more. It also made him deeply grateful for the life they had on the plantation...at least for now.

"Daddy?" John mumbled sleepily, his eyes widening when he realized it really *was* his daddy. "Daddy!" he shrieked.

They heard the pounding of little feet on the stairs. Moses laughed and sprang toward the door, opening it before John could. He swept up his son and swung him in a circle, laughing harder when John's giggles and screams split the still air.

Rose watched, a smile on her lips, until she heard the next sound she had been expecting. "Our daughter is now awake," she announced. "And I'm quite sure she's hungry." As she turned toward the house, she saw Felicia stationed next to the door watching Moses and John with a mixture of envy and pain. Another sharp pang of love shot through Rose's heart. She held out her hand invitingly. "Would you like to go meet your little sister?"

Felicia nodded shyly. She took Rose's hand and gazed up at her. "Are you really a teacher?"

"I am," Rose replied.

"My favorite thing in Memphis was going to school," Felicia revealed, her eyes losing some of their dullness. "My teacher said I learned how to read real quick," she offered.

"Very quickly," Rose said, figuring if Felicia loved to learn, they would start right away. Perhaps it would help take her mind off her pain.

"Huh?"

"You should have said, my teacher said I learned how to read *very quickly*."

Felicia ducked her head but not before she could hide her quick grin. "My teacher at home used to make me say things right, too," she admitted. Then she frowned. "It's real hard sometimes to know how to say all the words right."

"I agree," Rose replied. "Sometimes you wish you could just say them the way they come into your head."

"That's right!" Felicia replied. "Do you wish that sometimes, too?"

"Yes," Rose admitted, once more aware of the bright intelligence shining from the girl's eyes. She thought about her mama's prediction down by the river that Felicia would be a gift to her, and she became deeply aware it was true. She stopped outside Hope's room, glad the baby's cries had quieted, and knelt down, pulling Felicia around to face her. "I'm so very glad you're here, Felicia. I know I can never take the place of your mama, but I'm so glad you're going to be part of our family."

Felicia stared hungrily into her eyes. "They killed my mama and daddy," she whispered. "They be dead."

"I know," Rose said tenderly, pain squeezing her heart. "I'm so sorry that happened."

"Why did they kill them?" Felicia asked. "Did they do something real bad?"

Rose thought of all Moses had written her about the riot and shook her head firmly. "They did nothing to deserve what happened, Felicia."

"Then why did they kill them?" the little girl pressed, her lips quivering as she fought the tears pooling in her eyes. She held Rose's eyes with a fierce intensity.

Rose knew nothing but the truth would satisfy her. Felicia may only be ten years old, but she had lived a life that made her much older. She took hold of both of her hands, praying she could comfort this little girl as much as her mama used to comfort her. "There are people in the world who have a lot of hate and fear in their hearts, honey. Even though they shouldn't be, they are afraid of how their own lives will change now that all the slaves are free. They believe the only way they can live their lives the way they want is to get rid of black people."

Felicia looked confused. "There be an awful lot of us," she observed. "Won't we be hard to kill?"

Rose nodded, appreciating the astute observation. "Yes. And they won't be able to, but things are going to be hard for a while. There is a lot of hatred and fear." She knew it would not help to sugarcoat the truth.

"How can they be scared of me?"

Rose looked at the doe-eyed little girl and wondered the very same thing. "I don't know," she answered honestly. "There is no reason for white people to be scared of us at all, but the truth about fear is that it doesn't make sense. It just is."

Felicia thought about what she had said, her little face puckered in thought. "Moses said I wouldn't need to be afraid out here."

"He's right," Rose responded. She hoped she was telling the truth, but she also knew violence could find any of them at any time. The important thing right now was to make Felicia feel safe. "Moses and I are going to take good care of you."

Felicia nodded and flung herself into Rose's arms, the tears finally coming as her body shook with sobs. Rose held her close, knowing the tears were good for her. Sarah used to tell her holding tears was like trying to stop a raging river from overflowing the banks. No matter how hard you tried, they were going to come. You might as well let them come, because it was the only thing that would make you feel better. She crooned softly as she rocked Felicia, breathing a silent prayer of thanks that Moses had brought the little girl home.

Robert, not bothering to change into work clothes, ran to the barn eagerly. He wanted nothing more than to inhale the aromas that told him he was home. He took a deep breath as he entered the gaping barn doors. The smell of horses mixed with hay and saddle soap filled him with contentment. He smiled broadly as Granite stuck his head over the stall door and whinnied a greeting, but he wondered why the massive Thoroughbred was inside on such a beautiful day.

"Welcome home, Robert. Granite is inside because he makes Candy feel better."

Robert whirled around when Clint's voice lifted up from the stall next to Granite. He moved forward and peered over the door, crossing his arms on the sill. "She looks close," he observed, his pulse quickening as he echoed Clint's calm tone, not wanting to excite the mare. He wasn't going to miss any of the new births after all! "Are there any more?"

"She'll be the first," Clint said in a calm monotone as he stroked the bay's glistening neck, "but Shandy and Little Bit won't be far behind." His sparkling eyes shouted his enthusiasm.

Robert felt a surge of answering excitement. These would be the first foals born on Cromwell Plantation from Eclipse, the son of legendary Lexington who won six of his seven race starts. His dream of breeding top Thoroughbreds was coming true.

Candy broke out into a light sheen as her eyes shone with anxiety. She reached back to bite at her side as she snuffled out her discomfort. Robert watched her, seeing nothing to cause alarm. "Has her water broken?"

"About twenty minutes ago," Clint confirmed. "She was a little off her feed last night, so I brought her back into the stall after she had been out for a while this morning. I wanted to keep a close eye on her."

Robert nodded, saying a silent prayer of thanks that he had arrived home in time. He knew Clint was capable of handling things, but this was the boy's first foaling season. It would have been a lot to expect of him.

"I'm real glad you're back," Clint admitted. "I've read everything you gave me to read, but I sure would hate to mess something up."

"You won't mess it up," Robert assured him. "Horses have been giving birth on their own since God created them. They only need us if something goes wrong, and Candy seems to be coming along completely normally. If her water broke twenty minutes ago, she should be dropping her baby any minute. If it goes much longer than thirty minutes, there might be a problem, but I don't expect one. She looks great." He smiled when Candy gave a low moan, sank to her knees and then laid down heavily. He motioned for Clint to take a look. "You should be able to see the feet now."

Clint moved to the back of the stall, his eyes spreading wide when he saw the white sac protruding from the straining mare, two small front hooves sticking out as the foal struggled to be born. "Look at that!" he whispered.

Robert grinned. He remembered his first birth clearly. "Look at the feet," he instructed. "The soles are pointing down. Is that good?"

Clint nodded quickly. "Yes. They can point either down or sideways, but you don't want them pointing up," he said confidently as he moved forward to stroke Candy's neck again, murmuring softly.

Robert smiled. The boy had indeed done his homework. He watched as the foal's nose appeared, followed quickly by the rest of the neck, the front legs, the shoulders, and then the torso. Candy grunted and moaned, but she didn't thrash around. He knew the birth was progressing well.

"It's coming," Clint gasped, as the hips and rear legs appeared. Candy gave an extra grunt and the foal's entire body slid from the birth canal onto the clean straw Clint had layered around her.

Robert enjoyed the look on Clint's face as much as he savored the knowledge of their first foal from Eclipse. He had never lost his feeling that every birth was a miracle. He knew from the wonder shining in Clint's eyes that he felt the same way.

"Should we do anything?" Clint asked nervously.

Robert smiled, confident Clint knew the answer. "What do you think?"

Clint hesitated and then shook his head. "No. Candy did just fine." Moments later, the foal began to move around, gasping its first breath as the membranes and the umbilical cord broke. "It's a colt!" he said, keeping his voice as calm as possible.

Robert nodded, deep satisfaction filling him. He motioned for Clint to join him. "Let's leave them alone. Candy needs to rest for a few minutes. It will take the foal about thirty minutes to be able to stand and eat. She will be ready for him by then."

Clint stood slowly and reached out to touch the colt gently. He rubbed his hand down Candy's neck and then moved to the stall door with a look of wonder still on his face. "What are you going to name him?"

Robert smiled. "I'd say that is up to you."

"Why me?" Clint asked, looking back over his shoulder at the colt before he slipped into the barn aisle and securely latched the stall door.

Robert shrugged. "I figure a man likes to name his own horse." Silence hung in the barn for several moments. He watched with amusement as his words sank into Clint's mind.

Clint turned to stare at him, his wonder turning to disbelief and then edging into a shocked look of confusion. "His own horse?" he echoed slowly.

Robert nodded. "Every good horseman needs a horse of his own that he trains since birth. I want you to have Eclipse's first son." He knew what a huge gift it was. He also knew Clint deserved it.

Clint continued to stare at him until a broad grin slowly spread across his face. He whirled around to stare over the gate at the colt that had just risen to his sternum in the hay. He teetered there with a comical look on his face. "Look at him," Clint whispered. "He's a bay just like his mama, but look at that white star and the four white stockings. He's going to be a beauty." His voice was filled with awe and pride. He spun around and reached out to grip Robert's hand. "I don't know how to thank you," he said gruffly.

Robert shook his hand. "You're my partner in this venture," he said. "You're a natural horseman—I knew that the first moment I saw you ride Granite—but you have taken it much further by your thirst to learn all you can. I'm proud of you, Clint."

Clint swallowed and looked away for a long moment before his eyes swung back. "I have to think about his name," he murmured. "He's going to be the best horse ever."

"With Candy as his dame and Eclipse as his sire, I think you might be right," Robert agreed, joy filling his heart that he could put that look on Clint's face. "Now," he said briskly, "I suggest we check on our other mothers-to-be and let these two have some time to get to know each other."

Clint cast one more awestruck look over the stall door and then turned to join Robert.

Rose stood outside the door to Felicia's room and listened quietly, finally satisfied the little girl was sound asleep. She and Moses had spent the long afternoon showing Felicia around the plantation, thrilled to see her genuine smiles as John hugged her over and over. Without any prompting, her little boy had fallen in love with this stranger who had dropped into his world. He couldn't wrap his mouth around the name Felicia. After several failed attempts he had started calling her Fe-Fe.

Five month old Hope had smiled and gurgled nonstop. Rose had watched with delight as Felicia held Hope close to her chest, singing softly and laughing when Hope reached up to pat her face.

The little girl had been completely mesmerized by the horses, especially falling in love with Granite after he extended his neck over the stall door so he could blow her hair and nibble her shoulder. "He likes me!" she had exclaimed, throwing her arms around his neck.

She had been rendered speechless by the sight of the three tiny little foals standing in their stall suckling their mothers. If possible, she had been even more speechless when Clint gravely told her that Robert had given him one of the foals, which he decided to name Pegasus after the mythical Greek flying horse he had read about in Thomas' extensive library.

Felicia had finally fallen asleep on the porch, curled up in a rocking chair after a special dinner Annie prepared. Moses had carried her up to her bedroom and tucked her in bed gently. Rose sat beside her for a while, wanting to be there if she woke up frightened by the unfamiliar surroundings.

"She's asleep?" Moses whispered.

Rose nodded. "Felicia is exhausted. All three of the kids are asleep," she whispered back, not wanting to do anything to change that. She moved toward her husband, choking back her laugh when Moses swung her into his arms and carried her into the bedroom. The laughter died as she saw the intense yearning and need in his eyes. "I'm so glad you're home, Mr. Samuels," she said softly, pulling his head down for a long kiss. They needed to talk, but that could wait.

Hours later, they sat up against their pillows, watching the candlelight flicker as the breeze blew in through the curtains. Rose nestled contentedly against Moses' chest, her fingers playing across his tight muscles.

"It's time," Moses said somberly.

Rose leaned back and gazed into his eyes, too relaxed from their lovemaking to be concerned about anything he might say. "Time for what?" she asked lazily.

"Time for us to leave the plantation."

Rose stiffened and pushed back further so she could study his face. "What did you say?"

Moses nodded, pulling her back against him. "Going through the riot made me realize I truly do want to be a leader for our people."

Rose pushed clear again, crossing her legs into a sitting position so she could see him clearly. "Tell me," she invited, stunned by his sudden proclamation. She knew so little about the riot. Moses had brought home a pile of newspapers with the articles Matthew wrote, but she hadn't read them yet. She listened as Moses painted a picture of the horror he endured, her own horror growing with each word he spoke. Tears filled her eyes when he described Felicia's parents being killed, and she shuddered when he revealed how close he had come to taking on the police himself.

When he finished recounting the riot, Moses took a deep breath. The remaining anguish had fled as he told Rose everything that happened. The play of emotion on her face helped him release his own. "For the first time, I had a clear understanding of what every black person in this country is up against now that we are free. None of us are truly free as long as we are controlled by the hatred and contempt of people determined to keep us in the same conditions we endured as slaves."

Rose nodded but didn't respond. She was content to listen for now, watching the strong sense of purpose filling Moses' face.

"I realized during the riot that it was a lack of leadership that allowed the riot to happen in the first place. It's certainly what kept it going for as long as it did. No one wanted to step forward and claim leadership because it meant more risk." His voice held both contempt and anger.

Rose continued to sit quietly, letting him work through what he was feeling.

"You told me after the school fire that our people needed me. I didn't want to be needed," he admitted. "Now I realize I could never live with myself if I merely stand idle while other people fight for my rights. I want to be able to look my children in the eye someday and know they understand that I fought for them to have a better life." He reached over to take Rose's hand. "That *we* fought for them to have a better life."

"What do you have in mind?" Rose asked.

"We have to leave the plantation," Moses said again. "It's time for you to go to college. We made enough this year from the plantation to pay for the next year." He hesitated and then forged forward. "For both of us."

Rose's eyes widened. "*Both* of us?"

Moses nodded. "I'm going to become an attorney. Things won't really change until the laws change and until our people have representation from one of their own."

Rose's thoughts spun as she looked into his eyes. Suddenly she smiled. "You will be a fabulous attorney," she said softly, reaching up to touch his cheek. Pride swelled in her until she was afraid it would overwhelm her. "Moses Samuels, Attorney-at-Law. It has a nice ring to it."

"You don't think I'm crazy?" Moses asked. His voice was casual, but his eyes said he needed reassurance.

"Absolutely not."

"You really think I can go to college?"

Rose chuckled. "You will breeze through college. You learned to read so quickly, and I know how fast you have been devouring the books in Thomas' library. You have already absorbed more information than most people I know."

Moses hesitated. "Becoming an attorney might put us in more danger. The whites will see me as more of a threat."

"Yes," Rose agreed, surprised she could be so calm about it but knowing her feelings were still being carried by her mysterious conversation that morning with her mother. "I suppose they will, but it's true that neither one of us can live with ourselves if we don't do all we can to make sure our children and all the rest of our people have a better life. I thought we agreed we weren't going to let fear stop us from doing what we believe is right."

A smile played on Moses' lips. "Then we leave?"

"Yes," Rose said again, "but not yet," she added. She could hardly believe the words were coming out of her mouth, but she knew they were right.

Moses blinked. "What?"

"It's too soon. Hope is not old enough yet, and Felicia doesn't need more turmoil in her life. You saw her face when she was with the horses today. She needs time to heal in a place that is safe. She needs a sense of stability before we move her into another adventure. It's simply too much to ask of her now." As she spoke, her confidence in her decision grew. "It's not time to leave the school, and there are people right here who need you to lead them."

Moses stared at her. "I thought you were eager to leave."

Rose smiled. "I am." She told Moses what had happened down by the river earlier that morning. "We're going to leave here," she said, "but we still have some blooming to do right here."

Moses frowned, but his eyes said he agreed. "How long do we stay?"

"A year," Rose announced, a little stunned by her certainty. "One year." She smiled suddenly, and launched herself into Moses' arms. "I'm so very proud of you," she whispered. She kissed him deeply and then looked toward the window, stunned when she realized the glow in the distance was the sun coming up.

Moses' eyes followed hers. He laughed when he saw the glow lightening the horizon. "I have a perfect way to welcome a new day," he said quietly into her ear, stroking her hair back as he gazed into her eyes.

"You haven't had enough?" Rose teased.

"Of you? Never."

Chapter Twenty-Five

Carrie breathed a sigh of relief when she left school while the late afternoon sun painted the surrounding buildings with a golden glow. She loved every minute of her medical studies, but she was tired to the core. All she wanted was to go home and relax over dinner before she dug into her books for the night. "Thank goodness there is no one out here to harass us tonight!" she exclaimed. "I'm much too tired to ignore them right now. I'm sure I would say something I totally mean and wouldn't regret at all."

Janie grinned. "Why ignore them? I've been wondering what would happen if all of us joined together, rushed one of the hecklers, and beat them up. I believe it would be quite satisfying."

Carrie laughed but gave Janie a considering look. "Sometimes I hardly recognize you," she said, only half in jest.

"I hope so," Janie said. "I find that each day changes me a little more."

"Do you like who you are becoming?"

"I do. Do you?"

Carrie gazed at her. "Would it matter?"

Janie considered the question as they began to walk down the sidewalk. "It shouldn't," she admitted, "but I'm afraid it does."

"You're right that it shouldn't matter," Carrie replied, "but I'm also happy to tell you I'm thrilled with who you are becoming. I couldn't be more proud of you."

Janie flushed and her eyes glistened with gratitude. "I spent my first couple months here watching every man on the street because I was terrified Clifford would appear."

"And now?"

"And now there are times I wish he would so that he could see he has absolutely no power over me!" Janie answered. "Sometimes I can hardly believe I was the terrified woman in my memories. When I think about those months in Raleigh under Clifford's control, it seems I must be thinking about another woman."

The memory of Janie's swollen and bruised face when she had first arrived at the plantation after her escape never failed to fill Carrie with anger. "I wish Clifford *would* walk up to us right now. At least Robert had the satisfaction of beating him up. I would so love to have the same privilege."

Janie laughed but eyed her speculatively. "Would you really, Carrie?"

Carrie considered the question, but it didn't take her long to determine her answer. "Yes. I used to think anger was a *bad* thing..."

"And you don't anymore?"

Carrie spoke carefully, wanting to make sure she stated what she truly believed. "I don't think anger is a bad thing, but I think it can make us do bad things if it gets out of control."

Janie gazed at her. "You don't think beating up Clifford would be a bad thing?"

Carrie grinned at the hopeful tone in her friend's voice. "*Killing* him would be a bad thing—giving him a taste of what he did to you would be nothing but eminently satisfying!"

Janie chuckled and then fell silent for several moments. "You're changing, too," she observed.

"I hope so," Carrie responded. Almost a month had passed since the Women's Rights Convention. She had told Janie about her revelations during the conference, but her first full month of school had done nothing but intensify her convictions.

Janie continued to look at her. "Did something happen today?"

Carrie fell silent, not sure she was ready to talk about it. She took deep breaths of the spring air. June had brought sultry warmth to the streets of Philadelphia, but the evenings were still refreshingly cool. She let her thoughts simmer as she admired the window boxes full of colorful zinnias and purple coneflowers. Beds of blue flag irises waved proudly in the breeze, while peonies provided vibrant splashes of color against the brick townhouses lining the road. She knew Janie would wait for her to sort through her thoughts, and that her friend would also understand if she didn't want to talk at all. The last month of studying and living together had erased the long months they had been apart during Janie's marriage, making them closer than ever.

"Dean Preston asked me to meet with a doctor here in Philadelphia today," she finally revealed. Janie eyed her curiously but remained silent. As Carrie thought about her conversation with Dr. Henry Chambers, her anger grew. "He infuriated me!" she said in a sudden burst of emotion.

"Why?"

"He's an idiot," Carrie said bluntly. Janie snorted with laughter, her expression inviting explanation. "He started by telling me he didn't usually lower himself to speak to women medical students." Her eyes widened. "Can you believe he actually said *lowered*? I wanted to walk out right then."

"I'm surprised you didn't."

"I was too curious to leave. I wanted to know why Dean Preston had set up the meeting," Carrie admitted. "Dr. Benson recommended it, but I suspect there was another reason."

"Dr. Benson? From New York?"

"Yes. He recommended Dr. Chambers meet with me to learn about what the Metropolitan Board of Health has done in New York City."

Janie nodded somberly. "I've heard more cases are cropping up there."

"Yes. It's a matter of time until it begins to spread across the country. I don't believe New York will suffer like it has in the past, but there is no place else in the country that is as prepared as they are to deal with it. When it begins to spread, there will be many deaths," Carrie predicted.

"Why didn't Dr. Benson give Dr. Chambers the information he needed?"

Carrie had wondered the same thing. She stopped to consider it more fully, a smile of appreciation flitting across her lips when she figured it out. "Dr. Benson wants me to fully understand what I'm up against," she finally concluded. "I suspect that was also Dean Preston's reason for pushing it."

"I see," Janie murmured.

Carrie laughed at her confused expression. "I realize I'm not giving you much to work with here." She settled in to enlighten her friend. "After Dr. Chambers told me he didn't usually *lower* himself to talk to women medical students, he got a patronizing, fatherly look on his face and asked me if I understood what a risk I was taking being a medical student."

"Really?"

"Before I could even respond, he proceeded to enlighten me," Carrie continued. "He warned me that higher education and the autonomy it could provide would cause the degeneration of my reproductive organs, and that I was also contributing to the ultimate decline of civilization and the family."

"Oh dear," Janie murmured.

"Then he explained that he had been given the awesome responsibility as a medical professional to play a role in the debate over women's nature." She didn't bother to control the fury in her voice. "*Women's nature!*" Carrie was aware of several heads turning as she raised her voice with disgust, but she didn't care. "He is working with a group of local male physicians to write prescriptive literature regarding women's health, sexuality, and gender roles. Can you imagine? He then told me he feels a grave responsibility to give voice to the traditional definitions of femininity that must, of course, limit women's social role to staying at home and bearing children."

Janie chuckled.

Carrie swung around to stare at her friend with blazing eyes. "You find something humorous in that?"

Janie only laughed more loudly. "What I am waiting for is the end of this story. I'm quite certain I'm going to find your *response* to Dr. Chambers very humorous indeed. I wish I could have been there in the room when he was spouting his nonsense."

Carrie's anger melted as she smiled wryly. "I told him I was sure he would benefit from what I had learned in New York City, but that I found it completely offensive to communicate with a man who was afraid of a woman's strength."

Janie nodded. "I knew it would be good," she said with satisfaction. "What did he say?"

Carrie smiled. "He told me he wasn't surprised that I had fallen in with the *feminist* movement. I told *him* that some of my favorite feminists are the wonderful men in my life who recognize the equality and full humanity of women *and* men." She laughed as she remembered how red his face had gotten as he struggled for a response. "Before he had a chance to say anything else, I asked him if Edward Chambers was his son." She smiled at Janie's confused expression. She had only figured out the connection herself several minutes into their conversation. "Dr. Chambers looked as confused as you do. I then proceeded to tell him Dr. Benson had recommended he talk to me because I had saved his son's life at Chimborazo."

"You did?" Janie gasped.

Carrie nodded. "Edward was born in Georgia. His family moved north, but he stayed. When the war started, he fought for the Confederacy. He was brought into our unit after one of the battles at Cold Harbor. He was afraid he would lose his leg, but we managed to save it." Her expression softened. "We almost lost him during surgery, but he pulled through. He was there for several weeks, so we had a chance to get to know one another."

Janie stared at her. "How did Dr. Chambers respond?"

"I didn't give him a chance," Carrie said. "I told him that from what I could tell, his son had far more sense than he did because he had not cared one bit who treated him during the war, as long as they knew what they were doing. Then I left." She felt a surge of satisfaction as she retold the story. She could still see the man's mouth opening and closing, not a sound coming out, as she had sailed from the room.

"Does Dean Preston know?" Janie asked, her eyes dancing with laughter and admiration.

"Yes," Carrie said. At first she had been afraid of Dean Preston's response. She had grown to greatly admire her, and didn't want to disappoint her. "She laughed and told me she suspected it would go about like that. She told me she was proud of me for standing up to him."

The smile faded from Janie's face as she shook her head. "Do you really think it will ever change?"

Carrie pondered whether to tell her what she truly believed and then decided she didn't need to soften the things she said. "I do," she said firmly, "but I don't know that it will change in our lifetime. You said it yourself while we were in New York. The attitudes most men have about women have been developed over centuries. I believe we'll make great strides if we have the courage to press through the challenges, but I predict it will take more than our generation to see true change."

"I see," Janie murmured, disappointment shadowing her eyes.

Carrie laughed. "I think it is wonderful!" she proclaimed.

"Excuse me?"

Carrie laughed louder, understanding the expression on Janie's face. "Don't you understand? The women who follow in our footsteps may have it easier, but they'll never have the satisfaction that comes from being revolutionary. They won't be able to look back and know they battled through men's ridiculous ideas to open the doors for women to any field they wish to excel in." Her eyes glowed passionately. "We're becoming doctors because we want to make a difference, Janie. The wonderful thing is, by doing that, we're going to make a difference for every woman in the nation for generations to come."

Janie stopped walking and turned to look at Carrie for several moments. "Aren't you ever afraid?"

Carrie nodded. "Every day," she admitted easily. "I hate knowing that almost every man I see believes I am less than them. I hate knowing I am putting myself in danger every day simply because I want to be a doctor, but..." Her voice trailed off as a cable car rumbled by.

"But what?" Janie pressed, as the noise abated.

"But I am more afraid of not standing up to them. I couldn't live with myself if I let someone else's beliefs, whether they are from a man or a woman, dictate how I live my life." She shook her head. "I'm not really brave. I just refuse to let someone else control me."

Matthew swung off the train and grabbed his bag. No one knew he was coming home today, so there wasn't a carriage waiting for him. He didn't care. It was a beautiful day to walk through Richmond. He welcomed the exercise after the long train ride from Washington, DC.

He smiled when he felt the genuine optimism pervading the air. Many of the buildings that had been burned at the end of the war had not been rebuilt yet, but the entire downtown area was now free of rubble, and foundations were being laid for new structures to take their place. The streets were crowded with people laughing and talking as they went about their business. He let the good feelings propel him forward as he hurried up the hill to Thomas' house, but he wondered how these people would feel if Congress succeeded in moving forward with their plans for Radical Reconstruction. The aftermath of the Memphis Riot had made it almost certain they would get their way.

"Mr. Matthew!" Micah cried when he answered the door. "How many times I got to tell you that you don't need to be knocking on this door. This be your home."

Matthew smiled. "No one was expecting me. I didn't want to startle you."

"You go right ahead and startle me," Micah scolded.

May flung the kitchen door open. "Matthew! It's about time you got yourself back to Richmond. You been gone way too long."

Matthew smiled, warmed by their welcome. He hadn't been back in Richmond since he had pulled out on the train bound for Memphis seven weeks ago. Now that he was home, he let himself feel the fatigue that went bone deep. "It's good to be back," he said quietly.

May eyed him for several moments. "You come on in the kitchen. Dinner won't be ready for a while, but I got me a fresh strawberry pie I just pulled out of the oven. I reckon your skinny body could use some."

Matthew grinned and rubbed his hands together. "Lead the way."

Matthew had let May talk him into a long nap after he gorged on strawberry pie. He felt almost human when the rumbling sounds of a carriage pulling to a stop in front of the house woke him. He yawned and stretched, smiling broadly when he heard Thomas and Abby's voices as they entered the house.

"What? Matthew is here?" Abby's excited voice floated clearly up the stairs as he opened the door. "Where is he?"

May was in the middle of an explanation that he was asleep when he walked down the stairs.

"Matthew!" Abby cried. "Welcome home!"

Matthew grinned and pulled her into a hug. When he released her he shook hands with Thomas. "It's good to be back."

"Did you know Peter arrived yesterday?" Thomas asked.

"Peter? I had no idea. I haven't seen him since we left Memphis. Where is he staying?"

"Here, of course!" Peter walked in the front door as Matthew was speaking. "I heard rumors you were headed back to Richmond, so I decided to join you. I went down to the station to meet you, but your train arrived early. By the time I got back, you were already asleep. May told me if I woke you up, she would give you all my strawberry pie, so I let her have her way."

May snorted. "He might just get your pie anyway. It's time you figured out who runs things around here, Mr. Peter."

Peter laughed and gave her a hug. "He who runs the kitchen runs the house," he said playfully before glanced back at Matthew.

Matthew recognized the flicker in his friend's eyes. He knew Peter well enough to know he had something serious on his mind, but he also knew it could wait until after dinner. At that very moment, all he wanted to do was eat whatever was creating the delicious aromas wafting from the kitchen. "He doesn't sound sincere enough to me, May" he said. "I followed your orders when you told me to get some sleep. I think you should give me his pie."

May waved her hand. "The whole lot of you can go on in the parlor. There is lemonade and cookies waiting there. Dinner will be ready soon, though, so don't you be spoiling your appetite.

"Yes, ma'am," Peter said meekly. "Whatever you say."

May swatted at him with her apron and disappeared into the kitchen. Laughing, Matthew followed the rest of them into the parlor.

Abby was the first to speak. "I know social protocol says we should have idle chitchat since you have just arrived, but I'm not in the mood." She turned to Peter. "We all know you didn't decide to stop by Richmond for a casual visit. Talk," she commanded.

Peter nodded. "I did some more nosing around today. I didn't like what I discovered."

"About?" Matthew asked sharply.

Peter settled back into his chair and took a sip of the lemonade before he answered. "Have you heard of the Ku Klux Klan?"

Matthew frowned. He didn't know what he had expected, but it wasn't this. He struggled to remember what little he knew. "I've heard something about it. I understand it is a social organization founded by six Confederate veterans from Pulaski, Tennessee. They created it right before Christmas last year because they were bored. They wear white robes and hoods to hide their identities. They seem to be fond of bashing picnics and wedding ceremonies. I've heard people consider it great fun."

"That's how it started," Peter agreed.

"And now?" Thomas asked.

"I'm afraid it's becoming something more dangerous," Peter admitted. "They have grown quite a bit. From what I can tell, the trouble began when some of the people out playing pranks recognized the genuine fear black people felt when they saw them ride by, so they decided to take it further." He frowned. "It is turning into a secret, oath-bound organization committed to intimidating blacks."

"Like the vigilante groups springing up around the country," Matthew said heavily, visions of the Memphis Riot still fresh in his mind.

"Yes, but..."

"But what?" Abby asked. "You're not telling us everything."

Peter shrugged. "I'm still trying to learn exactly what is going on myself, but my instincts tell me this is more than a small band of vigilantes."

"What do you think it is?" Matthew asked, watching him closely.

"They have the power to organize," Peter answered. "Confederate veterans are flocking to their meetings. What started out as fun has turned into something deadly. I've been hearing stories about them burning blacks' houses. They're attacking and killing them."

"Like in Memphis," Matthew said bitterly.

"What happened in Memphis has made it worse," Peter revealed. "They seem to be picking up where the Memphis Riot left off. They sweep in at night wearing their robes and hoods so no one can identify them. They do their damage, and then disappear."

"Cowards!" Abby snapped.

"Yes," Peter agreed, his eyes troubled. "They are determined to reestablish white supremacy. The Ku Klux Klan has already spread to other counties in Tennessee and Alabama."

"And they're all attacking the blacks?" Abby asked with horror.

"No," Peter said quickly. "Right now the majority of them are still just playing pranks, but..." His voice trailed off as he looked at Matthew. "What is happening in Washington, DC, right now? I hear things from different people, but I wanted to hear it from you."

"And this is connected to the Ku Klux Klan?" Matthew was puzzled.

Peter sighed. "I don't know. I do know there are Republicans in Congress pushing for more strenuous Reconstruction Acts; especially after the Memphis Riot made it so clear that Southern governments can't be counted on to protect the freedmen."

"And you're afraid if the Republicans get their way, it will promote more vigilante violence in the South against the blacks," Abby stated.

"Yes," Peter replied. "I also believe that if the Republicans *don't* get their way, the blacks are going to continually face what happened in Memphis. I've been talking to some of my colleagues here in Richmond. Vigilante violence is increasing here in Virginia, as well." He shook his head. "I don't know what the answer is." He turned back to Matthew. "What is happening?"

"The Civil Rights Act was a victory," Matthew began, "but I have talked to many members of Congress who doubt they really possess constitutional power to turn the goals of the Civil Rights Acts into law. There are many pushing to seek constitutional guarantees for black rights. They don't want to have to rely on temporary political majorities, and they don't want the Supreme Court to have an opportunity to declare it unconstitutional."

"The Fourteenth Amendment," Peter said. "I understood the Joint Committee on Reconstruction proposed an amendment last year stating that any citizens barred from voting on the basis of race by a state would not be counted for purposes of representation by that state."

"Yes," Matthew agreed. "When slavery was abolished, that meant the full population of the freed slaves, not just the three-fifths compromise established in 1787, would be counted for determining representation in the House. Republicans are concerned about the extra power that will give Southern states, even though the freed slaves can't vote."

"So Republicans are looking for a way to balance that by getting the vote for the black man. They believe the blacks will vote with them," Abby said thoughtfully.

Matthew nodded. "The amendment was blocked by Democrats opposed to black rights, but it was also opposed by a coalition of Radical Republicans led by Charles Sumner. They didn't feel it went far enough in securing equal rights for blacks."

Peter leaned forward. "I understand a version of the amendment finally passed through Congress."

"That's true. They finally found a proposal the majority could agree on. It passed the Senate on June eighth, and then received approval in the House on the thirteenth. A resolution for President Johnson to transmit the proposal to the executives of all the states was passed on the eighteenth."

"Yesterday," Thomas murmured.

"And are the Radical Republicans happy with it?" Peter asked keenly.

Matthew shrugged. "They are satisfied they have secured civil rights for the blacks, but they are disappointed that they couldn't secure political rights for them."

"Meaning the Fourteenth Amendment still doesn't give them the vote," Abby stated angrily. "So Congress is still blocking both the black right to vote and women's right to vote."

"Yes," Matthew said quietly, knowing how disappointed Abby would be. "I'm sorry."

Abby frowned. "If they want real change, the blacks will have to be able to vote. As long as they have no voice, the South will try to rip all their freedoms away."

"I agree completely," Matthew responded hesitantly.

"What?" Abby asked. "What are you thinking?"

"It may work in our favor," Matthew said slowly. "Even though the Fourteenth Amendment doesn't go as far as we wanted it to, it is still going to be bitterly contested by every Southern state. I predict that most, if not all, will refuse to ratify it."

"And if they do?" Thomas asked.

Matthew lifted his hands. "I can't be sure, but President Johnson is losing more power and influence every day. I will be shocked if the Democratic Party retains its power after the fall elections. It is becoming more and more obvious that Johnson's lenient policies toward the South are a complete failure. The Memphis Riot was more evidence of that."

"Your and Peter's articles made that abundantly clear," Abby said warmly. "They were so well done. I've been proud of you for so long, but I don't think I've ever been quite *that* proud." Her shining gaze included Peter, as well. "You made sure the entire country knew what really happened."

Matthew flushed, pleased with her praise because he admired her so much. "It was nice to actually be a voice for change," he admitted. "Anyway, when Johnson's party loses this fall, and then when the Southern states refuse to ratify the amendment, I believe it will open the door for the Reconstruction Acts to go through."

"Turning the South into military states," Thomas said heavily.

Compassion filled Abby's face. "I'm sorry, my dear."

Thomas shook his head. "I wish there were another way to accomplish it, but I'm afraid there is not. President Johnson's policies have made the South believe they can do anything they want to without consequences. The state governments believe it, but now individuals believe it as well. That might actually be worse because it will be almost impossible to govern vigilantes who have no respect for the law. I'm afraid it will take a military crackdown to change things."

Matthew knew how much Thomas' admission cost him. He also wasn't sure that military governments would stop the chaos that was going to reign through the South. He exchanged a long look with Peter, knowing he was thinking the same thing. After their experience in

Memphis, they both knew the level of hatred had spiraled out of control.

Jeremy took a deep breath as he settled back in the carriage, exhausted from a long day. Thomas and Abby had left two hours before him because one of the machines had broken down. He refused to leave until it was fixed and in operating order for the next day.

"Tired?" Spencer asked, lifting the reins as he urged the horses forward.

"Yes, but it was a good day," Jeremy responded. "We got three new orders in. We are ahead of our projections by almost twenty-five percent. I can't complain about being a little tired."

"That's real good," Spencer replied, but he had an uneasy tone to his voice.

Jeremy looked up sharply. He and Spencer had become too close for him not to recognize when something was being concealed. "What is it?"

Spencer was quiet for a moment and then shrugged. "It's probably nothing."

"Just tell me," Jeremy responded. "I'm too tired to pry it out of you tonight."

Spencer chuckled but sobered quickly. "You been having any trouble with the workers?" he asked.

Jeremy frowned. "Not that I'm aware of. Things are always tense, but there hasn't been any outright trouble or violence." He was proud of the fact that their black and white employees were working together smoothly. They might not like it, but the wages they were earning compelled them to do it. He had even seen a few of them talking casually between shifts. He smiled as he realized the factory was making a difference in more than just family incomes. It was a small thing, but it was a beginning.

Spencer pulled his thoughts back. "What about a few weeks ago?"

Jeremy forced his exhausted mind to concentrate. "I had to fire a man," he remembered.

"A white man?" Spencer pressed.

"Yes. He refused to work on one of the new machines with two new black men I hired. He made a threat toward one of them."

"So you fired him," Spencer said gravely.

Jeremy shook his head impatiently. "What is the point of this, Spencer?"

"The *point* is that I been hearing things," Spencer replied. "Not so good things."

"There have been no more threats made against the factory," Jeremy protested. "Abby has been back for over a month. There have been no problems."

"Abby ain't the one who did the firing," Spencer said, his eyes searching every shadow as the carriage rolled down the street. "I been hearing threats against you, Jeremy."

"By who?"

"I don't know. I ain't heard the threats myself. Some of the fellas told me to tell you to be real careful, though. So I'm telling you."

Jeremy shrugged, too tired to be alarmed. "All right. I've been warned. Can you get me home to dinner now?"

Spencer chuckled as he slowed the carriage to turn a corner. "I reckon I can do that."

The large rock was hurled from the shadows. It barely missed Jeremy's head as it slammed into his shoulder. He grunted and fell back against the seat, stunned by the sudden attack.

Spencer groaned and yelled to the horse to run. It was too late. Four men appeared from the shadows, grabbing the horse's harness and holding them in place.

Six more men sprang from the darkness, swarming into the carriage.

Jeremy tried to fight back, but a vicious blow to the head blurred his vision and made him nauseated. He could feel the fists and boots slamming into his body, but he was powerless to stop the attack.

He closed his eyes and wondered if he was going to die. An image of Marietta's glowing eyes filled his mind, followed by Rose's laughing face. He struggled to remain conscious, but he could feel the blackness descending. He could hear Spencer's grunts as the darkness deepened. The last thing he remembered was the sound of yelling and running feet.

Chapter Twenty-Six

Thomas settled back in his chair, a broad smile on his face as he gazed around the dinner table. It was so wonderful to have Matthew and Peter with them for a few days. He glanced at the clock on the wall. "I'm hoping Jeremy will get home in time to eat with us." He had already explained the broken machinery that had delayed him.

Abby picked up her napkin, a troubled expression on her face. "Shouldn't he be here by now?"

Thomas shrugged. "I have no way of knowing how long it will take to fix the machinery." He watched her carefully. "Is something bothering you?"

"Nothing concrete," Abby murmured. "Just a feeling..."

Her words were drowned out by the pounding of hooves pulling a rattling carriage at a fast speed. "What in the world!" Thomas exclaimed, jumping up from the table to rush to the window. "No one should be driving that fast on this road. Someone will get hurt."

Abby was beside him in an instant, peering into the darkness. "Who is it?"

"I don't..." Thomas stopped speaking when the carriage plowed to a stop in front of the house.

"Mr. Cromwell! Mr. Cromwell!"

"That's Spencer!" Abby gasped.

All four of them raced down the sidewalk, while Micah and May stood on the porch, their faces grim with fear.

The light from the street lanterns revealed the open cuts and swelling on Spencer's face. One eye had already swollen shut, the other was a mere slit. "Spencer!" Abby cried. "What happened?"

Spencer shook his head and gestured toward the back seat. "They got Jeremy!" he gasped, pain making his voice hoarse. "They beat him up real bad!"

Jeremy was crumpled lifelessly in a heap on the seat. His face was even more battered than Spencer's. Both arms were cocked at odd angles.

"Is he...alive?" Abby asked in a broken voice.

Matthew stepped forward and held his fingers against his neck. "He's alive," he announced, motioning Peter forward. "We have to get him in the house."

"Should we move him?" Thomas asked between clenched teeth, fear and fury pulsing through him in equal measure.

May had joined them on the road. "Get him out of that there carriage," she commanded. "Take him up to Miss Carrie's old room and cover him up good with some blankets to keep him from going into shock."

Thomas blinked at his housekeeper.

"What? You think I didn't learn plenty from Miss Carrie when she been treating all them people in our house?" May's gaze swung back to Matthew and Peter. "Matthew, you go after Dr. Wild once you get Mr. Jeremy inside. I hear he still be in town. Somebody at Jackson Hospital gonna be able to tell you where he is. That's who Miss Carrie would want to treat these two."

Thomas felt completely helpless as he watched Matthew and Peter lift Jeremy as gently as they could. Matthew cradled his bloody head against his chest in order to keep him as immobile as possible.

"Thomas..." Abby whispered. "How could this have happened?"

Thomas bit back the bile in his throat as he fully realized how serious Jeremy's injuries were. His brother's face was an ashen gray. The only thing convincing him he was still alive was the sporadic heaving of his chest. "We had a guard for you," Thomas snapped, the sight of Jeremy's broken body fueling his anger and guilt. "I never thought to make sure Jeremy had one, too."

Abby spun around to face him as Matthew and Peter disappeared into the house. "This is *not* your fault," she said. "It's not possible for someone to be with all of us every moment. Jeremy and Spencer both carry guns." She shook her head. "How did this happen?"

"They came out of nowhere," Spencer gasped.

May had stayed outside while Jeremy was carried in. She turned on Spencer now. "You get out of that carriage right now," she ordered. "Get into the kitchen where's I can take care of you next."

"Nonsense," Thomas said quickly. He motioned to Micah. "Help me get Spencer into the bedroom behind the kitchen. I don't want him climbing the stairs to the upstairs bedrooms."

Abby rushed forward. "It will take me just a minute to get the bed changed."

"He'll be needing some..."

Abby interrupted May. "Yes, I know he needs some blankets. We'll get him settled, May. Please go check on Jeremy now," she said gently.

May exchanged a long look with her and then ran up the steps. Thomas put one arm around Spencer, waited for Micah to move in on the other side, and helped him up the stairs.

"Jeremy be the one hurt real bad," Spencer groaned.

"You're both hurt very badly," Thomas replied. "Thank you for getting him back here, Spencer. We'll get you settled and then check on Jeremy. There's not much we can do until the doctor gets here."

Thomas heard Matthew clatter down the stairs and run across the porch. Moments later, he heard the carriage rumbling down the road. He prayed Dr. Wild would arrive quickly. When they had Spencer prone on the bed and covered with a thick blanket, he and Abby raced upstairs.

Jeremy was lying unconscious under a mound of covers. His skin was clammy. Blood from deep gashes in his head had already turned his pillows bright red. His breathing was shallow and rapid.

May looked up when they walked in. "This boy be in shock," she said. She motioned to Thomas and Abby. "Get me all the pillows you can find. We gots to elevate his legs and thighs." Then she turned on Peter. "I ain't leaving Mr. Jeremy right now, so you gots to listen real close and do what I tell you."

"Anything," Peter said, his own face almost gray as he looked at Jeremy.

"I wants you to go downstairs and make me up a shock formula. You start with one cup of warm water. There should be enough in the tea kettle. Then you gonna add in two tablespoons of honey and one tablespoon of apple cider vinegar. You gonna find both of them on the first shelf of the pantry," she instructed. "Now this be the most important part. You gonna add in one teaspoon of cayenne. *One teaspoon.* You got all that?"

Peter nodded. "I got it. I'll be back as soon as I can."

May held up her hand. "I wants you to make up two batches. Make Spencer drink one of them. I don't care what he says. Just make him drink it. Shock don't always set in right away. He got beat up real bad, too."

Peter nodded and disappeared.

Thomas and Abby finished positioning Jeremy's legs on the pillows. "What now?" Thomas asked.

May inspected their work carefully before she nodded her approval. She turned to Abby. "I need you to go to Carrie's medicine cabinet and find that bottle of shepherd's purse tincture she made up last year when Moses be so sick. It needs to go in them drinks Peter be making, but I didn't think he could remember everything. That tincture be the best thing to bring up Mr. Jeremy's blood pressure and..."

Thomas knew what she wasn't willing to say. "He could have internal bleeding," he said quietly after Abby disappeared. "The tincture could help stop it."

May nodded reluctantly. "Don't know for sure, but he got beat up bad, so we gots to act like there be bad things going on in there." She closed her lips firmly, turning as Micah entered the room with a basin of warm water and a bundle of clean rags. "Thank you. I was gonna send Mr. Cromwell for that next."

"You ain't be the only one who learned things from Miss Carrie. The boy gonna be all right?"

"He will be if I got anythin' to say about it," May replied. "How's Spencer?"

"Complaining that we be wasting time taking care of him," Micah responded. "I told him if he moved out of that bed, that you wouldn't never be saving another piece of pie for him again. He's grumbling, but he's staying put. Mr. Peter almost got them drinks made. I made Spencer promise to drink it."

May nodded with satisfaction. "You go back down and see what you can do for Spencer's face. I's gonna need a big bucket of ice up here real quick."

"I'll do that," Thomas offered.

May shook her head. "Nope. I needs you to massage Mr. Jeremy's hands and feet to keep the blood movin'. Miss Carrie told me that be real important when someone be goin' into shock."

May began to gently wash Jeremy's cuts. She wrapped a long cloth around the one that was bleeding the worst, tying it securely to hold it in place. When Peter arrived with the drink, she directed both of them to hold Jeremy's limp body up against the pillows so she could ease the liquid down his throat.

Abby arrived moments later with a basketful of tins. May managed a smile when she saw what was in the basket. "I guess we all be learning something from Miss Carrie," she observed. "Give me some of that gypsy weed ointment to put in this water. It will help me get these cuts real clean."

"I also brought some plantain," Abby offered. "I saw Carrie use it on Clint's burns. I remember her saying it's also good for cuts."

"It sho 'nuff be," May said. "Honey be real good, too, but I'm figurin' Dr. Wild gonna have to stitch up some of these cuts on his head. I can't be putting nothing on them quite yet."

Abby eyed her. "How did you learn all this, May?"

May shrugged, talking as she continued to gently bathe Jeremy's head and arms, pulling the blankets back over him as soon as she had them clean. "I spent a whole lot of time helping Miss Carrie. First, it was Miss Georgia, and then Moses after he got shot. There weren't hardly no time before we were taking care of Mr. Robert. I learned me a little bit more with each one. I asked a whole lot of questions. Miss Carrie always be happy to answer them. I reckon she figured the day would come when I would need to know it."

"That day has certainly come," Thomas murmured.

"Oh, I done been using it right along," May said casually. "Lots of folks seem to know I learned a lot. They come to get me every now and again."

Abby smiled. "I'm glad they have you." She leaned down to look more closely at Jeremy's face. "Am I imagining that he looks a little better?"

"His feet are warmer," Thomas offered, "and his breathing seems to have slowed down some."

May stared at him for several long moments before she nodded. "He not be quite so bad," she announced. "I need him to wake up, though. We won't really be knowing how bad off he be until he wakes up."

Thomas stiffened at something he heard in her voice. "What are you saying?"

May hesitated before she answered. "Ain't no use asking for trouble before we get it," she muttered.

Abby was suddenly frightened. "Just tell us what you are thinking, May. Please."

"I ain't *thinkin'* nothin'," May protested, "but I seen men take beatings like this that ain't never quite right again," she said. "There ain't no reason to think that done happened to Mr. Jeremy. He's bound to have a concussion, but I know lots of people who come back and be right as rain after one. Ain't nothin' but time gonna tell us how Mr. Jeremy gonna be."

Almost two hours had passed before they heard the sound of a carriage rattling down the road. Abby leapt up and peered out the window. "It's them," she called over her shoulder. "Thomas, I'll stay here with May and Jeremy. You and Peter go downstairs and tell them what you know."

A few minutes later, Dr. Wild appeared in the doorway. "Good evening," he said. "I do manage to spend quite a bit of time in this house. I thought that would die off with Carrie gone, but I see y'all are determined to keep me coming around. It took Matthew a little while to find me, but I'm glad he did."

Abby smiled hesitantly, not sure how to respond to his cheerfulness. She was still too frightened for Jeremy.

Dr. Wild read the thoughts flitting across her face. "I believe Jeremy is going to be fine," he said quickly, moving forward to gaze down at him. "Thomas told me his color has come back and that his breathing is steady again." His face turned grim as he stared at Jeremy's battered face. "Who did this to him?"

"We don't know," Thomas answered. "We're hoping he can tell us when he wakes up."

"What about Spencer? Wasn't he with him?"

"Spencer is sleeping downstairs. We figured that would be the best thing for him."

"I ain't sleepin' no more." Spencer walked in slowly.

Dr. Wild gently pushed him into a chair. "You probably should be," he said sternly.

Spencer scowled. "I been beat worse than this on the plantation before I got free. It's Mr. Jeremy I'm worried about."

"Who did this?" Thomas snapped.

Spencer shook his head. "I ain't got no idea," he admitted. "It was real dark, and they came out of nowhere. The first thing they did was throw a rock that hit Jeremy real hard. Then a whole passel of them jumped in the carriage and beat Jeremy." He bit back a moan. "I tried to stop them, but two more men jumped on me before I could reach my pistol. I remember the bat, but it was too dark... It happened too fast."

Abby laid a hand on his shoulder. "We know you did everything you could," she murmured. "I'm so sorry you were hurt."

"Is Jeremy gonna be all right?"

"I believe he will be," Dr. Wild responded. "Thanks to May." He turned to her, his eyes warm with admiration. "When did you learn how to do all this? Peter told me about the drink you had him make for both of them. There is not one thing I would have done differently."

May grinned and ducked her head. "I did what Miss Carrie taught me how to do." She glanced up. "I cleaned his cuts, but I didn't put nothing in them. I figured you might have to sew some of them up. His arms don't look so good either, but Miss Carrie never taught me how to set bones."

Dr. Wild probed gently with his fingers. "Three of the cuts are going to require stitches. His right forearm is broken. So is his left wrist. Several of his ribs are broken, as well," he announced, his eyes flashing angrily. "Whoever did this did a real job on him." He reached for his bag and pulled out a needle and suturing thread. "I'm going to start with his cuts. Then I'll set his bones and wrap his chest to support his ribs. It will be easier if I do it while he is unconscious." He looked around the room. "If any of you have sensitive stomachs, you might want to leave the room."

No one moved.

"We're not leaving until Jeremy wakes up," Matthew announced.

"Except you," Abby said quietly, smiling at the look of surprise on his face. "Can I ask you to do one more thing? Jeremy is going to want Marietta here when he wakes up, and I know she'll never forgive me if I don't let her know what has happened. Until you got back with the carriage, I couldn't do anything about that. Do you need directions to her boarding house?"

"I know where she lives," Matthew assured her. "I'll be back as soon as I can."

Matthew had been gone about an hour when Jeremy moaned and moved his head a little. The slight movement made him moan more loudly.

Dr. Wild moved quickly to his side. "Nice to have you back," he said. "Try to not move your head. I'm afraid it's going to hurt badly for a few days."

Jeremy remained still. "What happened?" he whispered.

"We're hoping you can tell us more about that," Thomas said, relieved beyond words that Jeremy was awake and talking.

"My eyes," Jeremy murmured.

"They're swollen shut," Dr. Wild informed him. "We've been putting cold compresses on them, but it will take a while for the swelling to go down. You were beaten badly."

"Where...?"

"You're at home, Jeremy," Abby said tenderly. "Spencer brought you here after you were attacked."

"Spencer?" Jeremy gasped, the movement causing him to groan again. "How...?"

"I be fine," Spencer said roughly, coming to stand beside him.

"They got you, too," Jeremy whispered, confusion rippling across his battered face.

"They didn't get me as bad as they got you," Spencer said. "I'm real sorry, Jeremy," he muttered.

"Not...your...fault," Jeremy managed, pain twisting his face.

Dr. Wild looked at May. "Will you please make me some ginger tea? It will help with his pain. And will you bring me some honey to treat his wounds?"

May looked surprised. "You use the same stuff Miss Carrie use?"

Dr. Wild smiled. "There is a time for drugs, but Carrie taught me that nature has already provided most of what we need. I saw her treat every person who came into the black hospital with herbs and plants. I'd be a fool not to use what I learned."

"Do you know who did this to you?" Thomas asked, desperate for some answers.

Jeremy began to shake his head, but tears seeped through his swollen lids.

"No more talking," Dr. Wild announced. He looked around the room. "I want everyone out of here," he ordered. "Jeremy has suffered a severe concussion. He needs to remain quiet and still. You'll get your answers, but you're not going to get them tonight. May will stay with him through the night to monitor him for any additional signs of shock, but I don't want him to say one word," he commanded. "Is that clear?"

Thomas nodded. "Of course." He reached down and placed his hand on Jeremy's leg gently. "We're all going to be here for you, Jeremy. All you have to worry about is getting well." He understood the look that flitted across his brother's face. "The factory will be fine," he said. "And I will make sure both Abby and I have an armed guard with us at all times." He was relieved when the anxiety melted from Jeremy's features.

Dr. Wild nodded solemnly and smiled. "He's asleep again," he murmured. "It's what he needs more than anything. Even if he wakes up during the night, I don't want anyone talking to him."

"A young woman named Marietta is coming over," Abby whispered. "He is quite in love with her. Will it be all right if she sits with him?"

Dr. Wild considered the question. "Only if she is very clear that he is to not talk about *anything*. Any additional strain could do more damage, and it will certainly slow his healing."

May appeared in the door, her hands full of supplies. "Won't nobody be talking to him while I'm in this room," she said staunchly, her eyes flashing. "If I could keep that Moses quiet, it ain't going to be nothing to take care of Jeremy. He ain't near as stubborn!"

Dr. Wild chuckled. "I'm confident he will be in good hands." He turned to Thomas. "I'm going to stay here with him a little longer before I leave."

"Matthew will drive you home as soon as you're ready to leave. He should be back any minute."

It was almost twenty-four hours before Jeremy woke again. It took him a minute to remember where he was, but then the memories came roaring back. He was relieved when he could force his eyes open into a slit. He moved his head slowly, reassured when the pain wasn't quite as intense as it had been the night before. It still hurt, but it didn't feel quite so much like a train wreck in his head. He tried to take a deep breath, gasping as pain knifed through his chest.

"Jeremy?"

"Marietta?" Jeremy whispered. He wanted to reach out to her, but any movement sent waves of pain rolling through him.

"Yes, I'm here," Marietta said tenderly. "Matthew came for me last night." She interpreted the look on his face. "It's Tuesday night. You've been sleeping for the last twenty-four hours. May and I have taken turns putting cold compresses on your face to bring the swelling down."

"Thank you," Jeremy whispered. In spite of the unrelenting pain, he felt a surge of joy that Marietta had cared enough to stay with him. The last months had drawn them closer together, but he'd said nothing else about his love for her since that cold winter night. She had asked for time. He was willing to give it to her. His love had done nothing but grow stronger and more certain.

"I wouldn't have been anywhere else." When she spoke next, he knew she was crying. "I'm so sorry this happened to you."

Jeremy lay quietly, knowing any movement might render him unconscious again. "It was so dark," he whispered. "I didn't see...anyone."

"I know," Marietta assured him. "You don't have to talk about it."

"I want to," Jeremy gasped. His dreams had been full of the attack. Now that he was awake, he was anxious to tell Marietta what he remembered. It was only fair that she know the truth. He tried to look around the room to see if they were alone, but he couldn't move his head. "Is anyone else here?"

"We're alone," she said quietly as she took one of his hands.

He was suddenly aware of a pain radiating up from his arms when she touched him. "What...?"

"Both your arms are broken," she answered, anger flaring in her voice. "And several ribs. Breathing is going to be difficult for some time."

Jeremy lay still, trying to absorb what she was telling him. He wanted to scream and rage, but he knew any movement was more than he could handle. He was appalled when sudden hot tears scalded his eyes, but he couldn't stop them. If was as if his body belonged to another person.

Marietta stroked his hair softly, giving him time to regain control. "I'm so sorry," she whispered again. "So very sorry."

"You have to leave me," Jeremy managed to say.

"What?" Marietta sounded shocked. "Why?"

Jeremy wished he could see her clearly, but between his swollen eyes and the waves of pain still rolling in his head, it was impossible to focus. "They came after me because of what I've been doing," he said weakly, vivid memories raging through his mind as he forced the words out.

You think you can fire a white man?

You think we're going to let a nigger lover live in our city?

Their taunts had been followed with vicious kicks and bat blows to his head and body. He could vaguely remember the sound of bones cracking when he tried to use his arms to shield his head.

"Shh..." Marietta laid a hand on his lips. "It's too soon to talk about it."

Jeremy tried to shake his head, but the only result was another loud groan escaping his lips. He was desperate for her to understand. "You're not safe," he murmured. "Not safe..." More memories swallowed him.

You think we don't know, Mr. Anthony?

You think we don't know you're a nigger, too?

You think we don't know you're helping the niggers because you're one, too?

Jeremy closed his eyes to try to block out the vicious beating that accompanied the mocking voices, fear swelling in his chest until he could hardly breathe. Trying to breathe only intensified the pain roaring through his body.

You think we don't know about that white school teacher who is a nigger lover? We'll get her, too, Jeremy Anthony!

Frantic now, he forced his eyes open and tried to rise to a sitting position. He had to warn her! He had to make her leave.

Instead, he sank back into the blackness.

When Jeremy woke again, he was able to open his eyes more. He moved his head gingerly, glad when the movement caused only a dull throb to erupt.

"Better?" Marietta asked.

Jeremy's gaze flew to where she was sitting beside the bed. Her bright blue eyes were red with exhaustion, but she was still the most beautiful thing he had ever seen. The knowledge only intensified his pain. "You shouldn't be here," he said, glad to discover his voice sounded more normal.

"Where else would I be?" Marietta asked, amusement lacing her voice.

"I told you," Jeremy replied. "You're not safe." Desperation once more gripped his body. The nightmares as he slept had been terrible, but they were somehow easier to bear than the stark reality of facing the truth in broad daylight. "You must leave me."

"You don't love me anymore?" Marietta asked.

Jeremy searched for words. He fell back on the simple truth. "Yes, but..."

"I love you, too," Marietta said softly.

Jeremy stared at her, trying to make sense out of what she had said. "What?"

"I said, I love you, too," Marietta repeated. "As long as you haven't changed your mind, you should probably be glad about that." Warm humor sparkled in her eyes.

Jeremy wanted to shake his head vehemently, but he knew it would only make him pass out again. "You don't understand," he murmured, determined to remain conscious until she fully comprehended the danger she was in. "You can't be with me. I'm a mulatto. I'm going to mean nothing but trouble to you."

Marietta put a hand across his mouth. "Hush," she said. "I'm a lot of things, but I've never been a coward. I knew the risk I was taking when I came down to teach black students in the South. Every time I walk out of my boarding house, I am putting myself into danger."

"But..."

"I said to hush," Marietta repeated. "I have not fallen in love with either a white man or a mulatto. I have fallen in love with *you*. I am ashamed to admit it took me some time to figure out how I would feel about the possibility of raising a black child in this world, but the simple truth is that it doesn't matter. When Matthew arrived to tell me about the attack, I realized that nothing was more important than being with you. I understood how ridiculous it was to give up what we have simply because of what *might* happen. I also know that if we do have a black child, we will love that child and do whatever we have to in order to give it a good life." She fell silent for a moment and then leaned over to kiss him very lightly. "I love you, Jeremy Anthony."

Jeremy stared at her, joy obliterating the pain in his body as he heard the passion in her voice. He longed to reach up and pull her close, but he had to content himself with devouring her with his eyes. "I love you, too, Marietta Anderson. I will love you forever."

"That sounds about right," Marietta whispered. "All you have to do now is focus on getting well. Dr. Wild says it will take several weeks before you'll be ready to go back to work. Is it terrible of me to be excited we'll have so much time together? I told May I will be here every afternoon as soon as school is finished for the day. I've had someone take my students the last couple days, but it's time for me to go back."

Jeremy gazed at her, hardly able to believe Marietta really loved him. "Will you marry me?" he asked.

"Well, of course! How are you going to love me forever if we're not married, silly?"

Jeremy smiled, wishing he could release the laugh of joy burning in his chest. A flash of memories made him stiffen with fear instead. "You're not safe," he insisted.

Thomas walked in the room just then. "She will be, Jeremy. The purpose of money is to make sure the people you love are safe. The factory is hiring armed guards to accompany all of us for as long as it's necessary. That includes Marietta."

Jeremy gazed at Thomas for a long minute, reassured by the grim determination on his face. "She loves me," he said quietly.

"Well, of course she does," Thomas replied. "I tried to tell her you can be quite stubborn at times, but she promised me she can handle you, so I decided she knows what she is getting into."

When Jeremy fell asleep again, it was a healing sleep, free from terrifying images.

Chapter Twenty-Seven

Moses swung down from his gelding and took deep breaths of the morning air. Tobacco spread out in a green wave as far as the eye could see. Just as he had promised Thomas, every available acre had been planted. The crop was healthy and vibrant.

Summer had grabbed hold of Cromwell Plantation in a tight grip, but the early morning air didn't yet carry the sultry humidity that would hover over the tobacco fields by the afternoon. The men had started working as soon as there was enough light to see what they were doing.

Moses watched as a group of them ran harrows down the rows to turn under weeds and push dirt against the roots of the tobacco plants. He could almost see the towering plants responding by sending their taproots deeper into the soil where moisture was more abundant. They'd had plenty of rain, but deeper taproots made for healthier plants.

Another group of workers were topping and suckering, removing the emerging flowers from the tops of the plants, as well as removing the buds that were pushing out lower on the plants. It was tedious work that allowed all the nutrients to go to the leaves instead of to the flowers, causing the plant to grow longer into the summer and produce a greater harvest.

The worming was being done by the children, but Moses had set very strict guidelines for them. He only allowed them to work in the early mornings, and then they would go to school when it was too hot for them in the fields. He had also mandated that every child would receive payment for their labor. He would do nothing to make anyone feel they were still living in the days of slavery. If someone worked, they should be paid. He knew how disgusting it was to walk through the rows of the tobacco plants and pull off the horned, green worms, but it had to be done. The children were stuffing them into a large bag hanging from their shoulders. They would be tossed into a barrel later that day where they would be killed.

"Hello, Mr. Moses!" one of the children called.

Moses smiled at the gangly eleven year old with caramel-colored skin. "Hello, Stan. How are you doing?"

"Oh, I be doing real good," Stan said cheerfully. "I can hardly wait for the picnic later. My mama was up real late cookin'. Our new house sure did smell good when I got up this morning." The little boy beamed up at him. "We just got our new house finished two days ago. I heard my daddy tell mama that he didn't ever think we would ever have us our own house. He sure does like it."

"And you, Stan? Do you like it, too?"

"Why, sure I do. I ain't never slept on nothing but a blanket on the floor before this. When my daddy was off fighting, me and mama were in one of them camps. It weren't too bad, but now I got me a bed to sleep in." His eyes widened. "Can you imagine that? I got me my very own bed!"

Moses smiled. "I'm happy for you." A call lifted up across the tobacco plants and caught Moses' attention. "Keep working, Stan. I'll see you at the party later."

"Yessir, Mr. Moses," Stan quipped, but he didn't move. "Can I ask you just one more thing, Mr. Moses?" He ducked his head and then looked back up earnestly. "Is Felicia coming to the party?"

Moses smiled. "Of course she is. She wouldn't miss it. Now you get back to work."

A chorus of goodbyes from the other children followed Moses as he worked his way down through the tobacco plants toward Simon, chuckling over the look in Stan's eyes. He wasn't the only boy on the plantation who had his eye on Felicia. "The tobacco is looking great," he said as soon as he reached him.

"You say that every day," Simon observed.

"That's because it's true every day," Moses responded good-naturedly. "Everyone made good money last year in spite of how late we got the crop in. Now, with every acre planted, they should be excited about how well it is doing." Thomas' decision to pay everyone a portion of the profits had been brilliant. He had never seen men work so hard, or so cheerfully.

Simon grinned. "We're all excited," he agreed. "But right now everyone is thinking about tonight. None of us have ever celebrated the Fourth of July before."

"What was there to celebrate?" Moses asked. "The country may have been free from England but most of the blacks were slaves. I remember watching celebrations on the plantation where I grew up. I always wondered how they could celebrate freedom when they didn't care about mine."

"Well, now we're free," Simon said firmly. "And now that all the houses have been finished, this is the perfect time for a party."

Moses nodded, filled with deep satisfaction. The men had all worked together, finishing one home before they moved on to the next. They had decided the order by the undeniably fair method of drawing straws. After long days in the fields, they would go back to their land to build their homes. Robert, Moses, Gabe, and Clint joined them most nights. No one complained. They were creating something for *themselves*.

The last of the ten families had left their cabin in the old slave quarters for their own home on their own forty-acre parcel of land the week before. None of the homes were large, but Moses knew they would be added onto in the years ahead, and they were far bigger than anything any of them had lived in before. Most importantly, they were *theirs*.

While the men had been building, the wives and children had been putting in gardens and fencing off areas for their chickens and pigs. Everyone was eager for a party. It had been decided it would take place at Simon and June's new homestead instead of the plantation because everyone wanted to celebrate the first step in building their own community. Invitations had gone out to neighbors and friends.

Rose had called off school for the day in celebration of America's birthday. She, Annie, June, and Polly were cooking up a storm, as were all the men's wives. His mama had threatened him with her rolling pin when he had tried to snatch some of the sugar cookies off the table earlier, so he had retreated with empty hands, the women's laughter following him from the house. His stomach growled as he thought about it.

"I had to turn away four more workers yesterday," Simon announced.

Moses frowned. "That's twenty just this week."

"The news is spreading about how Cromwell Plantation treats its workers. Anybody with a lick of sense would rather work here."

Moses knew he was right, and he was proud of that fact, but his thoughts were troubled as he stared out over the tobacco.

"You're worried about the other plantation owners and their foremen. You have a right to be," Simon admitted. "They don't take kindly to anyone tempting their workers away from their contracts."

"Do you know where the men came from?"

"Two of them said they were working at Sowell's place. The other two told me they had been contracted to work for Cannon."

Moses sucked in his breath, his mind spiraling back. "You know who they are, don't you?" he asked.

Simon started to shake his head and then stopped, his eyes growing wide. "Two of the men who came to threaten Thomas on New Year's Day?"

"The same," Moses said. "How did the men take it when you told them we couldn't hire anyone right now?"

Simon shrugged. "They were disappointed. They said they would be back to try again because they hated working and hardly getting paid."

Moses sighed. He knew how most of the freedmen were being treated on the plantations. Even though the Civil Rights Act had passed, and even though the Fourteenth Amendment had been sent out to the states for ratification, it had done little to change the attitudes of Southerners. Even though the workers were free, they were still being treated like slaves. He knew many families were close to starvation because they were not being paid.

"You can't help everyone," Simon said with quiet understanding.

Moses clenched his fists as frustration surged through him. He knew Simone was right. He also knew Rose was right that they needed to stay on the plantation for at least another year, but he hated feeling helpless to make a difference. He knew life was better for the ten families who had received land from Thomas, and he knew the twenty extra workers he had hired for the summer were receiving fair pay, but he also knew they didn't even count as a drop in the bucket.

"There hasn't been any trouble since the schoolhouse burned," Simon reminded him.

That was true, but Moses could feel trouble brewing in the air, pressing down on him as heavily as the humidity that would hang over the fields soon. He had felt it in Memphis before the riot. After talking to Simon, he could feel the weight of it again. "Are the women and children alone on the homesteads?"

"Most of them. June and my boy are on the plantation today, but I think everyone else is getting ready for the party this afternoon."

Moses scowled. He didn't want to overreact, but he also wanted to be careful. He knew it was impossible for the men to work the fields and also watch over their homesteads, but he couldn't ignore the feeling that trouble was coming. Lives were more important than tobacco worms and profits. He listened to the cheerful calls of the men as they worked. He felt a deep responsibility to do all he could to keep everyone safe. Most of the men working the fields had also served with him during the war. When his eyes fell on the children intently plucking tobacco worms from the plants, he made his decision.

"Tell the men we are taking the rest of the day off," he announced.

Simon stared at him. "They have only been working for an hour."

"The tobacco plants aren't going anywhere," Moses responded evenly. "Today is a special day. Let's go ahead and make it one."

Simon continued to look at him. "You're that worried?"

Moses met his eyes. "I felt this same feeling in Memphis. There are a lot of dead people that would still be alive if someone had been willing to step up as a leader and take action to protect them. No one did." He took a deep breath, thinking about Felicia's parents. If they had taken heed of the warnings and come to Fort Pickering for refuge, they would still be alive. He doubted anyone had told them how dangerous things were. "I don't know if anything is going to happen today, but I couldn't live with myself if it did and I had done nothing to take care of everyone."

Simon looked out over the fields for a long moment. "I'll tell everyone we're starting the party early. They should go home, get their wives and kids, and come back to my place."

Moses managed a brief smile. "Tell the men to be on the lookout, but I don't want the wives and children to be worried."

Simon snorted. "You know Rose and June are going to see right through this, don't you?"

Moses' lips twitched. "Probably *all* the women will see right through it, but they will also let us think we are the big, strong protectors. I mostly don't want the children to be scared."

Simon hesitated. "You really think something is going to happen?"

Moses shrugged. "If it does, we'll be ready. Make sure all the men bring their pistols and rifles. We don't have to be afraid. We just need to be prepared."

Carrie pushed the errant tendrils of hair away from her face impatiently, determined to do more studying before the festivities began for the day. The cacophony of traffic noise flowing in the window, combined with the stifling heat, was making it difficult to concentrate. She glanced at the clock in her room, relieved to see there was still an hour before Matthew was due to arrive.

The door to her room slammed open. All four of her housemates poured into her room, dressed vibrantly in red, white, and blue.

"You are not going to study anymore today," Florence announced as she walked over and pulled Carrie's book from her hands.

"That's right," Alice said, as she removed Carrie's writing pad from her desk and held it aloft over her head. "You're done."

Carrie laughed, but she tried to reach for her book. "I just need to—"

"You just need to *what*?" Elizabeth demanded. "Prove you can be better than number one in the entire school in your studies. I hate to be the one to have to tell you this, but it's not possible to be better than number one."

Carrie flushed. "I'm not..."

Janie swooped in and placed a glass of cold lemonade in front of her. "Relax. We know you're not trying to make us look as bad as you do—it happens naturally," she teased, her eyes dancing with fun. "But you're done for today, Carrie. It's the Fourth of July! Philadelphia is about to host the largest parade in the history of this nation."

"I know," Carrie agreed, "but it's not starting for a couple more hours, and Matthew won't be here until noon. I still have time to get some work done."

The amusement died from Janie's eyes as she stamped her foot. "*When* did you get like this?" she demanded.

Carrie gaped at her, searching for words, but she couldn't come up with any.

"Even during the war you found ways to have fun," Janie scolded.

"Really?" Florence muttered, her voice making it clear she didn't believe her.

"Suddenly," Janie continued, "you seem to have forgotten the word *fun* even exists. All you do is study and go to school."

"That's not entirely true," Alice protested. "She eats sometimes, and she even sleeps a little."

"And then she goes back to studying," Janie insisted.

"That's true," Elizabeth agreed.

"It stops today," Janie announced. "I know you want to be the best doctor on the planet, and I understand you feel a responsibility to be a leader for all women, but you also have to live your life."

Carrie stared at her, wondering if what she was saying was true. Had she really changed so much?

Alice settled down on the bench and wrapped her arm around her. "We all admire your dedication, Carrie," she said gently, "but we're also worried about you."

"Worried about me?"

"Yes. When you first got here, you used to laugh and talk with us. Now all you do is come in from school and retreat to your room to study. The few minutes you're not studying, you only want to talk about medicine or women's rights. Obviously we agree with you on all those things, but there is more to life than that. Right now there are thousands of veterans beginning to line up for a parade. Our city is swarming with people eager to celebrate the rebuilding of a reunified country. They want to laugh and celebrate." Alice took a deep breath. "*We* want to laugh and celebrate. And we want you to do it with us."

"But only if you want to," Elizabeth added, ignoring Janie's snort. "We know it has to be your choice."

Carrie closed her eyes, realizing they were all speaking the truth. After fighting for years to come to medical school, she had been eager to ignore anything that kept her from her studies. But she knew it was more than that. The belief held by male doctors in the city that she was incapable of being a doctor had fueled a determination to prove them wrong. The battle to make her feel less than equal had ignited a fire that threatened to consume her.

Janie read the look on her face. She nudged Alice aside, sat down next to Carrie, and took one of her hands. "Carrie, there is nothing wrong with single-minded determination, but I've watched the joy disappear from your eyes in the last month. We really *are* worried about you."

Carrie opened her eyes and gazed into Janie's face. "You're right," she admitted slowly. Just saying the words made her feel better. She knew she would never lose her unwavering commitment to medicine and equal rights, but she had indeed lost the balance that gave her joy in living.

"It's one day," Janie said quietly.

Carrie grinned and jumped up from the bench. "Then I suggest we get on with it!" She turned to her closet and pulled out a bright red dress lined with white piping. Abby had mailed it to her a few weeks earlier. "I wasn't sure I would ever find an occasion to wear this, but today seems to be perfect."

"I have a hat for you!" Florence announced, pulling a straw hat from behind her back that was festooned with red, white, and blue streamers.

Carrie laughed and placed it in a cocky position on her head. She felt lighter than she had in weeks. Her expression sobered as she gazed around at her housemates. "Thank you."

Janie grinned and slipped her arm through Carrie's. "We have a little while before Matthew arrives. Let's go see what is happening in our city!"

The five of them threaded their way through the hordes of people lining Arch Street in preparation for the parade. In spite of the intense heat, everyone was in a marvelous mood. Laughter and conversation, peppered with the giggles of playing children, rose up like a cloud around them.

A sudden boom startled Carrie. "What was that?"

Janie looked at her. "That can't seriously be the first one you have heard today. They have been firing gun salutes from Penn Square all morning."

Carrie looked at her blankly. "I guess I was a little absorbed," she admitted. "No more," she said. "Tell me what is going on."

"Did you even know when I came in this morning to raise your window higher?" Florence asked.

Carrie shrugged. "I saw you do it. I figured you were letting more air in because it is so hot." She had been absorbed in reading the latest information on the cholera outbreak in Europe that was taking so many lives.

"That would have been reason enough," Florence agreed, "but the real reason is because we were told to raise every window in the house at least a foot so that the explosions from the cannons wouldn't break the glass."

"They have prepared the largest parade America has ever seen," Elizabeth said enthusiastically. "Last year the nation was still in mourning over President Lincoln. They have promised this year's celebration is going to be a climactic celebration of the ending of the war. They put out the call for everyone to decorate their homes and businesses."

"I'd say everyone responded." She laughed. "I've never seen so much red, white, and blue in my life."

Flags hung from every pole. Streamers floated in the breeze from every balcony. The front of every business was festooned with red, white, and blue buntings. It didn't stop there. Every person on the street, children included, wore a hat proudly proclaiming the national colors, and every carriage was decorated to the hilt.

"I'm surprised they haven't painted the bricks on the road," Carrie joked. "How many veterans will be here?"

"They are projecting at least ten thousand," Alice said proudly. "General Hancock is going to lead the parade, and then General Meade is going to present the Pennsylvania colors to Governor Curtin to officially signify the ending of the war."

Carrie felt a surge of energy as the laughter and confidence swirled around her. "This is wonderful!" she cried.

Janie nodded but took hold of her arm. "We have to get back to the house. Matthew should be here any minute. He came in on the train last night, but had meetings this morning. I don't want the house to be empty when he arrives."

"One very eligible man and five women," Alice said teasingly. "I don't like my odds."

"*Four* women," Carrie corrected with a laugh. "This one is very happily married. But if one of you gets Matthew, you'll be very lucky indeed."

Moses exchanged a long look with Simon when he rode into the clearing beside his house, relaxing a little when Simon shook his head to indicate he had seen no evidence of trouble. Rose had not pressed him for information when he went into the kitchen to tell everyone they were starting the party early, but he had known by the look in her eyes that she knew he was hiding something.

It had been his mama that set him straight before he could escape the inquisition. "You think there be stupid women in this kitchen?"

"Of course not," Moses said quickly.

His mama waved her infamous rolling pin under his nose, her eyes flashing. She had used it to make a point with him ever since he was young. "Ain't one woman in here don't recognize trouble when we see it. We been living it long enough to know when it be lurking around the corner. Now you tell us what is going on, son, or this rolling pin is gonna find a place on your backside."

"And we might just hold you down so she can get you good," June said mildly, her eyes flashing dangerously. "We don't need to be protected, big brother. We need to be prepared in case there is trouble."

How could Moses argue with that when he had said the same thing to Simon? He told them his suspicions, stressing that he had no evidence something was going to happen. That had seemed to satisfy them enough for them to put their focus on loading the wagon with all the food they had prepared, but he suspected they only quit pestering him because they wanted to make sure everyone was together as quickly as possible.

Rose eased up to him now and confirmed his suspicions. "We're all here," she said. "I want the whole story."

Moses met her eyes squarely. "There really isn't a *whole story*. It's just a feeling I have." He knew how inadequate of an answer that was, but it was the best he could do.

Rose gazed at him for a long moment. "When was the last time you had this *feeling*?"

Moses hesitated, realizing honesty was the only thing that would satisfy his wife. She would see through anything else. "Memphis," he admitted, trying to push back the memory of corpses and battered bodies.

Rose stiffened and looked around at the field full of laughing, talking people. Simon's forty acres had included a large field nestled into the woods. They built their home to one side of it. Since the field had not been fenced for animals yet, it was a perfect place for their Fourth of July party. Big tables had been hastily built to hold the mountains of food. Brightly colored blankets were spread everywhere in the shade of the trees bordering the field. Close to one hundred people were already there. The adults were clustered on the blankets, laughing and exchanging gossip, while the children ran wildly through the grasses, their giggles and shouts pealing through the late morning air. "What have you done to prepare?" she asked.

"All the men know my suspicions," Moses told her. "Everyone is carrying a pistol. There are rifles in the wagons."

Rose shuddered, horrified by what could happen if there was actually a gunfight. "This is not a battlefield, Moses. These are women and children."

"I know," Moses replied heavily, "but I've heard stories about vigilantes sweeping into communities shooting everything they see." His eyes flashed dangerously. "They won't get away with that here."

Rose was frightened by the picture he was painting. First, there had been the fire at the school. Then, Jeremy had been attacked. Thomas had sent recent news saying her twin was recovering well, but nightmares had haunted her. "Should we cancel the party?"

"I thought about it," Moses admitted, "but I have nothing except a feeling. I don't want to spoil everyone's fun after they have worked so hard. I've stationed two men at the intersections about a half mile from here. They know the trail to get through the woods, so they can beat anyone on the roads here if they suspect trouble. If we get advance warning, we can get the children and women into the woods where they will be safer."

Rose took a deep breath. She knew he had done everything possible. Now her husband needed to know she believed in him. "Then I suggest we join the party."

"Moses! Moses!"

Moses turned in time to catch Felicia as she hurled herself into his arms. He could hardly believe this was the same terrified child he had brought home from Memphis. Her cheeks had filled out and her eyes shone with vibrant life. She had bloomed on the plantation, just as Rose had predicted she would. He laughed as he swung her high in the air. "Hello, Felicia. Are you having fun?"

"I sure am!" she cried, her eyes glistening with joy. "Did you know the very last foal was born this morning?"

"I didn't," Moses replied. He enjoyed watching them every morning when he sat on the porch to drink his coffee. "Are you sure it's the last one?"

"Yes. Robert told me."

Moses hid his grin. "Well, if Robert says it, I believe it." Robert had become like a god to Felicia. She had fallen in love with all the horses, but the foals held a special place in her heart. She would sit for hours and watch them in the pasture. He had found her many times curled up in the straw with the foals in their stalls, sound asleep. Robert had already taught her how to ride. Her confidence was growing every day.

"I have a best friend," Felicia announced solemnly.

"Is that right?"

"Yes. Amber be by best friend."

"Amber *is* my best friend," Rose corrected gently.

"Amber *is* my best friend," Felicia repeated, smiling at Rose.

Moses nodded, holding her away so he could gaze in her eyes. "Amber is a good best friend to have," he responded. "Did y'all go riding this morning?"

Felicia's smile exploded on her face. "We sure did! Robert let us go all by ourselves this morning. We had to stay within sight of the barn, but I bet he'll let us go further soon."

"What makes you so sure of that?" Rose asked, not sure how she felt about Felicia and Amber roaming the plantation on their own.

"Because Amber told me about Robert's wife, Miss Carrie. She said Miss Carrie used to ride all over this plantation when she was hardly any older than we are. Surely Robert wouldn't keep us from doing something his own wife did," she answered with a cocky grin.

Moses choked back his laughter.

Rose sent him a scolding look and took one of Felicia's hands. "Miss Carrie lived here all her life, sweetie. She knew the plantation like the back of her hand. You have to promise me you won't go anywhere by yourself until you have been there first with one of us or Robert."

Felicia nodded quickly. "I promise," she said. "Will you let me down now? Amber is waiting in the woods for me. We're building a secret fort," she said importantly.

Moses smiled and lowered her to the ground, chuckling when she ran off. "Carrie's independence is legendary."

Rose rolled her eyes. "And her mother worried about her every minute. I'm beginning to understand how she felt." She laughed. "This is a beautiful day, and we are surrounded by wonderful people. I suggest we focus on having a good time. If trouble comes, we'll deal with it."

Moses nodded easily. "Let's go get some of my mama's potato salad before the buzzards eat it all." He had every intention of enjoying the party. He had done all he could to prepare for whatever was coming. He had said it was just a feeling, but it was more than that. Trouble was coming before the day ended. He knew it.

Matthew leaned against the lamppost, enjoying the music, the laughter, and the steady tromp of feet as thousands of veterans filed by. He was also quite sure he was escorting the loveliest women in Philadelphia. He had seen the many envious looks from men as he took his parade position with Carrie, Janie, Alice, Elizabeth, and Florence.

Janie edged up to him, her eyes sparkling with fun. "I'm glad you're here," she shouted. "After spending four years telling these men's stories in the newspaper, you should be here to watch the parade."

Matthew grinned. "This will be a fun story to write." He pushed away horrific memories of the battles he had covered. He was certain he would never entirely lose the images he carried in his mind, but their impact was lessening. Instead of paralyzing him, they inspired a jolt of gratitude that he had survived, as well as a determination to ensure the sacrifices had not been made in vain. As he watched the parade stream by, he was glad to see what seemed like an endless wave of men who had survived with him.

The majority of the parade-watchers were women, children and old men. Almost every other male of fighting age, which meant anyone from fifteen to fifty, was now marching. He felt curious eyes on him, but he was secure in his years as a war correspondent. He had served.

He forced himself to focus on the steady stream of soldiers moving past him. Many were minus a leg, hobbling with the aid of crutches and canes. Black patches covered blind eyes, while empty sleeves announced a missing arm. The thing every man had in common was the fierce pride on their faces as the crowd hollered and cheered until their voices grew hoarse. It took hours for the ten thousand men, accompanied by bands and colorful floats, to parade through the streets, but not one person moved until the last soldier had passed by.

Only then did the crowd begin to break up.

Matthew was aware of how loudly his stomach was growling. "I understand there is food at the house?" he asked hopefully.

Janie laughed. "Lots of it," she promised, laughing harder when Matthew rubbed his hands together and licked his lips.

Matthew reached into his pocket when they finally got back to the house. He had arrived with barely enough time to see the beginning of the parade. The envelope he carried had been burning a hole in his pocket ever since. He handed it to Carrie as they stepped into the foyer. "It's from Abby," he said in response to the question in her eyes. He smiled when she stiffened. "It's good news," he assured her.

Carrie relaxed and reached for the envelope. She opened it, read it quickly, and then smiled with delight. "Listen!"

> *Dearest Carrie,*
>
> *I know how much all of you have been thinking about Jeremy and praying for him. It will still be a few weeks before Dr. Wild removes the casts on his arms, but the last stitches have been removed from his head and the swelling has all disappeared. He is as handsome as ever. The deepest cuts were on his head, so the hair is growing back to cover them. Marietta has teased him about being as vain as a woman, but he merely retorts that he wants his beautiful fiancée not to have to start life with a scarred husband. I can assure you it wouldn't matter to Marietta. She absolutely adores Jeremy!*
>
> *Dr. Wild is confident the concussion has completely healed. He has cleared Jeremy to return to work on Monday but made him promise he would only work half days for the first two weeks. To my surprise, Jeremy agreed easily. I suspect he is enjoying his time with Marietta and is not eager to go back to work.*

Spencer is completely back to normal...at least physically. I've noticed he is much more nervous when he is driving, but he doesn't let it stop him. Of course, it could have something to do with the armed guards that ride with us everywhere. They are really quite impressive. I'm almost ashamed to admit how much of a relief it is to have a man with a rifle accompanying me everywhere I go, but I also realize what a dangerous time we are living in.

I'm sure we'll never know who attacked them, but, as odd as it sounds, it seems to have helped with tensions at the factory. Whites and blacks were equally enraged by what happened. We've had a steady stream of food coming into the house. May might never have to cook again. And Jeremy has been receiving so many letters. Even the employees who can't write have had someone transcribe a letter for them. They all want him to know how badly they feel. It's really quite remarkable. I guess it's more evidence that adversity can bring people together.

Please give everyone there my love. I have to close now so that Matthew can take this letter with him.

I love you dearest daughter,
Abby

All the women clapped enthusiastically. "That's wonderful news!" Elizabeth cried.

"Something else to celebrate!" Alice agreed. She waved everyone toward the kitchen. "Let's carry the food out onto the porch. I don't want to miss a minute of the fun."

Matthew gasped when he walked into the kitchen. "Where in the world did all this food come from?" He could hardly believe the piles of fried chicken stacked on platters surrounded by bowls of potato salad, fruit salad, and biscuits. Two apple pies completed the spread. He stared at the women. "You're all medical students. How did you have time to make all this?"

Florence laughed. "Ask Janie."

Matthew turned wondering eyes on Janie. He became acutely aware of how pretty she was. The realization took his breath away as he gazed at her blue eyes dancing in her animated face. He could barely conjure up the image of the frightened, battered woman he had last seen on the plantation the summer before. "Janie?" He fought to keep his voice even.

Janie shrugged. "We didn't make a thing," she admitted. "One of Opal's old customers opened a new restaurant when the old one burned down. Opal gave her permission to use her recipes. She feeds these hungry medical students quite often, and I've sent a lot of business her way. If it was up to us, we would probably survive off soup and sandwiches."

"It looks wonderful," he said warmly. He kept his eyes on Janie. "Can I fill a plate for you?" He was pleased when she nodded.

He chatted easily with the other women while they filled their plates, but his thoughts were on Janie. He had always liked her, but his mind had been too full of Carrie to truly pay much attention when they were together. He had celebrated when she married Clifford, and then supported her when she escaped to the plantation, but he'd never really gotten to know her. He watched her now, impressed with the intelligence and warmth radiating from her eyes. This confident woman was quite a change from the one he had known before.

Chapter Twenty-Eight

Moses stepped onto the makeshift platform that had been erected. The long day was winding to an end. Hours of play had tired even the children, and the mountains of food had been devoured. There was not one morsel left on the platters lining the tables. The sun had sunk below the treetops, casting a golden glow on the field. He knew his first Fourth of July party was one he would never forget.

Even with his concern about what might happen, he had still been able to have fun. It would have been impossible not to enjoy Felicia and John laughing hysterically during the games. He had loved dancing with Rose when several of the men tuned up their fiddles and banjos and launched into foot-tapping music that resonated through the sultry heat. He had sweated profusely, but he had enjoyed every minute.

As he stepped onto the platform, however, he felt a renewed heaviness press down on him. Every muscle stiffened as his gaze swung to the road, only slightly relieved when he saw it was empty. His eyes swept the crowd as he assured himself the men from his old unit were now stationed strategically in a protective semicircle around everyone else. The rifles were still tucked away in the wagons, but he knew every one of them had a pistol in their waistband, and their posture indicated they were ready for anything.

"Give us a speech, Moses!"

Moses smiled as one of the women called out to him. When he and Rose escaped the plantation almost five years earlier, he never would have dreamed he would return. He certainly never dreamed he would step forward as a leader to give a speech. As he looked out over more than one hundred of his people watching him expectantly, he felt a surge of emotion that almost left him breathless. He searched for Rose, saw her face glowing with pride, and then opened his mouth.

"Today is the Fourth of July. It's the day we celebrate the birth of a nation, but until today it meant nothing to me because I was a slave for too long in the land of the free. I despised the Fourth of July because it only seemed to mock the reality that I could never have what this country was based on."

Moses paused as his words rang out into the still air. This was the first speech he had ever set out to deliberately give. He felt both humble and strangely exhilarated as he realized he had something to give to his people. His voice grew stronger.

"Even though we have been declared free, we have only begun the battle that must be fought. The Congress has passed the Civil Rights Act. It has passed the Fourteenth Amendment that secures our equal rights. I know my wife has taught you all that, but I'm here to tell you that passing the laws is just the first step. It's a necessary step, but it's also one that will make life even harder for us for a while."

He watched faces grow grave with concern, but only truth would prepare them for what was coming. He had read everything Matthew had written. He had read the information flowing from Washington. He knew what every black in the nation was up against.

"The South is going to fight this. They are going to fight everything that secures our freedom. They are going to fight everything that secures our civil rights. They are going to fight everything that forces them to act as if we are equals. Let there be no mistake. We *are* equals," he called. "We *are* equals." His words hung in the air for a long moment. "But not just the men," he added sternly. "Every woman and man here today is *equal*. We all have a part to play in the future of our people.

"It is going to take great courage to press forward through this time. There will be people who come after us. There will be people who try to intimidate us by making us afraid. There will be people who treat us as if we are inferior. We are not inferior! There is not one person here today who is inferior in any way."

He watched as shoulders straightened and heads lifted. His heart soared as eyes brightened with confidence.

"We must fight for our rights. We must fight for the right to vote. We must fight for the right for education at every level."

A man stood up on the edge of the clearing. "And what if we ain't living on a place like Cromwell Plantation?" he called. "I had to sneak over here a little while ago. I ain't allowed to leave the plantation unless I got me a pass. That man, Sowell, he ain't handing out passes," he said angrily. "I done came anyway, but if I get caught, I gonna pay for it. He don't own me no more, but he still acts like he does!"

Moses took a deep breath and nodded. "I know it's tough. It's going to take time to change things for everyone." He knew many of the people watching him were from neighboring plantations. They had begun to arrive late in the afternoon after their day's work had been completed. "This country has only seen us as slaves for a long time. But there are people fighting for things to change."

"There must not be enough of them!"

Moses agreed. He also decided this was a good time to make his announcement. "You're right," he answered. "That's why Rose and I are leaving the plantation next summer. She is going to college to become an educator for all our people, and I am going to college to become an attorney. I figure the best way to make things change for everyone is to fight for the laws put in place to protect you."

He smiled when a shocked silence fell on the clearing. "There are many of you here who may never go to college, but that doesn't mean you can't still make a difference. Every one of you should learn how to read. People can't take advantage of you if you are educated. You have to make sure every one of your children goes to school. You have to refuse to be afraid," he added. "This country has controlled us by fear for too long. We have done things because we were too afraid not to. No more! There are a number of you who are property owners. More of you are earning fair wages for the first time in your life. Far too many of you are still being treated badly. The plantation owners want you to believe they still own you, yet you had the courage to leave your plantations and join us today. Every step you take toward freedom—a true freedom that you feel deep inside your own gut—will make the fear disappear."

Moses felt the approaching danger even before he heard the sound of pounding hooves. "Trouble is coming!" he yelled. "All of the women and children need to go into the woods. And those men who did not work for me need to go, too. Go in as far as you can and hide behind the trees." Surprised faces stared up at him. "Now!" He knew there wasn't much time.

Rose jumped up from the ground. She grabbed John's hand as she clutched Hope to her chest. "Let's go!" she cried. "Everything will be all right." She exchanged a confident look with Moses, and then turned and ran.

With the exception of a few muted cries, the women and children were silent as they fled into the woods. A handful of men—those who had left their plantations without passes—fled with them.

One of the men Moses had stationed at the intersections galloped into the clearing, his eyes wide with fear. "They're coming!" he yelled.

"How many?" Moses barked.

"Ten. And they all got rifles!"

"Did they see you?"

"I don't...think so," he said breathlessly. "I did what you told me. I waited till they got 'round the bend before I lit out through the woods. They mighta heard me, but I'm pretty sure they didn't see me."

"Good," Moses replied, forcing his voice to remain calm. He had planned for something like this. Now it was time to see if his plan would work. A quick glance told him the women and children were all in the woods. He prayed they would go back a long ways before they hid behind trees, but he was confident Rose would make sure of it.

Another look told him his men had claimed their rifles from the wagon. Simon was talking to them quietly as they formed a line in front of his house. The rest of the men he had hired for the summer, all veterans, had the pistols the other men had carried. He had twenty armed men ready to take on ten vigilantes. He didn't want there to be a battle, but if there was one, he liked their odds. He smiled at his men and then walked over to stand in front of the line, his rifle resting across his arms.

Ten horsemen, their faces covered with bandanas, galloped into the clearing with rifles held firmly in one hand.

Moses raised his hand, knowing all the men behind him had raised their weapons at the same time. "You're on private property," he called loudly.

The lead horseman pulled his horse to a stop, muttering a curse as he stared at the line of firepower behind Moses. "What do you think you're doing, *boy*?" he taunted, only his eyes showing his nervousness. He had obviously been counting on the element of surprise.

"I think, *Cannon*, that I am protecting privately owned property," Moses snapped. When he saw Daniel Cannon stiffen, he knew he was dismayed he had been recognized. "I suggest you leave now," he said, pulling his rifle to his shoulder and taking aim at the angry plantation owner. He knew the twenty men behind him had taken aim at the other horsemen, who had remained silent since their arrival, only their eyes betraying their nervous fury.

Cannon held his ground but his finger stayed away from the trigger. "You're the nigger running Cromwell Plantation, aren't you, boy?"

Moses decided he didn't owe the man any information. He stared back silently.

"You know that if we leave now, we're going to come back, don't you?" Cannon growled.

"We could go ahead and kill you now," Moses suggested. "Then we won't have to worry about that."

"You touch one of us and every white man in the county is going to come after you," Cannon warned, his eyes flashing with sudden panic.

"That could be," Moses agreed, "but the satisfaction of killing ten of you would probably make it worthwhile." His voice sharpened as he took a step forward. "You are on private land, Cannon. Get off." Moses' finger moved to the trigger. "I'm not patient enough to tell you again."

"Hey, Cannon!" one of the men yelled. "Look at all them blankets. They must have been having some kind of party, just like you said. I bet all the women and kids are hiding back there in the woods. I bet the niggers who left the plantations earlier are hiding in there, too." He pulled his horse away from the rest of the horsemen. "I bet they aren't armed!"

Moses knew by the sounds behind him that his men had shifted to form a barrier in front of the woods, but it was also obvious to him that he was going to have to do more than threaten. "Don't say I didn't warn you," he said grimly, as he took careful aim and pulled the trigger. The report of his rifle echoed through the clearing.

Cannon yelled. "You shot me, you filthy nigger!" His eyes widened with pained disbelief as his rifle clattered to the ground. He grabbed his arm as his horse skittered beneath him.

"Only in the one arm you have left," Moses said coldly. "And I only nicked you. I might not be so careful next time."

Cannon cursed loudly, his voice filling the late afternoon air as his eyes glittered with hatred. "You made a big mistake, boy!"

"That might be," Moses said. "But I'm feeling the urge to make a bigger one." He took a deep breath. "I've run out of patience, Cannon. I'm giving you ten seconds to go back down the road the way you came. In exactly ten seconds, the twenty men behind me are going to open fire. We don't usually miss what we're shooting at," he added.

"Ten...nine...eight..."

"We're coming back," Cannon yelled.

"Seven... six..."

By the time Moses had reached five, the clearing was empty. He had started to breathe a sigh of relief when he realized there was still one lone horseman hovering at the edge of the woods, almost hidden in the shadows. He stiffened and raised his rifle again, but he was too late to stop the vigilante from raising his weapon and firing several shots into the woods. Moses was thankful he had told everyone to hide behind trees. He prayed they had followed his orders.

"We'll be back," the man shouted, before he turned and galloped away.

Several of his men fired in retaliation, but the vigilante was already gone. The only sound was the drum of horse hooves as the horsemen fled. Moses didn't lower his rifle until the afternoon was once more silent.

"Look at them white men run!" one of his men hollered jubilantly.

"We did it! We scared them off!" another laughed triumphantly.

"Well done, men!" Moses turned and added his congratulations to their celebration, knowing how much it had taken them to overcome their fears and stand up to the vigilantes. Even though all of them were veterans, what they had done was a far cry from going into battle under the American flag. They had started a fight that would probably not end for a very long time. The reality would sink in soon, so he let them celebrate now.

He nodded to one of the men. "Please go into the woods and tell the women and children it is safe to come out." He believed the vigilantes were gone, but he also didn't want to give them an opportunity to find the trail through the woods and attempt to come up behind them.

"You heard them," he said quietly to the others. "They say they're coming back. We scared them off, but men like that operate from fear and pride. We made them look ridiculous. Right now we're all together, but once we go home it's going to be up to us to protect our families."

Simon nodded, his eyes narrow with anger and worry. "What should we do, Moses?"

"Keep your weapons handy," Moses replied. "And teach your wives how to shoot. Two of you are better than one."

"You want us to teach our wives how to shoot a *gun*?" one of his men asked in confusion. "I reckon I can take care of my family myself!"

Moses shook his head. "Don't be a fool. You can't always be around. What happens if you're out in the fields and they come back? You won't be able to protect them. You have to make sure your wife at least has a chance."

"He's right," Simon called. "We taught Rose and June how to shoot. I hope they never have to prove what good shots they are, but they're ready if they have to be. I'm going to set up a target range here on my land. Tomorrow night, I want you all to bring your wives."

"And any kids over fourteen," Moses ordered. "I fought with kids that age in the war. They need to have a chance to help protect their families."

"I thought the government was going to protect us once they let us go free," one of the summer employees complained. "Why ain't they doing nothing?"

Moses knew now was not the time for sympathy. "The government can't be everywhere at one time. I already told you things are going to be real hard for a while. I wasn't kidding. Things are out of control in the South right now. It's not going to change soon. You can wait for the government to show up, or you can make sure you protect your family."

The man stared at him and nodded slowly before he looked at Simon. "I'll have my wife here tomorrow night," he promised.

The women and children began to stream in from the woods. Moses watched as men greeted their families, laughing about their exploits. He was certain Rose would be the last from the woods because she would stay behind to make sure everyone found their way out. Still, he breathed a heavy sigh of relief when she appeared.

Suddenly, he stiffened. He held his breath as his eyes searched the group for Felicia. He couldn't find her. A frantic glance toward Rose told him his wife was looking for her, too.

"Amber! Amber, where are you?"

Moses spun around as Polly began to weave her way through the crowd looking for her daughter. Where were the girls? The last he knew, they were going off into the woods to build a fort.

Gabe was beside him in an instant. "Where's my girl, Moses? I thought she went into the woods with Polly."

Moses was sure there wasn't time for an explanation. "Come with me," he answered. He broke into a run as he headed for the woods. "Felicia! Amber!"

Before he could reach the woods, Felicia came stumbling toward him, tears streaming down her face. "Moses! Moses!" she screamed.

Moses reached her in seconds. He scooped her up into his arms and grabbed her close to him in a fierce grip just as Rose and Polly raced up to join them. "Where is Amber, honey?" He dreaded her answer.

"We were hiding in the fort," Felicia cried as she brushed away her tears. "We saw everyone running into the woods so we decided to stay in our fort."

Moses sucked in his breath. The branches they had surely used to build their fort had probably given them a sense of security, but they would have done nothing to stop a bullet. The look he exchanged with Gabe told him Amber's father was thinking the same thing. "What happened?"

"Amber got shot," Felicia whimpered, her face crumbling as her eyes filled with fresh tears. "We was hiding and then all of a sudden..." She buried her face into his shoulder again.

Moses knew Felicia was horrified for her new best friend, but it was more than that. He knew she was also reliving the moments she had watched her parents die. He rubbed her back gently and tried to speak calmly. "Can you show us where your fort is, Felicia?"

Felicia nodded through her sobs.

Moses caught his breath as he heard the pounding of hoofbeats again. He shoved Felicia into Rose's arms and sprang for his rifle. He could see his men doing the same thing. He groaned, knowing there was no way to get the women and children to safety again if the vigilantes returned with reinforcements. He had been wrong to think they had scared them away. He forced his thoughts away from Amber bleeding in the woods as he turned and raised his rifle.

Moses gasped with relief when Robert galloped into the clearing. He and Clint had stayed at the stables today to make sure his latest foal and the two who were just days old were all right. Moses shook his head to clear the roaring in his ears.

"What happened," Robert yelled as he slid Granite to a stop. "I heard gunfire!"

Moses nodded. "I can't explain it now," he said quickly. "Amber has been shot. We have to find her." He understood when Robert's face went ashen. Robert loved Amber like a daughter.

"Where is she?" Robert managed as he vaulted off Granite, handed his reins to a woman standing close by, and put a hand on Gabe's shoulder.

Felicia lifted her head from Rose's shoulder. "I can show you," she said bravely, as she gulped back her tears. She slid down from Rose's embrace and ran back into the woods. "Follow me!" she cried.

Robert grabbed Moses' arm. "You stay here in case something else happens. We'll find Amber."

Moses ground his teeth but stayed where he was. He knew Robert was right. The vigilantes could return at any moment.

It took less than a minute before all of them were standing in front of a flimsy, makeshift shelter fashioned from fallen limbs. Robert reached the fort first and saw Amber lying on the ground, a pool of blood surrounding her.

"Hey, Robert," she whispered weakly. Then she caught sight of her father. "Daddy!" she gasped. "It hurts, Daddy..."

"Amber!" Polly screamed, dashing forward when she reached the fort and caught sight of her daughter.

Rose held her back. "Let Robert and Gabe carry her out," she said. "They'll take her to the clinic. You and June can take care of her there."

Polly nodded, tears streaming down her face. "They shot my baby," she moaned.

Robert knelt down next to Amber. "Hey, honey," he said quietly. "Can you tell me where you hurt?"

Amber gulped. "My leg hurts real bad," she answered, the tears coming for the first time.

Robert moved her hand gently, wincing when he saw the hole in her thigh, but relieved that there wasn't more blood. The bullet hadn't hit an artery. He unbuttoned his shirt, pulled it off quickly, and tied it around her leg to stop the bleeding. "We're going to get you to the clinic, Amber. Will it be all right if your daddy carries you out of here?"

Amber nodded. "I think I'm ready to be out of my fort now," she agreed. She paused, her eyes grave with worry. "Am I gonna be paralyzed like you were, Robert?"

Robert shook his head. "Absolutely not. Your leg is going to hurt for a while, but you're going to be fine. Do you want to know how I know?"

Amber nodded her head, her eyes fastened on him.

"Your leg is hurting real bad, isn't it?" he asked tenderly. When Amber nodded, he gave her a big smile. "If you were paralyzed, you wouldn't be able to feel it. You wouldn't be hurting at all."

Amber gazed into his eyes and then looked past him to where her mama was peering into the fort. "Is that right, Mama?"

"That's right," Polly said soothingly.

Amber seemed to be satisfied. "I'm ready to go."

Gabe knelt down and pulled his daughter gently into his arms. "This is gonna hurt some, honey, but we have to get you to where Mama and June can make you better."

"Okay, Daddy," Amber said bravely as she blinked back her tears.

Felicia clung to Rose as Gabe carried Amber from the fort. "Are those men coming back to shoot us?" she asked in a terrified whisper.

"No," Rose said, praying she was right. She knelt down and pulled Felicia close. "You did the right thing coming to get us. That took a lot of bravery."

Felicia relaxed a little. "Amber is my best friend," she said, her voice still a whisper.

"She's lucky to have you for a best friend." They wouldn't know the full extent of the little girl's injuries until they got her to the clinic, but Rose's intuition told her it wasn't too serious. "Amber is going to be all right," she said soothingly.

Felicia clung to Rose's hand as they walked through the woods. Her little eyes never quit moving, but Rose couldn't fault her for watching out for trouble, because she was doing the same thing. She had stayed close enough to hear everything that had happened in the clearing. Carrie had told her after New Year's Day that Daniel Cannon could be a dangerous man. Sowell, the plantation owner who had led the men back in January, had been almost ready to listen to reason that day, but Cannon's anger had spurred him on. Rose knew a man with that much anger usually didn't let reason get in the way of impulsive, irrational action. If Cannon could find more men ready to face twenty rifles, he might return.

Rose took a deep breath when they reached the clearing. Gabe and Robert were just laying Amber down in the wagon on the pile of blankets that everyone had contributed. Polly was sitting in the wagon next to her daughter, and June was perched on the seat. As soon as they had her settled, Gabe leapt up to the wagon seat and picked up the reins. His face was tense, but his voice was easy as he slowly urged the horses forward, trying to not jostle his little girl any more than necessary. Robert fell in beside him on Granite. He was going to act as a guard for them, and he wouldn't leave Amber until he was sure the little girl was all right.

"Is the party over now?" Felicia asked in a small voice, her frightened eyes following the wagon as it rolled out of sight around the bend, dust forming a thick cloud behind it.

Clusters of family members were already making their way down the road. The laughter and easy conversation from the day had disappeared. Every face was drawn and frightened.

"Yes, honey," Rose answered. "The party is over. It's time for everyone to go home." She didn't add that no one was willing to be out after dark. Now that the sun had dropped beneath the horizon, she knew people were anxious to get within the security of their houses. She was also quite sure every man would be hunkered beside a window with his rifle tonight.

It was close to midnight when Moses tromped up the steps. Rose was waiting for him. It had taken her a while to sing Felicia to sleep, but the little girl finally drifted off when Rose promised she would wake her up if Moses didn't have good news about Amber. John and Hope, too young to understand what had happened, had fallen asleep even before she carried them to their beds.

"Welcome home," she said with a smile, as she handed him a tall glass of lemonade.

Moses nodded his thanks and sank down into his rocking chair heavily. He took a long drink and then settled his head back, remaining silent as he stared out into the night.

Even this late, the air hung heavy with sultry heat and the sweet aroma of honeysuckle. The steady drum of bullfrogs competed with crickets as fireflies ignited the trees and surrounding brush with hundreds of tiny golden sparks. Rose had almost been able to believe it was a peaceful evening. The reality of a loaded rifle across her lap kept her from relaxing, but it also gave her a sense of security as she watched every shadow for suspicious movement.

"Amber is going to be okay," Moses finally said.

Rose nodded. She had been sure of that. Moses would have said something immediately if there had been any reason to worry. "She's home?"

"Yes. June was able to get the bullet out. She packed it with salve to make sure it doesn't become infected, then wrapped it and sent her home. She's confident she will recover very rapidly." His voice deepened in admiration. "I had no idea my sister could do that. Carrie has taught her well."

"And your sister is very smart," Rose added. "Carrie taught her a lot, but I also see June reading the medical journals Carrie left behind. She is eager to learn everything she can."

"I know," Moses agreed. "My mama raised some mighty smart babies."

Rose chuckled. "That she did." She let the silence stretch on for a while, knowing Moses' thoughts had turned to Sadie, before she interrupted again. "Are you all right?"

Moses considered her question. "I'm honestly not sure what I'm feeling," he said. "I hate what happened, but I have to admit it felt good not to back away in fear."

"You know they're angry," Rose replied carefully.

"Yes, but they were angry before they got there. Do you think I could have done anything other than what I did?"

Rose had been thinking about that all night. "No," she said. "I'm so very grateful you were ready, and that you kept everyone safe."

"Everyone but Amber," Moses muttered as he clenched his fist.

"You couldn't know what would happen," Rose insisted. "The important thing is that, because you were ready for them, only one person in more than a hundred was hurt, and all the men who left their plantations were not discovered." She knew Moses needed reassurance. "Your speech was wonderful. It made every person in that clearing see you as a leader they could count on. When you told them to move, they moved."

Moses sighed. "What if doing what I did was a mistake? What if the vigilantes go to everyone's houses tonight?" His face twisted with fear as he stared out into the darkness.

Rose reached over to take his hand, her heart squeezing with sympathy. "Being a leader does not mean providing protection for everyone," she said. "It means that you prepare them to take responsibility for their own safety and for the safety of their families." She could tell by the look in his eyes that he was reliving what he had experienced in Memphis.

"I told everyone they should come back and live in the old quarters for a while," Moses revealed. "There would be safety in numbers."

"What did they say?" Rose asked, even though she already knew the answer.

"That they weren't going to be scared out of their homes," Moses said heavily. "That they would be ready if anyone comes." He stood and grasped the column at the edge of the porch.

Rose walked up behind him and wrapped her arms around him. "You've given them courage," she murmured.

"But what if that courage is an excuse for stupidity?" Moses groaned.

"Stop it," Rose commanded. She pulled Moses around and stared up into his face. "Being a leader doesn't mean you take responsibility for someone's life. *They* are responsible for their own lives. You are talking about men who served in the army for three years. They fought battles. They faced danger every day. You have given them options. You have warned them what could happen. They saw for themselves what happened today." She stomped her foot, impatient for him to understand. "Being a leader doesn't mean people are going to follow you around blindly like children. Your job is to open their minds and make them think. You are *not* responsible for the conclusions they reach."

Moses gazed down at her. His lips twitched. "I'm not sure you've ever stomped your foot at me before."

Rose stared at him, a slight smile forming. "I don't usually have to," she replied. "Moses, you are a voice that is going to be heard." She had a sudden inspiration. "When you put a tobacco seed into the ground, are you responsible for whether it will grow?"

"No," Moses said thoughtfully. "Not if I've planted it correctly."

"You just have to trust it to grow?" Rose asked.

"Yes," Moses admitted.

"And once it has started to grow, are you responsible for what happens next?"

"I'm responsible for taking care of the plant," Moses responded. "I can't ignore it and expect it to produce healthy tobacco leaves."

"And if it doesn't rain for months on end? If the soil has been depleted of nutrients from mismanagement?"

"I have no control over that," Moses said slowly. He gazed at Rose with warm admiration. "I see where you're going with this. I can plant seeds in people's minds, and I can nurture them, but I never have control of their lives. Things will happen that are out of my control. They might make decisions that are out of my control." He turned and stared out into the night. "It is impossible to carry the weight of every black person."

Rose gazed at him, her heart swelling with love. "Both of us are going to give all we can give," she said. "That is all we can do. We will both have to remind each other that the results are not up to us."

"And you're willing to live with the risks?" Moses demanded as he swung back around to look down at her again. "That could have been Felicia who was shot. Or John. Or Hope." His eyes burned with emotion as he looked at her.

Rose had thought of little else during the long hours she had waited on the porch. "It will break my heart if something happens to one of us, or to our children," she said huskily, "but something could just as easily happen if we do *nothing* to try to make a difference. You were right when you told everyone that the South is out of control. The only thing I know for certain is that nothing will ever truly change until there are people willing to take risks. All I can do is pray I will have the strength to go through whatever the future holds." She reached up and caressed his cheek. "The most important thing is that I will face it with the man I love."

Moses pulled her close and claimed her lips. "I am a lucky man," he murmured.

"You certainly are," Rose agreed as he led her into the house.

Carrie was surprised when her door swung open late that night. The heat was making it difficult to sleep, so she was sitting by the window staring out over the city, hoping for any breeze to cool her body. "Janie?"

Janie moved into her room. "Am I disturbing you?"

"Absolutely not," Carrie replied. She patted the seat next to her.

"I can't sleep," Janie admitted as she settled down, sighing when a soft breeze blew over her.

Carrie was quite sure it wasn't the heat keeping her friend awake. She waited quietly. The silence stretched out as she gave Janie time to decide what she wanted to say.

"I like Matthew," Janie said abruptly.

Carrie blinked in the darkness. "Oh?"

Janie took a deep breath. "I mean I have feelings for him. I've always thought of him as a friend," she hurried on, "but today I felt something else. And I'm pretty sure I saw something else in his eyes, too."

"Did you have a good walk with him tonight?" Carrie asked, a smile playing on her lips. She had been happy when she saw the two of them leave that evening, and she had also seen the envy sketched on the other women's faces.

"Yes," Janie said softly. "We just talked about things, but it was so pleasant. He's a wonderful man."

"I agree completely," Carrie responded, wondering how to continue. "The idea of having feelings for Matthew seems to be bothering you. Why?"

"My marriage to Clifford was a disaster," Janie reminded her ruefully.

"Matthew is nothing like Clifford!"

"I know…"

Carrie wished it was light enough to see Janie's face, but she didn't have to see her to know there was something else in her voice. They had spent many hours on window seats talking about life. "What is it?" she pressed. "You came in here to talk about it, so let's talk about it."

"I'm afraid," Janie said hesitantly.

"That Matthew will be like Clifford?" Carrie was confused.

"No," Janie said slowly. "I'm afraid…he will always love *you*." Her voice was vaguely defiant.

Carrie sat stunned as Janie's words hung in the air between them. "Excuse me?" she finally managed.

"Oh, Carrie," Janie murmured. "Do you honestly have no clue that Matthew has been in love with you for years?"

"That's not true!" Carrie cried. "Why would you say that?"

"It *is* true," Janie insisted. "All of us know it. Matthew has worn his love for you on his face for years."

Carrie shook her head, wanting to continue to vehemently deny it, but her mind carried her back to the first night they had met at the dance right here in Philadelphia. What had he said that night when he asked her to dance? *I would have to approach the only girl who is already spoken for.* Her mind whirled as she thought of all the years of their friendship. "He's never given me any indication," she protested.

"Of course he hasn't," Janie replied. "Robert is his friend. Matthew is a man of honor."

Carrie's thoughts continued to spin. Had Matthew stayed single all these years because of her? The very thought saddened her. "I'm not in love with him," she said.

"He knows that," Janie said quickly. "He knows Robert holds your whole heart."

"You've *talked* about it?" Carrie gasped. The idea horrified her.

"Of course not! I just know."

Carrie absorbed that in silence. "What are you going to do?"

It was Janie's turn to be silent. "I don't know," she admitted. "Even if he is over you and feels something for me, I'm not at all sure I could trust another man enough to marry him. I'm just becoming comfortable with myself."

"Matthew would never demand you bow down to his wishes."

"I'm sure of that," Janie agreed, "but I'm not at all sure..."

Carrie reached out to grasp her hand. "You're not at all sure of what?"

Janie sighed. "I'm not at all sure Matthew will ever be able to love another woman besides you. I want to believe he can, but I can't. Not yet."

Carrie latched on to the last words. "Not yet," she murmured. "Give it time, Janie. I can't think of anything that would give me greater pleasure than to see you two together." Janie remained silent, but Carrie could feel the tension flowing from her hand. "How long will Matthew be here?"

"He's leaving tomorrow. He is going back to Memphis for a week or so, and then he is heading to New Orleans for a constitutional convention." Janie hesitated. "He told me tonight that he has a bad feeling about it."

Chapter Twenty- Nine

Matthew walked slowly through the streets of New Orleans. The oppressive heat, even early in the morning, was almost more than he could bear. He wanted to claw at the humidity until it broke away from him, but it was useless to try to free himself from its cloying hold. He regretted that his trip to the fourth largest city in America had to be in late July.

The heat had demanded he rise early to have breakfast at a chic little restaurant down on the Mississippi. He had watched the busy port as he consumed a bowl of shrimp and grits, followed by a beignet that had almost melted in his mouth. He might abhor the heat, but he had fallen in love with the delicate pastries covered with powdered sugar. The famous beignet had been one of the things leftover from French occupation after the city nearly burned to the ground in 1788. The colorful stucco buildings decorated with elaborate ironwork balconies and galleries that filled what was known as the French Quarter were primarily built by the Spanish during their brief ownership of the city, but the beignet had held on.

While he sauntered down the riverfront, he thought about the fire that had almost destroyed the city on Good Friday. An alter candle in the home of Don Jose Nunez, the colony treasurer, had ignited lace curtains floating nearby. Gale-force winds blowing in through the windows fanned the flames into a blazing inferno that shot sparks onto nearby buildings. The wind spread the ensuing flames quickly.

No one in the city was alerted because tradition demanded that the bells on the Church of Saint Louis, used to rally citizens during an emergency, remain silent on Good Friday. The priests made certain they remained silent, but they also ensured that eighty percent of the city lay in a heap of ashes just five hours later. The 856 buildings that had taken seventy years to build were gone in just a few hours. Just six years later, another fire destroyed 212 more buildings. New Orleans, still under Spanish occupation, had responded by replacing all the wooden buildings with brick that was then covered with stucco.

Matthew, his stomach comfortably full, admired the architecture as he strolled along. He had especially fallen in love with the decorative wrought iron and the large arched doorways that provided the entry for multi-storied buildings centered with inner courtyards. He was determined to come back sometime during the winter so he could spend countless hours exploring the courtyards. The bubbling fountains and the cascades of bougainvillea everywhere could almost make him forget the humidity, but not quite.

"Hey, mister!"

Matthew jerked to attention at the sharp whisper from a shaded courtyard. He searched the shadows until he found the source of the greeting. Frightened dark eyes peered out at him from the face of a black man who almost blended in with the shadows.

"Yes?"

"You that fellow who wrote about the riot in Memphis?"

Matthew nodded. He had met a lot of people in the two weeks he had been in the city. The covert greeting made all thoughts of breakfast and luxurious courtyards flee his mind. The pressure that had been building in him during the days he had been in New Orleans came back in full force, pressing down so hard he suddenly had to fight to breathe the thick air. "What can I do for you?"

"I hear you be tryin' to make things better for black folks," the man said quietly, edging forward enough so that Moses could see his rough spun pants and shirt.

"I am trying," Matthew agreed, pushing down the immediate thought that he was failing dismally.

"So you think we ought to have the vote? You know about the convention tomorrow?"

"I do," Matthew said. He had thought of little else but the upcoming constitutional convention that would try to reverse the 1864 constitution that had withheld voting privileges from every black in New Orleans.

"You gotta warn folks," the man said sharply.

"About?" Matthew had a fairly good idea of what he meant, but his job was to collect information not only for the articles he was writing for the newspaper, but also for the section he was writing for his book about life in New Orleans now that the war was over. That meant he asked a lot of questions.

The man suddenly looked suspicious. "You don't know?"

Matthew gazed at him, recognizing the look of fear imprinted on so many black faces in the city. He knew they had very good reasons to be afraid. "I'm here to tell the story of the people who live in New Orleans," he responded. "I've heard a lot of things, but I also know I can learn more from every person I talk to." He understood when the man's eyes stayed narrow with suspicion. "The convention is coming up. You're afraid there will be violence, and you know there are going to be a lot of your people who will be hurt." His last statement released the man's tongue.

"It's gonna be real bad," the man insisted.

There was something in the man's eyes that made Matthew stiffen. "How do you know this?"

The man looked around furtively, making sure no one was close enough to hear. "I heard some white men talking this morning. They said...they said they were gonna wipe out every nigger in New Orleans."

The combination of raw pain and terror on the man's face made Matthew's stomach clench. "Who were they?" he asked sharply.

"I don't know. I was doin' some work right here in this garden 'bout an hour ago. I heard them talkin'. I was tryin' to be real quiet, but then I had to go and sneeze. They shut up real quick and took off." He continued, his voice dropping down to almost a whisper. "They was policemen." His eyes glittered with panic.

"Did they see you?" Matthew pressed.

"Nope. I made good and sure of that."

Matthew thought about what the man had said. The constitutional convention was taking place the next day. He had spent Friday night at an impromptu rally outside the Mechanics Institute where it was to occur. He had experienced the passion of the blacks who longed for freedom. "What's your name?"

The man hesitated a long moment. "Ralph," he said finally.

"Were you at the rally Friday night, Ralph?"

"Yes," the man hesitantly admitted. He anticipated Matthew's next question. "Most of the men are planning on going back tomorrow for the convention."

Matthew's mind spun as he thought about the speakers he had heard Friday night. He had stayed back on the fringes because he wanted to watch all the black faces, but also because he wanted to watch the reactions of the white people viewing the rally from porches and windows. The fury and hatred their faces had expressed added to the weight he had been carrying ever since he arrived in New Orleans.

"There's gonna be big trouble!" Ralph said more insistently.

Matthew nodded. "I agree."

"Can't you do something to stop it?"

"I'm trying to warn people," he said, "but so far no one is listening." He stared hard at Ralph. "So now I'm warning *you*. You tell me there is trouble coming. Does that mean you are going to stay away from the rally?"

Ralph's gaze wavered, but the determination on his face didn't. "Ain't nothing gonna change for black folks here unless we get the vote," he said. "We's got to stand up for our rights before things get even worse." He took a deep breath. "I reckon I gotta be there."

"You're walking right into trouble!" Matthew said, his insides seething with frustration, even while he understood the resolute expression on Ralph's face.

Ralph's expression was now oddly calm. "That might be, but I ain't had nothin' 'cept trouble since the day I was born." He took another step forward and spoke urgently. "They got to send soldiers to protect us. It ain't just the black folks they gonna go after. They's going after the folks who be trying to help us. There gonna be plenty of white people there tomorrow, too."

Matthew felt the pressure build in his chest even more. He knew Ralph was warning him, as well, but he had already made the decision to be at the convention. "I'll do my best," was all he could promise.

Ralph nodded and disappeared again into the courtyard.

Matthew continued down the street to his hotel, thinking about the conversation. The temperature had risen with the sun. It was only nine o'clock, but he knew it had to be close to ninety degrees already. He felt the hot pavement radiating up through his shoes as it rose to blast his face. He was grateful for the arching spread of the live oak trees draped with moss, but he couldn't always be in their welcome shade.

"You picked a bad time to be in New Orleans!"

Matthew raised his head and stopped dead in his tracks, unable to speak as he stared at the man in front of him.

"I should write this down. There are not many times I have seen you speechless. And you certainly don't look like a red-headed skeleton anymore!"

Matthew grinned suddenly. "Captain Anderson!" He shook his head and rushed forward to lock the man in a fierce hug. "I can't believe you're here!" He hadn't seen the Union captain since he plucked his emaciated body from the frigid waters of the James River after their escape from Libby Prison. Matthew had helped him make it to Fort Monroe and then headed off to a new assignment, while Captain Anderson had been put in a hospital to recover from his ordeal. "You look fabulous, Capt—" His stopped himself and another smile spread across his face. "I mean, *Colonel* Anderson."

Anderson shrugged. "There are less of us to compete for the ranks now," he said modestly. He grabbed Matthew's arm. "What are you doing here?"

"Writing about New Orleans. What else?" Matthew quickly explained about his book project, hardly believing he had run into his old friend. Their months together in the prison had forged a close friendship, but the events of the following years had kept them in different parts of the country. "It's so good to see you!"

"And you," Anderson replied with a brilliant smile. "I saw your articles about the Memphis Riot," he revealed. "What's happening there now?"

Matthew scowled. "I'm happy to tell you...once we get back to my hotel," he added. "You may be used to feeling like a baked pig, but I need some shade."

"You were always soft," Anderson scoffed, falling in beside him. "Where are we headed?"

"I'm staying at the St. Charles," Matthew answered.

"The newspapers must be paying better," Anderson replied with a raised brow.

Matthew grinned. "No, but my publishing editor seemed to think it important that I gain the true flavor of New Orleans while I am here."

The St. Charles was indeed the most luxurious hotel he had ever stayed in. The towering white building with stately columns made him feel he was walking into the Capitol Building every time he entered. He had spent hours lounging in the opulent lobby and bar listening to businessmen and politicians. They would probably be appalled at how much he had learned from eavesdropping on their conversations. He knew the first hotel had caught fire in 1851. The entire building had been destroyed, but miraculously there had been no fatalities among its eight hundred guests. It had been quickly rebuilt so it could continue its influence on the commerce and history of Louisiana.

Matthew turned off Canal Street and walked quickly to the hotel that loomed over St. Charles Avenue. He and Anderson wove their way through the crowded street, both of them breathing a sigh of relief when they entered the cavernous lobby that provided instant relief from the blazing sun. Matthew thought about claiming a table in the restaurant, reconsidered, and headed down the hall toward his room.

He was grateful for the slight breeze blowing in through his screened-in window as he pulled two chairs forward and waved Anderson into one of them.

"This feels rather clandestine," Anderson remarked with amusement.

Matthew was too hot and tense to bother with small talk. "This city is getting ready to explode," he said bluntly.

Anderson grimaced. "Do you think we'll ever have some time together when something dire isn't happening?"

"I hope so," Matthew said sincerely, "but that time is not now."

"No," Anderson sighed, "I'm afraid you're right."

"Is the military going to protect the convention on Monday?"

Anderson answered his question with one of his own. "How much do you know about the convention?"

"Enough. The city of New Orleans has created a chaotic political mess, helped along by Lincoln's desire to use them as an example of reconstructing the nation, even if they did it poorly, and exacerbated by President Johnson's ridiculous policies that have made the South believe they have full rein in how they deal with the freedmen. During the war, the Unionists had political clout because the city was under Union control. They have lost all that now, and the former Rebels have taken back almost complete control of their city." Matthew took a breath, thinking through what he had learned. "The Rebels are determined to keep the freedmen from having any freedoms at all. The Unionists have decided the only way they can hope to regain political control is to ensure the blacks have the right to vote."

"Do you believe the convention is legal?" Anderson asked keenly.

Matthew shrugged. "I'm not sure that *anything* happening here is legal. I know the Democrats believe the convention is illegal, but the Republicans, using the theory that Louisiana ceased to exist as a state because of their choice to secede, believe they can press the results of the convention by appealing to Congress."

"Do you agree with them?"

Matthew couldn't quite read Anderson's expression. "What I believe about the convention is irrelevant," he said impatiently. "What I *know* is that there is going to be violence on Monday. If the convention meets, and if the blacks turn out to support it—which they will—there is going to be a riot."

"Like in Memphis," Anderson observed.

"You don't want that here."

"How bad was it?" Anderson asked. "I read your articles, but it's hard to believe things like that actually happened in America."

"Believe it," Matthew said gravely. "I wrote what I saw. There was a lot I *didn't* see."

"What is being done for the people of Memphis?"

Matthew struggled to control his anger at what he had learned in Memphis during the few days he was there on his way to New Orleans. "Nothing. Oh, there is talk about compensating the blacks for their losses, but all anyone is doing is dodging responsibility. There have been commissions that have taken testimony from hundreds of witnesses, but..."

"But what?" Anderson pressed when his voice trailed off.

"But it is ultimately going to end up on President Johnson's desk, and I don't believe he will do a single thing about it," Matthew answered, uncertain whether Anderson shared Johnson's beliefs about Reconstruction. "He will put it back into the hands of the city and nothing will be done."

"And you think that is wrong?"

Matthew was running out of patience. He was glad to see his old friend, but he felt like he was being interrogated. "I think it's criminal," he said. "President Johnson's policies are turning back the clock to an America before the war. They are making the four years of war almost pointless. Most of the men in this city are conspiring against the United States, turning their nose up at every protection put in place for the blacks, and they believe they can do it because President Johnson's policies have let them believe it. Freedom for the slaves means nothing if they are not allowed to *live* in freedom, but the danger for Northerners is just as real as it is for the blacks. When the violence explodes, it will not only be toward the freedmen, but toward every person who doesn't wholeheartedly believe in white supremacy."

"You don't care much for New Orleans, do you?"

"No," Matthew snapped through gritted teeth.

"Good," Anderson said as he leaned back in his chair.

Matthew stared at him. "What?"

"I've been in this city almost since the end of the war. I totally agree with your analysis," Anderson said calmly, only his eyes showing his disgust. "I was fairly certain how you would feel about things, but I had to be sure."

"So, now you know." Matthew supposed he could understand, but he was still frustrated that Anderson had played this game with him.

Anderson read his expression. "I'm sorry not to answer you directly, but twelve months in this city has taught me to be cautious." He leaned forward and stared into Matthew's eyes. "You do realize speaking so bluntly could make you a target, don't you?"

Matthew battled his impatience again. "I don't care. I have very few people in this town who will listen to reason, so why bother? They tried reason in Memphis. It didn't work very well. Now I'm trying blunt truth."

Anderson smiled. "I'm glad you haven't changed."

Matthew slowly relaxed, taking a long drink from the water glass at his elbow. He decided it was safe to go back to his original question. "So is the military going to be at the convention?" He was dismayed when Anderson shook his head. "Why not?" he pressed. "Haven't you been listening to me?"

"Yes, and I agree we should be there, but unfortunately, I'm not the one in charge."

"General Sheridan doesn't understand the danger?" Matthew asked. "Could I meet with him?"

Anderson grimaced. "You could if he was in the city. He is in Texas reviewing troops on the Rio Grande. He suspected there would be trouble, but he left."

Matthew stared at him with disbelief. "The military commander of Louisiana and Texas *left*?" he finally managed. "*Now*? Who is in charge?"

Anderson answered only his last question. "General Baird."

"The officer who heads up the Freedmen's Bureau?" Matthew shook his head. "Is he aware of the danger?"

"He has been warned," Anderson said. "I received notice this morning that trouble is expected, but his hands are tied. Baird has done what he can. He has put both regiments on alert. He ordered a steamboat to maintain a head of steam all day tomorrow in case it is needed to ferry troops. He also ordered a tug to be kept ready at the wharf here in the city to provide rapid communication with the troops."

"Let me guess..." Matthew said bitterly, knowing that the barracks were three miles from the city. He envisioned the damage that could be done before the soldiers could receive word and reach the Institute. "He received a telegram from President's Johnson's office telling him to not interfere with the state or the city politics."

"I'm sure that will come, if it hasn't already," Anderson agreed, "but it was actually General Sheridan who ordered him not to place any soldiers around the Mechanics Institute. Sheridan wants to avoid the appearance that the military is supporting the convention. General Baird has been ordered to keep the troops in their barracks. They are only to be used in case of a civil disturbance."

"The barracks are miles downriver," Matthew protested. "How can they possibly get here in time to stop what is going to happen?"

Anderson shook his head heavily. "If I was the one in charge, I would do it differently, Matthew." He leaned forward and stared at him intently. "How can you be so certain there will be violence? The Mayor has put out orders to the city for everyone not connected with the convention to stay away. Baird has told him that if a riot breaks out, New Orleans will be placed under martial law. I don't believe anyone here wants that."

Matthew thought about Moses' certainty there would be violence in Memphis even before the riot had started. He had accepted it, even if he hadn't understood it at the time. Now he understood it. "I can feel it," he replied, understanding when Anderson's eyes narrowed. "If you had been in Memphis you would understand. After it was over, I realized I had felt it in the air even before it began. There is a feeling that wraps around you when there is so much hatred and prejudice raging through people. I'm not sure how to describe it."

"Are you sure it's not just humidity?" Anderson asked lightly. He frowned. "I know what you're talking about," he admitted. "It's almost as if there is a weight bearing down so hard you have trouble breathing."

"Yes," Matthew replied, relieved Anderson understood, but also dismayed because Anderson's agreement abolished any lingering hope that he might simply be overreacting.

Anderson looked out the window, staring down at the crush of carriages and pedestrians crowding St. Charles Avenue. "My understanding is that Mayor Monroe is going to use the police to maintain order."

Matthew groaned. "God help us!"

Anderson looked at him sharply. "I know Mayor Monroe is a radical Democrat, but—"

"You said you read my reports about Memphis?"

"Yes, but the police department here is different," Anderson protested, stiffening as he stared at Matthew's face. "What have you learned?" he asked.

"When Mayor Monroe took over the office a few months ago, he got rid of almost everyone in the police department with a Unionist bent and replaced them with Confederate veterans who are rabid supporters of white supremacy," Matthew replied, his gut twisting as memories of Memphis flashed before him. "He has a very clear agenda."

"The New Orleans police are not armed," Anderson replied, his left eye beginning to twitch.

Matthew knew his friend's eye only twitched when he was nervous. "Neither were the Memphis police," he said. "Until the riot started."

He let his words hang in the air. The only sound was the buzzing of flies and mosquitoes against the screen for several minutes. "I've been on the streets since early morning." He told him about the black man who had given him the warning.

"That's only two policemen," Anderson protested weakly, but his eye continued to twitch.

"Do you know who Lucien Adams is?" Matthew asked, desperate to make his friend understand the urgency of the situation. When Anderson shook his head, he continued. "He was a veteran of the Know-Nothing movement before the war. He basically served as a bully for the American Party that was so opposed to immigration."

Anderson nodded thoughtfully. "I remember President Lincoln wrote a letter about them in 1855. He said if they ever took power, the Declaration of Independence would have to be amended to say all men are created equal, except Negroes, and foreigners, and Catholics."

Matthew scowled. "He added that he would rather live in Russia, where despotism is out in the open, than live in such an America."

"What's that got to do with New Orleans?" Anderson asked with confusion. "The Know-Nothing Party died out right before the war started."

"True, but the thugs they hired to use strong-arm tactics during elections haven't gone anywhere. When the Know-Nothings used them, they could be counted on to intimidate, beat, or even murder a man to keep him from voting. Their party collapsed, they served in the war, and then they started looking for jobs."

"Lucien Adams?" Anderson guessed.

Matthew nodded grimly. "Your Mayor Monroe used these thugs effectively during his previous term as mayor, before he was escorted out of the city when it was under Union control. He used them again during the recent balloting when he was re-elected."

Anderson stared at him. "You've learned a lot in your two weeks here."

Matthew shrugged. "It's my job. Anyway, Lucien Adams is one of the worst. He fled New Orleans to escape being tried for murder in the fifties. General Butler threw him into prison during the war for sedition, but he escaped prosecution when Butler was recalled. His reputation is so bad that Adams, your chief of police—"

"Related?" Anderson asked sharply.

"No," Matthew clarified. "For which I'm sure he's very relieved. Anyway, Chief Adams refused to place him on the police force. Mayor Monroe went ahead and made him a sergeant. He now commands the First District substation on Pecaniere Street."

Anderson sucked in his breath. "I didn't realize..."

Matthew looked at him, knowing Anderson was powerless to stop what was going to happen. The thought made him sick. "I want to talk to General Baird," he said urgently.

Anderson shook his head almost helplessly. "I'll try Matthew, but General Sheridan and President Johnson have virtually tied his hands."

Matthew was suddenly anxious to return to the lobby where he could listen to men boasting about their plans. It was important he have as clear a picture as possible before the convention began. He quickly made plans to have dinner with Colonel Anderson that Wednesday night and then escorted him from the hotel.

Anderson grabbed his arm when they hit the street. "Are you going to be there?" he asked urgently.

Matthew nodded.

"If you're right about what you've told me, it's far too dangerous!"

"The life of a writer," Matthew said lightly, but the mass of tension growing in his chest told him it was going to be very bad. Still, it was his job to be there.

Matthew walked back into the hotel, stopping by the front desk before he went into the restaurant. He was smiling when he turned away, an envelope in his hands. When he was seated at a table in the midst of the chaos, he opened the letter.

Dear Matthew,

I love reading your letters about life in New Orleans. I dream of going there one day. I will also admit I am quite worried about you. From everything you tell me, the same thing that happened in Memphis could very well happen in New Orleans. Please be careful! If I wasn't so worried, I could almost laugh when I write that. I already know you are always in the middle of the trouble. My prayers are with you.

Medical school continues to absorb all my time, but I'm happy to say I love it! On a more somber note, cholera is spreading through the country. New York missed the brunt of it, but it didn't stop it from spreading. Cases have been reported in Baltimore, Cincinnati, Savannah, Chicago, Galveston, Little Rock and Louisville. The cases that concern me the most, though, are the ones that have been reported in New Orleans. Please be so very careful. New Orleans is not following the protocol that New York City is. The first cases have just been reported. I pray you will be out of there soon.

I hope you are coming back to Philadelphia when you leave. It's hot here, but not as dreadfully hot as you describe New Orleans to be. And so far we have been spared from cholera. We'll be ready with apple pie and fried chicken when you return. My Yankee housemates used to turn their noses up at our southern fried chicken. Now they love it as much as we do!

All the girls send their love, as do I.

Sincerely,

Janie

Matthew had been writing Janie regularly since he had left Philadelphia. She would not have received the latest letters he had sent. He knew that when she received them they would only concern her more, but he so appreciated having someone he could write the truth to. The one night he had spent with her after the Fourth of July parade had opened his eyes to what an amazing woman she was. After years of only being able to think of Carrie, Janie's warm vibrancy had captured his heart. He was eager to return to Philadelphia to spend more time with her, but he knew that he couldn't leave until after he had covered the convention.

Matthew smiled and gently folded the letter before he shoved it into his pocket. He would add it to the others he had received. If everything went as planned, he would be on the train to Philadelphia by the end of the week.

A harsh, hushed voice grabbed his attention. "It's quite true that the New Orleans police have a special interest in what happens tomorrow."

Matthew snapped to attention, trying to maintain a relaxed posture so he wouldn't alert the speakers that they were being listened to. He shifted slightly until he could see who was speaking. The two men huddled at the table next to him were obviously wealthy. Both of their faces were red with anger.

"If that convention is successful," the older of the men continued, "it's likely they will establish qualifications for public office that would prevent our Confederate veterans from serving as a police officer. I would say the prospect of losing a job that pays eighty dollars a month in a city with such high unemployment should give our police added incentive to make sure the convention does not convene." His voice dripped with satisfaction.

"But how will Chief Adams let them know if there is a disturbance? I heard Mayor Monroe was making them stay in the station houses," the other man asked.

"Oh, there will be trouble," the older man predicted confidently. "We're making sure there are enough whites there to start up a little trouble. Even if the niggers want this to be peaceful, they're not going to get their way."

Matthew clenched his fists under the table and forced himself to breathe evenly so that he wouldn't miss anything that was said.

"Chief Adams is using the fire-police telegraph system to get word out if there is any trouble."

Matthew listened intently. Philadelphia, New York, and Boston had similar systems to alert fire houses of a blaze. They were actually quite ingenious. The New Orleans alarm system consisted of sixty-five signal stations—cast iron, cottage-shaped boxes attached to the sides of houses, telegraph poles, or gas lamps. They were connected to the central office in the First District police station behind City Hall by a circuit of telegraph lines stretched overhead between tall poles. Normally, the boxes were locked, but every watchman and policeman had a key. If they spotted smoke, they would run to the nearest box, unlock it, and turn a crank inside to sound the alarm.

Turning the crank sent a signal to the central station indicating the district and box number from which the signal had come. The telegraph operator at the central station would then use a keyboard to activate any, or all, of the thirteen large bells located strategically throughout the city. Matthew knew most of them were on the steeples of prominent churches.

New Orleans was divided into nine fire districts. If the originating box was, for instance, number five in district three, the alarm bells would strike three times. Using another control, the central operator could send a second command to all of the signal boxes in the appropriate district. This command would cause a small bell inside each box to tap out the location of the signal box from which the initial alarm was sounded. Firemen were directed to the appropriate district by large alarm bells. Once they got there, they would be directed to the location of the fire by listening to the small bell inside of the signal boxes.

"I thought the alarm system was just for the fire departments," the man protested.

The older man smiled smugly. "It was obvious Chief Adams needed a way to summon his forces quickly should trouble arise. They have enabled the system to alert the police by using twelve strikes of the alarm bells. It won't be confused with a real fire alarm, but it will make sure our boys are there to take care of things."

Matthew tensed, hearing more in the man's voice than he was saying.

The other man must have thought so, too. "Do you know more than you are telling me?"

The older man shrugged. "I would make sure you avoid that area tomorrow. I'm sending my wife and children out of the city tonight."

"Why?" The younger man was obviously alarmed. "This isn't even the real convention. They're just meeting to find out how many more delegates they need to be able to even *have* the convention."

"And what do you know about that?" the older man asked sharply, his eyes narrowing with anger. "Are you one of the radical nigger lovers?" His voice dripped with suspicion.

"No, of course not!" the other man insisted. "I'm all for doing whatever it takes to keep the niggers from having the vote, but I also realize that if things get out of hand, the city could go under martial law. Is that what you want?"

"That won't happen," the older man scoffed. "President Johnson is on our side. He knows we have to take care of things our own way down here. Just because we can't force all the niggers back to the plantations, it doesn't mean we can't still control things."

The other man sounded doubtful. "What about the Civil Rights Act? What about the Fourteenth Amendment? I hate what is happening in our state as much as you do, but what if we lose control and they put us back under military law? What if things go terribly wrong and it opens the door for the Radical Republicans to gain control of the Congress? President Johnson will lose his ability to control things."

"That won't happen," the older man insisted again. He suddenly seemed to notice Matthew leaning slightly in their direction so that he wouldn't miss anything of what they were saying. His lips snapped shut as he scowled at Matthew.

Matthew reached down to pick up the napkin he had let slip from his lap, gave them a pleasant smile, and then went back to drinking the iced tea his waiter had placed in front of him. He kept his face neutral, but his thoughts were spinning.

The tension had been growing for years. Perhaps it was simply not possible to defuse the racial bomb that was going to go off in New Orleans the next day.

Chapter Thirty

Matthew was already sweating profusely as he took up a position next to a window on the second floor of the Mechanics Building. The imposing brick building was four stories high, but was actually only three stories because the middle hall was two stories tall. The cavernous hall was flanked on either side by tall windows that reached almost to the ceiling. Two large doors that opened outward onto the landing provided an entrance at one end. At the opposite end was a raised platform. A low rail in front of it divided the room into two unequal parts. Business was conducted inside the rail, while spectators stood or sat in the larger area outside.

Matthew glanced out at the growing crowd of black people and then turned back to what was going on inside the hall. The area behind the rail was populated with delegates sitting in chairs, waiting for the convention to start. There were three tables on the platform arranged into a horseshoe shape. Judge Howell, president of the convention, sat behind the table in the center. The table to the right had his secretary and assistants. The third table was populated with journalists, both local and visiting.

The larger area was slowly filling up with more men. Most were black, but there were white supporters scattered among them.

Matthew had opted to stand at the window so he could see what was going on outside. He wanted to be able to see what was going on because he was convinced the trouble would start on the streets. His concern grew as the number of black people milling around on Dryades Street in front of the building swelled. The atmosphere was festive, but he could feel the danger in the air as hundreds of black men, women and children dressed in their Sunday best sang and chanted about their right to vote.

Looking past the crowd of black supporters, he could see a group of white men gathered less than half a block away. He thought about the prediction of the man he had eavesdropped on the previous day. He could tell by the expressions on the men's faces that they were looking for trouble.

Howell had been forced to delay the start of the meeting by an hour because there were not enough delegates to form a quorum. Matthew had not paid attention to how they planned on fixing that because his attention had been focused on what was happening outside. He just knew Howell had left the room, promising to return when more delegates arrived. Matthew assumed he was downstairs in the governor's office.

His attention was pulled outside again when he saw another group of black men, one of them defiantly waving an American flag, moving down Canal Street. Their faces were set with determination and courage, and their military bearing said they were Union veterans. Matthew stiffened when he heard three young white men jeer at the flag bearer, their voices rising above the noise. The flag bearer's response was to wave the flag defiantly. Two of the men leapt from the sidewalk and tried to seize the colors, but they were beaten back, crawling back on their hands and knees as the group pushed on.

Matthew heard the pop of gunfire, but the group didn't falter. The drummers leading the procession beat the long roll just as they had during the war to rally the troops on the field of battle. "Fall in boys!" they cried. "Rally, boys!" The last of the marchers cleared the line of white men, their faces triumphant as they took their place in front of the hall.

Matthew continued to watch the white men, his stomach sinking when he saw their rage stiffen into cold purpose.

The supporters greeted the procession with exuberant excitement. The black veterans gave three cheers, and the crowd cheered in return. The flag bearer leapt to the top of the steps of the institute and waved the flag defiantly at the whites on Canal. The cheers grew louder.

As Matthew continued to watch, he realized some of the men in the crowd were acting drunk. He had seen bottles and canteens being passed around freely. He bit back a groan, knowing things could easily get out of hand. Suddenly, a black man ran down the steps of the Institute into the crowd. Matthew couldn't hear what he was saying, but it was obvious by the man's gestures that he was trying to get the crowd to be quiet and go away. Their response was to cheer louder. Another man came down from the stairs and tried to convince them to leave. He got the same response.

"This thing is going to explode."

Matthew glanced at a reporter from the *Boston Globe*. He didn't bother to deny it. The atmosphere was so tense and inflammatory that it would take hardly anything to provoke an explosion.

"I think we should get out of here."

"It's too late, Ben," Matthew snapped, wishing he could be anywhere but in this building. His gut told him he was standing inside a trap.

"What's that kid doing?" Ben asked, leaning further forward.

Matthew watched as a white teenage boy moved toward the black crowd yelling taunts and curses. Several black men holding sticks advance toward him threateningly. The boy retreated, but only when he reached a pile of bricks being used to construct a house. He grabbed a brick in each hand and turned toward the blacks defiantly, his face twisted with rage. Matthew felt a glimmer of relief when he saw a policeman come up behind the boy and pull him back, but he groaned when he saw several of the black men run up to the pile of bricks and begin throwing them into the white crowd.

"The fools," Ben muttered. "Don't they know they can't last against a crowd of armed white men? They are setting up the rest of the blacks for massacre," he growled.

Matthew watched in horror as he saw a black man pull a gun and fire.

That one shot was all that was needed to light the fuse of the bomb.

A cluster of blacks surged toward the windows in the hall to stare down on the street below. "Here they come!" one of the men yelled.

The white crowd rushed toward the Institute, firing as they came. The black men standing behind the pile of bricks, armed with pistols, retaliated with shots of their own. Matthew could only see the clash of colors as they met, the gunfire splitting the air. The festive crowd in front of the Institute fell silent. Several women screamed for their children and began to run, dashing through dark alleys that led to a parallel road.

Matthew almost couldn't believe it when the whites fell back. His throat tightened when he saw three black men lying in pools of blood on the street. The injured white men were carried off by their friends. No one dared attempt to rescue the blacks who had fallen.

As Matthew watched, he saw agitated movement in the white crowd, but for the moment they were staying in place. His gaze turned to the black crowd staring up at the building with frightened faces.

"Why don't they leave?" Ben muttered.

"They can't," a black man answered in a frightened voice. He motioned toward the other end of Dryades where another crowd of armed whites was gathering. "They ain't got nowhere to go."

"They can go through the alleys," Matthew responded, but he knew most of the crowd probably didn't know about that escape route. He still harbored a grasping hope that somehow this could all end without massive bloodshed. His hopes died when he saw a line of policemen advancing toward the Institute about fifteen minutes later. The alarm system had worked. They had been summoned. It sickened him that he had no confidence the men would simply restore order. He had heard too much. He could tell New Orleans' *unarmed* police force was heavily armed.

He also acknowledged there were blacks in the crowd who were helping to ignite the fury. If they had held their fire, it's possible the whole thing could have ended with jeers and taunts. Matthew knew most of the several hundred blacks crowded into the street and clustered in the hall had no desire for violence. They simply wanted to be free. A few hot-headed men had insisted on lighting the fuse. The white policemen were only too willing to let the bomb explode.

He groaned as a shot rang out from the black crowd. Twenty policemen immediately formed a military-style skirmish line, rifles drawn, as they advanced down the streets, their faces filled with a satisfied rage.

More black gunfire broke out as the shooters raced from one doorway to the next in their attempt to avoid the police. In spite of the fact that whites blocked both ends of the street, terrified blacks turned to flee. Many of them managed to race across the Commons, disappearing into alleys and shadows.

"Run!" Matthew whispered. "Run!" They may be heading straight into more trouble, but at least they would have a chance to escape.

Dryades Street was now empty, except for the three black bodies hit by the earlier gunfight. A line of police kept the white crowd back.

"I think they're going to keep it under control," Ben crowed.

Matthew, watching the policemen as they spread out and surrounded the Institute, felt his gut tighten into a hard knot. He fought not to believe what he saw in their faces, but everything he had heard came roaring back into his mind. "Get ready, Ben," he said grimly. "Those policemen are coming for us." He knew that being white wouldn't protect them.

"Get back!" Matthew yelled. "Get away from the windows!"

Ben looked at him as if he were crazy. "These are the *police*, Matthew. They are coming in to stop the convention, but they are going to protect us."

Matthew didn't have time to correct him. He pushed many of the black men away from the window, but one rushed past him, eager to see what was happening below. A shot rang out, shattering the window just above the man's head. The man stumbled back, his face a shocked mask.

Cries broke out among the crowd of more than one hundred blacks as more gunfire shattered windows. "What should we do?" one yelled. "We have no means of defense!" another hollered. Prayers and hymns rose from among the terrified chaos.

Cutler, one of the leaders of the convention, leapt onto the platform and waved his arms. "You blacks must go home! There will only be trouble if you stay!"

Matthew was horrified. Did Cutler not realize he was sending the blacks to their death, or did he just not care? He knew Cutler believed the blacks' presence would give the police reason to attack the hall. With them gone, he probably believed they would take the convention leaders into custody. Perhaps he wasn't thinking about the results of the blacks going out into the streets, but Matthew had a sick certainty that he didn't care. Cutler's focus was on self-protection.

Matthew watched as some of the blacks began to file reluctantly from the hall, their faces full of apprehension and fear as they glanced back. He took up his station by the window again, scanning the road to try to avoid gunfire. He was joined by the black men who had refused to leave. The police had sealed off both ends of Dryades Street and had now blocked the alleyways leading to the parallel road that served as an escape route for the rest of the crowd. When the black convention-goers reached the street, they stopped, staring back up at the building in confusion. They obviously didn't know what to do.

The lines of police and a large crowd of white civilians began to advance toward the Institute, yelling angrily as they pulled their weapons and began to fire.

"No!" Matthew yelled. Gunshots rose from the street like firecrackers as the whites fired into the crowd of unarmed black men. He watched in horror as men fell before the assault, blood darkening the bricked road.

The remaining men, almost all veterans, quickly broke into two groups and began fighting against the white advance. A few had pistols, but most fought back with bricks and stones. Slowly, they gave ground, retreating up the stairs until they were crowded into the vestibule of the Institute. The bullets continued their barrage.

Matthew could no longer see the men, but he didn't need to *see* what was happening. He already knew. He continued to watch, refusing to look away even as bullets shattered the windows of the hall. He had tried to stop this, but he had failed. Images of Memphis blurred together with the reality of dead men sprawled on the street below.

"Get away from the window!" Ben gasped, dragging him back through the shattered glass.

Matthew didn't resist. He knew the battle was coming inside now.

Cutler jumped onto the platform, his arms waving frantically. "Everyone who is not armed come into the railed area," he yelled. His face took on a greater panic when all but a dozen men moved forward, but he continued to shout orders. "You who are armed stay near the door. The rest of you must come forward and sit down. We are peacefully assembled. Sit down! Do not move." His voice rang through the hall.

The crowd responded slowly, their faces twisted with shock and anger, but convention leaders moved among them, pleading and directing. Matthew joined his fellow journalists at the table and waited. The large double doors leading into the hall had been left open as evidence that the convention did not intend to resist.

It was only five minutes before three policemen appeared in the doorway, pistols drawn, their eyes flashing dangerously. Seven more men were behind them.

Without a word, the ten policemen moved forward and opened fire on the seated crowd.

Matthew could only stare as blacks slumped to the floor, screaming in pain.

"Don't shoot!"

"We've done no harm!"

"We are peaceable!"

The policemen continued to fire, their faces cold with rage and hatred. Matthew couldn't look away, knowing with a sick certainty that he was watching the future of his beloved country.

When the police retreated to reload, several of the blacks jumped up, pulled the doors shut, and began to pile chairs in front of them in a futile attempt to stop the attack. Matthew watched numbly, knowing that because the doors opened outward it would be impossible to stop the assault.

Cutler remained on the stage, imploring them to stay calm. "The military will be here soon. They will be here in a few minutes." His eyes flashed with a desperate hope as his face revealed his horror.

Matthew stared at him, knowing the military was probably only now receiving word of trouble. It would be hours before they would arrive. "Don't count on it," he muttered.

"What do you mean?" Ben asked, his eyes glued to the set of double doors.

"They won't be here for hours." That was all Matthew had time to say before the police gathered outside tried to force the doors open again. There was a black man holding on to the handles with all his might, but when it became evident he couldn't hold them closed, he turned and rushed back to the railing area.

J.D. O'Connell, a former state senator during Union occupation, stepped forward bravely, both hands outstretched, a white handkerchief in one hand to signify surrender. "I implore you men to cease firing," he called. "These people do not wish to fight, and they have nothing to fight with. Every person in this room is prepared to surrender if the police will protect them."

Matthew allowed himself a flicker of hope when the police officer and O'Connell shook hands. Would it end with all of them being arrested? He watched as the former senator helped clear the chairs that were blocking the doors. His hope withered as he saw the cold calculation on the faces of the policemen who filed silently into the hall and formed a solid line across one end of it. He opened his mouth to yell a warning, but he was too late.

"We have them now, boys!" the officer yelled. "Give it to them!"

Once again the policemen opened fire, advancing further into the hall, emptying their revolvers as they came. More black men slumped to the ground, but the onslaught ignited the decision to fight back. If they couldn't surrender, they weren't just going to sit on the ground and be massacred.

One man jumped up and used a heavy stick to club down an officer who had advanced almost to the rail with his pistol. A few of the spectators pulled out their own weapons and returned fire. Many more jumped up, grabbed broken chairs, and rushed toward the officers, their defiant yells filling the hall. The police withdrew quickly, stumbling down the stairs toward the vestibule.

Several members of the convention, still desperate to be saved, followed the police onto the landing. "Don't shoot! Don't shoot!"

The response was almost immediate. An avalanche of bullets poured in through the windows. Matthew covered his head as shards of glass flew through the air. He knew more of the police must have taken up positions at the nearby Medical College to give them the vantage point. Most of the bullets went high and passed through the hall, but men still continued to fall.

Ben crawled over to Matthew, blood streaming from cuts on his face. "The military really isn't coming?"

"They were told to stay in their barracks. They're probably on their way here, but it will take them hours to arrive." He watched as one of the white spectators grabbed the United States flag standing by the platform, tied a white handkerchief to the tip of it and thrust it out through one of the shattered windows. His effort to signal surrender was greeted with another volley of gunshots.

"They aren't going to let us surrender, are they?" Ben asked, his face twisted with pain.

Matthew stared at him, not willing to abolish whatever lingering hope Ben still had. His eyes widened suddenly as he saw a spreading mass of blood on his colleague's shirt. "You've been shot!'

Ben nodded. "They got me a few minutes ago," he revealed through gritted teeth.

Matthew remained huddled against the desk as he pulled off his shirt. He tied it firmly around Ben's torso, grimacing as he groaned in pain. "We have to slow the bleeding."

Ben nodded. "I thought once I made it off the battlefields I was safe from gunfire," he gasped. "I figured being a reporter would be safe."

Matthew managed a tight smile, recognizing the look of shock beginning to glaze Ben's eyes. He bit back a groan as the double doors to the hall were forced open again. He pulled Ben under the protection of the table as the policemen rushed into the hall again.

This time it was the white minister, Reverend Horton, who stepped forward with a white handkerchief waving. All around the hall, people took out handkerchiefs and pieces of white cloth to signify surrender. Reverend Horton stepped forward bravely. "We surrender. We are peaceable. Don't fire. Take us prisoner, but don't fire."

Matthew watched in numb agony as the policeman raised his pistol and fired twice. Horton fell to the ground, blood pouring from his arm, but then struggled to his feet. A few of the spectators returned fire with their few remaining bullets. When a policeman at the door slumped to the ground, the rest retreated.

"They ain't gonna let us surrender!" one of the men yelled.

"We can't just stay here until they kill all of us," another hollered.

"We have to get out of here if we are going to survive," another cried.

"We have to escape!"

The cry rose up from the remaining black men standing angrily among their fallen comrades. Matthew understood their frantic desire to escape the slaughter, but he also knew their options were limited. He watched as the white leaders quietly discussed their options. He could tell by the looks on their faces that they had reached the same conclusion. Escape was their only hope of staying alive.

"Is there a way out of here?" Ben asked between gritted teeth.

"Most of the exits will lead them right into the mob outside. I don't know the building well enough to know how best to get out of here." He supposed he should have been prepared, but even in his wildest imaginations, he had not imagined this. The only way the policemen could continue to do what they were doing was if they were confident they would kill anyone who could identify them. That meant everyone in the hall. The sounds he heard out on the landing told him they were preparing for another assault.

The sound mobilized many of the convention-goers. He watched as men darted up the stairs to the fourth floor, and he saw more disappear down a back stairway that he supposed led to the back of the building. He grimaced when he saw men jump from the window to the street twenty feet below. Whether they made it or not, he understood they had to make the attempt.

"We've got to get out of here!" Ben grunted.

"We won't make it." Matthew did his best to sound calm. He knew Ben was too badly injured to escape.

Ben closed his eyes as a fresh wave of pain swept through him. His eyes flew open when it had ebbed. "You've got to leave me, Matthew!"

"I don't think so," Matthew replied, his mind racing as he tried to figure out what to do. As his eyes flashed around the hall, a man who had been sitting on the floor slumped to one side and crumpled to the floor. His eyes widened as he realized what he was looking at. It wasn't much, but it would have to do.

He rose to his feet, staying stooped over as far as he could to avoid the bullets still flying in the windows. "Come on!" he urged, pulling Ben up with him. Ben gasped with pain but struggled to follow him.

Matthew rushed forward, pulling Ben into a narrow cavity under the platform just as the doors were bashed open again. He tugged Ben back, holding his hand over his mouth to contain his cries of pain and then stopped, hoping he had pulled both of them far enough out of sight. "Be still!" he hissed. When Ben slumped against him, Matthew knew he had passed out from the pain.

Matthew pulled his legs in tightly against his chest, praying bullets wouldn't penetrate the platform. He had given them the best chance he could.

He could hear men talking in low voices above him, but he couldn't identify the hushed voice that suddenly became clear enough to be heard. "We have to get out of here. I expect to be killed. My only regret is that I don't have anything to defend myself with."

Matthew realized he was sitting in front of a narrow slit in the platform wood. He pressed his eye to the crack, his dismay growing when he saw the rows of men lining the landing outside the hall. Their clothing revealed they were not policemen, but members of the mob acting in concert with them. Anyone seeking to escape the building must pass through their gauntlet to reach the street.

Matthew was thankful for his hiding place. Ben's breath was shallow, but he was still alive. All he could do was hope the military would arrive before Ben died, or before they were captured.

Matthew watched through the crack as convention-goers began to move bravely toward the door. Once they passed the exit he was not able to see them anymore, but the cries of pain and the thuds he heard told him exactly what kind of beating they were being subjected to. He shuddered, forcing himself to swallow the terror threatening to choke him.

He should never have come. His determined stubbornness to report this story could mean it was the last one he would ever tell. When he closed his eyes, for the first time in six years, it was not Carrie's vivacious face that filled his mind. Janie's soft blue eyes gazed at him with sympathy and understanding, her hand reaching out to grasp his. He felt his breathing slow as an inexplicable peace filled him. Mistake or not, he was here. Silently, he began to pray.

More than two hours passed while Matthew huddled under the platform. The sounds drifting up through the window told him the riot had intensified. He fought to control his fear as he heard the never-ending pop of gunfire, followed by cursing and screams of pain.

The hall had cleared of people that were not dead or too wounded to move. His determination to know what was happening had disappeared. For the first time since his career as a reporter had begun, he was no longer hungry to tell every aspect of a story. He had thought living through the explosion of the *Sultana* had finished his thirst for journalism, but he had been driven forward by his belief that the stories must be told if change were to happen. As horrible as Memphis had been, he had felt satisfaction that his articles would make a difference. This was different. For the first time, he no longer had hope things would change.

He was sure he would never lose the images of cold hatred and calculating murder he had seen in the eyes of the police as they opened fire on unarmed, peaceful men, both white and black. Their only crime had been a belief in the black man's right to freedom. He had spent two weeks in a city full of such furious hatred and unreasonable fear that he no longer believed anything could change it. The Congress might enact laws, but who would enforce them? The United States military, even after four years of brutal war, had been held back from supporting what they had supposedly fought to accomplish.

Hundreds of men were rampaging through the streets, killing and maiming every black person they could find. Matthew didn't have to be out there to know it. He had seen it in Memphis. This was far worse.

Ben remained unconscious. Matthew was almost glad because it gave him an excuse to stay under the platform. When he glanced at his watch again, he saw it was after three o'clock. More than two hours since the violence had exploded, and the military was still not here. It made him sick to think of how many people had been killed and injured during that time.

He stiffened when he heard pounding feet on the landing again. The crack revealed a group of policeman as they swept into the hall. They began to work their way systematically through the room, nudging fallen men with their boot.

"This one ain't dead yet," one of the policemen said casually, and then laughed as he raised his pistol and fired. "He is now," he said just as casually.

Matthew's shoulders shook with silent sobs as the police roamed through the room, killing any man who was still alive. He no longer cared if they found him. He was quite certain he didn't want to live in a world filled with the type of men who could do what they were doing. Only the image of Janie's shining eyes and Ben's unconscious body kept him quiet.

Once they had killed everyone, the officers began to break up the room. Any remaining chairs were splintered against the floor, and then they moved forward to smash the tables and podium on the platform. Matthew sat numbly as the sound of boots hammered through his head. When he heard a vicious ripping sound, he realized they were tearing the United States flag.

"That will teach those abolitionists," Matthew heard one of them growl. When they were done, he heard them stomp from the room. He dared to stretch out his cramped legs, but he knew better than to come out of his hiding place. He didn't know how long he would have to stay there, but he was certain it wasn't safe to come out now. He owed it to Ben to give him a chance to live. His fellow journalist's breathing had become shallower, but he was still holding on.

It was almost four o'clock when Matthew heard footsteps again. He peered out of the crack again, breathing a sigh of relief when he saw a group of soldiers walk through the doors, their eyes wide with shock when they saw the dead bodies and the destruction.

"There can't possibly be anyone still alive in here," he heard one of them grunt. "Let's go back outside where we can do some good."

"Wait!" Matthew called, his voice weak from dehydration and heat exhaustion.

The soldier spun around. "Did you hear that?"

Matthew realized he was wedged into the opening by Ben's body. "Here!" he called. "Under the platform."

Moments later, two soldiers were kneeling in front of the opening. "Who are you?" one of them asked sharply.

"Matthew Justin. I am a reporter. This is Ben Conrad. He is a reporter for the *Boston Globe*. He has been badly wounded. He needs medical assistance."

"You sure he's still alive?" the soldier asked doubtfully.

"He's alive," Matthew said grimly. "He's one of the lucky ones."

The soldier stared at Ben's chalky face. "If you say so," he muttered, reaching forward to pull Ben's body toward him gently.

"How bad is it out there?" Matthew asked, more out of habit than because he actually wanted to know. Neither one of the men answered him, but the looks they exchanged told him everything. "Will you be able to get Ben to the hospital through the riot?" he pressed.

"We'll do the best we can," the soldier answered as he pulled Ben free from the platform hiding place. "Our squadron is waiting outside. More than five hundred of us arrived in the city a while ago."

"We'll get him there," the other soldier vowed, sympathy radiating from his eyes. "I'm sorry for what happened here."

Matthew crawled out behind Ben just as three policemen entered the room. Their eyes narrowed with hatred as they spotted him.

"Who you got there, soldier boys?" one of them called.

"I'd say that is none of your business," the soldier called back.

The policeman continued to advance. "Why, sure it is. You soldier boys were called in to keep the peace. You can't do that as long as these convention-goers are left to create havoc. We've been trying to create peace ever since the first blacks started firing at us. Why don't you let us take charge of these two?"

Matthew bit back his sharp retort, waiting to see what the soldiers would do. They exchanged uncertain glances, but moved to form a barrier in front of him and Ben. Another voice at the door made him close his eyes with grateful relief.

"What is going on here?"

The policemen whirled around when the sharp voice filled the hall. They straightened quickly. "Hello, Colonel," one of them called confidently.

Colonel Anderson advanced into the room, his eyes locked on the three officers. "Get out of here," he said flatly.

"Hey, you can't talk to us like that!" one of the police officers protested.

"If it were up to me, I wouldn't be talking to you at all," Anderson barked. "I would haul you off to jail and lock you up for the rest of your life. Or maybe I should follow the fine example you set here today and shoot you." His eyes narrowed with anger. "The Institute is now under the control of the United States military. Get out of here before I change my mind and do what I want to do."

The three policemen, their eyes blazing with fury, turned and stalked from the room.

Only then did Colonel Anderson step around the barricade his men had formed. His eyes widened with shocked surprise. "Matthew!"

"About time you got here," Matthew muttered, needles of pain shooting through his legs as they came back to life.

"What happened here?" Anderson demanded.

"I'll tell you later," Matthew replied. "Please get Ben to the hospital. He was shot in the side."

Anderson nodded to his men. "Pick him up and carry him downstairs. There is a wagon right outside the door."

His two men exchanged uncertain glances. "What if someone tries to stop us?" one of them asked.

"Shoot them," Anderson said bluntly. "Aim to kill. It's time we sent a message." He watched his men carry Ben out of the hall and then turned back to Matthew. "Do you need to go to the hospital?

"No," Matthew assured him faintly, the reality of everything swarming through him now that he and Ben had been rescued.

Anderson's eyes blazed as they swept the room. "My God!" he whispered. "How did this happen?" He shook his head and looked down at Matthew. "Do you need help?"

"I've been cramped up under the platform for a few hours," Matthew admitted. "My legs are still deciding if they want to work."

Anderson leaned down to peer under the platform, taking note of the blood pooled where Ben had been lying. He knelt down next to Matthew, wrapped an arm around his waist, and helped him stand, supporting him when Matthew swayed.

Now that Matthew was not limited to what he could see through the crack, he couldn't control the vomit that rose in his throat as the sight of bodies, already bloated from the heat and covered with flies, filled his vision. He leaned forward as his body expelled the horror he had experienced for the last three hours. Anderson held him firmly and then handed him a canteen full of water. Matthew reached for it gratefully, drinking until the canteen was empty.

"I'm so sorry."

Matthew sighed. "I know you had no control to stop it."

"No," Anderson agreed, bitterness lacing his voice. "What happened here was wrong. I am ashamed our government let it happen."

Matthew nodded. "I am, too," he said heavily. "Memphis was terrible, but this was far worse."

Anderson's eyes swept the room again. "How did this happen?" he asked again.

Matthew swallowed and told him.

Anderson stared blankly, his mouth opening and closing as he searched for words. He finally found them.

"The *police* did this? While the people were trying to surrender?"

Matthew nodded. The telling of the story had been almost as terrifying as living it. "I have to get out of here," he murmured. His lungs suddenly felt starved for air. His head started to whirl as he gasped for breath. "I gotta get out of here."

Anderson held him up as they moved toward the door.

Matthew fought to control his vomit as they squished through pools of blood on the landing, walking carefully around dead bodies that filled the stairwell. He broke down in tears when he recognized one of the men staring up at him with sightless eyes.

"Do you know him?" Anderson asked.

"That's Ralph," Matthew gasped. "The man who warned me yesterday."

The air wrapped around him while the putrid aroma of bodies bloated by the intense heat hit Matthew in the face. His heart began to pound wildly as he fought to pull air into his lungs.

"Somebody get over here!" Anderson shouted.

Matthew felt Anderson's arms grab him as the blackness swallowed him.

Chapter Thirty-One

Matthew woke to the feel of a cool compress on his head. He lay still, confusion swamping him. Where was he? Suddenly the events of the day came swarming back. He groaned.

"Mr. Justin?"

Matthew opened his eyes reluctantly, wishing he could just slide back into the oblivion. When his vision cleared, he identified an elderly white woman with snowy hair. Bright blue eyes shining with concern and compassion gazed down at him.

"Welcome back," she said softly.

Matthew could only stare at her. He didn't want to be back. He didn't want to have to remember the pile of dead bodies...the pleading voices...the hatred...He groaned and closed his eyes again.

The woman continued speaking softly. "The city is under martial law now. Most of the wounded have been removed from the jail and are now in the hospital."

"How many dead?" Matthew asked, his eyes still closed.

"They don't know yet."

The hesitant tone in her voice told Matthew just how bad it was. He gritted his teeth.

"My name is Abby Youngers."

Matthew's eyes opened reluctantly. "I know another woman named Abby," he said. This time he kept his eyes open long enough to inspect his caregiver. "You have eyes like she does." He moved restlessly. "Where am I?"

"My home on the far east side of New Orleans. Colonel Anderson had his men bring you here."

"You know Colonel Anderson?"

"He is married to my sister," Abby revealed.

Matthew looked at her with surprise. Her accent clearly identified her as a Southerner.

Abby smiled. "My sister left New Orleans years ago for school in the North. She was quite a bit younger than me. She never came back."

Matthew tried to remember what he knew about Anderson's wife, but he drew a blank. "She's not here in the city now?"

"No. She refused to come. She didn't want their children exposed to Southern bigotry." Abby's matter-of-fact voice held no rancor. "I have tried to give the colonel a feeling of home. He comes here for meals whenever he can get away."

"You don't resent him?" Matthew asked, trying to understand why he was here.

"Why would I?" Abby asked gently.

"He's a Yankee. He fought for the Union. Your city is now under military control once again."

Abby nodded calmly. "As it should be."

Matthew looked at her sharply. "You're a Unionist?"

"I prefer to not be labeled," Abby said evenly. "I would rather be seen as a woman who believes all people are created equal. I believe there have been horrible mistakes made on both sides during the last six years. I am quite sure more will be made."

Matthew appreciated her candor enough to respond with the same. "I've never seen such hatred as I experienced today." He closed his eyes as he fought off a shudder. "How will our country ever survive this kind of prejudice?"

Abby grimaced. "I learned a long time ago that there are some people with so little brains or ability that all they have to be proud of is the color of skin they happened to be born with. We've got a lot of those in New Orleans."

Matthew's lips twitched as he stared into her indignant eyes.

Abby laid another cool cloth on his head. "Hating people because of their color is wrong. It doesn't matter which color does the hating. It's just plain wrong."

"Yes, but there is a lot of it happening." Matthew wanted to blot out the images filling his mind, but they still swarmed in. He closed his eyes as they wrapped around his heart and squeezed it tightly.

"So you decide to hate, too? You believe that will make things better?"

Matthew's eyes flew to her. He didn't bother to ask how Abby could see into his heart. He shook his head, trying to make sense of the haze filling him. "I've tried not to," he murmured. "I was in Memphis during the riot there. I thought nothing could be more horrible."

"Until you came here?"

"Yes," Matthew said bluntly.

"And now you have no hope for our country." Abby stated.

Matthew turned his head to look out the window, seeing nothing but darkness. It was the way he felt inside. He didn't have an answer—at least not one he wanted to admit to.

"Can I ask you a question, Matthew?"

Matthew nodded, his insides churning.

"If you knew that hope and despair were paths to the same destination, which one would you choose?"

Matthew considered her question. The answer seemed obvious, but he knew she was asking for another reason. He mulled the question in his mind, knowing she would give him time to ponder it. As he stared into the night he realized that whether he liked it or not, the sun was going to rise on the United States in the morning. Decisions were going to be made, and lives were going to be impacted. A new day would begin...and would roll into months, years, decades and centuries. There was nothing that was going to stop the passage of time.

If you knew that hope and despair were paths to the same destination, which one would you choose? Matthew smiled slightly. "Are all women wise?"

Abby chuckled. "No, but most of us have far more time to think then men do because too many of you seem to believe we have nothing worthwhile to say."

This time Matthew was able to respond with a small chuckle of his own. "I know far too many wise women to ever think that," he protested.

"Yes, I know that."

Matthew looked at her. "I thought you said the colonel's *men* dropped me off?"

"The colonel told me all about you months ago," Abby said softly. "Did you think he would forget that you saved his life after the escape from Libby Prison?"

Matthew shook his head. "Neither one of us will ever forget that time. He helped keep me going..."

"When you were in Rat Dungeon," Abby finished for him. She laid a hand on his shoulder tenderly. "Matthew, you have experienced many reasons to give up hope."

Matthew appreciated the warmth of her hand. The feel of it gave him courage to gaze into her eyes. "I'm afraid," he said hoarsely.

"Of course you are," Abby agreed. "You would be a fool if you weren't. I've had many things to be afraid of," she said gently, "but hope has carried me through. I learned a long time ago that hope is some extraordinary spiritual grace God gives us to *control* our fears, not make them nonexistent." She reached up and stroked his hair. "Now go to sleep. The colonel will be back in the morning. You can get all your questions answered then."

Matthew stared into her eyes, drawing hope and strength from the light he saw shining there. Then he closed his eyes and let sleep claim him.

The sun was peeking over the horizon when Matthew opened his eyes again. He was surprised to see Abby still sitting beside his bed, knitting calmly. "Were you here all night?"

Abby smiled and set her knitting aside. "No. You slept peacefully through the night. I simply wanted to be here when you woke. I wasn't sure you would remember where you are."

Matthew was surprised how well he had slept. He knew Abby's tender words had banished the worst of the memories so that he could sleep. "Thank you for what you said last night."

Abby nodded calmly. "I'll be right back." When she returned, Colonel Anderson was by her side.

"Anderson!" Matthew exclaimed. He swung his legs over the side of the bed, relieved when the world remained steady.

Anderson stared at him for a long moment. Then, apparently satisfied with what he saw, he looked back at his sister-in-law. "Thank you for taking such good care of him."

Abby smiled. "He was a delight. There was nothing wrong with him except severe dehydration and heat exhaustion. Once I got enough water in him, I knew he would be fine."

Matthew smiled softly. The gift she had given him was far greater than liquid.

Abby's eyes twinkled at him as she turned to leave the room. "I'll leave you two to talk."

Anderson sat down in the chair Abby had just abandoned, his eyes heavy with fatigue. "You're sure you're all right?"

"I'm fine," Matthew insisted. "What is happening out there?"

"It was a long night, but the city is under control. Martial law has been declared. General Baird appointed Major General Kautz as military governor."

Matthew smiled slightly. "I wish I could have been there when Governor Monroe was removed from office."

"It was satisfying," Anderson revealed. "He protested, but he no longer has any legal authority in New Orleans."

"Abby dodged my question about how bad things were," Matthew said quietly. When Anderson hesitated, he reached out and grabbed his arm. "I lived it," Matthew said flatly. "I want to know."

"Close to fifty dead, I think. We won't know the final numbers for a while."

"Wounded?"

Anderson shrugged. "Hundreds," he said sadly. "But those are just the ones in the hospital. I have no idea how many are being cared for by friends or family. We may never know."

Matthew absorbed the information. "The police?"

Anderson hesitated again but met his eyes squarely. "They did exactly what you said they would do..." His voice thickened as it trailed off. "They killed or beat as many blacks as they could find. They also attacked white Republicans who have vowed to stand with the blacks." His eyes shifted away.

"But they'll probably get away with it just like they did in Memphis," Matthew snapped.

Anderson turned his eyes back. "I've already begun to hear their stories. They are blaming it on the blacks, saying they started it."

"And so that gives them the right to slaughter unarmed men?" Matthew felt ill. The massacre had been bad enough. The reality that there would probably be no justice made it even more unbearable. He pushed away the feeling of futility trying to consume him. He could face what had happened with despair or hope. As difficult as it was, he had decided to choose hope.

"All of this is going to backfire on the South," Anderson said. "This is going to do nothing but increase the perception in the North that white Southerners are determined to unleash a reign of terror on the freedmen."

"It's more than a *perception*," Matthew growled.

"And as horrible as it is, I believe it is the wakeup call that was needed," Anderson said thoughtfully. "The South has made it clear they have no intention of submitting to Yankee rule. It is clear they have refused to accept the verdict arrived at by four years of bloody war."

Matthew considered his words. "The elections are coming up," he added, feeling his first real spark of hope.

"Sentiment has already been turning away from President Johnson and the Democrats determined to follow his lead. People in the North have had all they are going to take. The elections will give absolute power to the Republicans. That is our only hope that things will change for the freedmen."

Matthew considered his words. The elections were to be held in November. Would they really change things?

He wanted to believe it, but his hold on hope was tentative at best.

Anderson watched him closely. "Are you going to stay in the city to write the stories the way you did in Memphis?"

Matthew considered the question carefully. He had been sure that he wouldn't when he was hiding under the platform the day before. Abby's gentle questions that had led him to renewed hope had also caused him to wonder if he should stay, but he slowly shook his head. "No. I have plenty of information to tell the story." He took a deep breath, feeling a surge of freedom when he made his decision. He would tell the story, but it was time for him to leave. "I'm going to Philadelphia as soon as I can catch a train out of this lovely city."

"I understand," Anderson said gruffly. He reached into his pocket. "I stopped by your hotel room on the way here to get you a change of clothes. They gave me this letter."

Matthew smiled when he saw Janie's handwriting. He tore it open and devoured the contents.

> *Dear Matthew,*
> *Wonderful news! We have discovered we have a ten-day break from school starting on Wednesday, August 1. Carrie's father has sent tickets for all of us to come home to the plantation. To say we are excited would be putting it very mildly! All of us are eager to get out of the city and breathe some real air. I don't know when you are going to be leaving New Orleans, but if it is possible for you to get away to the plantation, it would be so wonderful to have you there!*
> *Sincerely,*
> *Janie*

Matthew smiled and folded the letter.

"Good news?" Anderson asked.

"Very good news." Matthew felt a surge of energy as his heart pounded with anticipation. He stood and reached for the clothing Anderson was holding. "I'm leaving today for Richmond. Then I'm going out to Cromwell Plantation."

He was quite sure he would never return to New Orleans.

Thomas and Abby were waiting on the platform when Matthew swung from his train car. He hurried forward, surprised anyone had come to meet him. He had sent word of his arrival, but he had planned on walking up to the house as he was sure they would be working. His heart leapt with gladness as he waved at them. "What are you two doing here?"

Thomas hurried forward, his eyes dark with concern. "How are you, my boy?"

Matthew suddenly understood. "You heard about New Orleans?" He hadn't had the heart to do any more than telegram that he was coming home.

"Colonel Anderson sent us a long telegram informing us what you have been through. We received it early this morning. I am so sorry."

"Anderson sent you a telegram?" Matthew asked, reminded once again of just how good a friend he was. Abby stepped forward and wrapped her arms around him. Matthew sighed as her warmth spread through him.

"I know it was horrible," she finally murmured.

Matthew didn't bother to deny it. He finally stepped back, the ache in his heart not quite so searing. "When are the others arriving?"

Abby's look said she understood he wasn't ready to talk about it. "In about an hour." Her face lit up with a glorious smile. "We are so excited to have them home. To have you home, too, is just the icing on the cake."

"*All* of them are coming?'"

Abby laughed. "Yes. Elizabeth, Alice, and Florence can hardly wait to visit a real Southern plantation." She understood when Matthew hesitated. "Nothing has happened since the Fourth of July party. The vigilantes have not returned," she assured him.

Matthew thought about the looks of hatred and cold purpose he had seen in New Orleans. "They will," he said. He hated his certainty, and he regretted the concern that erupted in Abby's eyes, but it was best they be prepared.

Thomas frowned. "Perhaps, but I doubt they will do it when all of us are there. The vigilantes work under a cloak of secrecy. They are going to be less bold now that they know Moses is aware of their identity. They also prefer to prey on the weak—not armed men and women who know how to shoot a weapon," he added.

Matthew hoped he was right, but he doubted it. He would keep any more thoughts to himself, though, because he knew Thomas wanted to alleviate Abby's fears, and he wouldn't want the girls to be afraid. He was quite certain the vigilantes would return, however. He had seen the results of wounded Southern pride twice now.

He also knew how careful everyone was being. They couldn't do more than that. It would benefit no one if they walked around in constant fear of what could happen. He glanced toward the carriage, taking note of the armed guard seated beside Spencer. "How's Jeremy?"

"Both of his casts are off, and he's working full-time again," Abby replied. "He's also marvelously in love with Marietta. Just watching them together makes me happy!"

Matthew grinned, glad to have something take his mind off what he had left behind in New Orleans. "Have they set a date for their wedding yet?"

Thomas nodded. "This Christmas. They have decided to marry on the plantation."

Matthew's grin spread. "The plantation is always spectacular at Christmas. It will be even more so this year."

Thomas laughed. "I believe you're right. I hear that plans are already being made out there."

"Has Rose met Marietta yet?"

Abby shook her head. "Can you believe they haven't? When Rose last came to Richmond, Marietta had been called away from the city. That is about to be rectified, however."

"They're coming to the plantation with us?" Matthew felt the knots of pain unloosen a little more. "We're all going to be together?"

Abby nodded and pulled him toward the carriage. "We are!" Her eyes were shining with delight. "Let's get you and your luggage home so Spencer and Howard can return for the girls. It will be a tight squeeze, but I believe they can all fit in."

Matthew shook hands with both Spencer and Howard when they arrived at the carriage. There was no evidence of the attack on Spencer's face, but his eyes held a shadow that hadn't been there the last time he had seen him. Matthew understood all too well. Then he appraised Howard, liking the tall, lean man's steady brown eyes. Matthew knew Howard had served as a Union soldier, relocating to Richmond after the war to be closer to his wife's family. He wondered if the guard really understood what he was up against. He would talk to him later. The man was protecting people very precious to him.

Matthew listened as Abby chattered on the way to the house, but he was also covertly watching Howard. He was relieved when he realized the guard was constantly scanning the road, both in front and behind them. Howard responded to Spencer's quiet comments, but he never relaxed his vigilance.

Abby walked with Matthew into the house while Thomas stayed behind to get his luggage. "Are you satisfied with Howard?" she asked quietly.

"He seems competent," Matthew replied, his throat tightening when he walked into the house.

Abby read his face. "You weren't certain you would see this again."

Matthew took a deep breath, trying to keep his mind from going back to those terrifying hours in the Institute. In spite of his best efforts, Ralph's blank eyes staring up at him from the stairwell covered with blood would not be held back. He shook his head, biting back a groan.

Abby pulled him into the parlor and pushed him down into a seat. "My dear boy," she murmured.

Matthew managed a thin smile. Hearing Abby say *my dear boy* always had a soothing effect on him. He suspected, no matter how old he got, that it always would. He was aware when Thomas walked into the parlor, and then he watched as the carriage rattled off before he found his voice. "I'm done," he announced.

Thomas settled down in the chair across from him. "Done with being a reporter?"

Matthew nodded. "I thought covering the war was terrible, but what is going on in our country now is worse." He paused, trying to articulate what he had been thinking during his long train ride across the country. He had watched as mile after mile of the South rolled beneath the wheels, the constant humidity enfolding him in a smothering blanket. The only relief had been a thunderstorm in Alabama. It had relieved the cloying humidity, but it had done nothing to relieve his thoughts. "I had anticipated that rebuilding our country would be difficult, and I also expected racial tensions to be a reality, but..." He couldn't control his shudder.

"Take your time," Abby said softly, laying her hand over his.

Matthew stared at her. Talking about it was like opening the floodgates to his memories. He wasn't sure he wanted to, but he knew from experience that he had to. Holding it in would only destroy him from the inside. "I've never seen hatred like this. Soldiers fought on both sides of the war because their commanders told them to fight. They didn't see real people on the other side of the battlefield most of the time. They fought because that is what soldiers do." He turned to gaze out the window for a moment and then swung back. "Memphis and New Orleans were different. There was a certain mob mentality, but there was also a cold, calculating hatred that I had never experienced before. I was...I was ashamed to be an American."

Thomas and Abby sat quietly. He knew they were giving him time to get it out.

"President Johnson's policies have set something into motion that I don't think can be stopped. When the war ended, I believe the South was ready for change to be enforced. They expected it." He shook his head heavily. "After a year of Johnson's policies and virtually no consequences from the war, they have decided they will run the South the way they have always run it. Except now it is worse...and they believe they have the president's support. They know they can never go back to slavery, so now they are determined to either run the blacks off, kill them, or terrify them so they will never present a threat."

"You don't believe Congress can stop it?" Thomas asked.

Matthew shook his head. "No, I don't," he said honestly. "They will make laws, but the last year has released a fury and hatred so intense, I don't believe laws can shove it back into its box."

"You've lost hope," Abby murmured, her eyes dark with understanding and sympathy.

Matthew surprised himself when he shook his head again. "No, I haven't." Relief filled him when he realized he meant it. He pressed Abby's hand. "I met another woman named Abby when I was in New Orleans."

"Colonel Anderson's sister-in-law who took care of you."

A smile played on Matthew's lips as he thought about her. "Yes. She reminded me of you. She asked me a question the night of the riot. *If you knew that hope and despair were paths to the same destination, which one would you choose?*"

Abby absorbed the question for several moments before she responded. "How did you answer her?"

"She didn't expect an answer, but I realized what she was doing. She was making me acknowledge that life, and our country, was going to go on whether I wanted it to or not. I could live my life in despair, or I could live it with hope." He paused, wanting to make sure he meant his next words. "I chose hope," he said.

Abby pressed his hand, her eyes shimmering with tears. "I'm so glad."

Matthew looked out the window again. "I am going to live life with hope, but I am done immersing myself into the worst this country has to offer. I've spent the last six years following battles, senseless deaths, and riots." He took a long breath, once again feeling the freedom his realization had brought him. "There is more to life than that. There is more to *America* than that. I tried to walk away from reporting last year. The paper convinced me not to quit because they made me believe I could make a difference, and I thought writing a book about the South could heal the things that happened during the war."

"But it hasn't," Thomas observed thoughtfully.

"No, it's made it worse." Matthew shook his head to clear it of memories lurking close to the surface.

"So what are you going to do?" Thomas asked.

Matthew hadn't gotten that far in his thinking. "I have absolutely no idea. When Janie sent me a letter about everyone coming to the plantation, I decided to come here. That's the biggest decision I've been able to make so far."

Abby looked at him appraisingly. "So you've been communicating with Janie?"

Matthew smiled, knowing what she was thinking. "I have."

"So Carrie was right."

Matthew raised his eyebrows. "Carrie?"

"She wrote me after the Fourth of July that she suspected something was happening between you and Janie. She was quite happy."

Matthew sat quietly, relieved when the sound of Carrie's name did nothing to his heart. He met Abby's eyes squarely. She had been the first to realize the extent of his feelings for Carrie. He also knew she had agonized over the hurt caused by the unrequited love. "She's right," he said. "If I hadn't known Janie was coming here, I would have gone to Philadelphia first."

Abby smiled brilliantly. "Then I'm so glad she's coming." She glanced at the grandfather clock in the corner. "They should be arriving soon."

Matthew grinned. "In twenty minutes if it is on time."

Thomas smiled but went back to the earlier topic. "What if you have simply been writing about the wrong things?"

Matthew frowned as he turned his thoughts away from Janie's blue eyes and looked back at Thomas. He wasn't really in the mood to talk about his future, but perhaps it was best to think about it before he was distracted by Janie. "The wrong things?"

"You have focused on battles, senseless killings, and riots," Thomas said.

Matthew frowned more deeply. "I was covering the news."

"So what if you made your own news?" Thomas pressed.

"Made my *own* news?" Matthew echoed blankly. He didn't really want to be having this conversation but something told him it was important. "What do you mean?"

"Do you really believe every person in the South is full of rage and hatred?"

Matthew shook his head quickly. "Of course not."

"Who is talking about *them*?" Thomas asked. "Who is telling *their* stories?"

Matthew considered his words but remained silent, mulling over the words in his head. He sensed the questions were worthy of serious consideration.

Abby, still holding his hand, squeezed it tightly. "What a marvelous idea, Thomas!"

Matthew remained silent, not at all sure anything was a marvelous idea right now.

"Don't you see, Matthew?" Abby asked. "There are so many people that don't want the South, or our country, to become what you have experienced in the last few months. They are tired of the hatred and violence. Just like you, they are trying to figure out how to hold on to hope, but all they read about in the papers are the terrible things that cause the despair you have been feeling."

Matthew was silent, trying to absorb what they were suggesting, but he could feel the glimmerings of something waking in his heart.

"The book you were commissioned to write is about the South, right?" Thomas asked.

Matthew nodded, his mind whirling.

"Did they tell you it has to be about all the *terrible* things of the South?"

"No," Matthew admitted, feeling a small spark ignite in his mind.

"So, what if you wrote about the fire that burned down the school on the plantation? Instead of focusing on the destruction, what if focus on the courage and determination that had it rebuilt so quickly. What if you were to tell the story of children that won't let fear keep them from learning?"

Abby nodded vigorously. "And tell about Jeremy's attack, but focus on the good that has come from it. The factory employees are more united than ever. We have even had other factory owners approach us about how they can emulate what we are doing because they see our success. Isn't that worthy of a story?"

Matthew listened intently, the spark fanning to a flame as they talked.

"There are stories of people all over the South who are trying to rebuild their lives with an acceptance of the blacks and with the understanding that they lost the war. There are stories of blacks who are forging ahead to create something of their lives," Abby said excitedly.

Matthew's eyes opened wide as an epiphany filled him. "I have been feeling a responsibility to tell the stories of what has been happening. I thought if I told the stories, I could help create change. Believing that has created a tremendous burden." He sighed. "New Orleans was more than I could bear. The responsibility was suddenly more than I could carry." He stood and strode over to the window, sighing as a strong breeze blew in and cooled him. He smiled as he watched the waxy leaves of the towering magnolia tree shiver in the wind. "It's all in how I see it..." he murmured as sudden understanding blazed through him.

Matthew swung around with the beginning of a smile on his lips. "Writing about what I experience does not have to be a weighty responsibility. It's all about seeing the *possibility* in what I am doing. The *possibility* that my words can create hope instead of simply spread despair."

Abby jumped up and joined him by the window. "You're right! Have you been seeing change in our country?" she asked urgently.

Matthew frowned, searching his mind. He knew what the answer was supposed to be, but perhaps he wasn't ready to see it.

"Maybe even *glimmers* of change?" Abby asked.

Matthew nodded. He could acknowledge *glimmers.* "Yes," he admitted. The single yes was all that was needed. Suddenly, his mind was full of the stories he could write.

Thomas read his expression. "The kind of stories you are thinking about could ignite hope in people, instead of inflaming their fears. They could make people be willing to stand up and say they don't want to live in a country full of hatred. They could compel our Congress to make decisions that will actually change things."

"Glimmers of change..." Matthew murmured. He turned back to stare out over the city. "Doesn't that sound like the perfect title for my new book?"

"It does!" Abby exclaimed. Then she paused. "What about the one you are already writing?"

Matthew shrugged. "My publishers haven't set any solid parameters on my writing, but I know they have certain expectations. They won't feel it's a good book unless it covers the worst of who we are. Unfortunately, they believe sensationalism sells." His brow creased for an instant and then cleared. "I've had many publishers approach me about a book. I'm going to write a proposal for the book I have in mind. I'll find a publisher," he vowed, confidence blooming in him. "It's time to do things differently."

An Invitation

Before you read the last chapter of Glimmers of Change, I would like to invite you to join my mailing list so that you are never left wondering what is going to happen next. ☺

Join my Email list so you can:

- Receive notice of all new books & audio releases.
- Be a part of my Launch celebrations. I give away lots of Free gifts! ☺
- Read my weekly blog while you're waiting for a new book.
- Be part of The Bregdan Chronicles Family!
- Learn about all the other books I write.

Just go to www.BregdanChronicles.net and fill out the form.

I look forward to having you become part of The Bregdan Chronicles Family!

Blessings,
Ginny Dye

Chapter Thirty-Two

Matthew gazed around the porch as he sipped his lemonade, and then his eyes shifted to the pasture. He never got tired of watching the new foals frolic through the lush grass. Bays mixed with chestnuts and sorrels. He especially loved the dapple gray filly that pranced around the pasture as if she owned it. The pasture for the horses had more than doubled since he had last been here. Robert and Clint were indeed turning Cromwell Plantation into a thriving horse farm.

He watched with a lazy smile as Elizabeth, Alice, and Florence wandered through the field, Amber leading them confidently. Their peals of laughter and squeals of delight as the foals played around them rang through the air. Clint, his tall muscular frame outlined by the sun, kept watch over them from the door of the barn.

Amber still walked with a slight limp, but even Carrie had been impressed with how quickly her leg had healed. She had already begun riding again, but she and Felicia were never out of someone's sight. He knew Felicia was in the barn saddling up horses for them.

Carrie and Robert, thrilled to be together again, had disappeared on Granite and Eclipse almost as soon as she had arrived a few hours earlier. He could still hear her shouts of joy as they had raced off down the road toward the river.

Thomas and Moses had ridden out into the fields to inspect the tobacco crop.

Abby had enlisted Annie and Polly to help her and Janie carry in the groceries she had delivered from the city. Matthew could tell by the delicious aromas already wafting through the windows that the evening meal was going to be wonderful.

Rose had just disappeared inside to put John and Hope down for their afternoon naps. The last few hours had been full of laughter, questions, and stories as she had gotten to know Marietta. The two women had bonded immediately.

Jeremy and Marietta had just walked down the road to discover the hidden lake Carrie had told them about, their hands clasped tightly.

Matthew drew a long sigh, letting the peace of the plantation wash over him. He looked up as Janie walked out onto the porch. "There you are," he said quietly, his eyes locked on her face. It had been torture to be so close to her and not have time to be alone. Their train had arrived the afternoon before, but the house had been full to the brim with laughter and activity. They had risen with the sun and come out to the plantation. He had done little but watch her as the wagons had made their way down the dusty roads.

Janie smiled, settled down in the chair next to his, and accepted the glass of lemonade he held out to her. "Thank you." She sighed as she sipped the drink, breaking into a laugh when one of the colts butted Amber playfully with his head and then pranced away.

Matthew could see her relaxing.

"It's so beautiful," Janie murmured. "I think I'll always feel this plantation is my true home."

Matthew nodded, not able to take his eyes off her. He couldn't agree more. "Have you seen *all* of it?" he asked.

Janie turned to look at him, her eyes puzzled. She blushed when she felt the intensity of his gaze, but she didn't look away. "*All* of it?"

"I know about a special place down by the river," Matthew revealed.

"Carrie's special place?"

"No," Matthew responded. "*My* special place."

Janie cocked her head speculatively. "Then, no, I might not have seen that particular part of the plantation."

"Hmm...It seems a shame to have missed something."

Janie's lips twitched. "It would be a shame," she agreed.

"I think we should remedy that," Matthew said, his heart beginning to pound as her soft blue eyes gazed at him. He could only hope he wasn't reading more than he should into what he saw there. He stood. "We have time before dinner."

Matthew cleared debris from a large boulder on the edge of the river, thankful for the shade created by the arching branches of an oak tree, and for a breeze strong enough to keep any mosquitoes and gnats at bay.

"This is beautiful," Janie murmured as she watched the calm surface of the river reflect the puffy clouds gliding slowly by. After eight months confined by the crowded, noisy streets of Philadelphia, she was thrilled to be back on the plantation, but she couldn't use that as the excuse for why her heart was beating so quickly.

"I found this spot the very first time I visited the plantation. Since it was the dead of winter, it looked quite different. I was surrounded by snow-shrouded trees and ice chunks in the river." He shook his head. "That seems a lifetime ago."

"It *was* a lifetime ago," Janie replied. "Neither one of us are the same people we were six years ago. I, for one, am quite glad for that. I wouldn't want to still be that person."

"You were wonderful!" Matthew protested.

Janie smiled. "I was a young girl with idealistic dreams of what life was like."

"And now?"

Janie's gaze swung out over the river as she considered his question. "And now I hope I am a woman with a clear vision of who she is and where she is going."

"Is there room in that vision for someone else?" Matthew dared to ask, forcing himself not to hold his breath as he waited for her answer.

Janie's eyes swung back to stare at Matthew. "I..."

"I'm sorry. I know it is probably too soon to talk about my feelings for you," Matthew said apologetically.

"It's not that," Janie murmured. She had grown beyond the point where she was interested in playing games. She recognized the increasing openness and intimacy in the letters they had shared over the last month. She recognized the look in Matthew's eyes, and she wouldn't deny how she felt about him.

"What is it?" Matthew asked, encouraged by what he saw flitting across her face. He reached out to take her hand, feeling a quick disappointment when she pulled it back.

Janie sighed and turned to face him. "Do you really believe you can ever love anyone but Carrie?" she asked.

Matthew should have been surprised by the question, but he wasn't. He had long since realized that as much as he had tried to hide his feelings for Carrie, he had failed. Of course Janie would have seen them. "I will always love Carrie," he said honestly, "but I've realized in the last month that I was never actually *in love* with her." He couldn't blame Janie for the look of skepticism that blazed in her eyes. "My mama used to tell me I was always determined to get the one thing I couldn't have. She warned me that I would spend my whole life unhappy if I closed my eyes to the beauty of what was right there waiting for me."

Matthew paused, his eyes turning toward the water before he continued. He knew Janie would give him time to explain. "My daddy used to tell me that he loved mama from the minute he laid eyes on her, and that he would never be able to even look at another woman. He told me that *Justin men* loved for life. When I met Carrie, I thought she was the most beautiful woman I had ever seen. When I realized, that very first night, that Robert was courting her, I decided I was doomed to always love a woman I could never have. The chaos and the pain of the war kept me from considering things could be different. It was just one more source of pain for me. I buried myself in my work, deciding that being single would allow me to make more of a difference through my writing..." His voice trailed off as the feelings swamped him.

"And now?"

Matthew smiled and swung around on the boulder. "And now I realize that the most amazing woman I have ever known was right there all the time." His expression grew somber as he reached out and took Janie's hands. "When I was in New Orleans hiding under the platform with Ben, watching people being beaten and murdered, your face was the only one I saw. It was *your* eyes gazing at me that kept me sane. You were the only thing that kept alive my desire to live."

Janie's face whitened, but her eyes held his steadily.

"Janie, I love you. I love your strength and your passion. I love your ability to laugh and keep moving forward even when life hands you nothing but pain and struggle. I love that you are going to be a doctor. I love that you are a strong woman who has the courage to speak your mind." Matthew took a deep breath. "And I love how your blue eyes become soft with compassion and sympathy when someone else is hurting. I love that you make me better than I really am."

Janie shook her head. "You are the most remarkable man I know," she said.

Matthew eyes widened as hope bloomed. "You don't mind that I love you?"

"Mind?" Janie asked, a smile lighting her eyes. "If you had ever done more than look at Carrie every time I was in the room, I probably wouldn't have married Clifford. I loved him in the beginning, but I never felt about him the way I felt about you." Her smile softened with emotion as her eyes shimmered with tears. "I have loved you almost from the day I met you."

Matthew laughed loudly, lifted her from the boulder, and pulled her close. "I love you, Janie," he whispered, just before his lips claimed hers.

When Matthew finally released her, Janie still had one important thing to talk about. "It truly doesn't bother you that I'm a divorced woman?"

Matthew smiled tenderly. "Other than the fact that I wish I had been the one who had the privilege of beating

Clifford up when he came to the plantation instead of Robert, it makes no difference to me at all." He held her shoulders and gazed down into her eyes. "You were remarkable before, but you are even more remarkable now. My mama used to tell me that hardship usually creates the most beautiful people if they don't become bitter. You are the most beautiful person I know."

Janie blinked back tears of gratitude, hardly able to believe Matthew actually loved her.

"There's something else I need to tell *you*," Matthew said.

Janie smiled, knowing that nothing he could tell her would change her feelings for him. "Go ahead."

He told her about his earlier conversation with Thomas and Abby, and then waited for her reaction. He was suddenly aware of just how uncertain his future was. He wondered if that would bother Janie.

Janie smiled. "My grandmother called that 'shifting with the wind.' " When Matthew blinked at her, she laughed. "Change has always been hard for me. My grandmother used to tell me that it was usually in the winds of change that we find our direction. I didn't like that very much because if things were going along smoothly, I wanted them to keep going that way."

"And they never do," Matthew murmured. "Things always change."

Janie smiled. "*Glimmers of Change*. I really think that title says it all, especially right now. Everything seems hard, but there is still reason for hope." She gripped his hand tightly. "We will find our way together, Matthew."

Matthew felt a powerful surge of joy. He laughed, picked Janie up, and swung her through the air, laughing even harder as her peals of merriment rolled over the water and echoed back from the woods.

To Be Continued...

Available Now!
www.DiscoverTheBregdanChronicles.com

Would you be so kind as to leave a Review on Amazon?
I love hearing from my readers! Just go to
Amazon.com, put Glimmers of Change into the Search
box, click to read the Reviews, and you'll be able to
leave one of your own!

Thank you!

<u>The Bregdan Principle</u>

Every life that has been lived until
today is a part of the woven
braid of life.

It takes every person's story to create
history.

Your life will help determine the course
of history.

You may think you don't have much of
an impact.

You do.

Every action you take will reflect in
someone else's life.

Someone else's decisions.

Someone else's future.

Both good and bad.

The Bregdan Chronicles

Storm Clouds Rolling In
1860 – 1861

On To Richmond
1861 – 1862

Spring Will Come
1862 – 1863

Dark Chaos
1863 – 1864

The Long Last Night
1864 – 1865

Carried Forward By Hope
April – December 1865

Glimmers of Change
December – August 1866

Shifted By The Winds
August – December 1866

***Many more coming... Go to
DiscoverTheBregdanChronicles.com to see how
many are available now!***

Other Books by Ginny Dye

<u>Pepper Crest High Series - Teen Fiction</u>

Time For A Second Change
It's Really A Matter of Trust
A Lost & Found Friend
Time For A Change of Heart

<u>When I Dream Series</u> – Children's Bedtime Stories

When I Dream, I Dream of Horses
When I Dream, I Dream of Puppies
When I Dream, I Dream of Snow
When I Dream, I Dream of Kittens
When I Dream, I Dream of Elephants
When I Dream, I Dream of the Ocean

<u>Fly To Your Dreams Series</u> – Allegorical Fantasy

Dream Dragon
Born To Fly
Little Heart

101+ Ways to Promote Your Business Opportunity

All titles by Ginny Dye
www.AVoiceInTheWorld.com

Author Biography

Who am I? Just a normal person who happens to love to write. If I could do it all anonymously, I would. In fact, I did the first go round. I wrote under a pen name. On the off chance I would ever become famous - I didn't want to be! I don't like the limelight. I don't like living in a fishbowl. I especially don't like thinking I have to look good everywhere I go, just in case someone recognizes me! I finally decided none of that matters. If you don't like me in overalls and a baseball cap, too bad. If you don't like my haircut or think I should do something different than what I'm doing, too bad. I'll write books that you will hopefully like, and we'll both let that be enough! :) Fair?

But let's see what you might want to know. I spent many years as a Wanderer. My dream when I graduated from college was to experience the United States. I grew up in the South. There are many things I love about it but I wanted to live in other places. So I did. I moved 42 times, traveled extensively in 49 of the 50 states, and had more experiences than I will ever be able to recount. The only state I haven't been in is Alaska, simply because I refuse to visit such a vast, fabulous place until I have at least a month. Along the way I had glorious adventures. I've canoed through the Everglade Swamps, snorkeled in the Florida Keys and windsurfed in the Gulf of Mexico. I've white-water rafted down the New River and Bungee jumped in the Wisconsin Dells. I've visited every National Park (in the off-season when there is more freedom!) and many of the State Parks. I've hiked thousands of miles of mountain trails and biked through Arizona deserts. I've canoed and biked through Upstate New York and Vermont, and polished off as much lobster as possible on the Maine Coast.

I had a glorious time and never thought I would find a place that would hold me until I came to the Pacific Northwest. I'd been here less than 2 weeks, and I knew I would never leave. My heart is so at home here with the towering firs, sparkling waters, soaring mountains and rocky beaches. I love the eagles & whales. In 5 minutes I can be hiking on 150 miles of trails in the mountains around my home, or gliding across the lake in my rowing shell. I love it!

Have you figured out I'm kind of an outdoors gal? If it can be done outdoors, I love it! Hiking, biking, windsurfing, rock-climbing, roller-blading, snow-shoeing, skiing, rowing, canoeing, softball, tennis... the list could go on and on. I love to have fun and I love to stretch my body. This should give you a pretty good idea of what I do in my free time.

When I'm not writing or playing, I'm building I Am A Voice In The World - a fabulous organization I founded in 2001 - along with 60 amazing people who poured their lives into creating resources to empower people to make a difference with their lives.

What else? I love to read, cook, sit for hours in solitude on my mountain, and also hang out with friends. I love barbeques and block parties. Basically - I just love LIFE!

I'm so glad you're part of my world!

Ginny

Join my Email List so you can:

- Receive notice of all new books
- Be a part of my Launch Celebrations. I give away lots of Free gifts!
- Read my weekly BLOG while you're waiting for a new book.
- Be part of The Bregdan Chronicles Family!
- Learn about all the other books I write.

Just go to www.BregdanChronicles.net and fill out the form.